Larry—

The Astronaut
from
Bear Creek

Hope you
enjoy the book!

The Astronaut from Bear Creek

A Novel
by
Nick Allen Brown

Harrowood Books
2015

Trade Paperback Edition
ISBN-13   978-0-915180-53-0
ISBN-10   0-915180-53-7

LIBRARY OF CONGRESS CATALOGING-IN-PUBLICATION DATA

Brown, Nick Allen, 1978-
  The astronaut from Bear Creek : a novel / by Nick Allen Brown. -- Trade paperback edition.
    pages cm
  ISBN 978-0-915180-53-0
  1. Orphans--Fiction. 2. Astronauts--Fiction. 3. Widows--Fiction. 4. Adoption--Fiction. I. Title.
  PS3602.R722426A88 2015
  813'.6--dc23
                        2015003359

10 9 8 7 6 5 4 3 2 1

First printing: April, 2015

Harrowood Books
3943 N Providence Road
Newtown Square, PA 19073
800-747-8356

This book is dedicated to my friend Steven Dyer.
You are kind and selfless and I am honored to know you.

Also by Nick Allen Brown:

Field of Dead Horses

ACKNOWLEDGMENTS

Julie Jones
Thanks for helping me with the research I needed for this book.

Jessica Seibert
You are a wonderful editor and friend.

Cari Small
You are brilliant!

Laura Tenpenny
Thanks for your help with editing, your input was a big help.

Leslie Witty
You helped me more than you know.

Becky Brown
This book wouldn't have been possible without you.

Chapter 1

BEAR CREEK, PENNSYLVANIA

Next to Justin sat his hedgehog of a wife, finishing off her order of loaded cheese fries. Painted on her chubby lips were remnants of melted cheese, sour cream, and a smattering of grease. She reached for the last of her margarita as Justin signaled the barkeep.

"Another wing platter and a tall one."

"Margarita too," Judy Creeson said. Her voice sounded as if her throat were packed with gravel...a byproduct of twenty years of discount cigarettes. She was twelve when she started smoking, a vain attempt to look cool while wearing powder-blue eye shadow and red lipstick. From the beginning of her pre-teen years till now, she had amassed two miscarriages and a stretched-out stomach, which advertised her alcoholic and caloric achievements. Using the back of her Cabbage Patch hand, she wiped the slop from around her mouth before she turned her head back toward the TV. The barkeep, a thin, thirty-something brunette wore a tight, black tank-top, and tried her best to look inconvenienced, hoping her last two customers got the point. She hurriedly punched in the orders on the touch screen at the end of the bar as she exhaled in frustration.

Justin looked down at his digital watch. 1:29 AM. Hearing a *swishing* noise, he looked up at a man sweeping sawdust and peanut shells into a dustbin. The kitchen crew bustled behind a stainless steel swinging door as they noisily put away pots and pans. Justin watched as the tank-topped barkeep filled up a tall glass of frothy light beer that he considered free-of-charge.

Earlier that day, Justin had been asked to watch the counter for a few hours at Edwards Auto Garage. It was a nice change from his daily routine of replacing alternators and installing brake pads. With no customers around and being that he was the only employee at the front, it gave him the chance to slip several twenty-dollar bills from the register and into his front left pocket.

Justin loved to splurge on food and as a result, his waistline splurged over the top of his jeans. After forty-three wings and seven mugs of beer, he felt gastrointestinal pain and was forced to stand up for relief. The loaded cheese fries and margaritas were testing the limit of Judy's brown T-shirt and brown sweatpants giving her the appearance of a potato wearing a leotard. She grunted as she shifted uncomfortably on her barstool before laying her head on the bar.

Once 2:00 AM arrived, the barkeep gladly handed them their check. A few minutes later, Justin and Judy Creeson stumbled out the front doors of Wild Bill's Sports Bar and clumsily walked across the wooden plank porch. Their discount sneakers clopped and puttered about as they headed for the parking lot in a drunken haze.

Once on the roads of Bear Creek, Justin Creeson drove his forest green '92 Camaro with his eyes wide open, as if he was able to focus past his intoxication. He managed a left turn and used both hands on the worn and sticky steering wheel. What once was a cool sports car now resembled a heap of metal, fiberglass and Bondo. The engine seemed to cough like an elderly man with pneumonia and could be heard inside the houses as they drove down Sycamore Street. The throaty rumbling engine woke a few light sleepers as it sped down the road.

"You're weaving. Don't weave."

"I'm not weaving."

"You're weaving, and the cops gonna pull you over," Judy said as she tried to light up a cigarette. Her alcoholic haze and the lack of shock absorbers in the junkmobile prevented her from successfully igniting the tobacco. She spoke as she held the unlit cigarette in her mouth and her eyes on the flame of her lighter. "You're not supposed to be driving anyway." Justin let up off the brake and hit the gas pedal too hard, sending the Camaro down a hill.

"How am I weaving? I'm straight as an arrow."

Judy took the unlit cigarette out of her mouth and yelled, "You're going way too fast. Slow down, moron. Arrows don't weave."

The front left tire abandoned the road first. Justin tried to steer it back onto the asphalt and overcorrected. Skidding tires. Screaming. The telephone pole snapped when the passenger side slammed into it with jagged, splintered wood piercing Judy's skull like a toothpick into a watermelon. Her unwashed, stringy hair whipped around as the car flipped over. Her body broke free of the wreckage and smacked the road with sounds of cracking bone and slaps of fat. Her body skidded to a quick halt and left a trail of blood with bits of skin and tissue ground into the road. The car came to a stop on its roof, the tires spun freely, mangled hoses bled fluid onto the asphalt. Justin remained in the drivers seat upside down. He looked at the shattered windshield in front of him as his unwieldy weight bore down on his broken neck. Paralyzed and unable to correct the restricted airflow, blood gurgled and spurted from his mouth just as the pools of gasoline around him caught fire.

Chapter 2

Jerry Pike and Alan Toms were known to other pilots in the flying community as "Tom and Jerry." Decades ago when they were both in flight school at the U.S. Air Force Academy, they roomed together and had been like brothers ever since.

Sitting in the cockpit of a NASA-owned Cessna Citation VII, they talked while they waited for their passenger. The overhead lights in the hangar were off, but the sunlight from the mouth of the giant structure let in plenty of light. While the hangar could hold five airplanes, only the Citation VII was parked inside. Carrying on a casual conversation, they each held an overpriced cup of coffee.

"As soon as I see it, I throw it in the trash. Gone. The whole, entire loaf of bread," Jerry said before taking a sip of his steaming coffee.

"I swear, my wife will take out a slice and pick around it."

"Mine too. What's the matter with people? Mold is bacteria."

"Well, it's a fungus."

"Even worse." Jerry looked out the window of the plane for their passenger. No sign of him.

"Do you eat blue cheese?" Tom asked before stirring his hot coffee and blowing on the surface to cool it down.

"Sure."

"Me too. Blue cheese has mold in it, and we eat that."

"Yeah, but isn't that the good kind of mold?"

"I don't know. How can mold be good?" Both of their heads turned toward the front of the plane as they watched a late model Honda Accord enter the giant mouth of the hangar. The sedan drove past the Cessna and headed toward the left corner. Jerry continued.

"Mushrooms are fungus."

"Yeah, you're right. But, mushrooms aren't mold."

"There has to be good mold and bad mold. Just like bacteria."

"I suppose. We eat yogurt, and it's full of bacteria."

"I don't eat yogurt."

"How can you not eat yogurt?"

The Honda Accord parked, and the driver exited and placed his worn tassel loafers onto the polished concrete floor of the hangar. In his left hand was a brown, zippered case containing a tablet computer. In his right was a cup of coffee from the same coffee shop as Tom and Jerry's expensive java. A blue button-up shirt displayed a coffee stain— the spillage from a hazardous sip taken while approaching a red light, while his old, faded blue jeans hid similar splattering from a hairpin turn taken at thirty-five. The late-as-usual Dr. Daniel Stanton, 52, looked at the coffee stain on his fresh shirt and continued as if it were completely okay that it featured a noticeable, brown stain. He walked lazily up the stairs of the Cessna while carefully balancing his coffee. The heels of his loafers *thunked* on each metal each step until he entered the cabin of the plane, still wearing his sunglasses.

"I thought penicillin had mold in it," said Jerry.

"Does it?" replied Tom.

"I don't know."

Dr. Daniel Stanton bent slightly with a grunt as he sat in a plush leather seat, still keeping his coffee level. He looked at the pilots through his dark sunglasses and nodded as he said their names: "Tom, Jerry." They shifted around in their seats and leaned on their armrests as they looked back at Dr. Stanton.

"Hey, Stanton. What's all this about?" Tom asked.

"What do you mean?"

"Our flight plan is for Pocono Mountains Municipal Airport in PA."

"So?"

"So there's a rumor going around that you're going to meet with Jim Crazyfield," Jerry said with a mischievous smile.

"It's not a rumor."

"You are actually going to see him?" Jerry asked, and Tom added, "In person?"

"Why else would they give me a private jet to the middle of nowhere?"

"We're not picking him up, are we?" Tom asked.

"Yeah, he's not getting on the plane, right?"

"You guys ever met him?" Stanton asked.

"I saw him once," Tom said.

"Where?" Jerry asked.

"The propulsion chamber. He was testing something. That was fifteen years ago."

"I evaluated him eleven years ago for spaceflight. He was nice. Seemed normal then," Stanton said as he shrugged his shoulders and slid his sunglasses to the top of his head. "All I know is I have orders to pick him up, and he has to wear a straitjacket during the flight," Stanton said nonchalantly, never smiling once.

"Are you serious?" Tom asked.

"I knew it," Jerry said with a look of worry and fear.

"Yep," Stanton said as he casually took a sip of his hot coffee before continuing. Tom and Jerry hung on every word. "He's a flight risk. He has to wear a scream helmet too."

"What? What's a scream helmet?" Tom asked.

"Aww man…this is crazy. I didn't know we were picking him up."

"You guys are soft. What the heck is a scream helmet anyway? I just made that up."

"Geez, I swear I thought you were serious," Jerry said as he released a deep breath.

"Not me. The scream helmet thing isn't real. I knew that."

"No you didn't," Jerry said.

"Mayfield," Stanton said in a corrective tone.

"What?" Tom asked.

"I wouldn't go around calling him Crazyfield."

"Why not?" Jerry asked.

"I am actually supposed to pick him up. No straitjacket though."

"Is he really a flight risk?"

"Of course not. You're both flight risks," Stanton said as flopped his tablet computer in the seat next to him and settled into his leather seat. He pulled his sunglasses down over his eyes, ready for a nap.

"You catch the game last night?" Jerry asked, changing the subject.

"Fell asleep at the half," Stanton said, eyes closed as he spoke in a sleepy tone.

"Duke won," said Jerry.

"Figured," Stanton said during a yawn. "Seems a couple cold beers makes me sleepy now. I'm getting too old."

"Nachos, cheese and jalapeños. I stay awake through the whole game," Tom said. Jerry nodded as if it were a confirmed secret.

"I love jalapeños. Good tip," he said as he closed the shade to his window.

"Hey, Doc," Jerry started, "if you open a loaf of bread and you see only one slice of bread with mold on it, what do you do?"

"Trash. Whole loaf," Stanton said. Jerry turned his head toward Tom with a look of confirmation.

"It's a smart move."

"Makes sense that my wife keeps it then," Tom said as he rolled his eyes. Jerry laughed, and Dr. Stanton cracked a smile with his sunglasses still hiding his eyes.

The procedure for takeoff began. Switches were flipped. Headsets were placed and fitted, and screens displayed scrolling flight data. Dr. Stanton took another sip of his coffee, returned it to the cup holder, and leaned to one side of his plush leather chair and found a comfortable napping position. Tom initiated with the tower, speaking into his headset microphone. Stanton could feel the slow roll of the plane as it inched toward the end of the hangar. Before the plane reached the runway, Dr. Stanton was asleep, slouching like a careless teenager.

Chapter 3

At Pocono Mountains Municipal Airport, the Cessna Citation VII sat near the smallest hangar. Tom and Jerry exited the plane before Dr. Stanton stood up from his plush, leather seat. Tom opened the luggage compartment, removed two golf bags and set them on the asphalt. Jerry took off his shoes and replaced them with golf shoes. Tom did the same as they talked.

"I couldn't do it. The pig was laying there on a table with an apple in its mouth, you know, like you see in the movies," Tom explained.

"And it was cooked? People were eating it?" Jerry grunted slightly, showing his age as he tied the laces on his shoes.

"Yep. They were just cutting into this poor animal. It doesn't feel right eating out of a carcass."

Dr. Stanton stepped out of the plane yawning, still donning his sunglasses. His hair was a puffy mess from napping, and his coffee-stained, blue button-up shirt was partially untucked. Even though he looked like a wreck, he seemed comfortable with his appearance.

"You sure about bringing Crazyfield on board?" Jerry asked with a smile. Stanton looked at the open gate to the airport and searched for his ride, then glanced at his old Movado watch as he came down the stairs.

"Doubt he'll even come back with me. This thing is more of an evaluation," Stanton's tattered loafers clicked, clacked and scratched on the asphalt. "You guys playing a course nearby?"

"Yeah. Buck Hill. Call us on the cell if you need us back sooner," Jerry said as he put on his sweater vest. A mini-van taxicab entered the gate of Pocono Mountains Municipal Airport and headed cautiously toward the Cessna.

"I got the mini-van. You guys can have the next one."

"You know, you could end up buried beneath the floorboards of his motel if you aren't careful," Tom said. He and his golf buddy laughed as Stanton's loafers lazily smacked the pavement. The sound of the mini-van's weak four-cylinder engine almost drowned out the laughter from Tom and Jerry. Almost.

In the mini-van taxi, an old black man named Del looked at his clipboard and confirmed the address. He looked up and watched in his rearview mirror as Stanton got in the backseat. Del's voice rattled off the address as if his throat had a motor in it while his eyes peeked over the top of his drug store reading glasses.

"164 Bear Mountain Road?"

"Yes, sir."

"Bear Creek Inn, huh?"

"Yep."

"You know it's closed, right?" Del asked as he turned around and looked at him over the top of his glasses.

"I do."

"Okay," Del nodded, "we're on our way." He set the clipboard in the front passenger seat and shifted the cab into drive.

"Actually, I want to grab something to eat first. Can you recommend anywhere?"

"Well," Del said as he looked at his watch. "I could use something to eat myself. If you don't mind Murray's Diner, I'll get something too. You won't lose your ride and you won't have to eat on the meter."

"A diner sounds good to me."

"Alright then," Del said as he turned the steering wheel. "Best Reuben sandwich in PA"

Chapter 4

Murray's Diner had been around since the 1970s. The Formica lunch counter and the swivel barstools reflected the era of its inception. Bacon, eggs, grits, hash browns and the occasional omelet made up the limited, but delicious and quick breakfast fare. BLTs, ham sandwiches, chicken tenders and Murray's famous Reuben were the favorites of the lunch crowd...especially the Reuben. Darla Pettigrew, a big-boned, 55-year-old waitress sliced cabbage with a chef's knife behind the lunch counter. She always wore her hair up, which did nothing to compliment her thick, dangling cheeks that resembled Richard Nixon's jowls. Her cheeks jiggled slightly as she managed the cabbage on a wooden cutting board. In her younger days, she was a third base softball player and built up a muscular physique. Her eating habits stayed with her over the years as her athleticism declined. With the grip of a commercial fisherman, she used a chef's knife to slice the cabbage into thin strips, adding salt every so often to help draw out the moisture. The water and salt helped create the brine in which the cabbage could ferment without spoiling. It's no secret that Murray's famous Reuben was famous because they made their own sauerkraut.

When Stanton walked into Murray's, the place was packed. While it was more of a local diner, tourists would wander over from the Poconos Mountains to patronize the boutiques and antique shops from time to time. Murray's was one of the few lunch options in Bear Creek.

Stanton sat down at a small table in the middle of the hungry diners, looking out of place. The locals knew what a tourist looked like and since they couldn't place him, they shot odd looks his way from the corners of their eyes. When Darla first approached him, he was looking at the menu.

"You don't look like a tourist," Darla said.

"You guessed it. Just passing through," Stanton said as he pointed to the Reuben on the menu. "Cab driver said you have the best Reuben in the state. Set me up and I'll take a cup of coffee, too."

"You got it," said Darla, thinking it curious that a man who was passing through used a cab driver. After putting in Stanton's order, she sidled up to Del who came in shortly after parking his cab. "Hey, Del, who's the stranger?" she asked as she set a steaming cup of hot coffee in front of him.

"A big wig, I guess. He flew in on a private jet."

After thirty minutes of serving guests, clearing tables, refilling soda and cups of coffee, Darla brought the check to her mystery customer. Speaking to Stanton in a friendly way, trying not to sound too nosey, she asked him a question as if they were acquaintances.

"You work in the Poconos or something?"

Stanton looked up at her friendly face while she crookedly held a half-full coffee pot in her right hand.

"Nope. I'm here to visit a local over at Bear Creek Inn," Stanton answered. The people sitting around him overheard him and stopped eating. They turned their head to see who had said the name.

"Bear Creek Inn? The astronaut?" Darla asked, a little too loudly. Now everyone was silent. The entire diner looked at Stanton. All of a sudden the thought of being hacked up and buried underneath the inn didn't sound so ludicrous. Before Stanton could answer, Darla broke the silence as she looked out the front door.

"Daggone it," Darla said under her breath. Dr. Stanton turned his head and saw a truck sporting a Pennsylvania State Parks logo. The truck parked and Steven Burns exited followed by a co-worker wearing the same blue-collar attire. Darla hung her head and reached into her apron, and pulled out a check for Stanton. "Pay at the counter when you're ready." Darla said as she prepared herself for Steven.

He entered the diner, his eyes searched for a table. The patrons quickly went back to their food and periodically glanced at Stanton from the corners of their eyes. Steven and his co-worker found an empty booth at the far back corner.

After Stanton took the last bite of the Reuben sandwich, he moved his plate to the other side of his table and sat back in his chair, sipping his coffee. He glanced at Del, hoping that he was nearing the end of his lunch so he could escape the uncomfortable, shifty stares from the surrounding lunch crowd. Two elderly men sitting on barstools at the lunch counter surrendered their typical conversation of fishing to discuss the astronaut instead. Stanton couldn't help but eavesdrop.

"I heard he was seen in town once."

"Where?"

"Over at the hardware store on the square."

"What'd he do?"

"I don't know, just bought a few things and left."

"Was that this year or last?"

"I don't know, four or five years ago, I think. Who knows, probably wasn't even him."

At the far end of the lunch counter sat a thick, burly man named

"Bull". He wiped his mouth and paid for lunch by reaching into his pocket and produced a thick wad of fives and tens. He peeled off fifteen dollars and placed it on top of his check as he looked around the diner. Bull's real name was Jeremiah Dower, but it had been fifteen years since anyone had called him by his first name. Back in his high school days, his teammates wore out the "Jeremiah was a Bullfrog" song during his four years as an offensive linesmen on the football team. By the time he graduated, the name "Bullfrog" stuck. In his later years, he just introduced himself as Bull. He turned his head toward the back of the diner and saw Steven Burns and his co-worker. He grabbed his cup of coffee and walked over to the booth.

"Hey, big guy," said Steven.

"My lunch hour is almost up."

"Have a seat if ya want," Burt Poole said. Burt wasn't the dumbest of the three, but he was close. He and Steven had been friends since junior high and wherever Steven went, Burt followed, including working in the local State Game Lands. Bull squeezed his linebacker frame into the booth, sitting next to Burt and set his cup of coffee on the table.

"You guys missed it," Bull said.

"What's that?" Steven asked. Bull's eyes darted in the direction of Stanton as he spoke.

"Fella over there said he's going to see the astronaut."

"At that motel?"

"Yep."

"Have you ever seen him? I haven't," Steven asked.

"Nope. Never. I heard he's crazy," Burt said.

"Of course he's crazy. You'd have to be out of your mind to lock yourself up in your own motel for ten years," Steven explained.

"I had forgotten about him," Burt added.

"You know about his visitors, right?" Steven said quietly. "I've seen green lights over there in the sky." He gestured by pointing straight up. Bull looked up at the ceiling.

"You should go talk to that guy and see what's going on," Burt said. Steven's eyes darted between Burt and Bull as if he was about to accept the dare.

Stanton had paid and just finished the last sip of his coffee when he sensed that the man approaching his table was going to speak to him.

"Are you visiting the space man?" Steven asked as he crossed his arms and looked down at a seated Dr. Stanton. The patrons around them stopped talking and waited for him to respond. Noticing Steven's structurally compromised, country accent, Stanton slightly mimicked him.

"Is that what he's known as 'round here?"

"Yup. Well, crazy space man or crazy astronaut or…" Steven tried to continue until Darla interrupted him.

"Steven, go sit down, and I'll take your order," she said.

"Crazy? *Everyone* calls him crazy?" Stanton asked.

"Yeah. So, is he?"

"I'm a psychiatrist, and I'm here to see him. So what do you think?" Stanton asked.

"You're a shrink?"

"Yep. I wouldn't come up here to see a sane person."

"So, he is crazy."

"Pretty much." Stanton stood up, forcefully lost eye contact with Steven and grabbed his tablet computer, implying he was done with the conversation.

"What happened up there?" Steven asked.

"Up where?"

"Space."

"What do you think happened?" Stanton asked. Steven had heard the rumors late one night while hanging out at the rock quarry with friends and drinking cheap beer. He thought about his response before saying it out loud while the diners around him waited for his answer. Finally, he spouted it off.

"I don't know…little green men?" Steven said. Darla shouted as she started to push him toward his seat.

"Daggone it, Steven. Go sit! You're a nuisance," Darla said.

"No, no! Looks like the doc wants to answer. Let him answer," Steven said, stopping Darla from pushing him. Darla turned her head thinking the answer might surprise her. The diners once again sat in silence waiting for Dr. Stanton's answer.

"I am legally bound to the physician-patient privilege."

"What's that?"

"Means I can't tell you."

"Ha! I knew it!" Steven shouted with laughter as he slapped the formica top of a nearby table.

"All right! Go. Go sit. Leave him alone," Darla shouted as she made him walk toward his seat while he yelled out to Stanton.

"I knew it anyway, Doc. It's our secret. I won't tell anyone!" Darla waited until Steven sat back down before leaving his side. She walked back toward Stanton.

"I can't stand that boy," she said under her breath. The customers looked at Stanton and then at Darla. "I'm sure sorry about that."

"It's okay. Every town has one," Stanton responded softly causing several of the patrons in the diner to laugh.

After lunch at Murray's, Stanton once again sat in the cab. On the way there, they passed by two cop cars and a tow truck. On the other side of the road was a telephone pole, ripped in half, but moved out of the way of traffic. Officer Lancaster motioned for Del to go on through. Del couldn't help but notice a Camaro in the shape of an accordion sitting atop a flat bed tow truck.

"Good lord," Del said.

"Doesn't look good," Stanton added.

As Del drove on, Stanton was able to see some of the small town of Bear Creek. They passed by quaint boutiques selling trinkets and antiques. A little further down, he saw an ice cream parlor that looked inviting and family-oriented. Most of the houses seemed to be from the 1950s with many of them sporting white picket fences and brass knockers on the front door. The mini-van cab turned onto Bear Mountain Road, a steep incline that cut through a thick forest of trees. Stanton looked out the windshield seeing that they were in a tunnel of trees with sunlight peeking through the foliage. The engine of the mini-van seemed to breathe a sigh of relief once they approached Bear Creek Inn. Just off Bear Mountain Road, a quaint entrance to the inn was built with stone pillars and an iron gate. A path made up of pebbles and loose rock wound through the dense forest which obstructed the view of the inn from the road. Once a welcoming accent to guests, the gate appeared as if it had been riddled with bullets from an automatic rifle. Scraggly weeds poked through the stonework causing much of the bricks to shift and crack. Long ago, a tree had fallen during a thunderstorm and knocked the silver and black call box to the ground.

Del's taxi came to a stop outside the gates.

"Seventy-eight dollars and thirteen in change," Del said as he read the meter. Stanton handed Del a hundred dollar bill as he stared at the disheveled gates wondering how he would get past them.

"Keep the change," Stanton said, never taking his eyes off the gate.

"You sure?" Del said handing him a receipt.

"Go ahead. I'll call you when I need a ride back."

"Much obliged. You be careful in there," Del said tucking the bill into his shirt pocket. Stanton got out of the cab and slid the van door shut just before Del drove off.

He stepped off the asphalt and onto the pebbled road in front of the gates to Bear Creek Inn. The pebbles crunched beneath his loafers as he approached the fallen call box. He bent over and used his hand to brush the leaves and grass off of the front and located a red button. After pushing it, he quickly decided it was a lost cause and stood up.

Stanton looked at a space between the stone pillar and a maple tree. Deciding that was the only way past the gate, he began to maneuver through the opening. He pulled himself clear of the ironwork and looked to his left. He noticed a large wooden sign on the ground that once hung on a tree. The worn and tattered sign read *Welcome to Bear Creek Inn*—once a warm greeting—and to Stanton it seemed eerie and foreboding as invasive plant life had grown through the rotted cracks. Stanton walked up the gravel trail and spotted a deer. He stared at it as he slowed his walk and stepped quietly. The deer dropped its head and picked at a sprawling maidenhair fern and brought its head up to chew. Stanton's shoes caused a pebble to crack as he took a step. The deer stopped chewing and noticed him before scampering off deep into the forest. He continued around the gravel path as he breathed in the clean mountain air while taking in the beautiful near-silent scenery.

When he finally came to the end of the path, the gravel trail opened up to a clearing with a cobblestone driveway that ended at a large two-story inn tucked away at the base of Bear Mountain. The grounds were in dire need of a landscaper. Tall grass had taken over the lawn. Shrubs and bushes looked as if they hadn't been tended to in years. The roof over the wrap-around front porch was missing enough shingles to cause concern. Stanton stood in front of the inn and looked up at a pair of beautiful French doors made from thick oak. In the center of each door, a pane of beveled glass was covered by a window shade. On the right door a black sign hung with orange text that read – *Closed*.

Stanton imagined that at one time the grounds were well kept, the porch was inviting and guests came and went. Looking at the overall condition of the front porch, he saw that it needed to be repaired or even replaced due to the splintered and weathered wood. Inviting it wasn't.

Dr. Stanton climbed the warped, wooden stairs that had endured decades of swelling and contracting every time it rained. He stepped up onto the porch allowing his loafers to loudly smack the wooden planks under his feet, announcing his presence. The hollow thud of each step resonated around him as he looked to his left at a parking lot. Except for an old, rusted, red truck, the lot was completely empty and overtaken by grass and weeds. On the driver's side of the truck, written in faded letters were the words *Bear Cr* with the rest of the letters worn off. Stanton looked back at the doors in front of him.

"You ready for this?" Stanton said to himself.

Just as he reached out for the door, he heard a noise coming from inside.

Chapter 5

The city of Wilkes-Barre was only fifteen minutes from Bear Creek, and when the good people of Bear Creek said, "I'm going into town", they meant Wilkes-Barre.

Mallory Cain sat at her desk surrounded by cupcakes and birthday cards. Her shoulder-length hair and petite figure made her look younger than forty-five. With a birthday celebration waiting for her after work, she focused on a file in front of her. Mallory had been given the Abbey Creeson case, a nine-year-old girl in Bear Creek who was orphaned after her aunt and uncle were killed in a DUI car wreck at 2:15 A.M.

Mallory's boss walked across the government office that was crowded with desks, lamps and load-bearing I-beams. Mallory turned toward him as he approached, fully expecting him to give her more bad news. Grady Davis, a former college basketball player for Oklahoma, could talk your ear off about playing in the National Championship and losing to Kansas. Most of his employees had heard his story more than twenty times. His build was thick and his height would have made him intimidating, except his mannerisms were more like Superman than a villain. Nearly a year ago, Mallory was walking to her car in the office parking lot at night when she saw two men wearing disheveled clothing. After considering that there was a real possibility of getting mugged, she hurried to her car and quickly drove away. Ever since her close encounter, she fantasized that Grady would have appeared from the shadows and disassembled the attackers limb by limb with his bare hands. He spoke with the tone of an educator, both pleasant and helpful.

"It ain't much, but here's what I got. There will be a service but no proper funeral. The state is transporting their bodies to the forensic science program at Penn and the service will be held in four days, so make sure the little girl is there. Now the hard part, the children's home isn't quite closed, but it will be in a few weeks so they won't intake any children. For the time being, all orphans go to Philly. Problem is Philly is overcrowded, and you'll have to wait until they transfer some of the children. You may have to find a home for a few weeks."

"Weeks? Mallory asked. "All the homes around here are already full because of the orphanage closure."

"Who knows? Could be sooner. Maybe just one week. See if there are any available foster parents in the county, and if there aren't, let me know." Grady left her desk in a hurry and headed to the next fire. Mallory looked at the contents of the manila folder once again. She was familiar with the file, as she had been assigned Abbey's case twice in three years. The first time was when her mother abandoned her at the age of three, leaving her little girl at pre-school and never picking her up. The second time, Abbey had been playing on a junk pile in her aunt and uncle's backyard, only to slip and fall onto an old pane glass window. A shard of glass sliced Abbey's leg, and after incessant screaming, she was eventually retrieved from the junk pile. Justin and Judy Creeson gazed upon her deep wound knowing they were without any kind of medical insurance, and the free clinic would just send them to the hospital. After a week of bandages and first aid tape, the wound became infected, and a visit to the hospital became necessary. When the hospital discovered Abbey's leg was infected to the point of amputation, the child protection agency was called. A negligence complaint to the state concerning the welfare of Abbey was filed, and Mallory assisted with the investigation.

The file on her desk had several photographs of the home where Abbey resided—a small house built in the 1960s without central heat and air. From the photos one would easily come to the conclusion that the Cresson's were sloppy, filthy people who had little respect for themselves, let alone anyone else. When the investigation into Abbey's injury concluded, Justin and Judy were ordered by family court to undergo a series of mandatory classes for three months. Instead of making every available class in order to get Abbey returned to their home as fast as possible, they would miss a class here and there, show up late and fail written assessments. What should have taken three months became six. Abbey didn't mind the long absence as she stayed in a clean foster home with a comfortable bed, central heat and air and better food. Recovering from an amputation would have been torture in her aunt and uncle's home, but being with friendly and caring foster parents made it easier.

The newest stack of papers in the file was the police and coroner's report on the accident and death of Justin and Judy Creeson. She flipped through the papers, noticing a new addition to the file, a death certificate of Abbey's biological mother. Just as she began to look it over, one of her co-workers walked up and handed her a birthday card and spoke in a happy, sing-song voice, "Hey there, Birthday girl!"

Tescily Kennedy, called Tess by her friends, has had to endure life-long questions concerning her famous last name. After her first child, she put her dreams of being a fashion designer on hold indefinitely. Since she only wore pastel colors, her friends considered it a good move.

"Please, I'm hardly a girl." Mallory took her hand off the file and let the manila flap lay open, exposing the contents of Abbey's life.

"You're not that old, and you look much younger than you are. You shouldn't be sad about it." Tess reached out and tugged Mallory's hair playfully. She noticed a picture of Abbey among a coroner's report in the file. Fearing the worst, she covered her mouth, as her eyes grew large. She looked at Mallory. "Oh no. Tell me she's okay. It's that Creeson girl isn't it? Is she okay? Tell me she's okay."

"She's fine."

"Are you working her case again? Why is her file out?"

"Well, I suppose it is good news although we probably shouldn't think so."

"Yeah? What?" Tess said with an expression as if she was about to be told a secret.

"Her aunt and uncle were killed last night in Bear Creek. DUI."

"No way!"

"Yep. She's an orphan."

"That is good news. Well, you know I don't want anyone to die or anything, and I don't want a little girl to be orphaned but…"

"Abbey is better off," Mallory said as she opened the birthday card. Kittens in party hats adorned the cover and interior.

"I should say so. Karma, huh?" Tess said as she watched Mallory open the card.

"I hate it for Abbey, but I'm glad for her too. Thanks for the birthday card."

"No problem. Lunch is on me tomorrow. Mulligan's has half-priced appetizers from eleven to one."

"Spinach artichoke," Mallory said mimicking Tess's sing-song voice.

"Happy birthday to you." Tess walked away toward the other side of the office strutting in her lavender and honeydew outfit while Mallory flipped through Abbey's file. The file photo of little Abbey was taken at her school on picture day and was paper clipped to a child abuse/neglect investigation report. Mallory rubbed her thumb over Abbey's pretty face, thinking that the little girl had finally caught a break.

Chapter 6

Mallory Cain hung up the phone after a frustrating hour of making calls to foster homes in Luzerne County. Due to the closing of the Wilkes-Barre Orphanage, all participating foster homes were at full capacity. Little Abbey Creeson was officially homeless. An idea sparked in Mallory's head and she quickly spun in her chair and faced the other side of her desk. She opened a drawer packed tightly with files and fished out a folder marked *State Placement Guidelines: Minors and Emergency Placement.* She opened the file and scanned through several stapled documents. Using her index finger, she found the paragraph she was searching for.

ARTICLE 21;SECTION 4 – PUBLIC/PRIVATE SHELTERS AND LODGING. *Minors under the ages of 18 can be granted approved lodging under section 4 and 5 of Pennsylvania child placement law should the minor(s) and or agency not have access to immediate approved placement home(s) and or state facility. For child endangerment protocol see AR.22;SEC9.*

APPROVED LODGING.

Mallory fumbled through her desk in a mad search. Upon opening a drawer, she removed three blank forms. Purse. Keys. Sunglasses—and out the door she went.

At Bear Creek Elementary, nine-year-old Abbey Creeson was deep in thought as she calculated answers for her fourth grade math quiz. The 61-year-old Mrs. Watt took a stroll around the desks, watching the students for signs of cheating. A forgotten relic in the Bear Creek school system, Mrs. Watt was nearing retirement and the end of her cruel reign over the students who were unlucky enough to be placed in her fourth grade class. Feared by her students, loathed by the other teachers and an enemy to the staff in the lunchroom, she carried on day-to-day with a frown. Abbey came to the last three questions on the math quiz with her shoulder-length hair falling on either side of her face. Even if another student wanted to copy her answers, they wouldn't be able to see her paper due to the curtain of hair covering both sides of her paper. After she answered the last question, she turned her paper over and popped her head up, pushing the bridge of her glasses to the top of her nose. Her glasses were a constant reminder of an uncomfortable day when she picked them up at the county health clinic. Under the assumption that the glasses were paid for by the state welfare office, Abbey's uncle, Justin Creeson yelled at the office manager of the free clinic. Being forced to pay a ten-dollar co-pay angered Justin to the point of swearing at everyone behind the counter while Abbey stood behind him.

Mrs. Watt glanced at Abbey's math quiz, noticing an error. A teacher worth her salt may have pointed out the error to further educate the student on the subject they were working on. Instead, she casually picked up Abbey's quiz and walked between the desks, inciting fear in the children's souls while she silently laughed at Abbey's mistake.

When the school bus arrived outside of Abbey's home that morning, she was standing beside the mailbox in a worn coat and pink backpack she bought at a garage sale with her own money. Her aunt and uncle never came home from their late night out, which wasn't anything new, and she was left to get herself ready and to the mail box by 7:35 AM. Getting ready in the morning wasn't easy for her as she had to hobble around on one leg until she was dressed and ready to force the end of her knee into the one-size-too-small prosthetic leg. Thankfully, the bus driver was aware of Abbey's disability and would honk the horn and wait for her to waddle the gravel driveway if she was ever running late. The day proceeded like any other, until shortly after lunch, when she was called to the principal's office.

A victim of discount fashion, Mr. Phelps, the school principal, saved money by buying all of his clothes from discount stores that sold irregular clothing. Sweater vests, button-up shirts and dress pants all bought at a fraction of the price with the small caveat that most were ripped, torn or damaged in some way. He was an unattractive man, destined to live a life with novice sewing skills that mended most of his flawed clothes. Thinning gray hair and a fast-food build, he walked toward his office where little Abbey waited for his arrival.

The sheriff's office had placed a call to Mr. Phelps early that morning and explained that Abbey Creeson's aunt and uncle were killed in a car accident the night before. Mr. Phelps was asked to keep the information to himself until arrangements were made for Abbey. After a second phone call stating the sheriff and a state social worker would be arriving shortly, Mr. Phelps had Abbey summoned to his office.

"Hello Abbey," he said with a half smile as he walked in.

"Hello," she said as she sat on the edge of the chair. She had removed her prosthetic leg and sat it next to her. Since it was a size too small, Abbey loved to take it off whenever she had the chance. Her other leg dangled and swung back and forth freely in the air.

"There are some people coming to see you, and I thought we could wait in the music room, okay?"

"Okay," Abbey answered as she pushed the bridge of her glasses up to the top of her nose and pulled her prosthetic leg to her knee and forced her appendage into the top. She stood up and limped out of the office. On the way to the music room, Mr. Phelps walked slowly and asked her questions to break the silence.

"Did you have a good day at school today?"

"Yeah."

"What did you do?"

"We did spelling words this morning, and after lunch we took a math quiz."

"How was recess?"

"We didn't have it today."

"What? Why?"

"Mrs. Watt said that if we couldn't spell our words we wouldn't have recess."

"Your class didn't go to recess today?"

"No. Sometimes we miss it."

"You've missed it before?" he asked in a near state of shock.

"Yeah," Abbey answered. Mr. Phelps bit his bottom lip while his memory brought up all the instances in which Mrs. Watt had caused him problems. Protesting fun and educational field trips, proposing to increase the amount of homework, and attempting to shorten recess were just a few. Mr. Phelps opened the door for Abbey upon reaching the empty music room. As she limped in, footsteps could be heard approaching behind them. The school secretary walked up to Mr. Phelps and spoke in a low tone. Aware of the situation, she couldn't bring herself to make eye contact with Abbey.

"They're here," she said softly and walked away.

"Oh, okay," Mr. Phelps said before turning to Abbey. "Abbey, could you wait in here momentarily?"

"Can I play the piano?" she asked.

"Of course," Mr. Phelps said with a smile. Just as he closed the door, Abbey limped toward the upright piano. Mr. Phelps walked back to his office as he looked himself over. A small tear in his sweater vest had been mended, but it was still noticeable. With an attempt to conceal his cheap nature, he covered it with his left hand as if he was patting his stomach. Once in view of Mallory Cain and the sheriff, he expressed his professionalism by holding his head up high as he extended his right hand for a handshake as if he were a politician.

"Hello. I'm Principal Phelps," he said as he shook hands with the sheriff.

"I'm Sheriff Coleman, and this is Mallory Cain."

After the introductions, a meeting commenced in Mr. Phelps' office. School bus routes were discussed, notes about grief counseling during school hours, notification of Abbey's plight to teachers and staff, and the preparation of her school records for when she transferred. Once Mallory had completed the necessary forms and cleared everything with Mr. Phelps, she was ready to see Abbey.

Chapter 7

Weeks before Stanton flew to Bear Creek, Pennsylvania, an email was sent to Jim Mayfield. The email asked if they could send someone to speak with him about a mission that NASA would be working on and that it pertained to Jim's area of expertise. The email was lengthy, explaining some of the details, and within an hour, they had their response.

From: Jim Mayfield [mailto:Jim.Mayfield@canyonmail.net]
Sent: Monday, 8:55 AM
To: 'dthomas'
Subject: RE: Proposal

No thanks.

A few more emails were sent to Jim that explained in further detail that crates would be sent with computers, servers, and touch displays. He would be given access to NASA's SHELL satellite, and a gigabit internet connection. A few days passed, and then a second email from Jim Mayfield hit the inbox of the mission director.

From: Jim Mayfield [mailto:Jim.Mayfield@canyonmail.net]
Sent: Friday, 6:12 PM
To: 'dthomas'

Subject: RE: Proposal

Will consider.

Stanton knocked on the door, unsure if he should knock or just go in. He looked down at the porch taking notice that it could be entirely possible that theJim was casual and relaxed with his right leg resting on his left knee. He had let himself sink into the chair and looked comfortable as he spoke and sipped from his near empty bottle of beerre were bodies piled up underneath, just as Tom and Jerry said. When there was no answer to his knocking, he decided to try the door. When the door opened, Stanton pushed it open, but stayed on the front porch.

"Hello?" Stanton hollered out and smiled out of uncertainty. "Hello?" he said again. "It's me, Dr. Stanton." He walked in and took notice of a massive stone fireplace to his right that extended twenty-five feet in the air and into the knotty pine rafters. Exposed wooden beams supported the high ceilings, and the walls were covered in dated, beige patterned wallpaper. To the left of the hearth were worn leather couches and chairs angled toward an analog rear-projection television. Stanton could imagine families gathering and watching TV shows and ballgames. He closed the door behind him and took several steps in the lobby.

The *click* and *clack* of Stanton's loafers on the hardwood floor echoed throughout the expansive lobby of Bear Creek Inn. On his left was a long check-in counter with half of the wall covered by small wooden boxes used to keep messages for guests. On his right were French doors leading to a dining hall. Standing in front of the grand staircase,

Stanton could see a hallway behind it with rooms spanning down the right and left hallways. At the top of the staircase, Stanton could see another hallway with numbered doors. He looked around the lobby and listened for signs of life. Nothing. From the second floor, something caught his eye. In the air, floating quietly was a paper airplane. Stanton watched it sail through the air before it lost momentum and the nose tipped downward and gained speed before making a soft landing near Stanton's feet. Confused, Stanton looked around, then back at the airplane and ultimately decided to pick it up. Unfolding the paper, he read a handwritten note.

I'm here.
Just give me a second.

Stanton looked up at the second floor railing where the airplane started its flight then back down at the note. Not knowing how long he would have to wait, he set the paper airplane on the check-in counter and walked to the worn leather couch and sat down. The cushions were broken in and very comfortable. Next to him was a remote control with duct tape keeping the battery cover secure. Stanton pushed the power button, and the old rear-projection TV came to life. Talking heads on ESPN discussed spring training. Stanton turned down the volume and waited patiently, sitting through a string of commercials. Bored with the commercials, Stanton turned off the TV. The door to the dining hall began to open, and Stanton stood up and faced the door. Jim Mayfield appeared from behind the open door and looked at the first guest under his roof in ten years. Stanton put his hands in his pockets and cleared his throat.

"Hey," Jim said sporting a full beard and a dark flannel shirt. His denim jeans and shirt looked twenty years old, but his Merrell Vibram

Sole Hiking Shoes looked brand new.

"Jim." Stanton said as he nodded, "Thanks for seeing me."

"Sorry for the welcoming, but it took me a bit to get used to the idea of someone else being here," he said. His right hand held the doorknob with the other gripping side of the door. Stanton took notice.

"No one has been in here?"

"Well, a couple times over the years I've had family visit, but no one else. No outsiders," Jim took a deep breath and looked down at the hardwood floors.

"You okay?"

"Yeah, it's just strange."

"Do you remember me?"

"Sure, you evaluated us for spaceflight."

"That was a long time ago."

"Yeah, it was."

"Can we have a seat?" Stanton said, wanting to get started.

"Sure. Of course. You wanna beer first?"

"That would be great," Stanton said taking notice that it was the first sign of normalcy in his brief encounter. Jim left the comfort of the French doors and disappeared into the dining hall.

Stanton's first thoughts about Jim were that he appeared to be more reserved than unsociable. Jim didn't seem afraid of his presence as much as he was bothered. When he came back into the room, he was handed a beer with an illustration on the label of a black bear roaring in a stream with salmon flipping out of the water. The words *Black Bear Alaskan Ale* were sprawled across the top of the label.

"Alaskan ale?"

"It's a craft beer. It's good," Jim said as he took a sip. Stanton followed Jim's lead and placed the end of the bottle to his lips. His eyes grew large as the freezing-cold, amber liquid sloshed around his mouth with hoppy flavor igniting his taste buds. The sudsy liquid went down smooth as he swallowed leaving a bold note.

"That's beyond craft. Wow. That is really good."

"Took me three years to find one that good," Jim said taking another sip. Stanton looked at the label.

"How do you get supplies, groceries, and things if you don't leave the inn?"

"The beer I order online. For my groceries, there's a guy in town that owns a grocery store," Jim said taking another sip. "I send him an email of what I need, he delivers it to the back porch. I pay double the price of everything I ask for which isn't bad since I buy mostly produce."

"What's his name?"

"Charlie. He comes over once a week or so."

"You ever talk to him?"

"Nope. Just email."

"How long have you been living here all alone?"

"Ehh, I guess I'm going on ten years now."

"Do you feel alone living here?"

"What's with all the questions?"

"That's why I am here. To determine if you're insane or of sound mind."

"I see. What's the verdict so far?"

"You look like a thinner version of Jerry Garcia, and you have good beer."

"Nice."

"Can I ask how you earn money?"

"You know, I haven't ever thought much of psychiatrists."

"Me, either."

"How's that? Isn't that what you do?"

"After being in the profession for as long as I have, I have met so many blowhards."

"Your colleagues, you mean," Jim said as he downed the rest of his beer.

"Yep. Everyone likes to think they know what they're talking about. Buncha squirrels."

"So you think the profession is a crock?"

"Not all of it. Maybe eighty percent."

"That's a high number, but I tend to agree." Jim said as he sat his empty bottle on the coffee table. Feeling better about Stanton, he leaned back in his chair. "What was the question?"

"How do you earn money? Are you currently working?"

"Well, all this came from my parents," Jim said as he gestured his hands in a grandiose manner.

"It's nice. Has a cozy feeling. How long have you owned it?"

"My parents had it for thirty years, and then it went to my sister and me."

"Lot of people stay here?"

"Used to. The Poconos are a few miles east of us, and this always served as a place to stay for families on a budget. We would stay at capacity for most of the year."

Stanton opened the leather cover of his tablet computer and pulled out a pair of reading glasses from his shirt pocket. After Stanton took time to read a paragraph, he looked up and removed his glasses.

"What is Hatherton?"

"Hatherton? Why?"

"It says here you work for them."

"Hatherton is a contractor for NASA and the U.S. Military."

"What do they supply NASA with?"

"I don't know the full scale, but I know they work on module couplings, module concepts, and in-orbit propulsion."

"How long have you worked for them?"

"Almost ten years but I wouldn't say that I work for them."

"It says here that you do."

"And what is that?" Jim said as he pointed to the tablet computer.

"It's your profile. Its mostly about your education, your career, and work history. So you don't work there?"

"I'm more of a consultant. I check their calculations, look over schematics, and review their measurements. Sometimes I conference with some of the crew on the ISS, but it's nothing major. I'm more of a contractor or a consultant than an employee."

"Are you paid a salary or by the job? You don't have to answer if you don't want to."

"I'm paid well for my work on a per job basis. They use me because I'm not expensive, and I'm very thorough."

"Do you have any other sources of income?"

"Weird questions."

"They are, but I am required to ask. I gather from what little I have been told that the mission director wants to hire you for something. These questions lead me to believe that they want to know if you need money."

"I didn't spend much of my income from working at NASA. I was always too busy, so I have plenty in savings. I also make and sell handmade rocking chairs."

"What about the text books?"

"How'd you know about that?"

"*They* told me."

"*They* know a lot don't they?"

"Not a lot. That's why I'm here. They didn't know about the rocking chairs."

"I work with a group of professors on the text books. The pay scale for one book is pretty remarkable, but I only do one every few years - so far anyway.

"How many have you completed?"

"I don't know. Six or seven. I started out editing. Checking and re-checking calculations, things like that. But the last one I co-authored."

"What is it called?"

"*Stellar, Galactic, and Extragalactic Astronomy*. My part was the radio propagation in the interstellar medium and gravitational lensing. I edited the sections containing calculations and graphs for Eddington luminosity, cosmic microwaves, and the Sunyaev–Zeldovich effect."

"Sounds fun." Stanton said alluding to the fact that he had no idea what Jim was talking about. Jim returned a smile, acknowledging Stanton's gesture, but continued speaking.

"It keeps my brain going. Some of it is fun. Most of it is work though." Stanton wrote down Jim's answers and looked at his empty beer.

"Want another one?" Jim asked as he held up his empty bottle.

"Does the Pope wear a funny hat?" Stanton answered with a smile. The next couple of hours were spent with Jim answering a multitude of questions as they both drank Black Bear Alaskan Ale.

"You live alone, but you seem to stay busy."

"I suppose. I have thought about cutting ties with Hatherton and stop writing textbooks. I think I'd like to just focus on making rocking chairs."

"You like it that much?"

"I love it. Crafting something so difficult and having it turn out perfect is a great feeling."

The evaluation came to a close when the final question was asked. Stanton had travelled over a thousand miles to ask one question. Not wanting to get it wrong, he glanced down at the notes on his tablet computer before looking up and uttering the words.

"Why did you choose to lock yourself inside this place? Why not be more social?"

"I don't know," Jim said immediately as if he knew the question was coming. Stanton paid close attention to his mannerisms. Jim was casual and relaxed with his right leg resting on his left knee. He had let himself sink into the chair and looked comfortable as he spoke and sipped from his near empty bottle of beer. "It didn't start out that way. I wanted to take a year off. A year off from everything and not answer to anyone. That turned into two years and two became three and so on. Now I feel like I don't ever want to leave or have to deal with anyone again."

"Are you afraid to leave?"

"No."

"Would you leave if you were asked to?"

"I don't know. Probably not."

After their lengthy conversation, Stanton briefly left the inn to make a phone call outside on the cobblestone driveway. Even though he was outside, he spoke quietly in case Jim could somehow hear him.

"Stable. Social withdrawal disorder or even avoidant personality disorder. Nothing serious by any means," Stanton said on his end of the conversation. While he listened, he saw a deer eating budding vegetation on a small bush. He stared at it, wondering if it was the same deer he saw earlier as he answered questions. "I think he would be receptive to it. I'll ask."

Stanton called Del the cab driver before he walked back inside. Jim wasn't anywhere to be seen. Stanton stood by the leather couches, noticing that the sun coming through the skylight cast warm rays on the leather cushions. The room felt warm and made him long for another nap. Since reaching the age of fifty-two, sleep had become a much bigger priority than it used to be. In mid-thought, Jim walked in from the dining hall carrying a bowl of fruit.

"Sorry, I'm getting hungry and thought I would grab something. You want anything?"

"Nah. I ate before I got here," Stanton said.

"So what'd they say?"

"Well, they want to know if you could come to Houston for a meeting. Private jet. You won't have to deal with anyone or talk to anyone else," Stanton said. Jim looked off into the distance in thought while he chewed on a piece of fruit.

"I refuse to leave. I mean, I'm open to the idea of a remote workstation or something, but that's it. I like being here, and I don't want to leave."

"I understand. At this point, they definitely have to play by your rules."

"What details do you have about this? Why do they want me?"

"I don't know for sure, but the mission they are discussing seems vital—imperative even. Both the mission director and the administrator have had meetings about you in particular."

"The administrator?" Jim said as he chewed on a honey crisp apple. He looked at Stanton, leaning forward with his elbows on his knees. Small bowl of fruit in one hand, fork in the other, he quickly popped a banana slice into his mouth and continued to speak as he chewed. "Must be something going on if both the director and the administrator are talking about me."

Chapter 8

Hitting the keys on the upright piano, Abbey attempted to play a song with one finger. Mallory entered and set down her things and walked over to the piano bench and knelt beside Abbey.

"What were you playing?"

"Old Dan Tucker."

"I used to play that when I was your age," said Mallory. "Do you remember me?"

"I think so."

"I came to your house and took you to the Lang's home. Remember them?"

"I remember," Abbey nodded.

She reached out and held Abbey's hand and looked in her eyes. "Abbey, can we go sit at the table over there?" Abbey nodded again. Once seated, Mallory began her difficult task, a task she had been trained to do.

"I am sorry to have to tell you this," Mallory said and then took a deep breath. The words wouldn't come. She hesitated like a sixteen year old pulling out into heavy traffic. "Last night, your aunt and uncle were in a car accident. Their car ran off the road, and they didn't survive," she explained. Abbey's distant stare and furrowed brow signaled to Mallory that she may have to explain it again. Before Mallory could say anything, tears started to collect in Abbey's eyes and fall to the rim of her glasses. Mallory hugged her, and Abbey wrapped her arms around Mallory's neck.

Mr. Phelps walked toward the door to the music room and peered inside the small, slender window. Peeking into the room, he saw little Abbey Creeson hugging Mallory, her small fists tightly gripping the fabric of Mallory's shirt.

Questions were asked. Some were answered; some weren't. Abbey would cry and calm down, only to sob once again into Mallory's shoulder upon getting difficult answers to her questions. After an hour of one-on-one time, Abbey Creeson sat in the passenger seat of Mallory's car. She stared out the window as the scenery flew by at dizzying speeds, although Abbey didn't even seem to notice. Trees, rocks, guardrails and the houses blurred together. Her attention was brought toward the driver's side as Mallory's cell phone rang. Abbey watched as she picked up the phone and silenced it before putting it back in her purse. Abbey went back to the blurred scenery as Mallory reached out to hold the hand of a newly orphaned girl. As she steered the car around a curve, she looked for a certain street sign. Mallory took the long way around, as the shorter route would bring her past the scene of the accident. Without knowing if the wreckage had been cleared off the road or not, she avoided the street. After Mallory found Abbey's house, she parked in the gravel driveway.

A small three-bedroom, one-bath home with cracked vinyl siding wasn't much to look at from the outside and was even worse once they opened the sliding glass door. Mallory remembered the sloppy and cluttered home of the Creesons, but was welcomed by a new odor produced by half-eaten food left on the end tables, TV trays, and the kitchen counter. Abbey didn't seem to notice the odor—she'd gotten used to it.

Mallory followed Abbey to her room.

"Abbey, we need to get your clothes, toothbrush, and toothpaste. We don't need to worry about anything else. We just need your clothes, toiletries and any toys you want to keep."

"I'm supposed to have my vomit syrup."

"What?"

"In case I eat fake sugar. I have to have the syrup."

"Is it medicine?"

"Uh huh," Abbey said. Mallory excused herself and headed out to the car. She grabbed her file and flipped the pages while she stood between her car and the open driver's side door. She found a medical form and used her finger to scan the conditions section and found *advanced aspartame disorder* written in pencil with a description: *Patient cannot digest aspartame. Kidney failure imminent upon digesting aspartame. In the event of accidental ingestion, treat with ipecac followed by medical treatment.*

Mallory closed the folder. "Artificial sweetener," she said aloud to herself.

Back inside the filthy house, Mallory stepped over piles of dirty laundry in an attempt to get into the bathroom and open the cabinets.

"Abbey, honey? Is your syrup in here?" Mallory asked out loud. Abbey answered from her bedroom.

"Should be in a green bag with a zipper." Mallory looked for an item fitting the description. Behind her was a slim linen closet. She opened it finding towels, sheets, newspapers, empty plastic Wal-Mart bags, and a green zippered case. She grabbed it and unzipped it—four pre-loaded syringes with *Ipecac* on a white label on the side of each syringe. Mallory squinted to read the instructions.: *One syringe equals one full dose. To be administered orally. Squirt ipecac into mouth and swallow.* She zipped it up and walked back into Abbey's room.

"I got it."

When she finally made it to Abbey's bedroom, Mallory's eyes began to tear up. Abbey's bed was on the floor and she didn't have a dresser or a closet, but her room was clean. Her clothes were folded and stacked neatly against the wall under her window. Toys and stuffed animals were organized opposite her bed. There was room to walk without stepping on laundry, old pizza boxes, and beer cans.

"Do you always keep you room this clean and organized?"

"Sometimes it's messy, but not always. I like it straightened."

Trying to hide her emotions and focus on getting her out of the house for the last time, Mallory found a camouflage duffel bag and began to pack the clothes folded neatly on the floor.

Chapter 9

Del drove his taxi through the opened gate of the Pocono Mountains Municipal Airport. He parked twenty yards away from the jet just as Tom and Jerry put their golf clubs in the luggage compartment. They stared at the cab looking for signs of Jim Mayfield.

"He in there?"

"Doesn't look like it."

Stanton paid Del his fare and included a tip.

"I may be back. Hope to see ya when I am."

"You, too. Appreciate the tip."

"Take it easy," Stanton said as he got out of the cab.

"He's alive," Tom shouted.

"Did you have to run for your life?" Jerry said with a laugh.

"You guys wouldn't believe it if I told you," Stanton said as he climbed aboard the plane. Tom and Jerry looked at each other as if Stanton really did experience something out of the ordinary. Once they boarded and took their seats in the cockpit, they prodded Stanton with questions to no avail. He had already reclined in his leather seat and pulled the window shade down.

"Did something happen?" Tom asked.

"Is he certifiable?" Jerry added. Stanton put his sunglasses on and got comfortable. With his eyes closed and ready for his second nap of the day, he spoke without making eye contact from behind his dark sunglasses.

"I can't tell you because he is my patient, but if I could, you wouldn't believe it anyway," he said. Deciding to let them think the worst.

"Is he messing with us?" Tom asked.

"I bet he is."

"Do you believe him, though?"

"Yeah, I believe him," Jerry said as he nodded slowly.

. . .

Mallory steered her car up the side of Bear Mountain Road with one hand—her other hand on her cell phone.

"I am just now becoming aware of this, and I need to understand a little better. I've never heard of this condition," Mallory said as she navigated the curves.

"She's not supposed to ingest artificial sweetener. No diet soda or tea with aspartame in it. No food or candy that says sugar-free or even sugarless-gum," the nurse said. "It's not just aspartame though. It's all artificial sweeteners."

"What needs to happen if she does?"

"Give her one full syringe. There's no needles or anything. Just have her squirt it in her mouth. Ipecac causes you to vomit so once she regurgitates what she ate or drank, get her to the ER. If aspartame makes it to her kidneys, they could fail. We keep syringes and a bottle here at the school, but she knows what she shouldn't eat or drink." Mallory listened intently and missed the entrance for Bear Creek Inn. She applied her brakes and put the car in reverse while thanking the school nurse and hung up her phone.

Mallory parked her car outside the gate to the inn and helped Abbey exit the passenger seat. After she wiggled and scooted to the edge of the passenger seat, Abbey attached the prosthetic leg to her knee. She stood in front of the exterior of the gate and looked at the eerie and disconcerting stone and ironwork overtaken by plants and weeds.

"See the space between the tree and the pillar?" Mallory said, suggesting that's where they were headed. Abbey clutched her tattered, stuffed Panda Pillow a little tighter as she limped and waddled next to Mallory toward the gate.

"Here, let me help." Mallory said as she took the Panda Pillow momentarily in her arms and held Abbey's hand while she guided her between the pillar and the maple tree.

After an unsettling walk down a gravel path, they reached the cobblestone driveway and arrived at the unkempt exterior of Bear Creek Inn. The sky was getting dark, multiplying Abbey's fear. Mallory walked like she had been there a thousand times while Abbey limped cautiously behind her, trying not to listen to the noises of the forest that surrounded her. After she helped Abbey up the steps, Mallory reached for the handle on the front door and found it unlocked. The only light source in the dark lobby came from the TV, illuminating the soft, leather couches and bottles of beer that sat on the coffee table. Mallory walked around the couches and grabbed a bottle off the table. Still cold. Abbey watched as Mallory shouted out into the darkness.

"Jim?" Her voice echoed against the hardwood floors and the emptiness of the high, wood beamed ceiling. No answer. "Jim?" she yelled out once again. Nothing. Mallory reached to the left of the doors and turned on the lights.

The height of the ceiling and the size of the grand staircase startled

Abbey as the lights flicked on. Without saying a word, she slowly raised her arm and pointed toward the second floor. Mallory looked at Abbey and turned her head to see what she was pointing at. A paper airplane sailed through the air and landed near the check-in desk. Mallory saw the plane and glared at the direction of where Jim might be. Familiar with Jim's paper airplane communication, she wasn't amused. Without even picking up the airplane, she answered his note.

"She's a little girl, and she doesn't even know who you are."

"What is this place?" Abbey asked.

"It's like a hotel. It's closed though."

"Oh."

"Come on Jim, where are you?"

Jim's arm appeared from behind the wall on the second floor. He pointed toward the paper airplane with a furious motion. Mallory exhaled in frustration and walked over, picking up the paper airplane and unfolded it.

No outsiders!

"She's a child," Mallory shouted.

"Especially children," Jim yelled out before he slammed a door shut.

"Who is that?" Abbey asked, still concerned about her surroundings.

"Well, you wouldn't believe it, but he's an astronaut. Well, *was* an astronaut."

"Really?" Abbey asked. Mallory spoke loud enough so that Jim could hear her.

"And my stupid brother!" In her loud, outdoor voice, she continued to speak. "We're staying the night. You're welcome to join us. Hope you have something to eat in the kitchen." Mallory put her hand on Abbey's shoulder. "Come on."

Mallory hadn't been to see her brother in over a year. She normally visited him around Christmas, but was out of town with her own family the previous year. Since they talked on the phone every few months or so, Mallory made it a point to stay away from the inn. While she didn't understand her brother's behavior, she respected him and kept her distance.

Mallory guided Abbey behind the grand staircase. To their right and left were long hallways with doors numbered beginning with Room 101. Mallory noticed Abbey looking around at the massive lobby.

"Big, isn't it? It has gotten smaller over the years though. When I was a kid, I thought this place was the biggest building in the world." She opened the door to Room 101 while Abbey stayed out in the hallway. Mallory walked right in and started taking plastic coverings off the floor, the bed, the desk, in-wall HVAC, lamps, and nightstands. Abbey watched from the hallway while Jim stood out of view on the second floor landing and listened to the rustling in the room below.

"I will be sleeping in this bed here, next to you. You can put your things here." Mallory said as she pointed to what would be Abbey's bed. "Come on in." Pink backpack, Panda Pillow and a bottle of water were placed neatly on the bed. Mallory watched Abbey from the corner of her eye as she sat on the bed and removed her prosthetic leg to massage her sore knee.

After they got set up in their room, Mallory gave Abbey a piggyback ride toward the dining hall. Now only an open space, the dining hall was once full of tables, chairs and hungry guests. Years ago, Jim gathered all of the furniture in the dining hall and stored it in the utility barn out back. Mallory's footsteps echoed around the large basketball court-sized room. To the left was a workbench with sawdust scattered around the floor. A small lamp illuminated a block of wood clamped down with carving tools neatly positioned on a board above the bench.

"What's all that?" Abbey asked.

"He's a woodworker. He makes furniture. Well, mostly rocking chairs," Mallory answered.

As they walked toward the kitchen, Abbey looked at the work area. She squinted to see two computers sitting side by side near the workbench. On the wall was a hook that held a woodworkers apron. Mystified as to what the equipment and tools were, she turned her head as they entered the kitchen.

The kitchen looked desolate—industrial. Mallory set Abbey down and walked to the commercial grade refrigerator. Upon opening it, she saw containers of strawberries, cantaloupe, mandarin oranges, diced pears, peaches and other fruit, all cut, prepared, and neatly stored. Mallory closed the door and opened a cupboard. Inside were canned green beans, spinach, sweet corn, sweet peas, celery, new potatoes, okra, and diced carrots.

"Fruit and vegetables," Mallory said to herself before she closed the cupboard. She glanced over her shoulder. "I am kind of on vacation tonight, and I don't like eating fruits and vegetables when I am on vacation. Are you up for a pizza?" Mallory asked. Abbey shrugged her shoulders, seemingly up for anything.

Chapter 10

While there are many conference rooms on NASA's campus, the most elaborate one is adjacent to the administrator's office. The frosted glass walls feature large framed photographs of nebulas and planets adhered to the glass interior. The massive conference room table is more like a giant tablet computer with a touchscreen surface. The entire room never failed to impress presidents, governors and senators who attended meetings with Frank Navasky, NASA's director.

Mr. Navasky entered the room and the lights automatically increased their brightness. He took a seat at the head of the table and slid his finger across the slick surface launching documents, prepared drafts, and statements. Frank's assistant, Mike McCara entered the room quietly and took a seat.

"Where's Dave and Dr. Stanton?" Frank asked without looking up from his email. Mike looked at the time on his watch. 4:45 P.M.

"Dave is talking to someone in the hallway. He's coming. I haven't seen Dr. Stanton yet, but he was supposed to have landed by now."

Mission Director, Dave Thomas, entered the room and closed the glass door behind him. Unfortunately, Dave bore the same full name as the founder of Wendy's fast food restaurants. For most of his life, Dave had been asked "Where's the beef?" and endured fast food orders left on his voicemail from hilarious co-workers over the years.

"Stanton's coming. He's running behind," Dave said as he took a seat. Using the touchscreen table in front of him, he began to pull reports off a server by tapping and sliding his finger. Mike McCara watched both men prepare for the meeting, making the mistake of looking at Dave's necktie. As always, it was cinched tight and appeared as if it was closing off his airway. While Dave didn't enjoy being strangled by his ties, he did prefer a clean, and tight neckline free of wrinkles with a perfectly tied knot. When his constricting ties caused Dave to slightly choke, his solution wasn't to loosen the knot. Instead he constantly tugged at his collar throughout the day by tucking his index finger in between his throat and the collar of his dress shirt and pulled it for temporary relief. Mike slowly reached for his own collar and kept an eye on Dave as he made a covert move to loosen his own tie. Once the quick maneuver was completed, Mike cleared his throat as nonchalantly as possible.

"Good lord, don't tell me he's jet lagged," Frank said as he looked at the time.

"We can start. I have enough info to begin," Dave said.

"What have we got so far? Is he crazy or not?" Frank asked as he closed his email with a swipe of his finger on the slick glass. Dave looked down at the touchscreen and read a report from Stanton.

"Dr. Stanton evaluated Jim and believes he's of sound mind. He notes that he has a disorder known as social withdrawal, but explains that it is nothing serious."

Frank had been the administrator of NASA for three years and even before he took the job, he had already heard the rumors concerning Jim Mayfield. Frequent words the staff used to describe Jim were words like eccentric, insane, mentally ill, and abnormal. Those words were usually paired with others such as genius, mastermind, innovator, flawless, and super engineer. The rumors were widespread, but Frank knew that most of the negative descriptions were unfounded. Jim's reputation among those who had worked with him, was nothing short of brilliant.

"Is he on his way?" Frank asked.

"No. I am told that he is open to a discussion, but he does not want to leave his residence," Dave answered.

"So how about a video conference?"

"Well, normally I would say yes, but something of this magnitude, what we are requesting of Jim, should be done in person."

"You gonna go up there?" Frank asked.

"Probably. I would like to hear what Stanton has to say first," Dave responded.

Mike McCara was quickly aging from thirty-five to forty under the workload that Frank Navasky brought him. Press releases, taking notes during meetings, setting up travel arrangements, and managing his boss's laptop and email were just some of the tasks he had performed since lunch. Mike had heard the rumors of Jim Mayfield since working for Navasky and considered Jim to be a legend. Since news of the mission director seeking out Jim Mayfield had spread, the stories and rumors of Jim began to circulate the building like a wildfire in dead grass. With the possibility of accompanying Frank to the town in which Jim resided, Mike spoke up in hopes of getting a seat on the private jet to Bear Creek.

"Your schedule is currently clear on Friday. Weather looks good and would be a good day for you to travel," Mike said as he looked up from his smart phone.

"I'm not going to hicktown to see Crazyfield," Frank said. Mike instantly gave up. Frank sounded certain and sincere.

"Well, it seems that I will make time to go up there, but only if you agree that this is important enough to do so," Dave said.

"This mission is ours. Japan and Russia are relying on us at this point and if we announce that we are sending a flight engineer who helped design the coupling and has 81 EVA hours, they will calm down."

"I will make arrangements," Dave said as he pulled on his collar. Mike cleared his throat.

Chapter 11

Papa John's Pizza was busy since college basketball season was in full swing. With the oven cranking out a pizza every minute, Melissa took the 73rd phone call of the night.

"Your phone number?" Melissa asked. The response came through the line. She lazily typed in the number. The screen showed no record of a previous order. She asked for the address and typed it in. "Okay, what would you like?" She typed in pepperoni, sausage and an order of parmesan breadsticks.

"Okay, your order is $16.22. We'll have it out to you in about forty-five minutes," Melissa said and thanked the customer before hanging up. She printed the ticket and looked at the address. While looking over a map of Bear Creek pinned to the wall near the cash register, she searched for 164 Bear Mountain Road using her index finger to find the address. The map wasn't any help. She turned around to her busy co-workers as they yapped, pounded dough and banged pans and pizza rings. Melissa yelled out above the clatter and noise.

"Hey! Where's 164 on Bear Mountain Road?" she shouted. The clanging stopped. The pounding of the dough quickly subsided. Her co-workers stared at her in her red apron, holding a delivery ticket. "What?" Melissa asked. Silence.

"Bear Creek Inn?" One teenage boy questioned. Three delivery drivers sprinted, clamored, and dove at Melissa. A wad of hands reached and grabbed for the ticket, with one young man emerging victorious. Clutching his prize closely to his chest, he yelled: "It's mine! I got it! It's mine! Ha ha! WHOOOO!" The other two drivers admitted defeat.

The lobby of Bear Creek Inn used to be a gathering place for guests of the inn, waiting out snow storms or playing board games while watching a movie, TV show, or sporting event. Mallory sat on one of the three worn, leather couches that surrounded the oversized coffee table and looked over a file that was spread out in front of her. The amount of paperwork to get Abbey transferred to an orphanage in Philadelphia could have fed a family of goats for months. Hungry and impatient, she looked over at the other end of the sofa. Abbey seemed content with her prosthetic leg sitting on the floor in front of her. She used her index finger to push up the bridge of her glasses while she changed channels on the TV.

A car with a Papa John's illuminated sign on top drove in front of the entrance to Bear Creek Inn. Familiar with the dilapidated entrance to the inn, the driver exited his car and quickly maneuvered his youthful, thin frame between the stone pillar and maple tree. While keeping the pizza level, he exited the tight squeeze and made his way up the gravel path.

Mallory finished filling out a form and returned it to the folder. She picked up all of the papers, held them horizontally and racked them on the coffee table, evening out the edges of the stack. She placed them in a folder just as there was a knock at the door.

"Pizza's here!" Mallory said as she jumped up and walked over to the front door as she fished out a twenty-dollar bill from her pocket.

The driver was surprised when a female answered the door. With the expectation of getting to meet Jim Mayfield, the only town celebrity, he didn't give up when he saw Mallory at the door instead.

"How much?" Mallory asked.

"Sixteen twenty-two," The driver said as he peered over Mallory's shoulder, looking for a glimpse of Jim. He was handed the twenty. Mallory noticed him looking past her.

"Something wrong?"

"No, I mean. No, not at all." Hearing a TV to his right, he looked in the direction of the sound. Maybe Jim Mayfield was sitting in front of the TV, he thought. Mallory realized the driver was looking for a glimpse of her brother and took the pizza box from his hands.

"Thank you," she said and closed the door. The driver was left standing on the porch, still holding the twenty and unsatisfied. "Dang it," he said as he turned around and headed toward his car.

Once the pizza box was open, and slices were placed on plates, the TV provided enough ambient noise to break the silence.

"This is really good," Mallory said after chewing on a slice, trying to start a conversation.

Abbey was thinking of a time when she came home to her aunt and uncle's house after school. Macaroni and cheese for dinner while watching a reality show on TV was commonplace and an expected routine. With no family of any kind, she suddenly felt alone and abandoned. As Mallory took another bite of pizza, she turned her head to see Abbey as she held a piece of pizza, her eyes shut tight, her mouth wide open, but silent. Tears streamed down her face as Abbey dropped the pizza, took off her glasses and held her face in her hands. Mallory moved to Abbey's side and held her. Sobbing noises finally emanated from Abbey, soft at first before becoming loud and uncontrollable.

"Abbey. I am so sorry. So sorry," she said as she wrapped her arm around Abbey's shoulders. She embraced Abbey tightly, coming to tears herself. From the second floor, Jim looked in on them before he disappeared into the dark hallway and walked down to a room and silently closed the door.

. . .

After dinner, Mallory sat on the leather sofa with Abbey asleep next to her. Abbey's head rested on a pillow as Mallory placed her hand on Abbey's back, the way she would one of her own children. Mallory made circles with her hand while applying slight pressure, giving comfort to an orphan who had one of the worst days in her life, but Mallory also knew it was the beginning of a better one. She had placed many children with families that were caring, loving, and very compassionate.

When it came time to get Abbey to bed, Mallory had a difficult time deciding what to do. With her own kids, it was as simple as waking them and getting them to trod off to bed in a zombie-like state. She thought about the prosthetic and how best to get Abbey to bed. Deciding to muscle up and carry Abbey, she hoisted the nine year old up and onto her chest as if she were carrying a sack of potatoes. Mallory grunted and squirmed momentarily and plunged each foot forward, trying to be even keeled and not jostle Abbey. Once in the bedroom, she hobbled over to Abbey's bed and laid her down and covered her up.

Mallory returned to the lobby, retrieved Abbey's prosthetic and put it beside her bed. She then promptly walked out of the room and closed the door behind her. Now, it was time to search for her brother.

The search didn't take long after she made it to the second floor.

Out of all the rooms, only one door had light coming from underneath. She gave a courtesy knock and opened the door.

"Jim? I'm alone," she said as she slowly entered.

"Hey, I figured you'd come find me," he said out of view. When Mallory entered, Jim had been seated, but quickly stood up and hugged her. Mallory embraced him back and kissed him on the cheek.

"Missed you."

"Who's the rugrat, and what are you doing here?"

"Glad you missed me too."

"You know I can't stand it."

"That young girl's aunt and uncle, her only living relatives, were killed at two a.m. this morning. She is an amputee and has a medical condition."

"I figured. If a random kid is with you, it's never good."

"I need help."

"I'm sure you'll find it tomorrow. When you leave."

"I am your sister. I need *your* help."

"I don't ask anything of you. Why do you need me to allow you two to stay here?"

"Not me."

"What?"

"I won't be staying here."

"Are you kidding me? I am not looking after a disabled kid with a medical condition. And people think *I'm* crazy."

"You're not crazy—just mean and inconsiderate."

"You should know me well enough to not ask."

"I need this. I need your help," Mallory said as she crossed her arms in frustration.

"I can't," Jim said. "I live here, away from everyone for a reason."

"I wish you didn't. I wish you were normal." Mallory said and turned around and walked out of his room.

"I can't change the way I feel and the way I want to live."

Speaking out of view of Jim, "Yes you can. Doesn't matter. We will be out of here in the morning."

Jim closed the door to his room and went back to watching TV. A weather report showed a thunderstorm approaching with a high wind advisory. After he decided that he couldn't tolerate the smaller TV screen any longer, he turned it off and headed for the lobby.

. . .

The thunderstorm arrived in the middle of the night and began pelting the inn with rain, high winds and the occasional knocking of a tree bending far enough to slam into the side of the roof. Garbage cans flew, bouncing along the cobblestone driveway and into the side of the wooden planked porch. The porch light flickered before going out.

Abbey sat up in her bed, trying to remember where she was. She could see brief glimpses of the room with every flash of lightning that blasted through the window. She decided it was too dark and searched for her prosthetic leg and forced the end of her knee into the uncomfortable circumference. She waddled over to the bathroom and turned on the light. Nothing. The power was out.

The thunder and violent noises of objects that flew in the wind didn't wake Mallory as she rested peacefully with her face smashed into a down pillow. Abbey quietly walked back to her nightstand and put on her glasses before searching for her Panda Pillow. While it may take a child a small amount of time to search for a lost toy, it takes a child with limited mobility much longer. Looking under the bed was a chore as she had to remove her leg, bend down and peer underneath. When she didn't find anything, she used her upper body strength to hoist herself up and then back on the bed, attaching her leg once more. Thinking that the Panda Pillow may be out in the lobby, she took a deep breath as the thunder crashed above the inn.

She opened the door to the hallway and calmed herself, before limping quickly out of the room. She hid behind a thick, round timber that reached all the way to the incredibly high ceiling. The thunder and lightning frightened her, but the thought of having her Panda Pillow to share the burden of the threatening storm was comforting. She broke away from the large timber and limped and waddled to the leather couch. Between the couch and the table, she found her Panda Pillow and grabbed it and held it close. Before she turned around and headed back to the security of her room, she noticed several bottles on the table—in fact, five of them. The flash of lightning illuminated a black bear on the labels of the craft beers. Then, a man appeared from the dining hall carrying a candelabra. The flames flickered with each step and before Abbey could scream, Jim whispered, "Dang it!" and quickly stepped back into the dining hall. Terrified of the bearded man, Abbey attempted to walk quickly back to her room. *Step, clonk, step,* and with each hurried motion, her knee began to slip causing quick, immense pain.

"Ouch," Abbey said as she fell. The left side of her face hit the hardwood floor as Jim witnessed her fall. Sharp ringing filled her ears. Instinctively, he rushed to her side to help. Setting the candelabra on the floor, he crouched over her, unsure of what to do. Abbey was in pain, tears formed in her eyes, and real fear set in when she looked up at the giant man hovering above her. His hands were thick and appeared to be the size of car tires. His head resembled a lion. His mane was illuminated by the candles, which allowed her to see his eyes. He appeared to be concerned and gazed upon her with eyes drawn in worry. Abbey looked away and tried to not make eye contact.

"I'm sorry. I didn't mean to scare you," Jim said. His voice was muffled in her head and sounded deep and robotic.

"Where's Mallory?" the giant asked. Abbey tried to sit up only to receive unwanted assistance from two large car tires. She rubbed her head, and the ringing began to subside.

"She's asleep." Her own voice sounded muffled in her head as she spoke.

"Figures," Jim said, still kneeling over Abbey.

"Can't she hear the storm?" Abbey asked in a distressed voice.

"A train could burst through here, and she still wouldn't wake up," Jim said. His voice started to sound normal, since the ringing in her ears had stopped. Abbey continued to rub her face. "Are you bleeding?" he asked.

"I don't think so," she said as she looked at her palms after she touched her face while still avoiding eye contact.

"I'd turn on the lights, but the power went out."

"My face feels huge."

"You must have smacked the floor pretty hard."

"I need my leg," Abbey said as she held her face. Jim glanced over and saw that her prosthetic leg had come off. He reached and grabbed it by the shoe. Unsure of how best to hand it to her, he set it on the ground in front of her, standing it straight up. She now felt as if the giant wasn't a threat and looked at him directly.

"I need to sit on the couch to put it on."

"Oh, okay," Jim said and offered her his hand. She grabbed it as Jim, acutely aware of how strange it felt to offer a stranger any sort of assistance, helped her up onto the couch.

"Thanks," she said as she uncomfortably jammed her leg into the opening. Jim stood in front of her and looked at a broken child with messy hair and a well-used prosthetic leg. Unaware of his gigantic appearance, he towered over Abbey with his hands on his hips.

"Do you need help back to your room?" Instead of addressing his question, she posed another:

"Is there any pizza left?"

"Pizza? Shouldn't you go back to bed?"

"I didn't eat much at dinner. I'm starving."

"Um…let me check," Jim said and disappeared into the dining hall, taking the candelabra with him and absent-mindedly leaving Abbey in the dark. Ten minutes passed and just as Abbey considered he might not come back, he arrived with a plate of pizza.

"It was in the fridge. I had to heat it up in the gas oven. It would have been quicker in the toaster oven, but the power is out. Sorry it took so long."

"Thank you," she said and blew on the pizza to cool it down. After she had taken two bites in silence, Jim decided to speak up.

"So uh…how'd you lose the leg? In the war?" Jim said with a smile as he leaned against the stone fireplace. Without laughter or even a smile, she responded, "I was playing in the backyard and cut my leg. It got infected."

"Oh. Sorry to hear that," Jim said as Abbey took another bite of pizza. "Sorry to hear about your aunt and uncle, too. Mallory told me." He immediately regretted bringing it up by the look on her face. "My mother and father passed about fifteen years ago," he said, trying to relate to her. Abbey got a better look at Jim in the candlelight and quickly decided that he wasn't a giant. He seemed normal, even with the unkempt beard.

"Do you miss them?" Abbey asked.

"I do. I think about them all the time."

"Do you feel alone?" Abbey asked. Jim thought back to standing outside the funeral home. *It was snowing, and his face was cold. His right hand was warm as Mallory held it tightly.*

"No. I don't feel alone. I've had Mallory by my side," Jim answered as he stared at the floor. Abbey was silent—then tears. "I'm sorry. I didn't…I'm sorry. Should I go wake…uh…," Jim said as he righted himself, no longer leaning against the fireplace.

"No. I'm just sad. I don't like being all alone," Abbey said through her tears. Jim looked at the little girl and couldn't feel anything but sorry for her. A flash of lightning blasted through the windows, accompanied by the ferocious sound of thunder. Abbey jumped as she wiped her tears away.

"Can I do anything for you?"

"I'm tired."

"Do you want me to walk you to your room?"

"No, thank you," Abbey said as she set her plate of half-eaten reheated pizza down on the coffee table. She made sure her prosthetic leg was secured and stood up. "I'm going to go lay down. Thank you for getting me the pizza," she said as she headed toward her room. Halfway between the leather couches and her room she stopped and turned around, looking over her shoulder.

"My name is Abbey. Abbey Creeson." Abbey seemed to wait for Jim to say something.

"Hi," Jim said, stunned at the little girl and her mannerisms. Just before she turned around, he added, "I'm Jim."

She nodded and continued toward her room and closed the door quietly after she went inside. Jim grabbed a near empty bottle of beer and downed the last of it as he thought of Stanton and the little girl. Two guests in one day – *no thanks*, Jim thought.

Chapter 12

The storm clouds over Bear Creek Inn had dissipated enough to let the morning sunlight break though. The skylight in the lobby allowed warm rays to illuminate the check-in desk while Mallory talked on the phone. Her voice echoed throughout the vast space around her as she spoke to her husband in Wilkes-Barre. She asked questions about what her kids had for dinner, how the baths went, and which bedtime story they read. Once caught up on her household, she hung up feeling perplexed as to where Abbey could stay.

In the kitchen, Mallory opened the refrigerator and looked over the fruit once more. The previous night, the healthy selection didn't seem satisfying enough for her appetite, but for breakfast the fruit selection before her was a welcome sight. As she evenly mixed blueberries, raspberries and grapefruit in a bowl, Jim walked into the kitchen. Mallory glared at him as she closed the lid on a piece of Tupperware, snapping the lid tight.

"You're still upset with me?"

"I'm not fond of you right now," Mallory said. Jim leaned over and looked into the bowls of fruit she was preparing for herself and Abbey.

"Aww, man. You're eating all my berries."

"I'm gonna go through hell trying to find a place for Abbey to stay. I wish you would reconsider."

"I actually thought about it."

"You're so generous, a humanitarian. You are so kind and selfless, and the world will one day celebrate your giving nature."

"Isn't it against the law for a child of the state to stay with an un-approved guardian?"

"Yes. But that's not what this is. She's a ward of the state staying in an approved lodge. It helps my situation and hers that this place is registered as an inn. As a favor to me, while I'm away, I wanted you to look after her. Since you own it and I'm your sister, I thought it would be a good solution."

"It's not."

"I just didn't count on my cruel and heartless brother to turn me down."

"Suppose I allowed her to stay here, how long are we talking?"

"Days."

"Not weeks?"

"Probably a few days."

"The *probably* part bothers me. I know how you are."

"Days. I promise."

"I met her."

"Who? Abbey?"

"Yep."

"No you didn't."

"Last night. Midnight or so."

"What? Why?"

"I was reading a book, and the power went off."

"Why'd the power go off?"

"Due to the raging storm outside."

"There was a storm?" Mallory asked. Jim shook his head.

"I remember one night we camped out back with some friends when we were little kids," Jim said, pointing to the back of the inn. "A family of raccoons started scratching at our tent in the middle of the night, and we all screamed and ran out. When we got inside the inn, we didn't know where you were."

"I know. I slept through it."

"You would sleep through a Helen Keller drum solo."

"Abbey came out here?"

"I was watching a game on TV and reading a book. When the power went out, I went into the kitchen and got one of the old candelabras. When I came back, she was out in the lobby."

"That's it?"

"Not hardly. She looked at me, got scared and tried to hurry back to her room, and she fell. She's okay though."

"Did she scream?"

"Nope. She was hungry. I made her pizza."

"Pizza?"

"She said she was hungry, so I heated it up in the oven."

"Then what?"

"We talked, she ate and then went to bed."

"I can't believe you would even speak to her."

"I know. I had a pretty good silent streak going. Well, except for the psychiatrist earlier."

"So the power is out, you heat up pizza for her and then talk about…what?"

"I told her I was sorry to hear about her aunt and uncle, I told her that we lost mom and dad, and that was it."

"What'd she say about her aunt and uncle?"

"She said she was sad and felt lonely. She cried a little," Jim answered. Mallory looked into Jim's eyes to the point of a cold stare. She spoke softly, continuing to stare a ray of death into Jim's eyes.

"And you…can say *no* to that?"

"Saying it out loud like that is making it more difficult."

"Oh please, oh please, oh please," Mallory said as she clasped her hands in front of her and bounced slightly.

"Sorry."

Mallory grabbed Jim's shirt and tugged in desperation, "She has a prosthetic leg!"

"Still, I can't do it. She has a medical condition. I'm not qualified."

"Sweeteners. She can't ingest artificial sweeteners. You eat fruits and vegetables all day. It's fine!"

"You mean, like Aspartame?"

"You don't even have artificial sweeteners in this whole building," Mallory said as her voice took on a higher-pitch. "It's not even a big medical condition! It's like a small, inconsequential medical condition."

"No."

"I hate you! I freaking hate you!" Mallory said as she punched Jim in the arm. She grabbed the bowls of fruit and left the kitchen.

Before Mallory started making desperate phone calls to foster parents who weren't able to take on another child, she decided to take a shower and get Abbey packed. Abbey ate her bowl of fruit and watched TV while she sat on the edge of her bed. Jim stood in the dining hall at his workbench. He clamped the seat of a rocking chair with multiple clamps, securing it to his workbench. After carefully selecting his starting point, he applied the head of a broad-head chisel to the seat and carved out a small strip of wood. He walked over to a computer screen to check his plans displayed on the monitor in CAD format.

He was focused on the rocking chair until he heard noises coming from behind him. *Step. Clonk. Step. Clonk.* The repeated sound caused him to turn his head away from his project. Abbey was carrying an empty bowl and was heading toward the kitchen. She hadn't yet noticed Jim as she hobbled her way toward the large, metal kitchen door. When she started looking around the massive room, she spotted Jim and gave him a wave that would imply, "Hello, friend." Jim took his time before he waved back. He wore a woodworker's apron and stood among sawdust and curved peels of wood he had carved. *Step. Clonk. Step. Clonk.* Despite the discomfort, her prosthetic leg, got her to her destination as she disappeared behind the swinging door.

After setting her bowl in the industrial-sized, stainless steel kitchen sink, she pushed the bridge of her glasses up to the top of her nose and hobbled back out into the dining hall. Jim turned away from his work as the sounds continued. *Step. Clonk. Step. Clonk.* Curious as to what the computers were for and what Jim was working on, she hobbled over toward him. He noticed her curiosity and set his carving tool down.

"Where's Mallory?" Jim asked.

"In the shower. What are you making?" Abbey asked as she looked at the seat clamped onto the workbench. The wood for the seat was very thick but as smooth as a river rock.

"A chair," Jim answered. Abbey glanced over at the computer screen and saw mathematical calculations next to images that resembled blue prints.

"Do you like math?" Abbey asked.

"Yeah, I guess. I live and breathe it."

"I like it, too."

"What are you learning now?"

"Fractions."

"What grade are you in?"

"Fourth. My favorite part is the math races."

"What's that?"

"We stand in front of the board and the teacher gives us a math problem. As soon as you're done solving it, you turn around. First one wins."

"Do you win a lot?"

"I didn't used to because I couldn't turn around as fast. Now the teacher just makes me put my hand up."

"Mathematics is what got me into astronomy."

"We study astronomy in our science book. We're working on science fair stuff now."

"Are you entering the science fair?"

"I don't know. I'm thinking of entering the science symposium instead of making an exhibit."

"I went to the international science fair in Houston when I was in high school. I didn't win, but I got to go."

"We can't go to nationals yet, not old enough."

"Abbey?" Mallory yelled out from the lobby.

"Gotta go. See ya later," Abbey said as she turned toward the door.

"Okay. Good luck."

"Thanks." *Step. Clonk. Step. Clonk.*

Jim had been working for nearly an hour on the seat of the chair when he heard Abbey's familiar steps and Mallory's halfhearted goodbye shouted from the lobby.

"Goodbye, Jimmy!" Jim stopped carving.

"Mallory?" he yelled.

"What?"

"Come here a second."

"Ugh, what is it?" Mallory said as she trudged toward the dining hall door while carrying Abbey's pink backpack on her shoulder and suitcase in her left hand. She flipped her sunglasses to the top of her head and held her car keys as they dangled in her right hand. She poked her head around the corner. "Whhaaaat."

"If it'll help her out, and you too, I guess. She can stay."

"What?" Mallory said as she dropped Abbey's suitcase and let the backpack slip off her shoulder and onto the floor. She walked over to Jim with a look of disbelief and her hands on her hips. Just as she got within whispering distance, she threw her hands out to the side, dumbfounded, and loudly responded, "What is your deal?"

"I don't know. She seems intelligent and polite."

"The fact that she is a child and needs help doesn't incite hospitality and kindness? She has to be intelligent and polite to be able to stay? Isn't that a little pretentious and heartless?"

"Nope. There are plenty of bratty kids running around who are perfect reflections of their brain-dead parents." Mallory seemed to stop and think before answering.

"Yeah, okay. You're somewhat right."

"I'm right."

"Well, she's not a bratty kid, by any means."

"I can see that. She can stay for a while if it helps you both out."

"Geez. It's like pulling teeth from a bobcat."

"I can't apologize for who I am."

"I am not asking for an apology." Mallory turned her head and shouted toward the lobby. "Abbey?" After several steps and clonks, Abbey appeared. "Would you be okay staying with Jim until we can get you moved?"

"Sure. I like it here."

Getting Abbey unpacked didn't take long. Mallory looked at the time on her cell phone and decided that if she hurried she could get to her desk at work, start Abbey's paperwork and still make Mulligan's for her birthday lunch with Tess. She hugged Abbey and spoke softly in her ear. "You be careful around here. I don't want you to fall on this hard floor again."

"Okay."

"If you need anything, you have my number. I'll be back to check on you."

"Okay," Abbey replied.

"Jim is a little weird sometimes, but he's nice. If you need something and he can't get it for you, then call me. You don't need to be afraid of him."

"I'm not."

Jim was still working in the dining hall when Mallory yelled out to him.

"Thank you. Call me if you need anything."

"Yep," Jim answered as he used his broad-head chisel.

Since Abbey was on a bereavement absence and didn't have to go to school, she threw herself on the old, tattered leather couch and turned on the big screen TV. She changed channels until she found cartoons before removing her prosthetic leg. Instead of sitting up, she stretched her leg out toward one end of the couch and rested her head on her right arm. With a sideways view, she watched an animated episode of *Wonderland.* Within an hour, the sunlight broke through the skylight and warmed the room.

Just days before, Abbey had been asleep on her aunt and uncle's couch, a plaid tragedy with bits of sticky residue on one end and an entire cushion missing from the other. When Justin Creeson had arrived home from work, he shouted at Abbey to wake up and get off the couch. Cigarette, beer, and an untucked filthy shirt, Justin took his niece's spot on the couch as he changed the channel. In comparison, her surroundings at the inn were much cleaner with infinitely more room, and the couch was extremely comfortable. Feeling safe and warm, it was no wonder that within minutes little Abbey Creeson was asleep.

Chapter 13

Atlanta International Airport was busy as usual with weary travelers. Men in suits moved at blurring speeds and children eager for spring break to begin talked incessantly. Small wheels on suitcases rolled over brief separations of square tiles while announcements carried through the large space over the P.A. system.

Outside the airport dressed in his Marine Dress Blue Bravo uniform was Corporal Drew Bredenburg. He wore white gloves and held a tightly folded American flag in one hand, ready to escort the wife of a fallen soldier through the lively airport.

While Cpl. Bredenburg didn't stand at attention, he wasn't at ease either. His eyes glanced around while travelers exited vehicles and embraced their loved ones, saying their goodbyes. He quietly watched with interest until a black car pulled up in front of the terminal. The windows were tinted, and the driver was the first to exit after the trunk was released. Wearing black gloves, a black suit and donning a chauffeur's hat, the driver retrieved a suitcase and quickly closed the trunk. He nodded at Bredenburg, confirming the arrival of the widow and sat the suitcase on the sidewalk. The driver opened the rear door on the passenger's side and waited patiently for his passenger to exit. Kelly Mae White, 28, swung both legs out of the car and stood up. Cpl. Drew Bredenburg was taken aback by her "girl next door" look and noticed that she wasn't wearing any makeup. Instead of brand name clothing, Kelly wore a small black dress from Target that seemed a size too big for her. Corporal Bredenburg watched as she quietly thanked the driver who simply nodded with a slight smile and returned to the driver's seat. Kelly turned toward the soldier standing before her. Hiding his nervousness and attraction to Kelly, Corporal Drew Bredenburg introduced himself.

"Mrs. Adam White?"

"Yes."

"I'm Corporal Drew Bredenburg, and I will see you and Staff Sergeant Adam White to Bear Creek, Pennsylvania." Kelly nodded and broke eye contact with her escort. It wasn't the mention of Adam's name that stung like an electric shock, but the quick, fleeting thought of never seeing him again.

"Of course."

"Please follow me." Corporal Bredenburg promptly turned around, placing his hand on the handle of her luggage and pulled it behind him as he guided her toward the long lines of the security-screening checkpoints.

One of the many private lounges in the airport had been reserved two days in advance for Kelly Mae White. Oftentimes the rooms were reserved for corporate VIP's, celebrities, high-ranking government officials, and military personnel. Instead of the uncomfortable adjoining chairs most passengers sat in while waiting at their gate, cushioned leather furniture awaited those who entered the private lounges. The plush chairs faced a massive window that offered a full panoramic view of the jetways, taxiways, runway, and an orange windsock off in the distance. The door opened, and Corporal Bredenburg turned on the lights while he held the door for Kelly to enter.

"This is the assigned waiting room. Please stay here. You will see me out there with Staff Sergeant White within the hour. I will be back to get you, and should you need anything, just pick up that phone," he said as he pointed to a small, wooden table with notepaper and a plain, black phone. "Food, drink or any item that you may require is provided." Kelly hardly listened, as she was still processing the previous words spoken by Corporal Bredenburg - *you will see me out there with Staff Sergeant White within the hour*, as if Adam were still alive.

"Okay. Thank you."

"Yes, Ma'am," he said as he closed the door. The thought of seeing Adam alive brought tears to her eyes as her memory ignited.

"You can't feel it now, silly," Kelly said as she looked down at Adam's hand on her stomach. Sitting in a booth at a restaurant, they sat side by side.

"I know. I'm just excited." Adam said. With hardly an ounce of body fat on him, his face was thin, and his jaw seemed razor sharp. Adam smiled as he rubbed his hand on her stomach, as if trying to feel for the life inside Kelly.

"What if it's a girl?" Kelly asked.

"I thought of a name for a girl," Adam said.

"You did?" Thinking it would be a family name or a sweet name that would only leave her hoping it was a girl. She looked down and wriggled her hand between her stomach and his rough and rigid bear paw. She gazed up at Adam, revealing a smile she couldn't hide if she tried to.

"What's the name?" she asked.

Kelly wiped away her tears and glanced out the large window as an airplane took off down the runway.

Chapter 14

Dinner at Bear Creek Inn consisted of mangoes, kiwi, seaweed salad, and steamed spinach. Abbey had been used to a diet that consisted of greasy foods and beverages with high caffeine and sugar content. She hadn't ever seen a mango or a kiwi before, but quickly took to the kiwi. Jim had set the bowls of food on the table in the lobby and walked back into the dining hall. He continued to work while he sat alone and ate intermittently. At one point, he peeked in on Abbey and saw her as she sat by herself and watched TV. Looking at her caused him to think back to when he was a child sitting on that very couch. He would use a pencil on ruled notebook paper and would solve a homework problem as he sat alone. Sometimes Mallory would come out and sit next to him and watch TV. He liked it when someone else was out there with him, even if it was Mallory. He opened the door and walked into the lobby.

"Are you okay out here?" Jim asked. Abbey looked up at him and shrugged her shoulders.

"I suppose," she responded. Jim thought she was kind and polite and felt he hadn't been as nice to a recently orphaned girl as he should have been. Instead of leaving her out in the lobby all by herself, he brought his food into the lobby and sat on the floor as he held his bowl in front of him. The spinach was her least favorite, but the seaweed salad, as bad as it sounded to her, was actually the best part. To his surprise, she spoke up almost as soon as he sat down.

"When you said we were eating seaweed, I was worried, but I actually like it."

"Yeah, it's not what you think," Jim said.

"I like that it's stringy and cold," Abbey said as she took a bite of the seaweed salad.

"This is a super food," Jim said as he took a bite.

"What's that?"

Speaking with his mouth full, Jim answered, "A food with high nutritional content. It gives you benefits like energy, helps with your circulatory system, and even concentration."

"Super food," Abbey repeated out loud as she looked at the seaweed. "I like it."

"I do, too."

When dinner was over, Jim returned to working in the dining hall and moved back and forth between his computers and his workbench. As the night wore on, Abbey got tired of watching TV and wandered into the dining hall. Abbey stood silently as she watched him grab a piece of sandpaper and apply it to the block of wood on his workbench. The work lamp illuminated the particles of dust floating in the air. With each sanding motion of the paper, more particles would sweep up and float away. She looked at one of the computer monitors and stared at the screen. Jim had worked without interruption through Abbey's stepping and clonking through the dining hall. Knowing she was standing behind him, he eventually turned around.

"Are you going to bed?" Jim asked as he wiped the sweat off his brow and onto his woodworker's apron.

"I don't have school tomorrow."

"Right. I guess I wouldn't go to bed either."

"Can I look at your computers?"

"Well, I can set you up on one of them if you like."

"Okay," Abbey said. After Jim had closed a few programs and opened a browser, Abbey was off and running. She immediately visited a website as if she had done it many times before and began playing a game. Jim had been momentarily distracted by the sound effects from the game and before he could say anything, she quickly maneuvered the mouse and brought the volume all the way down. For the next half-hour Jim saw from the corner of his eye the number of times Abbey pushed the bridge of her glasses to the top of her nose. A mouse click. Typing on the keyboard. Mouse click. Pushing the bridge of her glasses up. Abbey repeated these steps unknowingly, but Jim couldn't help but notice.

"Are your glasses broken?"

"No," Abbey replied, never taking her eyes away from the screen.

"You keep having to push them up."

"Yeah, they slide a lot," Abbey answered, eyes still locked on the game.

The next day proved to be similar to the one before it. Jim worked in the dining hall, Abbey watched TV and took a nap on the couch. Dinner was diced peaches, green beans, and steamed carrots covered with a honey glaze. Abbey ate everything on her plate and drank a glass of ice-cold water.

"I like the honey."

"I always eat it in the spring."

"Why spring?"

"It's local honey. The delivery guy gets it from a local beekeeper.

Helps with allergies."

Abbey eventually wandered into the dining hall where she played on the computer once again. And for the second night in a row, Jim struggled as he watched Abbey push up on the bridge of her glasses repeatedly. He set his sandpaper down and walked over and pulled up a chair next to Abbey.

"Can I see your glasses?" Jim asked. Abbey thought about it for a second and then took them off and handed them over. Upon inspection, Jim noticed the frames were cheap plastic, and the hinges appeared as if they had been repaired before. Instead of making a comment, he just handed them back to her.

"Do they bother you? The sliding down all the time?"

"Sometimes, especially when I take a test."

"Hang tight," Jim said and left the room through the kitchen door. Abbey went back to her game and played for some time before Jim came back. When she heard his footsteps, she paused her game and turned her head, seeing him with a power drill in tow. "Let me see your glasses again." She removed them and handed them over. "This is a small drill bit," he said as he held it up. "See? Very small. No one will notice the hole, okay?" Jim explained.

Still unsure as to what he was doing, but fearing to question him, she nodded her head. Jim held the frames in his hand and started up the drill. Abbey covered her ears with her hands and watched the drill bit plunge into the end of the frame just above where her ear would be. Jim drilled two small holes, one on each side and set the drill down. He reached into his pocket and pulled out fishing line, a plastic bead and a pocketknife. After ten minutes of Abbey putting on and taking off the glasses for purposes of measuring the fishing line, Jim methodically tied the line to each end and attached the bead to the middle of the string. He held up Abbey's glasses and nodded for her to take them and put them on. She did as asked.

"Now reach behind your head and feel that bead."

"Okay."

"Now, hold onto the line, and push the bead toward the back of your head," Jim explained with hand motions. As she moved the bead closer to the back of her head, she immediately felt tightness around the frames that she wasn't used to. It wasn't too tight, but the pressure felt good. "Now let go," Jim said. Abbey let go and felt the frames firmly attached to her face. When she looked down, the frames didn't slide. They didn't even move. Abbey smiled.

"I love it!" she said. "Thank you!"

"You're welcome. The only problem is, the line kind of sticks out. You might look a little funny." Abbey felt the back of her head. The line did stick out like a small ponytail.

"That's okay."

"It doesn't bother you?"

"No. My glasses feel great now," she said as she still donned a big smile while moving her head around in circles. Jim couldn't help but smile himself.

"That's very utilitarian of you."

"What's that mean?"

"It means you're not a snotty brat. You're a good kid," he said as he got up and took his tools with him and disappeared behind the kitchen door. Abbey resumed her game and smiled as she moved her head up and down and enjoyed the feeling of her upgraded glasses.

Chapter 15

Kelly was sitting down in the waiting room facing the large window. For the past half-hour, she had been watching as an airplane docked at a jet way and luggage was being unloaded from the hold. Several men were working around the plane performing certain tasks, but she couldn't identify what they were doing or what their purpose was. Never fully sitting in her seat, she remained on the edge and looked down at her black shoes and black dress. Her pregnancy was noticeable while standing up but even more so sitting down. She brushed off minuscule pieces of lint from her stomach and tucked part of her shoulder length hair behind her ear. As she looked out the window, she could see the maintenance workers as they quickly moved out of the way. A small vehicle with a large conveyor belt attached to the side drove up and parked with the belt flush to the door of the hold of the airplane. With quick, snapping movements, Corporal Drew Bredenburg appeared from the right side of Kelly's view and walked toward the small vehicle as he held the flag tucked under his arm. Kelly stood up and walked to the window. Her hand covered her face as tears began to stream down her cheeks when six men in Marine Dress Blues brought out the coffin. They carried it to the conveyor belt, set the end on the belt and stopped. Kelly watched through tears as two soldiers released the casket and walked up to Corporal Bredenburg. Once he handed the flag over, the two solders unfolded the flag and draped it over the coffin. Each corner was secured and the two soldiers returned to the position closest to the conveyor belt. Corporal Bredenburg stood at attention while the belt began to move and the six men guided it up the conveyor. With a quick prompt, all seven men saluted as their fallen brother was loaded onto the plane. Kelly took several steps back and sat down as she sobbed uncontrollably.

Chapter 16

Ring. Ring.

"How's it going?" Jim asked.

"We are waiting for a spot at the Philadelphia orphanage. I don't think the people that closed the orphanages here in Wilkes-Barre and Allentown thought about overflow in Philly."

"So what's that mean?"

"Can you keep her there until they have room?"

"How long?"

"Well, we should be able to move her in a few days or less I hope. That okay?"

"I guess."

"I have to put her back in school though. She can't miss too many more days."

"Fine by me. How is she getting there?"

"I have it covered. Since she was already enrolled at Bear Creek Elementary, it makes it easier on me."

Since Abbey was classified as disabled, Mallory requested that the school district make special arrangements to pick up Abbey at the inn. Bear Creek Road was not on the district's pre-planned route, but was an easily achieved request. The wrought iron, rusted gate closing off the inn was the only obstacle between Abbey and the school bus. The night before Abbey went back to school, Jim had taken his truck to the gate and secured the truck's winch to the iron gate. He threw his truck in reverse, forcefully pulling the right side of the gate open, just enough to let Abbey walk through with ease, and no more.

The next day in the lunch line at Bear Creek Elementary, Abbey was bombarded with classmates tugging on the small loop of fishing line that stuck out from behind her head. Her glasses fit better, but were now a target kids could pull on. While the intention wasn't to bully Abbey, it might have seemed so when one of the boys pulled too hard on the line, breaking the hinge on the right side of her glasses.

"Ouch!" Abbey said as a tiny screw lightly scraped her temple when it broke.

"Sorry," said the boy. When Abbey found a teacher, she showed the glasses to her.

"What happened, Abbey?" Mrs. Tisdale asked.

Back at Bear Creek Inn, Jim was working on the seat of the rocking chair. While looking at a measurement on his plans, his phone rang. Jim put it on speaker.

"Hey," Mallory said.

"What? You have another abandoned child in need of a place to stay?"

"If I did, I wouldn't call you. Abbey's glasses broke, and she's getting a headache from not being able to see, so she needs to be picked up. I am having a deputy take her back to the inn."

"I just fixed her glasses."

"You fixed them? What was wrong with them?"

"Too loose."

"Well, I gotta find a way to get her new ones. I'll call you when I can."

Deputy Corbin arrived at Bear Creek Elementary to pick up Abbey Creeson. It was a difficult drive for Corbin as he was part of the cleanup effort when Abbey's aunt and uncle were scraped off the road. However, he also knew Justin Creeson whom he had put in the back seat a few times himself. Thinking it somehow wrong for Abbey to ride in the same backseat as her drunk uncle, he made arrangements by putting his front seat disaster of files, empty soda bottles, and a nearly-finished box of donuts in the back.

Abbey's address sounded familiar, but he couldn't place it in his head as he steered his way to 164 Bear Mountain Road.

"Sorry to hear about your glasses," Corbin said as he tried to make small talk.

"It's okay. I know someone who can fix them."

As Deputy Corbin drove his cruiser up the slight incline, he began to recognize where they were headed. Upon approaching the entrance to Bear Creek Inn, he looked at the address again on the paper, then back at the gate.

"You staying at the inn?" Corbin asked. Abbey nodded her head. "You see the astronaut?" he asked as he furrowed his brow in disbelief. Abbey simply nodded her head again. "What's he like?" Abbey shrugged her shoulders as she answered.

"I don't know. Nice, I guess. He works a lot and is pretty quiet." The cruiser parked in front of the gate. Abbey grabbed her backpack.

"Wait. Don't you want me to drive you up to the inn?"

"Gate won't open anymore than that. I'll just walk."

"Oh," Corbin said as he watched Abbey struggle to get out of the car. "You need some help getting out?" he asked.

"I think so."

Deputy Corbin helped Abbey get out of the cruiser and then assisted her through the opening in the gate. Once on the other side of the broken entrance, Abbey thanked Deputy Corbin. He nodded his head and thought how Abbey was nothing like his obnoxious daughter who seemed to be constantly caffeinated and rude.

Jim could hear Abbey open the front door and *step-clonk* in the lobby.

"Now, how did your glasses break?" he asked as he opened the door from the dining hall.

"Andrew! He and every other kid thought it was funny to pull on the line that stuck out from behind my head. They were fitting me so good too. It was an accident though. He even said he was sorry."

"Well, let me see if I can fix them. How bad is your vision without the glasses?"

"Just a lot more blurry. My headache comes and goes."

"More blurry? You mean your vision is blurred when you have your glasses on?"

"Yeah, but it's not that bad."

"They're not supposed to be. You should see clearly. That's the point of wearing glasses. Do you have headaches while wearing your glasses?"

"Yeah, sometimes."

. . .

Mallory was sitting at her desk when her phone rang. She saw that it was Jim calling and quickly answered it.

"Hey."

"Did you know that Abbey's vision is blurry when she has her glasses on?"

"No? What do you mean?"

"Her prescription is off."

"I already called, and the clinic is overrun with flu and strep patients. The optometrist who runs the vision center at the clinic has the flu. Said it will be late next week before Abbey can be seen."

"Next week?"

"Can you fix her glasses until then?"

"She can't even see properly. It's obviously not the right prescription."

"At least she can see better with them than without."

"Can't you take her to a regular optometrist?"

"They don't take Medicaid."

"I thought that was for old people."

"C.H.I.P. – Children's Health Insurance Program is like Medicaid for kids. She has to go to a clinic around here unless she goes to a bigger city with more C.H.I.P. participants."

"This is one hundred percent garbage."

"It is," Mallory agreed quickly. "Welcome to a typical orphan's life. But it's not that bad. I've seen worse. Way worse."

"So next week? That's it?"

"Yep," Mallory answered. "Sounds like you care, Jim. I'm not used to that."

"She's nine. She can't see and doesn't deserve this," Jim said. Mallory tapped her pencil on her desk calendar while she exhaled in frustration. "If I make an arrangement, can you pick her up?" Jim added.

"I can't be running back and forth between Wilkes-Barre and the Inn all the time. She's not my only case."

Click. Jim hung up, and Mallory was left on the other end. She cursed as she put the phone down. Jim opened up a browser and typed in a search term, *Bear Creek, PA Optometry*

Jim found only one search result for Bear Creek with the rest being from Wilkes-Barre. *BC Eye Care.* Jim clicked on the website and discovered they sold children's frames and made their lenses at the office. He picked up his phone, and dialed the number.

"Bear Creek Eye Care, this is Tonya. Can I help you?"

"When do you close?"

"Five p.m."

"Do you ever see patients after you close?"

"No sir, would you like to make an appointment?"

"Who owns this practice?"

"Doctor McCoy."

"Is he in?"

"Yes, but he is with a patient."

"I'll wait," Jim said as he put the phone on speaker. While he waited, he worked on the rocking chair after he slipped into his woodworker's apron. Finally, when someone answered, Jim picked up his phone.

"This is Doctor McCoy."

"Hi. I am looking after a little girl that is nine years old, and she needs new glasses. Do you take C.H.I.P. insurance?"

"We do not. I'm sorry if that is an inconvenience."

"Fine. Do you make house calls?"

"We do not."

"That's inconvenient. What if I explained to you that she is handicapped? Does that make a difference?"

"Does she have a prescription?"

"She needs a new one."

"My equipment isn't able to be transported."

"I see. Thanks," Jim said before he hung up.

Mallory looked at the time on her cell phone. Ready to leave work she shut down her computer and swiveled around in her chair as she grabbed her keys.

Ring. Ring.

"Hello," she said without looking at her caller ID.

"Can you come over?" Jim asked.

"Not tonight. We have practice at the pool for Lilly, and then we are going out to dinner."

"When?"

"At six."

"That's two hours from now. Could you come and get Abbey and take her to the optometrist? Shouldn't take but a half hour."

"No way. I have to get ready, and I'd like to spend some time with my kids."

"Her glasses suck! She can't see."

"I might be able to tomorrow."

"Fine. Don't worry about it."

"She'll be fine until then. Can't you fix them temporarily?"

"Yeah, I'll think of something."

Chapter 17

Once Kelly Mae White was in Wilkes-Barre, she had a car service drop her off at Economy Car Rental. After renting a red compact, she drove to the Roadside Lodge and Bar, the cheapest motel in town. The motel was overdue for remodeling a decade ago and each room's sun-faded door faced the uneven and pothole-ridden parking lot. Room 122 was given to Kelly and once she opened the door, she wished she had spent a little extra for a better room. The carpet was grimy and discolored. The ceilings and walls were covered in a popcorn material that had flaked off in many spots, mostly at the height of a small child.

The chill in the room prompted Kelly to search for a thermostat. She finally discovered a black knob on a silver plate, but the instructions had worn off long ago. Without anything else in sight that seemed to resemble a thermostat, she blindly turned the knob to the right, which started a rumbling sound inside a vent above her head. In time, the vent emitted heat, and Kelly could comfortably rest on her bed. She didn't eat much for lunch that day as there was too much going through her mind at the airport to be concerned with food, but now she felt weak and shaky.

Using her phone, she found a place that delivered by the name of Pennsylvania Bread Company. After she ordered potato soup and a salad, she decided to bide her time by making another phone call, one that she was unsure if she should make. Unzipping a camouflage duffel bag, she found a folder and looked through important documents. Marriage certificate, passports, bank account information, and pay check stubs. Then she found what she was looking for, a piece of paper with a phone number written in Adam's handwriting. She dialed the number.

Ring. Ring.

"Hello?" A woman answered. Kelly hesitated, but pushed forward. "Alma?"

"Yes?"

"It's Kelly Mae," she said. With the full expectation for Alma to slam the phone down and end the call, Kelly was intrigued when she heard a muffled swooshing noise, followed by quick footsteps and a door being shut. Alma whispered,

"You shouldn't be calling here."

"I'm in town."

"It doesn't matter," Alma continued to whisper.

"I'm going to be there tomorrow."

"That's fine, but don't say anything to him," Alma's voice seemed to ease out of the whisper, before speaking in a matter of fact tone, "Don't call here again."

Click.

Kelly plopped her phone on the bed and exhaled in exasperation. She walked to the bathroom and splashed water on her face before she stood straight up and turned sideways, looking at her medium-sized belly in the mirror. She placed her hand gently on her tight bulging stomach. She closed her eyes, trying to reach down deep and feel the life inside her. She slowly opened her eyes and looked at herself in the mirror knowing that even though Adam was gone, he left behind something worth living for.

Chapter 18

At BC Eye Care, the phone rang with only forty-five minutes until closing time. Tonya answered the phone, ready for after-work adult beverages with friends.

"Can I speak with Dr. McCoy?" Asked Jim.

"He's with a patient."

"I'll wait," Jim said. Tonya put Jim on hold and went back to scanning a patient's insurance card. After fifteen minutes, Dr. McCoy picked up the phone.

"This is Dr. McCoy."

"Hi, Dr. McCoy. I called you earlier about the handicapped girl."

"Yes."

"Could you see her at five? I know you close soon, but it would really help us out," Jim explained. Dr. McCoy exhaled and pondered over how generous he was feeling.

"Does she need to be tested for deficiencies and fitted for frames?"

"Yes. How long does it take?"

"About an hour or less. We have an in-office lens molding system here, and we make our lenses. You won't have to wait a week to get the glasses."

"Good."

"You asked about C.H.I.P. earlier. I'm sorry but we don't handle C.H.I.P. patients. A child's exam and a pair of glasses can cost around three-fifty or so without insurance."

"No problem. We'll pay cash."

"Cash? Fine. Five o'clock. Please don't be late."

Out at the main gate, Jim was once again in his truck securing the winch to the wrought iron. He pulled the gate open with enough space for the truck to fit through. Jim saw several cars zip past on Bear Mountain Road, which quickly reminded him that he hadn't been out on the open road in over a decade. He only used his truck to haul wood back and forth from the forest to the inn. Another car zipped by, as did a hint of anxiety. Jim hadn't been off his property, nor had he seen many people for nearly ten years. Sure he had seen teenagers crossing his front lawn, staring at the inn with cautious and fearful faces from time to time. Jim had even managed to avoid Charlie, his dependable deliveryman. As he sat in the truck, he decided he would drive Abbey to the optometrist's office, but he wouldn't go inside. Assuming that Abbey had endured nine difficult years, he didn't want to contribute any more to her detriment. and so it came to pass that Jim would leave the inn for the first time in ten years.

With the gate open, Jim turned his truck around and drove back to the inn, pulled up to the front porch and waited for Abbey to come outside. His hands gripped the steering wheel and the anxious feeling came over him once again. Abbey soon appeared and *clonk-stepped* down the few steps off the front porch. She struggled slightly to lift the door handle. Once the door was cracked, she used her hands, arms, and body weight to open the rusted door of the truck, and grimaced at the height of the seat. Jim looked at her, waiting for her to get in, when he quickly realized she couldn't do it on her own.

"Oh. Hang on," Jim said as he got out of the driver's side and jogged to the passenger side. He started to bend down and made a gesture as if he was going to pick her up but paused.

"Uh, I'm not sure, I just, I don't want to hurt you," Jim said with a guarded look on his face.

"It's fine. It won't hurt," Abbey said in a reassuring tone. Jim bent down and carefully wrapped his left arm around her back and his right arm behind her legs. In one easy motion, Abbey was gently lifted off the ground and carefully set into the passenger seat of the truck.

"There. You okay?"

"That was fast," Abbey said with a smile.

She had her broken glasses with her under the assumption she was getting her glasses repaired. She held the broken frames in her lap.

"This is going to be very strange for me," Jim said as he slowly steered down the winding gravel path toward the gate.

"What is?" Abbey asked.

"This little trip," Jim answered as he put on an old University of Tennessee ball cap and pulled the bill down as far as he could without blocking his vision.

"To the eye doctor?"

"Yeah. Very much so."

"Why?"

"Weeeell, it's a long story," Jim said as he came to the gate. He applied the brake just before the main road. "I haven't left my place in ten years," Jim said in a confiding tone.

"Mallory told me."

"Yeah, what'd she say?"

"Said that you were funny about people, and you hadn't left in a long time."

"That's pretty accurate. Now listen, for the rest of your life, you cannot tell Mallory that I left the inn. In fact, once we get back here, you forget all about it. Okay? This never happened."

He looked left and right and saw no signs of traffic before he pulled out onto Bear Mountain Road. Abbey thought of a question.

"What does 'funny about people' mean?"

"She's referring to me not wanting to be around other people. I don't like people, in general, but it's more that I would rather be alone."

"You don't like people? Does that mean you don't like me?"

"Well. I refused to leave the inn for over ten years, and I'm breaking my impeccable and glorious streak so you can see better. You think I would do this if I didn't like you?"

"No," Abbey said with a grin. She glanced over at Jim who was also smiling, one of the first expressions she had seen from him. He steered with both hands on the wheel and never took his eyes off the road while talking to Abbey.

"Remember that people will tell you anything. They will tell you what you want to hear. They will lie to you, but actions always speak louder than words," Jim said. He applied the brake at the stop sign as he came to the end of Bear Mountain Road. He looked around, completely unfamiliar with his surroundings.

"What is all this?" he said as he stared at a McDonalds on one corner and a 12-pump gas station on his left. The road was much wider than Jim remembered. "You have to be kidding me."

"What's wrong?"

"This has all changed," Jim said as he looked around and then turned onto Summit Drive. "Here, look at my phone. See where the directions are telling us to go." Jim took in the landscape as if he was surveying damage caused by an atomic bomb. "The steakhouse is gone. Aww, man," Jim said to himself as he looked to his left. They drove past boutiques, local restaurants, fast food joints and a sports bar called Wild Bill's Saloon. "I don't know. What did I expect? It's been ten years," Jim said not expecting a response from Abbey. "Where is the next turn?"

"Willow. Turn left on Willow."

"Okay," Jim said keeping an eye out while searching for recognizable landmarks. "This is weird."

After Jim made the turn on Willow, Abbey was helpful in finding the office of BC Eye Care. The parking lot was empty except for two cars parked on the side of the building. Abbey unbuckled her seat belt just as he parked the truck.

"Abbey, I'm not going in. But they will take care of you." Jim removed folded cash from his pocket. "Here, take this and give the doctor this after you get your glasses."

"All of it?"

"All of it, but make sure you tell him 'thank you'."

"Okay."

"You need help getting out?"

"No, but I will need help getting back in the seat."

"Okay." Jim said as he watched her open the door and set her broken glasses on the seat. "Why did you bring those?" Jim asked. Abbey slowly slid off her seat and landed on the asphalt of the parking lot. She reached out and grabbed her broken glasses. She looked as if it was obvious what she was doing.

"I brought them...so they could fix them."

"Oh. I guess I didn't explain. You're getting new glasses."

"New glasses?"

"Yeah. That's why we came here."

"Oh, wow."

"Well, you need new ones don't you?"

"I sure do. I thought we were coming here to fix these. This is great."

"Be careful, and Abbey?"

"Yeah?"

"Don't mention my name or the inn or anything. Okay?"

"Okay. I won't."

"See you soon," Jim said as she tried to close the passenger door. "Here, I got it," he smiled as he and reached out, grabbed the handle and closed the door. Jim looked up and saw Abbey limping to the front door just as a woman wearing brightly colored scrubs unlocked and opened the door for her.

Jim looked around for signs of people nearby and pulled his ball cap down even further. Every other business in town was either closed or in the process of closing. He picked a book up off the seat and opened it. *Quantum Transport Modeling* was a book written by one of Jim's colleagues. Already on page two hundred, Jim was on pace to finish it by tomorrow.

After twenty-five minutes, something caught his eye. At the big picture-window of BC Eye Care, Abbey was wearing a pair of frames. When Jim looked at her, she shrugged her shoulders and threw her hands out to the side, as if to say *"whaddaya think"*. Jim smiled and gave her a thumbs up. He watched Abbey turn around and limp toward Tonya as she held out the frames while she spoke. Jim went back to his book and was once again distracted by Abbey who was now wearing green colored frames. She made the same gesture to which Jim replied *"not so much"* by making a snide expression and shaking his head slightly.

Upon the third time… he considered assisting her to be more entertaining than reading. Finally the decision came down to two options. Abbey stood in front of the window with light pink colored glasses. Jim rocked his head from side to side to signal, *"those are pretty good,"* and then waited for her to try on the second pair. Navy blue frames with a thin white stripe on both sides that were sleek and somehow still girly. Jim thought she looked studious. *"I like them,"* Jim mouthed while as he gave a thumbs up. Abbey's decision was final. Jim watched as she handed them to Tonya who smiled and set them aside. She then took Abbey to the back of the office where they disappeared into a room.

While Jim sat in his truck and read his book, Abbey and Tonya waited at the reception desk while her lenses were cast and set by Dr. McCoy. Once Abbey was handed her new pair of glasses, Tonya fitted the frames to Abbey's face while Dr. McCoy turned out the lights in the office, except the one over the receptionist's office. He leaned over the computer, and after several mouse clicks, the total came up on the screen.

"The total comes to three hundred and forty-nine dollars and seventeen cents," he said. Abbey reached into her pocket and handed him the folded cash.

"I'm supposed to hand this to you and say thanks," Abbey said just as Tonya finished fitting her glasses.

"There you go, Abbey. All set," Tonya said. Dr. McCoy unfolded several hundred-dollar bills. He separated them and counted four hundred dollars.

"This is great. I love my new glasses," Abbey said. Dr. McCoy held the money in his hand.

"You have change coming to you," he said.

"I was told to give you all of it." She smiled and felt the sides of her new glasses. Tonya saw her to the front door, and Abbey took a step outside, thanking her as she limped back to the truck. Jim waited until Tonya was inside before he got out and ran over to the passenger side. He kept his head down and out of view.

"I love them. They feel great," Abbey said. Jim quickly opened the door and scooped her up and sat her down gently on the seat and closed the door. Once in the driver's side, Jim looked at her frames.

"I'm glad you like them."

"They are so light, and I can see forever, and it's so clear."

The trip home was faster than getting to the doctor's office. Jim kept a lookout for local police while going ten miles over the speed limit. He sped up to fifteen miles over the speed limit once he got onto Bear Mountain Road. Once past the gates, Jim maneuvered his truck's bumper against the wrought iron gate and backed up, closing the gate so only Abbey could walk through. He parked in back, and they entered the inn through the back porch. While it wasn't a spy mission, it felt like one to Jim, as if he had gotten away with something.

Chapter 19

The morning of the funeral in Wilkes-Barre, Kelly drove her red compact rental onto Highway 117 while turning the dial on the heater to the maximum setting and cranking the fan up as high as it would go. She thought of everything but Adam and the fact that with every second, she was moving closer to a funeral in which her husband would be lowered into the ground.

Once her rental car was in the parking lot, she took deep breaths and slowly released her grip on the steering wheel. Kelly brought her head up and looked around for people she might recognize. Some men that looked to be Adam's age were dressed in their military uniforms with their significant others on their arms. They walked from their cars with long strides and spoke to each other softly. Some couples appeared to be too sad to talk. Then, a familiar face appeared.

Alma White was walking up to the front door with Grant White. Grant wore his thick miner's coat over his discount white shirt and blue tie. Coal miners weren't known for style, and his frugal nature led him to dress like a laborer on a budget. They walked with hesitant steps and wore heavy frowns on their cold, wrinkled faces. Kelly remembered sitting in the living room with Grant, Alma and Adam when he explained to them that he was joining the Marines.

"This isn't what you are supposed to do," yelled Grant. He had been raising his voice ever since Adam said the words. Kelly, feeling out of her element,

stared at the floral print wallpaper that clashed with the floral print couch. "I make a good living in those mines. What? Are you too good for it? Being a soldier is dangerous."

"The mines are just as dangerous as the military, Dad," Adam said. Grant's face reddened, and it seemed like steam was going to expel from his ears. Instead of yelling, Grant screamed.

"Thousands, hundreds of thousands die in war. A single war, and you're telling me that it's just as dangerous as mining coal?"

Adam grabbed Kelly's hand and stood up. They headed for the door, but not without further lashings from Grant. "You are making the biggest mistake of your life, and I do not support this." Adam walked Kelly to the car, opened her door and promptly closed it once she was inside. Adam turned toward his father who was on the front porch and pointed at Kelly.

"She supports me, Dad! I lean on her, not you," Adam said with a firm tone before he got in the driver's seat. Grant went inside and slammed the door. By that time, Adam and Kelly were only married three months.

Kelly sat in her car, not wanting to go inside the funeral home. Instead she preferred to be one of those girls attending another soldier's funeral while she held on tightly to Adam's arm—walking slowly, talking to him softly.

"What rank was he?"

"Staff Sergeant," Adam would say.

"Oh."

The chill in the air warranted the heavy coats, as they would be out in the cold for a full-length military burial. Kelly had purchased a black pea coat to keep warm at the graveside service. She wrapped it around her and left enough room to hide her bump from the twentieth week of pregnancy and got out of her car. The interior of the funeral home was warm, almost hot. Kelly took a few steps inside before the funeral director, who offered to take her coat, greeted her.

"No, thank you. I'm quite cold," she lied. The room was very warm, but she thought it improper to attend her husband's funeral and announce her pregnancy at the same time. People she didn't recognize stood in the hallway and spoke quietly outside the visitation room. Many of the uniformed men were from the honor guard and didn't even know Adam. She looked down and could see her small bump through the top opening of her coat. The outside was buttoned and seemed to hide her stomach. Walking toward the viewing room, the heat became more intense. Kelly thought she should take her coat off to prevent from fainting, but felt as if she could get through it.

From the door of the viewing room, the funeral looked more like a church service. People were seated in rows of pews while waiting for the service to begin, speaking in low, respectful tones. Kelly looked toward the front and saw the coffin. Tears began to stream down her face as the sudden reality of the funeral abruptly hit her. The casket was open. Adam's face could barely be seen over the edge from where she stood. She covered her face with her left hand while the crowd of people began to realize the wife of Staff Sergeant Adam White was standing in the back of the room. Their heads turned just as Kelly's eyes rolled upward. Her legs no longer held her weight. She lost consciousness a few feet away from Sergeant Lawry. His cat-like reflexes kicked in as he thrust his arms and hands around Kelly in mid-air. With great ease, he supported her weight entirely and gently laid her down on the carpeted floor.

"Can someone get an electric fan over here?" he asked as he unbuttoned Kelly's pea coat only to discover that she was expecting.

Chapter 20

The wind that came off the mountain made the inn slightly chilly, and with a young girl sleeping on the first floor, Jim built a fire and turned the heat up to seventy-three. It was early in the morning, and the sun had yet to break the horizon.

He opened a closet door in the dining hall meant for cleaning supplies and mop buckets. Instead, the closet housed a folded up treadmill that leaned against the wall. Jim wheeled it out toward the back patio door. Sweatpants, sweatshirt, and a knit hat kept Jim warm while he ran rhythmically on the electric belt. As he made strides toward his three-mile goal, he stared out over the backside of Bear Creek Inn. An old barn, where his father used to keep landscaping equipment, had seen its better days. The thick forest beyond the barn showed signs of constant movement, with forest critters and deer bounding carelessly, mostly unseen. Jim's feet treaded lightly at a swift pace. He wiped the sweat off his brow as he came close to his three miles. Suddenly, he could hear Abbey's voice behind him.

"I what that was."

Jim stopped the treadmill and stepped off before he turned around. Abbey was peeking around the corner of the door with only her head and hand visible.

"What was that?" Jim asked.

"I didn't know what that noise was," Abbey said pointing to the treadmill.

"Oh. Sorry. I hope it didn't wake you."

"I was up."

"You still like your new glasses?"

"I do. I was excited to put them on this morning."

Blueberries, sliced bananas, and two cups of green tea were arranged by Jim with a little help from Abbey. She used a paring knife to slice the bananas and divided the slices into two small bowls. Instead of carrying their breakfast into the lobby, they stood up and ate off the stainless steel, commercial-grade prep table.

"What are you studying today?"

"Um, this week we're doing cells."

"Plant, human or marine life?"

"Bacteria."

"Wow, I was in seventh grade when I learned what bacteria even was."

"We are learning structures."

"Structures? What do you mean?" Jim asked as he ate a slice of banana. Abbey couldn't remember the full name, but for some reason, the word "flag" kept repeating in her head. Instead of saying what she knew would be incorrect, she simply shrugged her shoulders. "You mean like capsule, flagella…," Jim said trying to jog her memory.

"Yeah. Flagella. I have to give a report on it, like out loud in front of the school. Instead of doing an exhibit, I am presenting in the science symposium."

"You do? Flagella? You feel you got a good handle on it?" Jim asked, taking a sip of tea. Abbey nodded her head.

"We were assigned different parts of the structure, and I was assigned flagella."

"I'm sure you won't have any problems with it. You're a smart girl."

"You think so?"

"I know so. I can tell."

"My uncle didn't."

"What? What do you mean?"

"He would say I didn't have much sense, and I was ignorant."

"Why?"

"I don't know. My leg, I guess. Said I shouldn't have been playing around on a junk pile. Other things, too."

Jim looked away as he chewed on a piece of fruit, wondering how anyone could tell a little girl she was ignorant.

"Do you believe you're smart?" Jim asked as he turned his head and looked her in the eye.

"I guess."

"What kind of grades do you get in school?"

"C's and B's."

"How about A's?"

"Yeah, sometimes."

"Abbey, I know a lot of smart people, and I have also known some ignorant, brain-dead individuals, and I can tell the difference between someone who is intelligent and one who is not."

"What do you think about me?"

"Here's the thing. In your case, you were born with it. You did nothing to earn it or deserve it. You are smart whether you want to be or not. Luck of the draw."

"I'm lucky?"

"Yeah, but what you do with it is up to you. I promise you that you're smart. Without a doubt."

"Thanks," Abbey said soaking in the comment from Jim. She chewed on a berry while he looked at her from the corner of his eye, hoping she believed him. The thought of a grown man telling a child that she was senseless was maddening and sickened him. Abbey looked at the clock on the wall.

"I gotta go. See ya after three," Abbey said.

"Okay. Bring home your science book, and I'll help you go over flagella if you want."

"Okay, I will," Abbey said as she hobbled out of the kitchen door and into the dining hall. Jim finished up eating and drank the rest of his tea. In the lobby, he peeked out the window and saw Abbey as she walked down the path to the gate to catch her bus. It was a long walk, but she never complained. Jim had been meaning to repair the gate for some time, but hadn't a real reason to do so. With Abbey leaving soon, he could close it up and not have it repaired, which suited him well enough. The phone rang. Jim walked into the dining hall and answered it.

"Hey, Mallory," he said after he saw her number on the display.

"Hey, I got an appointment with an optometrist next week."

"Next week? Forget it. Already done."

"What?"

"Already taken care of."

"What do you mean?" Mallory asked. Jim stood up and put on his woodworker's apron.

"She's got new glasses."

"How?"

"Dr. McCoy here in Bear Creek."

"Wow. They take C.H.I.P?"

"No," Jim said. Suddenly he felt like he was getting too close to a fire. He didn't want to tell Mallory he left the inn. There would be an onslaught of questions. She would tell everyone she knew, thinking he had made a breakthrough. No way. She couldn't know. Abort! Abort!

"Who took her? Is there a bill or an invoice?"

"No invoice, look I'm kinda busy here," Jim said as he tried to end the call.

"I don't understand."

"How much longer is she going to be here?" Jim asked as he pretended to sound hurried.

"Should be soon. I have to pick her up tomorrow morning for her aunt and uncle's service."

"Okay. Let me know," he said with a tone that implied he was done.

"Wait, Jim."

"Gotta go!"

"Dang it!"

"Call me later," Jim said and then hung up. He felt he had escaped the questions for now although he knew he would have to answer eventually. Before another thought entered his mind, he received an email.

From: 'dthomas'
Sent: Tuesday, 2:54 PM
To: Jim Mayfield[mailto:Jim.Mayfield@canyonmail.net]
Subject: RE: Proposal

———————————

Jim,
We would like to visit with you and explain our proposal to you. If you

*are open to the idea, Dr. Stanton and Frank Navasky would accompany me
tomorrow or the next day at 1pm. Let us know what works best for you.*

Jim quickly replied to Dave that the following day was fine. He
closed his email and began laying out tools and sorting out slender
pieces of wood on his workbench. He worked nearly seven hours
straight with very few breaks until he heard Abbey *step, clonk* up the
stairs and onto the front porch.

"Is she here already?" Jim said to himself. He looked at the time.
Without knowing it, Jim had been busy. Hearing the familiar *step, clonk*
coming up behind him, Jim turned around and saw Abbey carrying a
piece of paper.

"What's that?"

"A note from the guidance counselor."

"Wow. I forgot about guidance counselors. Mine wasn't worth
much. What's the note say?" Jim asked as Abbey approached him and
he reached out his hand. She noticed the wood particles and shavings
that hung on the hair of his forearms. She handed him the paper. As
soon as Jim read it, he looked on his desk for his phone.

. . .

Ring. Ring.

Mallory was sitting at her desk about to wrap up for the day when
Jim called.

"Who took Abbey to get new glasses? You never leave the inn, and
you don't know anybody, so who took her?" Mallory started in. "I've
been thinking about it all day, and please don't tell me you just put her

in a cab and sent her on her way." Jim ignored her question and started in with the note Abbey brought home from school.

"Abbey's guidance counselor is requesting a meeting with her guardian. I guess that's you since I'm not going."

"What is it about?"

"I don't know. The letter is pretty straightforward," Jim explained. Mallory exhaled thinking she should get it over with.

"Okay. I'll call and see what's up. It's probably nothing, but no matter what, she'll be in another school in a week anyway."

"How soon?"

"Oh, I don't know, a few days. I'll be by tomorrow morning to pick up Abbey for the service. I'll take the letter from the guidance counselor then."

"Okay. Gotta go," Jim said in a hurry. Mallory tried to slip in another question, but he had already hung up.

Later that evening, Jim made two chef salads and they sat in the lobby at the coffee table. While he wasn't big on television shows, he opted to watch an inane reality show that featured kids and adults at a summer camp that Abbey seemed to enjoy. During commercials, Jim and Abbey spoke about school, and he asked her questions about cell structures. When they finished eating, Jim brought up the subject of Abbey leaving.

"Did Mallory talk to you about moving to Philadelphia?"

"A little. She said I would be moving there at some point."

"Are you okay with that?"

"I think so. It's a little scary, I guess," Abbey said as she took a bite of her salad. Jim could see that she didn't really want to talk about it.

"Remember what we were talking about this morning?"

"About what?"

"About you being smart."

"I remember."

"Well, there isn't a smart or intelligent person in this world that got that way on their own. You have to read and research and ask questions and learn from people who know more than you do," Jim explained. Abbey nodded her head. "So, I happen to know someone who can help you with your report. Would you like some help with it?" Jim asked.

"Yes."

Moments later, Jim and Abbey sat in front of the computer and looked at the screen with the words, *connecting*, in small letters in the center of a window. Abbey waited patiently with two sheets of ruled notebook paper and a pencil. Her prosthetic leg sat next to her, and she kicked her other leg freely in the air. The window came alive as the video feed connected, showing a black man wearing glasses. His hair was nearly all gray and the wrinkles in his face appeared to be more stress than old age.

"Jim Mayfield," the black man said as he looked at his computer screen. "Is this the young girl you emailed me about?"

"It is. Abbey, this is Dr. Woodward."

"Hello," Abbey said as she waved her hand.

"Hello there, Abbey. I hear you are doing a report on cell structures."

"I sure am."

"Well, I can certainly help you with this. I'm not sure if Jim told you or not, but I am a biomedical engineer here at MIT, and I have studied cells nearly all my life."

"Really?" Abbey said. "Just cells?"

"That's right. I engineer bone, cartilage, blood vessels, skin, and muscles on a cellular level. My work is mostly for the repair and healing of damaged tissue." Abbey listened and took all of the information in, but seemed nervous and unsure of what to say. Jim sensed her nervousness and stepped in.

"Dr. Woodward, as long as it is okay with you, I'm going to record our conversation in case she would want to use any part of your explanations in her presentation," Jim said with a quick acknowledgement from Dr. Woodward. Jim continued: "So, I guess if you could walk us through the functions of bacterial flagellum, Abbey will take notes."

Dr. Woodward began explaining the protein flagellum and went into detail about basal body rings while Abbey feverishly wrote down his explanations. Every so often, Jim asked Dr. Woodward questions, giving Abbey more material for notes. Then came the most advanced subject, when Abbey's new teacher described the cylindrical shape of flagella, how it was well-matched for locomotion and went into great detail about the Reynolds Number. The Reynolds Number explanation was going above and beyond Abbey's fourth-grade level, but Jim didn't stop Dr. Woodward. Abbey continued to take notes and followed right along.

"Jim, I am going to send you a link to our model library with a username and password. Once you log in, you can access animation of bacterial flagellum. You can download some videos, and she can use it in her report if she likes."

"That's great. I will make sure she uses it."

"If her school videos the students reports, I would like to see it," Dr. Woodward said with a smile.

"They do sometimes," Abbey said nodding her head.

"Well, make sure you send me a link, ya hear," Dr. Woodward added before he and Jim said their goodbyes. Once they disconnected, Jim looked at Abbey.

"Nice guy, huh?"

"Yeah. He sure knows a lot about cells."

"He sure does. Let's take a break, and then we can go over your notes," Jim said as he stood up.

"I've been looking up and down all day and I haven't had to push my glasses up once," Abbey said. Jim reached out and pushed the end of her glasses just behind her ear, causing them to slip and sit crooked on her face.

"Until now," Jim smiled.

"Hey," Abbey said with a laugh as she readjusted her glasses.

Chapter 21

Kelly opened her eyes to a dimly lit room. She saw speckled ceiling tiles and heard muffled voices, then a louder voice that was directed toward her.

"Hello there. You fainted, but you're okay," a man said as his slender face came into view above her. Daylight came in through thin lace curtains that covered a nearby window. The soft light allowed her to see that the man who knelt beside her was wearing a military uniform decorated with ribbons. She watched as he removed a stethoscope from around his neck, placed the buds in his ears and placed the metal disk to her heart.

"Good. Sounds good. You don't need to sit up just yet. Take it easy."

Kelly could hear muffled voices coming from the next room.

"Where am I?"

"An office. You're lying on a couch. I have the lights off, and the door closed. Take your time."

"Oh my God. My husband. The visitation," Kelly's muscles tightened and anxiety spouted from her face like a fountain.

"Don't worry, Mrs. White. You've only been out for ten minutes or so."

"Ten minutes?"

"Just take it easy. All of your vitals are fine. You didn't even hit the ground when you fell. I think you just got a little warm. I'm sure your baby is fine, but you should still get checked out by your O.B. as soon as possible."

Kelly took a deep breath and relaxed her muscles.

"Are you a doctor?"

"No, Ma'am. I'm a medic. I knew your husband pretty well. Adam spoke of you often. I'm sorry for your loss."

Knock. Knock. "Don't get up," Sergeant Lawry whispered.

The door opened. Alma White stuck her head inside as he stood up, placing the stethoscope back around his neck.

"Is she awake?"

"She is."

"May I come in?"

"Sure."

Alma entered and spoke with Sergeant Lawry quietly. Kelly couldn't hear what they were saying, but felt anxious when Sergeant Lawry left the room and Alma pulled up a chair next to her.

"Grant can be very difficult at times," Alma said as she sat down. "He wouldn't approve of me talking with you, but I don't care. I have to be upfront with you. Without this child, this conversation would be non-existent," Alma explained. Kelly thought her tone of voice sounded more pleading than demanding or forceful.

"This changes everything. In time, maybe Grant will come around. I can work on that," Alma placed her hand on top of Kelly's and offered a half smile.

"Thank you."

"Well, you're going to be a single mom. You are going to need help, and I will make sure you get what you need. Where are you currently staying?"

"A motel. Not far from here."

"Are you going to move up here?"

"I already have. I mean, I have all of my things with me. I moved off the base."

"You know, you should have told me this on the phone."

"I know. I didn't know exactly know how to bring it up."

"Well, I will start talking with Grant and see if I can't work it out for you to stay in the apartment above our garage."

"That would be nice."

"It may take some time for me to convince him, so be prepared to stay at the motel for a few more days."

Still feeling weak and tired, Kelly closed her eyes. For the first time since Adam's death, Kelly felt a connection to someone that felt like family.

. . .

Mallory pulled into a parking lot and put the car in park as she checked the time on her phone. Abbey opened the car door and pushed it wide open before setting her prosthetic leg on the cracked and pitted asphalt. The parking lot of the Second Street Christian Church wasn't full and most of the cars belonged to church staff. The church had about 400 members and served the county by offering funeral services to low-income families for a reduced fee.

The service for Justin and Judy Creeson wasn't heavily attended. The only other attendees were co-workers from Edwards Auto Garage, at which Justin was employed. They stood in the hallway outside the chapel talking in hushed tones while still wearing their mechanic's uniforms.

"I heard he was at eighty miles an hour. That can't be right, can it?" Abbey heard one man say to another as she walked past.

The mechanics looked at Abbey, but were unsure of who she was. When the service was about to start, Mallory guided Abbey down the aisle of the chapel and took a seat on the left side. A photo of Judy and Justin taken at a department store photo studio sat on an altar with a small bouquet of flowers behind the black frames.

When the pastor finally entered the chapel and took the pulpit, he raised his arms to signify that everyone should stand up. As he looked out into the congregation, he counted only eight people. Mallory looked at Abbey as she placed her hands on the pew in front of her and used it to help her stand up.

"Let's bow our heads and pray," the pastor said. Before Mallory did as asked, she watched as Abbey bowed her head, clasped her hands and closed her eyes.

Chapter 22

When Abbey returned to the inn, she took a nap before eating an early dinner with Jim. Once the plates and water glasses were cleared, she sat on the couch with her prosthetic leg on the floor and waited anxiously for questions from her new study partner. Jim sat on the other end of the couch with his feet underneath him and a notebook in his lap. While the initial assignment was to give a short report on what flagellum was, Jim took Abbey's research far beyond.

"The rotational speed of flagella varies in response to what?" Jim asked. Abbey thinks a moment, but doesn't seem to have a viable answer. "This is what we thought sounded like a movie title."

"Oh! Proton motive force!" Abbey said with a smile.

"That's it!" Jim said with a grin.

Ring. Ring.

Jim excused himself to find his ringing cell phone in the dining room.

"Looks like tomorrow is the big day," Mallory said.

"Tomorrow?"

"Got the papers emailed to me today. She doesn't have to go to school tomorrow, so let her sleep in. She's going to have a long day."

"Where is she going?"

"St. Nicholas Orphanage in North Philadelphia."

"Is it nice?"

"I suppose. As nice as an orphanage can be, I guess."

"Should I tell her, or do you want to?"

"I will if you would prefer it."

"Nah, I can tell her."

"How is she doing since I dropped her off?"

"Fine. She hasn't talked about the service. How was it by the way?"

"Sad. Only six other people were there besides us. I think they were her uncle's co-workers, too. They never said a word to Abbey."

"That's depressing."

"Yeah, but not uncommon. I'll see you tomorrow."

Jim hung up and walked toward the lobby, while he wondered how to break the news, and was curious as to how she would react.

"Hey. That was Mallory."

"Is she coming over?"

"Yes, but not until tomorrow. It seems that you're moving to Philadelphia." Without knowing exactly what to say or how to tell her, he had taken the opportunity as soon as it had presented itself.

"Tomorrow?" Abbey asked. Jim didn't respond. He could see fear filling her eyes like tears. Abbey removed her glasses and cupped her face as he stood at the foot of the couch.

"I'm sorry. I didn't know how else to tell you," Jim said. Abbey began to emit sounds of sobbing. He thought he could have said it more gently than just coming out with it, but it was too late. He looked at her as she cried, unsure of what to do. He took a few steps and sat close to her, but not too close. He reached to pat her on the back only to retract his gesture before touching her.

"I don't mean to cry. I just…"

"It's okay."

"I like it here, and I like my school, or at least my friends." Jim shrugged his shoulders trying to think of something to say.

"You know, I would never have let you stay here if you weren't such a good kid. You are kind and polite. That goes a long way in life."

"Thanks."

"And smart. You know more about flagella than any kid in your class. Guarantee it. You probably know more than the teachers at this point." Jim said as Abbey wiped away tears and put her glasses back on.

"Do I need to go pack?"

"No, I wouldn't bother with it. Let Mallory handle it."

"I will miss the seaweed salad."

"You don't have to. Ask the orphanage about it. Tell them you require it."

"You think they will get it?"

"No. But you can try."

"I will try."

The night ended with Abbey falling asleep on the couch while watching an animated movie. Jim retired to the dining hall and picked up where he left off working on the rocking chair. Near midnight, he took a break and opened a browser on his computer and began typing in a search engine.

St. Nicholas Orphanage, Philadelphia

Jim clicked on the website for the orphanage and was greeted by a home page featuring the orphanage's courtyard. Stone walkways and willow trees with bright yellow, pink and purple flowers planted in rows. *It looks nice,* Jim thought. He clicked around on the site and found a menu featuring breakfast, lunch and dinner. Sausage biscuits, pizza, spaghetti and meatballs were on the menu for tomorrow. Then there was a gallery of photos that displayed the living quarters. The first photo showed long hallways with doors lining the walls similar to the hallways of Bear Creek Inn. The next set of photos showed the individual rooms, only instead of one or two beds, there were four crammed in each. Every bed frame was constructed out of pinewood and large, protruding bolts. Disconcerted with what looked like overcrowding, Jim clicked around and discovered a news article about the orphanage. After he read it, Mallory got a late night phone call.

Ring. Ring. Her phone rang on the nightstand near her head. Her husband, Barry, woke up and nudged Mallory.

"Hey. Honey? Hey, Honey? Wake up," he said trying to wake her to no avail. He moved on to shouting. "Wake up," he yelled with a not-so-gentle push.

"What is it?" Mallory asked as she pulled her sleep mask up on top of her head. By now, her phone had stopped ringing and went to voice-mail.

"Your phone rang," Barry said. Just as she looked at her phone, it began ringing again. It was Jim. She stood up in fear that something had happened to Abbey. She took a few steps toward her closet, thinking she was going to have to throw on clothes and bolt out the door, which wasn't an uncommon occurrence in her line of work. When she answered, Jim began.

"Did you know that this orphanage is at maximum capacity?"

"Jim? What's wrong?"

"The orphanage, that's what."

"Are you kidding me, Jim? It's midnight," Mallory whisper-yelled.

"This is important. I wouldn't call you if it wasn't."

Daniel, one of Mallory's kids, walked into the room with tired eyes. He rubbed them as he spoke.

"I heard shouting."

"It's nothing. Go back to bed," Mallory replied as she reached for her silk robe on the corner post of her bed.

"Mallory, do you hear me?" Jim asked.

"Yes. I hear you. What are you talking about?" she asked as she punched her arms through the thin silk sleeves.

"This orphanage has way too many kids there. They serve red meat all day, and they are low on funds. I just read an article where this place is in financial turmoil," Jim explained. Mallory continued to whisper-yell into the phone while her son looked on.

"Jim, that's like, every orphanage in the country. They all suck. They're all over-crowded. That's the way it is. What did you expect?"

"I don't know. Can you just talk normal and not be so rude?" Jim asked. Mallory took the phone away from her ear in disbelief. She placed the microphone next to her mouth and spoke directly into it.

"It's midnight."

"What if I let her stay here?" Jim asked. The silence on Mallory's end was longer than Jim was used to. "Hello?"

Mallory hurried across her bedroom, the silk robe flapping and snapping behind her. She closed the door to the master bath as she walked in, now speaking in a normal tone.

"What? You want her to stay there?"

"Well, she likes it here. We're working on a report for school, and at least here she can eat real food and not be surrounded by a million kids all day, every day."

"I have gone through mountains of paperwork trying to get her transferred. I finally see light at the end of the tunnel, and you tell me it wasn't even necessary."

"Mal, think about her for a second. I don't care about how much paperwork you had to do."

"Yeah, okay. Fine. I will see what I can do. They are already expecting to intake her tomorrow evening. I guess I can retract it."

"Please do."

"This is more work for me. Besides you didn't get me anything for my birthday."

"You told me you hated birthdays."

"I hate getting older, but I still like presents."

"If there is anything I can do to help, please let me know. I will do whatever I can."

"I don't know how this will work though."

"What do you mean?"

"You are not set up as a foster home. You've never taken the classes, or gone through registration, so I don't know how I can make this work. All I can do is continue to file lodging extensions."

"Can you just keep doing that?"

"Not really. I'll have to figure something out. There's also the possibility of a nearby foster home opening up as they send more kids to Philadelphia."

"As long as she doesn't go to an orphanage."

"I'll call you later."

Jim walked back into the lobby and found the credits to the animated movie rolling over a song. On the couch was Abbey, fast asleep. Her face was smashed into the leather cushions, still in her school clothes.

"Abbey? Hey, Abbey?" he spoke softly as he gently shook her shoulder. She began to move her arms and leg only to roll over toward the cushions and fall back asleep. *If I leave her here, she could roll over and fall on the floor,* he thought.

Unsure of how best to get her to her room, Jim bent down and carefully ran his muscular arms between the soft leather couch and Abbey's lanky body. As if she only weighed a few ounces, Jim lifted Abbey off the couch with ease, but did not hold her close at first. Her body lay like a rag doll between the tracks of a roller coaster. He slowly brought Abbey toward his chest, and her head rested against his bicep.

Jim walked carefully, keeping Abbey level without jostling her as his bare feet made silent steps across the hardwood floor and into Abbey's room. With slow, steady movements, he lowered her down on the bed and after a few clever maneuvers, he got the covers from underneath her and tucked her in. Back out in the lobby, Jim grabbed her prosthetic leg. Before walking back to her room, he examined it, looking at its construction and felt the weight of it in his hands. He moved the components to simulate walking while he studied the clunky aluminum joints. He placed the prosthetic leg beside her bed where she could easily find it and turned off the light before he quietly left her room.

Chapter 23

Kelly parked her car and looked for lip-gloss in her purse. Her movements and concerns mimicked someone who wasn't attending the funeral of her husband. She shut the driver's side door and put her hands in the coat pockets of her black pea coat. Walking toward the burial site, she stared at the ground instead of risking seeing the coffin. Her mind went back to a time when she and Adam helped out another couple by babysitting their four-year-old boy for a few hours.

Adam and Kelly were watching over Caleb Zachary Parker, the son of Sgt. Parker, on a snowy afternoon at Quantico. Open fields of grass and trees made the perfect setting for playing in the snow. Snowballs and snow angels were made, and a snowman rose from the ground that day.

"It's cold but I'm having so much fun," Caleb said as he helped pack in the mass of the snowman with his small, colorful mittens.

"You have a name for him?" Adam asked.

"I don't know. Maybe Whitey," Caleb said, causing both Adam and Kelly to laugh.

"Maybe there's a better name," Adam replied with a smile. "Pack it in good, and we can use these rocks for eyes," he explained to Caleb as he held out two dark, gray rocks. Kelly watched them together while paying close attention to Adam. He interacted with Caleb in a kind and polite manner, which made Kelly smile with thoughts of parenthood.

"When we're done we could tackle him!" Caleb said, making Adam laugh

out loud.

"I'm for it if you are, big guy," Adam said as he hurriedly packed the snow into the body. Once the snowman was put together, Kelly watched little Caleb take a running start toward the creation he named Snowbot. Once Caleb got close, his feet left the ground as he jumped and wrapped his arms around the snowman only to make a slight dent in the three snow spheres. Caleb landed on the ground and laughed when he saw he caused little damage to Snowbot.

"Oh! Good try though," Adam said.

"You do it! You're bigger than me," Caleb said. Without the ability to refuse a four year old's request, he asked for Caleb to stand back. With the speed of a bull, Adam started out jogging, then burst into a full run. He charged the snowman and leapt, tackling it as if trying to force a fumble. The packed snow exploded into a fine powder and Adam's built frame of muscles hit the ground hard. Without flinching, he got up and dusted the powder off.

"Amazing!" Caleb yelled as he threw up his hands, his eyes as big as quarters.

"Oh, poor Snowbot!" Kelly exclaimed as she picked up two rocks that were once his eyes.

"It's okay, Miss Kelly. I'm gonna rebuild him," Caleb said as he started to remake the snowman. Adam then tackled Kelly to the ground, using his hands and large forearms to help her fall gently. She screamed and laughed before laying her head into the cold snow. Once on top of her, he kissed her gently before rolling over and lying on his back, staring at the cloudy sky. While Caleb continued to make his snowman, Kelly and Adam talked, lying on their backs and staring at the sky.

"So, you want a boy now?" Kelly asked as her eyes took in the gray clouds floating above them.

"No, I'd like a girl just as much." Adam moved his arms and legs, making a snow angel. Kelly turned her head and looked at Adam. "Why? What do you want?" he asked.

"It doesn't matter. Health matters more to me," Kelly said as it started to snow. Small, dainty flakes fell wayward while Adam propped himself up on his elbow and looked at Kelly. He gazed into her eyes as a snowflake fell on her right cheek. She felt it and smiled. Another flake landed on the tip of her nose. Feeling the cold, but not brushing it away, she giggled.

"You feel that?" Adam asked.

"Of course. It's like a piece of frozen confetti."

"You look pretty in the snow."

"I do?" Kelly asked and got a kiss in response as Caleb ran over to them, excited about his snowman.

"Snowbot is done," Caleb said. Both Kelly and Adam looked at a snowman with awkward tree branch arms. The three spheres were more oblong than circular, with its body leaning sadly to the right like the Tower of Pisa.

Kelly walked to the gravesite and was greeted by Cpl. Bredenburg. She kept her eyes to the ground as he carefully guided her to her seat —a folding chair covered in a purple velvet drape next to teary-eyed Alma White. Before she sat down, Kelly noticed Grant as he stared at her from the other side of Alma. He seemed to nod briefly to her. He looked away, but Kelly could feel that something had changed. Possibly he would accept her, if anything, so he could see his grandchild.

Chapter 24

When the burial was over, all Kelly remembered was the folding of the flag, shots being fired into the sky and a lone bugler playing "Taps." Feeling sick and uneasy from crying so much, she retreated to her motel room to rest. Pregnancy had taken its toll on her body along with the grief and stress that masked the feeling of hunger. After another delivery order from Pennsylvania Bread Company, she ate a tuna sandwich on toasted wheat in between taking off her black dress and slipping into a pair of jeans and one of Adam's old faded T-shirts. It was comfortable and soft to the touch. No matter how many times she washed it, it still smelled like him.

Desperately needing a nap, she climbed into bed, and before long, she was dreaming of Adam. Kelly could see his face while walking in a park. It was autumn, and the leaves were every shade of yellow and orange. Kids could be heard off in the distance building piles of leaves. Laughing. Running. She could feel her hand in his and smiled at the way he looked at her. He didn't speak, and neither did she. They weren't walking, but instead they were strolling. They were taking their time and enjoying the fall. His face slowly began to change until she realized his face was melting, and his voice was muffled when he tried to scream from the pain. He was in agony, and he was terrified. When Kelly woke up, she was in pain. Stomach pain.

Ring. Ring.

"911 what is your emergency?"

Chapter 25

Jim was up early as usual. Once again he cranked up the heat to give Abbey some warmth when she woke. On the headrest of the rocking chair, he used a smoothing plane to shave the ends of the wood to a rounded shape. After working for some time, he looked at his aviator's watch, noticing it was nearly mid-morning, and Abbey wasn't up yet. While Jim liked to think of himself as a pragmatic and an indifferent person, the thought of telling Abbey she didn't have to go to the orphanage excited him. He took off his woodworker's apron, hung it on a hook and returned the plane to the board above the workbench with a smile before heading out of the dining hall. He took quick steps and made his way to Abbey's room filled with good news.

Abbey was in the small bathroom packing her toothbrush and ponytail holders into a small travel case when she heard footsteps approaching from behind. Jim knocked on the open door to her room and heard her moving around the bathroom out of view.

"Hey. I'm just packing my things," Abbey said. A wave of regret toppled over Jim, who was wishing he had woken her up and explained that she didn't have to leave. She had been managing her morning under false pretenses. Before he could explain, she started to speak as she hobbled out of the bathroom. "I am usually excited to be going somewhere but not this time."

"Why?" Jim said as he stood in the doorframe, curious as to what she would say. Abbey walked to her bed and placed her toiletry case in her duffel bag. She turned around and looked at Jim.

"I like it here, and I wish I could stay," Abbey said as tears started collecting in the corners of her eyes. Feeling terrible for not telling her sooner, thoughts rushed through his head. *Maybe I should have woken her up the way my mother would wake me when school was closed due to heavy snow. "There's no school today so you can sleep in. Go back to sleep."*

Okay mom.

Jim, still standing in the doorway, took a few steps inside as she stood next to the twin bed.

"Abbey, I called Mallory and told her to let you stay here."

"You did?"

"I don't want you to have to go to the orphanage either," Jim said with eyes determinedly dry. Abbey took several steps toward Jim, surprising him with a hug. Jim bent down on one knee, and she wrapped her arms around his neck. She began to cry uncontrollably as if the stress had built up pressure and now released like a steam whistle. She sobbed into his thin T-shirt while he awkwardly placed his hands on her back slightly hugging her, unsure if he should. Taken aback at her embrace, he was hesitant to say anything as she cried and sniffled. *It's okay,* he thought. *It's okay.* He felt he did the right thing, but acting like a guardian to a child felt foreign.

The next day when Abbey put her backpack on and walked into the dining hall, Jim turned around as he stood in front of his workbench, slipping his carving tool into the front pocket of his apron. Instead of sending Abbey out the front door to head to her school bus, Jim thought he could offer another option.

"Would you like me to walk you to the gate?" Jim asked. Abbey nodded her head *yes*, without having to take any time to think about it.

Jim stepped off the front porch with ease, while Abbey held onto the railing and stepped down on her own.

"Are you ready for your report? It's coming up in a few days."

"I know. I was nervous about it before, but now I'm excited."

"You think that any other kid in your class will be as prepared as you?"

"No. There's a kid in my class named Ben, and he smells and never does his homework."

"He smells? What's he smell like?"

"Like wet dog," Abbey said. Jim smiled at her response.

"I think Mallory is going to see your guidance counselor soon."

"She is?"

"Yep. Any idea what it would be about?"

"No."

"Mallory is supposed to find out. I'll speak to her sometime today."

While Abbey walked beside Jim, he noticed that she was hunched over while carrying her backpack. She seemed to be taking soft, easy steps to suit the end of her knee that was seated in her prosthetic.

"Is your backpack heavy?"

"Yeah, it's always heavy."

"Here, let me have it," Jim said as he reached down and grabbed the loop at the very top. Abbey slid her arms out of the straps and felt her backpack lift up.

"Is that better?" Jim asked as he slung the backpack over his shoulder.

"Yeah. Thanks."

Abbey talked more about school while Jim listened. When they came into view of the gate, Jim handed Abbey her backpack and stood back out of sight just as the bus pulled up. Abbey waved at Jim, saying goodbye with a smile as she walked up to the gate and slid through the opening.

. . .

Just as Jim and Abbey were getting along, a woman by the name of Margaret Philhours sat at her desk in a Philadelphia social office. She looked down at Abbey Creeson's file as she reached her craggy tree limb arm toward her blue and white teacup. Her face would resemble the moon—if it were wrinkled and had two beady eyes. Her pale, cratered complexion, formed by a bad case of childhood acne, made her appear much older than sixty. She took a sip of her morning tea as she had every day of her adult life, letting the hot liquid flow over and in between her stained teeth, a flaw that went unnoticed by everyone since she never smiled. Working in a plain cubicle with gray pincushion walls, she looked over the transfer request submitted by Mallory as she returned her teacup to the saucer with a *cling* and a *clank*. Her hair was long and gray, but no one had ever seen her hair out of a bun. It was always rolled up and pinned, often times with a pencil stuck in the thickest part of her hair.

"Good morning, Miss Philhours," a co-worker said as they made their way down the row of cubicles. Some people spoke to her out of fear, even though they never got a response; some spoke to her out of pure spite as they aimed for a "kill her with kindness" tactic. All five of the "good morning" greetings to Miss Philhours were returned with silence. Her co-worker's nerves were grated daily by the irritating sound of the quaint *clinks* and *clanks* that came with the removal and return of her cup to the saucer. She flipped through the file of Abbey Creeson and used her wrinkled stick fingers to peck on the keyboard in front of her, yet another sound that aggravated the adjacent cubicle inhabitants. *Peck. Peck. Peck.* Her computer screen displayed a database of awaiting parents to be matched to a child. She continued to *peck* and *click* until a page was printed while she took another sip of tea. Her veiny, wrinkled tree branch hand reached for the printed page and slipped it into Abbey's file, set it aside and moved on to the next child's folder in front of her.

"Good morning Miss Philhours," another co-worker said as he walked by her cubicle. No response, just the *clank* and *clack* of her cup and saucer.

Chapter 26

Murray's Diner was in full swing at lunchtime, serving the good folks of Bear Creek. Some patrons came in overalls, some in sweaters and jeans, but none of them were dressed up. When Del's mini-van cab pulled up and four men exited wearing suits, vests and ties, half of the diner looked out the big picture-window and stared. When the front door to the diner opened and all four men walked in, nearly every diner looked up from their plates and stared at the out-of-place suits. The music of Patsy Cline could be heard playing softly while ceiling fans spun on the lowest setting.

"This is interesting," Dave said.

"It's good. I promise," Stanton stated. Frank Navasky looked around at all the eyes staring at him. Mike couldn't help but speak up.

"I feel like I'm in a movie."

Stanton led them to the counter where Darla was trying her best to look casual. The four outsiders sat down on the red swivel bar stools and each grabbed a menu. Behind them, the door opened, and Del walked in after parking the cab. No one noticed Del because the local diners were still focused on the four men at the counter.

"Back again?" Darla said as she walked in front of Stanton.

"Yep. Brought some friends this time."

"Welcome," Darla said as she pulled out her notepad and pen from her apron. "What can I get you fellas to drink?"

"Could we place our lunch order too?"

"Of course," Darla said with a smile.

"Waters all around. Four Reubens with fries," said Stanton.

"Wait. No cheese for me," Dave said.

"No cheese? That's the best part," Stanton said as he leaned back in his chair.

"I'm allergic."

"No, he's not," Navasky said with a smile as he looked at his co-workers and glanced up at Darla, including her in the conversation. "He just says he's allergic. He actually just hates cheese."

"Butter, cheese and ranch dressing. Hated it all since I was a little kid."

"Huh. I never knew that," Stanton added. "I could probably eat a cheese and butter sandwich."

"It's called a grilled cheese," Darla said with a grin. She looked at Dave as she pointed her pen and winked. "Got it. No cheese." She turned her head and shouted to the cook.

"Four roos with fries, eighty-six wax on one."

The door to Murray's opened, and Steven Burns walked in holding a thermos. Darla looked up from her notepad. After she mumbled a few expletives under her breath, Frank, Mike, Stanton and Dave turned around and looked at Steven. Steven stared at the four men and then recognized Stanton. Before Steven could speak, Darla walked toward him and began pushing him out the door.

"Four shrinks now? He must be insane!" Steven said with an ornery laugh as Darla grabbed his thermos and pushed him outside before locking the door.

"Who's that?" Frank asked.

"That's the hayseed I told you about," Stanton replied.

The entire diner watched as Darla filled up Steven's thermos. Their eyes followed Darla from the counter to the door and watched her unlock it and hand the thermos to Steven.

"Courtesy of Murray's Diner," Darla said as she handed it to him and closed the door. Steven seemed to get the point and walked back to his truck as he glanced numerous times at the four men through the window. "Sorry about that guys, but if I let him in here, he wouldn't leave you alone."

"What'd he ask you last time?" Dave asked Stanton.

"Something about aliens."

"Why?" Mike questioned.

Darla interjected, "Your astronaut friend up there has been the talk of the town for years."

"He has?" Frank asked.

"Yep. Just when people start to forget about him, you guys show up." Darla gestured toward Stanton. "Since you've been here, the whole town has been talking about him, speculating what's going on."

Dave looked over his shoulder and caught the majority of the diner quickly going back to their plate lunches. In the window to the kitchen, four plates were put on the sill.

"Order up!" the cook said.

"Hope you guys are hungry. This Reuben is huge," Stanton said.

By the time they bit into their sandwiches, talk was reduced to silence as their teeth sank into hot rye bread and corned beef.

Chapter 27

Kelly Mae White struggled with tubes in her arm as she awoke from a deep sleep. The rhythmic beeping of a heart monitor could be heard from her left side. The drugs that flowed from her IV revived jumbled memories. Adam's funeral seemed like a dream and that his death wasn't real. Kelly shifted from one side to another, feeling a sudden pain in her stomach. She felt for the baby just as a nurse came into the room.

"Mrs. White?" the nurse whispered. Kelly turned her head and looked at a fuzzy outline of a woman dressed in peach-colored scrubs. "I'll go get the doctor." The nurse left as Kelly closed her eyes. Her stomach felt as if it was split wide open, exposed to the air. Just as the doctor came in, she clinched her eyes from the pain. Tears begin to form.

"Mrs. White, I'm Dr. Ward," she heard a young man say, followed by sounds of a metal clipboard and pages turning. "I regret to inform you…" Mike Ward was a new doctor, and the hesitation in his voice was obvious. Fumbling, he gathered the words and did his best to sound professional and courteous. Trying to remember his training from residency, he uttered, "…the baby didn't survive."

Kelly Mae turned her head away and sobbed with both hands on her face. Nervous, and regretting being a physician at the moment, Dr. Ward took a step back and allowed Kelly some privacy. He stared at the floor with his hands clasped in front of him. After some time, Kelly's crying subsided. He then delivered the rest of the news, ready to bolt and vomit in the nearest men's room.

"Mrs. White, we performed a D&C under anesthesia which required intubation. You may notice that your throat is sore," Dr. Ward continued, but Kelly could barely hear him. Losing the only thing left of Adam had numbed her senses completely. Tennis shoes squeaking on a clean tile floor and the sound of a door shutting were the last things Kelly heard before she lost consciousness.

. . .

In Bear Creek, Del drove his mini-van up Bear Mountain Road and stopped in front of Bear Creek Inn. As they exited, Stanton paid Del, including the same tip as last time.

"I'll call you when we're ready," Stanton said as Del nodded. Frank, Dave and Mike looked at the broken gate with crumbling and disheveled stone pillars on each side. Stanton looked at the gate, which was now slightly open. "Last time the gate was fully closed. Guess we can squeeze in through here," he said as he pointed to the opening. All four men made it past the gate and walked up the pebble road to the cobblestone driveway. Their dress shoes tapped and clapped on the stones beneath their feet as they marveled at the exterior of Bear Creek Inn. Stanton led the way to the front door and stepped up on the front porch. Mike McCara carried Frank's briefcase yet fidgeted with it in excitement and nervousness, unsure of which hand to hold it in. Stanton pressed his thumb on the latch of the front door and pushed it open.

Chapter 28

Mallory had put off the meeting with the guidance counselor until she had free time to drive into Bear Creek. A bittersweet drive, since she was angry at Jim for not being a normal member of society, but at the same time, she was proud of him for looking after Abbey. Mallory steered the car around a corner thinking of how good Abbey had it living under the same roof as Jim. All the healthy foods she could eat, cable TV, quiet surroundings, and more space than any little girl could ask for. Mallory had been to many orphanages, and while the living conditions were often better than the homes the kids came from, they weren't ideal. Comparatively, Abbey was living in luxury.

After checking in with the front office at Bear Creek Elementary, she took a short walk down a hallway and peered into classrooms every so often out of curiosity. Some kids were at their desks writing and some were watching an instructional video projected on the wall. When she found the guidance counselor's office, she opened the door and found Mrs. Tilda Harris pecking away on her keyboard.

"Mrs. Harris?" Mallory asked as she entered.

"You must be Mrs. Cain. Glad you could come."

Mallory took a seat across from her desk. They spoke at length in friendly tones about their day and their jobs, and finally on to Abbey.

"How is she doing in school?" Mallory asked.

"Seems to be slipping a bit which is expected under the circumstances, and that's why I wanted to speak with someone. I have to say that she had a hard time before, and now, she seems even more despondent and in need of assistance."

"Before? You mean before her aunt and uncle passed?"

"She had some self-esteem issues. Her situation seems to be magnifying those problems, and her grades are suffering a little." Mallory began to take notes. Mrs. Harris continued, "While it isn't anything to worry about this moment, it could mean much bigger problems down the road."

"Sure. I understand," Mallory said.

Mrs. Harris pursed her lips and seemed to hesitate before speaking up. Mallory furrowed her brow, confused and curious.

"Between you and me, and this doesn't leave this office," Mrs. Harris said. "Abbey's teacher is Mrs. Watt. Unfortunately."

"Unfortunately?"

"She isn't the best teacher in our school system. In fact, she is the absolute worst."

"Then why does she teach here?"

"I wish I could tell you, but I'm just a GC, and in our district only the principal can make that decision. Problem is, Abbey might need help from a more compassionate and caring teacher. I don't have the power to even recommend that. It isn't my place."

"Aren't there only two months left in the year?"

"A little less than two, yes. I suppose that's where we pick our battles. Maybe this isn't one we fight."

"Well, Abbey may have to go to Philadelphia soon if we can't find a foster home in the area."

"You know, if Abbey were to be placed in a foster home and stay in the school district, I have one last recommendation. Abbey is attending the science symposium soon. She will be standing up on stage and giving a report in front of all the kids in her grade level, which is really good for her."

"Of course."

"I would recommend that Abbey take part in another school event," Mrs. Harris said as she picked up a legal pad and glanced at her handwritten notes. "In November, we have a school play that we put on every year. Roles are assigned in late April or early May so that parents can work with their child to help them memorize their lines during the summer. When school starts again in the fall, they practice every other week."

"Seems like a bit much for a school play."

"It is. But it is also a fundraiser. Tickets are twenty a piece, and we do a fair amount at the concession stand."

"Must be a big production."

"Some parents really get involved, and we raise enough money in one night to fund all the field trips the following school year."

"And you want Abbey to be in it?"

"Yes. I do. She will see her classmates more often, and these kids become good friends. It would be good for her. Plus the role is perfect for her. This year we are putting on the play *Peter Pan*."

"Oh, wow! That's one my favorites. What role were you thinking of?" Mallory asked.

"Well, last year we invested in a pulley system for the play *Cinderella*. We put one of our teachers on a harness, and she acted out the role of the fairy godmother. So, I was thinking that Abbey would be perfect for Peter Pan. Especially since the pulley system would be easy for her to get around the stage considering her mobility issue."

"It sounds like a good fit, but you think it'll be okay even though it is a role for a boy?"

"Certainly. Traditionally, at least for the stage, Peter Pan is almost always played by a female."

"You think Abbey could pull it off?"

"I know she could."

Chapter 29

Stanton entered Bear Creek Inn with Frank, Mike, and Dave following closely behind. The first-timers took in the high ceiling, stone fireplace, the worn leather couches, and the older model television.

The *click-clack* of loafers echoed throughout the expansive lobby as Frank glanced up at the large, wooden support beams. Stanton looked around the lobby and listened for signs of life.

"Is he home?" Mike asked as a joke, but no one smiled. From the second floor, something caught their attention. Floating quietly toward them was a paper airplane.

"What's this?" Frank asked as it landed near their feet.

"Hang on." Stanton said as he walked over to pick it up. The other three watched as he unfolded it and read the words on the paper. They watched with interest as Stanton looked up from the paper and stared at the second floor railing. He yelled out to the dark hallway at the top of the staircase.

"He's Mike McCara, assistant to the administrator," Stanton shouted.

"What is it?" Frank asked in a near whisper. Stanton slowly turned the paper so they could read it. To Mike's dismay, the note read.

Who's the kid?

"What's the deal?" Dave asked Stanton.

"I think Mike should wait out on the front porch."

"Why?" Frank asked. "This is weirder than I thought it would be."

"Well, we are here on his terms," Dave said. "Mike? Will you wait outside?" Dave added.

Mike breathed a sigh of disappointment and set Frank's briefcase down before he walked out the front door. Stanton strolled over to the old leather couch and sat down. Frank and Dave followed suit.

"What now?" Dave asked. Before Stanton could answer, the door to the dining hall opened. Jim walked out with his arms crossed and stood at a distance. Stanton noticed Jim's beard seemed thicker and fuller. It complimented his flannel shirt and thick khaki pants that confirmed the lumberjack description he had given to Frank and Dave.

"Sorry. I'm particular about people," Jim said as he shifted his weight from one leg to another. Stanton noticed Jim was nervous, prompting him to introduce Frank and Dave as a way of breaking the ice.

"Jim, this is Dave Thomas and Frank Navasky." They tried not to stare at his appearance, but couldn't help it. After they shook hands with Jim, Dave and Frank sat next to each other on the soft cushions of the leather sofa.

"Dave, I remember you from the old days. No big surprise you're mission director now." Jim said with a grin.

"Thanks. It's definitely a dream job for me," Dave replied. While Jim walked around the couch and sat down, Frank started the meeting.

"Jim, what we are about to tell you, we haven't made public yet. In fact, this will be the first time Dr. Stanton hears of this," Frank said. Thinking this would be a boring meeting, Stanton had already slouched down into the soft leather cushion next to Jim only to perk up and pay attention. "On February 23rd, the ISS sustained a shower of debris and it damaged the Zarya module. It's not life threatening, but it is a heightened risk. It could become unstable, and we would lose that module. Frank gestured for Dave to take over.

"Currently, the module is shut down and sealed. At one point, the plan was to repair the exterior of the module with a routine spacewalk." Dave added.

"The ISS has sustained many leaks over the years. Why is this one different?" Jim asked.

"Well, the holes have been repaired, but it wasn't a through-and-through incident," Dave said. Frank sat forward on the leather couch and used his hands as he spoke.

"The debris damaged the coupling rings on the ISS. We have to remove the existing coupling rings and replace them." Dave handed Frank a tablet computer. Frank powered it up and launched schematics that looked very familiar to Jim.

Over a year ago, while Jim was working on a project with Hatherton, he helped design a new type of coupling ring that connected the modules on the Space Station. The rings were made of a stronger material and were easier to lock and unlock. When Dave Thomas called Hatherton, he spoke with one of the lead designers after the ISS had sustained damage from the debris. Dave was asking so many questions about the coupling rings that the designer finally replied, *"You know, the guy you really want to talk to is Jim Mayfield."*

"Mayfield? Why?"

"It's more his design than anyone else's, and if you need to retrofit them, he'd be the guy to talk to."

Before meeting with Jim, Dave had obtained the schematics of Jim's design and loaded them onto the tablet. When Jim saw the plans, he instantly recognized them.

"You have logged 81 EVA hours. We project this repair to take an estimated eight to twelve hours, possibly more. The coupling ring needs to be not only retro-fitted, but installed and you have the experience we need for this mission. Especially with such short notice."

When Jim first saw the schematics on the tablet, he thought they simply needed his advice as a mission consultant, but now it sounded like they wanted him to go back to the space station.

"Short notice? How short?" Jim asked.

"November."

"Is that it?"

"Well," Dave said, looking at Frank for approval then back at Jim. "In a nutshell, yes, but you know there's a lot more."

"Essentially, we need someone to go through the training quickly. We only have eight months, but you've served as a flight engineer, and a mission specialist with the most EVA experience. These qualifications along with the fact that you assisted in the design of the coupling makes you our best candidate," Frank said.

"And you can help with the retrofitting," Dave added.

Outside on the front porch, Mike McCara looked at his smartphone and checked sports scores. Then he heard something coming from the gate. Strange, repetitious sounds beyond the trees, brush and weeds - *Oh God, I hope that isn't a bear*, Mike thought.

Instead of turning them down flat, Jim wanted to feel out the mission. "Who's currently on board?"

"Commander Anatoly Grechko, Mission Specialist Benjamin Akers, and Science Officer Susan Basset."

"Any of them able to complete the repair? Seems a little out of the way to send me. Or anyone for that matter."

"Russia is already sending up cargo that includes resupply. They are sending up Vitali Popov and a seat is available for one of ours. All agencies involved want the most experienced flight engineer available. Being that you were part of the design team with the contractor and you have the most EVA time and appear to be healthy and able to perform this task, that makes you our first option."

"What was the mentioning about the remote workstation? That part I'm interested in," Jim asked. Dave quickly answered as he thought he might have his fish on the hook.

"It's part of your compensation package," Dave said as Frank removed a white envelope from his briefcase and set it on the coffee table. Dave put his hand delicately on the envelope as he spoke, "Everything in here is already agreed upon and signed. It includes financial compensation, computers, servers, and access to NASA's SHELL satellite," Dave explained as he moved to the edge of his seat. "This mission will require eighteen months on your part. Eight months preparatory, two weeks aboard the ISS and ten months working remotely. The ten months will be minimal involvement, but still a part of the mission."

Outside, Mike stood up from the rocking chair and walked to the edge of the front porch. He stared in the direction of the noise. A glimpse of bright colors could be seen between the spaces of the brush. *It can't be a bear.* Mike watched until a little girl with an artificial leg came into view. *Step, clonk, step, clonk.* Wearing school clothes and a small pink backpack on her shoulders, she made her way to the front porch, as Mike watched in confusion.

Abbey kept her eyes on the ground and watched each step her prosthetic leg made on the cobblestone driveway. When she got close, she looked up and saw Mike.

"Oh! Hello," Abbey said with a startled tone, but still produced a smile.

"Hi," Mike replied. He watched as she struggled slightly to climb the few stairs to the porch.

"Are you here to see Jim?" Abbey asked.

"Sort of. I'm waiting out here. He's in a meeting."

"Oh. Well, hope you don't have to wait long."

"Me, too. Who are you?"

"I'm Abbey."

"Are you his daughter?"

"No. Just a friend. He's letting me stay here for a while."

"Do you get to talk to him?"

"Yes. All the time."

"What's he like?"

"He's nice."

"Oh."

"Well, gotta go," Abbey said as she started inside.

"Bye."

Dave sat back in the comfortable leather cushion while Jim picked up the white envelope. Instead of opening it, he simply held it and looked at Frank.

"It's two weeks max. You will come back with Anatoly Grechko in the Soyuz capsule once the repair is completed," Frank said.

The door opened, and Jim peered around Frank and saw Abbey. Frank and Dave turned and looked. She *stepped and clonked* toward her room. Stanton looked at the little girl and then at Jim. He leaned over and whispered in Jim's ear.

"Who is that?" Stanton asked.

Jim whispered back, "Long story."

Both Dave and Frank tried to ignore that a little girl with a prosthetic leg had just walked in.

"The other agencies are aware of our proposal, and they anticipate your answer. If you could review the package…" Dave stopped speaking when Jim set the envelope back on the coffee table with an apologetic expression.

"I don't want to waste your time. I'm not interested."

"You don't even want to review the offer?" Dave asked.

"Not if it means leaving here. I appreciate the opportunity. I found a life here that I like, my finances are in order, and I am only willing to work remotely," Jim explained. Dave and Stanton seemed stunned.

Outside the inn, Mike McCara stood on the cobblestone driveway and looked at his email on his smartphone. The front door opened and Frank stepped out with his briefcase. Mike turned around as Frank forcefully closed the door behind him.

"Something happen?" Mike asked. Frank stepped off the front porch, his shoes clicking and clacking on the cobblestone. Dave exited next, appearing more disappointed than angry. A long flight home, Dave thought as he eased the door closed. Mike, not getting an answer from Frank, looked at Dave.

"Everything okay?" Mike asked. Dave stared off at the mountains in the distance without answering.

Inside, Stanton was standing with Jim.

"Well, you just turned down an opportunity to go back to the International Space Station. What else are you up to today?"

"You think I'm crazy?" Jim said with a smile and his hands in his pockets.

"A little. Working where I work, I meet hundreds of people that are all vying for a chance to go to space. They hand you a seat, and you turn it down."

"You know, that little girl needed glasses, and I took her to the doctor's office to get new ones. I drove her in my truck and back. I didn't even like that. Not that I can't do it, I just don't like it."

"Wait. You left the inn?"

"I did."

"Interesting. You haven't left in a decade, and the person that gets you to leave is a little girl. At this point, she has more power than NASA."

"One needed me to take her four miles. The other needs me to travel two hundred and seventy miles straight up. There's a bit of a difference in requests."

"What's with the girl? She a relative?"

"No. She's an orphan that needs a place to stay."

"How'd you end up letting her stay here?"

"My sister is a social worker and an overall clown. My hand was forced."

"You know, last time we met, I asked if you felt this way pre-flight, before you even went to space. You said you were sociable and didn't have any social withdrawal tendencies."

"Right."

"Post-flight, since you've been in space, you've felt a need to stay closer to home."

"Yeah, I guess," Jim said. He watched as Stanton stood silent in thought. "What?" Jim asked. Stanton looked at Jim with eyes that reminded him of a college professor from decades ago.

"The psychological impact of spaceflight on humans is still new to us, and we as a species have barely scratched the surface."

"Last time we met," Jim said with a smirk on his face, "you said that your profession is eighty percent crap."

"Yeah, well now I'm talking about the twenty percent," Stanton said with a smile, which drew a slight laugh from Jim. He leaned sideways to peer through the window, watching Dave and Frank speak in the driveway. "I better go. It's going to be a fun flight home."

"You know how you go on vacation, you're glad to be there, but when you get home you just feel…"

"Good?"

"I was going to say 'relaxed'."

"Yeah, I know that feeling."

"It's kinda like that. I feel like that every day."

"I see," Stanton said as he started toward the door.

"I'm not crazy. I just like what I like, and I don't have to compromise."

"Jim," he said as he opened the door. "I know you're not crazy." Stanton slapped him on the shoulder. "You take care."

"Keep in touch." Jim closed the door and headed for his workbench in the dining hall.

Chapter 30

Mallory drove up Bear Mountain Road and parked her car at the front gate to Bear Creek Inn. After she made the trek to the front porch, she opened the door and walked inside.

"Hey, Mallory," Abbey said. Mallory did a double take when she saw her brother on the couch sitting Indian style with Abbey next to him, reading from a book with the same thickness as *War and Peace*. Mallory froze.

"What are you guys doing?"

"Studying for my report tomorrow."

"She has to stand up in front of the school tomorrow and give a report on flagellum."

"Jim, can I see you in the dining hall?" Mallory asked. Jim, not thinking, brought the book with him while keeping their place with his index finger. Once in the dining hall, Mallory closed the door behind him.

"You're helping her with her presentation?" Mallory asked, looking a little bothered.

"Yeah. What? What's wrong with you?"

"Nothing, I just didn't think you would be interested in helping a little girl with her homework."

"I wouldn't use the word *interested*. She needs help and I'm helping her. What's the big deal? You act like it's wrong."

"No, no. I just…I don't know. It's just strange."

"What's is?"

"My brother has locked himself away for ten years and doesn't want to talk with anyone or see anyone, and then all of a sudden you're helping a small child. I'm not used to it," Mallory said as she looked at the textbook. She reads the words *Chemiosmotic Theory and Membrane Bioenergetics*. "Wait. You're reading this book to her?"

"No. Just a chapter or two."

"Chemiosmotic theory? She's nine."

"I know. We aren't reading the whole thing. Calm down."

"Where'd you get the book?"

"It was delivered today. Bought it online."

"You going to her presentation too?" Mallory asked although she already knew the answer.

"They are supposed to video it. I hope I get to see it."

"You should get out more. Ten years? This is ridiculous."

"Not a chance. Besides I'm working. I don't just sit around here and do nothing."

"I know. I just came by to check up on you both and to tell you something pretty cool."

"What's that?"

"You remember one Halloween when mom and dad made us dress up like Peter Pan and Tinkerbell?"

"Yeah."

"You don't think you still have your old Peter Pan costume do you? Maybe somewhere upstairs in the attic?"

"This is the weirdest conversation I've ever had."

"What? Why?" Mallory asked. Jim smiled, and slightly laughed. He hung his head and took a step back. It wasn't like her brother to be mysterious. "What?" Mallory said. Jim was still smiling. He took another step back and walked toward his desk. "What are you doing?" Mallory asked, now thinking her brother was insane. Jim said nothing. He stopped at his desk, reached for an object and turned around and walked back to Mallory. As he got closer, she could see green wrapping paper and a bow. Jim handed it to Mallory, and she took it from his hands.

"You said you like presents but not getting older. I didn't buy it. I found it in the attic in a box," Jim said. Mallory looked at the present, then back at Jim.

"Are you kidding me? Is this what I think it is?" Tears started to collect in her eyes, but she pressed on and opened the gift. Tearing the paper, she removed enough to see that it was what she thought—a ceramic night-light in the shape of Tinkerbell. It was old and a little discolored, but still in good shape.

"Mom made *me* dress up like Peter Pan because you were obsessed with Tinkerbell. I wanted to be a ghost or a monster for Halloween, but I was forced into green tights and a stupid hat," Jim said. Mallory held the ceramic night light in her hands as if it were a precious jewel. "Anyway, I thought you might like to have it. Maybe it would remind you of being young again. Get it? Not growing older?" Jim said. Mallory wiped tears away before she spoke.

"This was in my room from when I was a little girl until I left for college."

"I know. I found it next to our costumes. You also had Tinkerbell window decals but I didn't see them in the attic."

"Thank you," Mallory said while tears streamed down her face. She looked at Tinkerbell's face as her mind transported her back to her seven-year-old self. She remembered lying down in bed late at night with a walkie-talkie and talking to Jim who was in the next room. The soft glow of her Tinkerbell ceramic night-light barely illuminated her surroundings.

"This has to be my favorite present I have ever gotten. It means a lot." Mallory collected herself as Jim patted her on the shoulder.

"I didn't think it would make you cry," Jim said. Mallory laughed through her tears.

"It's unexpected. And thoughtful."

"What were you talking about Peter Pan for?" Jim asked as Mallory finished composing herself.

"This is a weird coincidence. Today I spoke with Abbey's guidance counselor, and she is going to ask her to be in the school play. They're putting on *Peter Pan*."

"Really?" Jim asked. He crossed his arms and asked with curiosity, "That is a coincidence. What character do they want her to play?"

"Peter Pan," Mallory said with a chuckle.

"Aaaaaaaand do they know that Abbey is a girl?"

"Of course. The counselor said that females traditionally play the part anyway. Apparently there are quite a few lines to remember and thinks that Abbey could do it. They even have a harness that will allow her to fly around the stage."

"What about Tinkerbell? Seems more appropriate."

"I don't know. She said something about a light or a laser that portrays Tinkerbell on stage. Not an actual actor."

"Is that why you were asking about the Peter Pan costume?"

"Yeah, maybe she could wear it."

"That costume is thirty-five years old. It's got holes and dust all over it. I couldn't even find the hat."

"Oh. Well okay. Don't say anything to Abbey yet. They're not telling the kids anything yet."

"I won't."

"Thanks again for my present."

"Get it? You said you didn't like getting older," Jim said as he pointed at the nightlight. Mallory stared at her brother with an expression that successfully conveyed, *"You're so clever"* and, *"You can't be serious right now."*

"Yeah, Jim. I got it," she said with a charitable grin.

Chapter 31

Kelly Mae White awoke and looked at the clock on the wall. Although she was still hazy from a night of drug-induced sleep, she could see that it was six in the morning. She reached her hand out, searching for something to drink. Her eyes stared at the ceiling while her hand moved about until she felt a plastic handle. She tilted her head upward and saw a half-full hospital mug with a flexible straw. Water. Her throat was incredibly sore from the intubation and breathing through her mouth all night. She gripped the handle of the cup and brought the straw to her lips and felt temporary relief as the cool water splashed down her raw throat.

"Glad to see you're up," a nurse said as she entered the room. Kelly sat the cup back on the table and tried to clear her sore throat. "Looks like you're being released today."

"I am?" her voice squeaked and sounded suppressed.

"Probably not until after lunch. Either way, you should make arrangements to be picked up. You can't drive home," the nurse said as she took the mug off the table and refilled it in the small sink by the bathroom.

Home.

Where will I go? Kelly thought. The plan was to attend Adam's funeral, stay in Wilkes-Barre and raise her daughter. *What now?*

The nurse sat the cup down and started out the door. "The doctor will be by before lunch. I'll get your meds for today and I'll get you some of that great crushed ice we have. That'll feel good on your throat."

Kelly looked to the left for her cell phone.

. . .

In the dining hall of Bear Creek Inn, Abbey was dressed and ready for school earlier than normal. She sat next to Jim at his desk in the dining hall and looked at a slideshow they had prepared the day before. Together, they reviewed fifteen slides of material for the science symposium, especially slide eight, which featured an animation sequence that showed how cells used flagellum to move. While the video played, Abbey read out loud from her stack of note cards.

"Cells use flagellum to travel, and when viewed under a microscope, the cells appear to swim as seen here," Abbey said while Jim watched the video and listened to her notes, making sure they matched. Once she finished he nodded his head, satisfied with the presentation.

"Sounds good. Should work just fine," Jim said.

"We skipped over Dr. Woodward's video."

"It's embedded in the slideshow now. Here, take a look." Jim said as he clicked to slide thirteen. Dr. Woodward was shown on screen, and Jim pressed play. The video was a recorded segment of Abbey's interview with the doctor. "It will start just like the animation video when you advance to the slide, so make sure you say what's on the note card before you move on."

"Okay," Abbey said as Jim removed a flash drive from his com-

puter. He put it in her pink backpack and zipped up the small compartment.

"If you lose the flash drive or the file is corrupted in some way, I
emailed the slides to Mallory, and she forwarded them to your guidance counselor."

"Thanks!" Abbey said with a smile. "You are prepared for everything."

"Must be the Boy Scout in me," Jim said as he followed her out of
the dining hall. *Step. Clonk. Step. Clonk.*

Jim and Abbey talked about not being nervous on the way to the
front gate. He spoke at length about breathing with control and not
thinking about anything but the report. When Abbey got on the bus,
Jim stayed out of view behind the brush.

As Abbey boarded the school bus, Jim thought about fixing the
gate or removing it altogether. He took his time as he made his way
back to the inn, staring down the cobblestone path. Abbey didn't
seem to have a big problem with the stairs, but walking all that way
seemed unnecessary. The only thing that prevented her from being
picked up in front of the inn was the gate. *Maybe that would be a good
idea*, he thought. *Maybe Abbey could stay here a while longer.* Jim settled
on no certainties, but he briefly considered the thought.

. . .

Kelly had called Alma White three times with no answer. Instead, a
cab ride back to the motel would have to suffice. After a thorough
post-op exam, she was informed that she must walk from one end of
the hallway to the other in order to be released. If the pain was too

much, she was to return to her room, and the doctor would be called. With no wish to delay her departure, Kelly uncovered herself and accepted assistance from the nurse to sit on the edge of the bed. Upon standing up, she felt pain in her stomach, and her legs were weak. While bearing most of her weight on the nurse's arm, Kelly took a step. Minutes later, Kelly was in the hallway and making the trip toward the end, using the IV pole for balance. The nurse at her side used both hands to help Kelly move forward, being very cautious with her in case she started to fall, but Kelly stopped walking. She bent over slightly and began crying while holding her stomach.

It took some time before the nurse could get it out of Kelly what was wrong. It wasn't the pain; it was something else. A feeling of emptiness came over her, the loss of Adam and the loss of their daughter. When the nurse realized her problem, she stood beside Kelly, placing her arm gently around her shoulder. Speaking softly to her, the nurse repeated encouraging words,

"I'm right here. It's okay, you're going to be okay."

Chapter 32

The wrinkled hand of 60-year-old Miss Philhours reached for the receiver of her phone that sat on her desk. She cleared her prissy throat as soon as she was connected with Mallory.

"CPS, this is Mallory."

"Mallory, this is Miss Philhours with the DHS in Philadelphia."

"Oh yes, hello."

"I have a transfer form in front of me for Abbey Creeson, and I have yet to receive a follow-up for this child."

"Yes. I am sorry. I informed someone there at DHS that we are temporarily canceling the transfer until further notice."

"I see. I am having trouble with a section on the form that was left blank."

"Okay. Which part?"

"The foster home number or orphanage where the child resides."

"I have it taken care of at this point, so no need to have it filled out."

"Mrs. Cain, on paper this child resides with the State at St. Nicholas Orphanage. We cannot release a child unless we have accurate records of the child's temporary residence."

"I asked to have the child's transfer retracted."

"I filed all forms, Mrs. Cain. I can send you a transfer back, but I need the child's residence and or foster parent's name, address, and state-issued residence number. Is this child currently in a foster home?"

"No."

"Is the child in an orphanage?"

"No."

"Mrs. Cain, where is the child?"

"In approved lodging."

"Approved lodging? Is the child in danger?"

"No. We had no access to housing for the child since our orphanage closed and all the foster homes are full."

"Mr. Cain, we have a perfectly good orphanage here in Philadelphia, and I must tell you, that we might have a family in Arizona that is looking to adopt, and this little girl luckily meets one-hundred percent of the criteria."

"Well, that's good to hear, and I am sure your orphanage is just fine."

"If you leave the transfer as is, she could be adopted by this time next week as long as the family agrees to meet with this child. While I don't have it set in stone yet, I believe that she would be a good match. I will have to call you back."

"That's fine. However if the prospective family doesn't pursue Abbey, I will require the transfer to be cancelled."

"Understood," Miss Philhours replied, although it was a complete lie. She ended the call with a tone of voice that sounded pleasing and cooperative. It was odd to her that the child wasn't in an orphanage or a foster home. The red flag that was raised in her mind caused her to reach for her dainty teacup. As she lifted it toward her shriveled lips, a *clink* sound came from the cup as it lightly hit the rim of the saucer. Whenever the *clink* and *clank* of the cup and saucer rang through the air, the high-pitched sounds sent chills and shivers down the spines of Miss Philhours' co-workers in the surrounding cubicles. Her dead cold fingers reached for a pen and began filling out Abbey's name at the top of the court order.

. . .

Ring. Ring.

Jim answered his cell phone after checking the caller ID. He cradled the thin cell phone between his ear and shoulder as he worked on the slats of the rocking chair. Bent over, looking closely at the Bubinga wood, he sanded the surface by hand.

"Hey, Mal."

"Hey, I just wanted to call and give you a heads up. There is a family in Arizona that might be looking to adopt Abbey."

"Really?" Jim stopped sanding the wood and stood up straight. "Who are they?"

"I don't know."

"Well, do they have any kids? Do they have stairs, and if so, are they able to give her a room downstairs?"

"I don't know anything at all. Nothing. All I know is what I told you."

"Well, thanks for the call. Helpful and informative. Good job."

"Sometimes I wonder why I even bother."

"In this case, you shouldn't have. Call me back when you have more info."

"Ugh. Forget it."

. . .

In the auditorium of Bear Creek Elementary, the kids of the fourth, fifth and sixth grades were only excited about the science symposium because they got to get out of class. Backstage, Abbey stood with nine other students who were ready to give their presentations. A total of three kids were using the projector, and the rest just had note cards. Abbey reviewed her notes and waited for the symposium to begin.

The lights dimmed in the auditorium, which prompted hoots and hollers from the kids and shushes from the teachers. A video was projected on the screen showing footage of plant and animal cells with a voice-over that explained the visuals. Once the video faded to black, a teacher walked on stage and introduced the first presenter, Haley Wright, a sixth-grader who chose note cards for her five-minute presentation.

Abbey stood backstage watching the other kids give their presentations. Quick explanations on their areas of study were rambled off from their notes while their teachers sat in the dimly lit audience grading their performances. The presentations covered the nucleus, chromosomes, ribosomes, and unfortunately for one sixth-grader, endoplasmic reticulum.

The handful of mispronunciations by the presenters should have inspired a few laughs from Mrs. Watt, but she was unaware they were committing any errors. Mrs. Watt had only one child to grade for her class, and little Abbey Creeson was ready after five of her fellow presenters had appeared on stage. Mrs. Tisdale had loaded Abbey's presentation onto the school's laptop and handed Abbey the presenter's remote before she *step, clonked* to the middle of the stage.

Speaking into the microphone, Abbey started her presentation. While the other students had stayed far away from the microphone, Abbey didn't know it was bad form to speak with her lips almost touching the mic. Her voice, usually cute and high-pitched, boomed over the auditorium, causing a slight echo. "When we swim in a swimming pool, we use our arms and legs. When a cell swims, it uses its flagellum," Abbey explained while a photo highlighting the cell's lash-like appendage appeared on the large screen. With her pen ready to assign a grade, Mrs. Watt watched Abbey as she gave her report. Toward the end of the presentation, Abbey explained that she spoke with a biomedical engineer at MIT, as the video of Dr. Woodward appeared behind her. She placed her thumb on the remote's *"Next"* button.

"Here, Dr. Woodward explained how the tube shape of flagella is well-matched to locomotion of these organisms, operating at a low Reynolds number."

Abbey pressed the button, and Dr. Woodward came alive.

"These organisms operate at a low Reynolds number. The surrounding water, taking its viscosity into consideration, is more important than its mass or inertia."

When Abbey finished her presentation, teachers shared puzzled looks while kids stared vacantly, dazed by information beyond their grade level. Mrs. Watt looked down at her notepad and wrote down Abbey's grade. Finally Mrs. Tisdale, confused by such verbiage from a fourth grader, walked onto the stage.

"Let's give Abbey a round of applause." A smattering of applause began and quickly ended.

"What was that?" One teacher asked another in a whisper.

"MIT?" the other teacher asked. "Did she say from MIT? Like, the school?"

Mrs. Tisdale placed her hand on Abbey's back and encouraged her to walk to the right of the stage. Abbey smiled as she limped from the microphone to the side of the stage, feeling a genuine sense of accomplishment.

Chapter 33

After a lengthy discharge process, Kelly sat in a wheelchair near the front doors of the hospital. An orderly stood behind her with his hands on the handlebars of her wheelchair while he bobbed slightly from side to side. He wore blue scrubs and white earbud headphones that emitted loud music and prevented him from hearing Kelly's question.

"Is that my cab?" she asked as she pointed toward a white, 2002 Buick Regal painted to look like a taxi. Her question was overpowered by hip-hop music being blasted into the orderly's ears while she watched the old Buick that had been converted into Lucky's Taxi Service greet her with a deep throaty cough. Lucky's was a one-man operation and the brainchild of an old barfly who made the bulk of his income transporting people from the local jail and hospital. Kelly sat still in her wheelchair as the orderly pushed her to the curb and prepared to help her into the cab. Once seated inside and the door was closed, she looked at Lucky in the rearview mirror as he spoke.

"Where we headed, Ma'm?"

"Roadside Lodge on Campbell Lane."

Kelly cradled her small, ballooned stomach to help soften the up-and-down jolts from potholes and speed bumps.

Once at the Roadside Lodge, Kelly saw her rental car and remembered that she would have to turn it in soon. Dismissing the thought, she entered her room and considered lying down and sleeping. Food also crossed her mind. She looked around the room at the uncomfortable bed, filthy carpet and discolored tile in the bathroom. She removed her smartphone out of her back pocket and searched for another place to stay. Perhaps a hotel with room service and a bed she could disappear into.

Despite the pain, Kelly had quickly packed her bags, checked out of the Roadside Lodge and drove to the Wilkes-Barre Plaza Hotel and Convention Center. While it was harder on her wallet than her previous accommodations, the hotel made up for it in convenience and comfort. She felt she could use a good dose of both while she recovered from the most painful experiences of her life. Kelly drove cautiously and avoided bumps and potholes to the best of her ability.

. . .

Jim was sitting in his office chair at his desk talking on the phone. When Abbey opened the front door and entered the lobby, she could hear talking in the dining hall. Jim was speaking with a contractor in Wilkes-Barre about his less-than-satisfactory gate and told the man on the other end of the line he was ready to pull the trigger on the project.

"If it is going to cost that much to fix it, then just tear it all down and start from scratch," Jim said. Details were suggested, such as installing a remote camera with a feed directly to his desktop computer. Jim ended the conversation, insisting the gate be torn down as soon as possible and rebuilt by mid-summer. Jim hung up the phone and spun around in his chair and looked at Abbey as she stood in the doorway still wearing her pink backpack.

"Well?" Jim asked.

"It went great."

"Really? Did they video it?"

"Yep. It's supposed to be online on our school's site."

Jim immediately spun back around in his chair and navigated the school's page. After a few minutes of searching, he was unable to find the video.

"They must not have posted it yet."

"Oh. I thought it would be up by now," Abbey said, disappointed.

"We'll check later. Since it went so well, we should celebrate."

Two bowls filled with apple slices, cashews, sunflower seeds and mandarin oranges were brought out to the lobby where Jim rented a movie online. An animated adventure with a small boy and a giant robot filled the lobby with Jim and Abbey's laughter. When the movie was over, they went back into the dining hall and checked the school's website for the video.

"Well, maybe they'll post it tomorrow," Jim said when he couldn't find it. Abbey kept looking at the screen hoping they had overlooked it. Saddened by the missing video, Abbey decided to take a shower and get ready for bed.

"Can I play a few games on the computer before I go to bed?"

"I would say you've earned it," Jim said, slightly smiling. When Abbey returned from her room with wet hair, she found Jim working on the rocking chair. Curious, she walked past his desk and came up to the workbench.

"Can I see what you're working on?" Abbey asked.

"Okay, can you get that chair? Bring it over here so you can stand on it. I'll help you," Jim said. In no time, Abbey was standing on a chair looking at the pieces of wood on his workbench. "See, this is the back of the chair," Jim said as she looked at slats of wood and a headrest.

"You sell these rocking chairs?"

"I do."

"People come up here and buy them?"

"Nope. I have a website. People order them, and I ship them."

"A website? Can I see it?"

Jim took Abbey over to the computer and typed in his URL.

handcarvedrockingchairs.com

The website was simple. On the homepage was a gallery of rocking chairs Jim had created over the years. After giving Abbey control of the mouse, she clicked over to the order page. There were four photos of four different styles of rocking chairs. By each photo, instead of a price, there was an email address.

J@handcarvedrockingchairs.com

"How much do they cost?"

"It varies."

"How much does that one cost?" Abbey said as she pointed to the workbench.

"Five thousand dollars."

"Really?"

"Yep."

"Do they all cost that much?"

"No."

"Some cost more."

"Really? Like, how much?"

"I had one family send me blocks of walnut cut from a tree. They asked me to make a rocking chair out of it. So it cost more."

"Why did they send you wood?"

"The wood was from a tree that was planted by the grandfather of a woman who was going to have a baby. It was a sentimental thing. That's most of my business. Women that are expecting."

"Why does it cost so much?"

"Because it is hand-carved, and I mostly use an expensive wood from Africa called Bubinga. It's the best wood on earth. But I'm not just making a rocking chair, it's a family heirloom passed down from one generation to the next."

Jim went into detail about the precision and the meticulous process in carving the wood until finally he had explained all he could. When he decided to get back to work, Abbey navigated the mouse to her favorite website and began playing a game. Jim would sometimes look over at her screen and notice she would check for the video on the school's website from time to time. When it was apparent that she was very tired, Jim spoke up.

"Why don't you go on to bed? We'll watch the video tomorrow."

"Okay," Abbey said as she closed the window on the computer and rubbed her eyes behind her glasses. "Goodnight."

Jim worked on the rocking chair until about midnight and finally felt the tiredness creeping over him. He checked his email on his computer and found a message from Mallory.

From: Mallory Cain [mailto:Mallory.cain@cservice.east.gov]
Sent: Friday, 6:12 PM
To: 'Jim.Mayfield'
Subject: Ride for Abbey

If she sticks around Bear Creek, Abbey will need a ride after school when she is done with the meeting for the school play. I am sure you won't do it. Do you have any ideas?

–Mal

Jim didn't answer right away. Instead, he decided to look once more for Abbey's video on the school website. A few clicks and there it was. An embedded video posted on the events page with the title *Bear Creek Science Symposium*. Before Jim clicked play, he hesitated but finally convinced himself that it would be okay to watch without Abbey.

Play.

Jim watched as the video displayed footage of plant and animal cells. Skipping forward, he stopped and briefly watched a sixth grader's report. The kid was nervous and read from note cards.

"Ribosomes are found in all living cells,"

Jim immediately skipped his presentation and searched for Abbey. Finally, he found her after the fifth presentation and played the video.

Step, clonk, step, clonk.

Jim smiled as he watched her walk out onto the stage and stand in front of the microphone. The projector lit up the screen with the first slide.

"When we swim in a swimming pool, we use our arms and legs. When a cell swims, it uses its flagellum." She seemed calm and poised. He had told her not to be nervous, to be confident. She was. Jim watched as she advanced the slides and continued her oral report. While the video continued, Jim started to feel something. He smiled as she stood on stage, articulating the details of her report before the video clip of Dr. Woodward began.

Once the clip ended, Abbey continued and without warning, Jim felt the stream of tears flowing down his face. Feeling so proud of Abbey overcame his senses. Jim saw the final product of working with her, seeing her learn and grow. When the video clip ended, Jim closed the browser. Wiping away the tears and his slight shame for crying, he continued to replay Abbey's report in his head and smiled at how well she had presented it.

When Jim woke the next morning, the sun had just come over the horizon. He had a quick morning run on the back porch followed by a shower. Once in the kitchen, Jim used a paring knife to cut up a kiwi into thin slices and placed them in a single bowl. He washed grapes in the sink and took great care to scrub each red grape on the vine without squishing them. He placed the grapes on top of the sliced kiwi and walked out of the kitchen.

After Abbey had gotten ready for school, she put on her pink backpack and walked out with Jim to the bus stop. In no hurry, Jim explained to Abbey that the video was posted last night.

"Last night?" Abbey asked as Jim held the bowl and let her pick at the fruit as they walked side by side.

"Yep. Sometime between ten and midnight."

"Did you watch it?"

"I did."

"You watched it without me?"

"I'm sorry, but I couldn't help myself. I was excited to watch it."

"That's okay. What did you think?"

"Well, do you remember when we were talking in the kitchen, and I asked you if you believed you were smart?" Once Jim asked the question, he thought about where he was heading with the conversation. A knot formed in his throat and his face became very warm, a feeling he hadn't had in decades.

"Yeah,"

"Do you remember what your answer was?"

"Um...I don't remember."

"You said, *'I guess'.*" Jim stopped walking. Abbey ceased *stepping* and *clonking* and watched to her surprise as Jim knelt down and looked at her as he spoke.

"When I watched that video," Jim stopped and turned his head. Abbey thought he was going to sneeze but instead she could see his eyes redden and glaze over. "I saw one of the brightest and smartest girls I have ever seen." Unable to control his emotions, tears formed in his eyes. "I am so proud of you." Jim sat the bowl down on the cobblestone driveway as Abbey reached out and hugged him. "You are very smart. You learned so much, and you presented it to your school perfectly."

She felt secure and protected as his strong arms wrapped around her. For the first time, Jim embraced Abbey without awkwardness. When he let go and stood up, he left the bowl on the ground.

"Can we watch the video when I get back?"

"Of course," Jim said. Side by side, they walked toward the gate.

Chapter 34

After four days of recovering in her gentler accommodations at the Plaza Hotel and Convention Center, Kelly Mae White left her room for the first time. Walking down the hall, she felt little pain from her surgery, which she attributed to the medication and the soft-as-a-cloud bed where she had been sleeping. She looked at the time on her cell phone and noted that she had an hour and a half before going back to the hospital for a check-up on her progress—doctor's orders. She had considered another attempt to speak with Alma and Grant White, although she hadn't made up her mind yet. In the restaurant on the first floor of the Plaza Hotel, eggs, bacon and toast were placed in front of her with a glass of orange juice. Kelly sat alone in a booth thinking about Adam and the time when she spoke with him via videoconference late one night.

"I slept in today so I wouldn't be tired when you called," Kelly said as she *stared at the screen of her laptop.*

"I have been thinking about talking to you all day," Adam said. He reached *into his camouflage fatigues and removed an envelope. "I want to show you something."* He unfolded a piece of paper that looked like a printout of an of- *ficial military document. "I got a promotion yesterday."*

"What? You did?" Kelly said with a smile.

"I went from a corporal at E four to a sergeant at E five."

"That's great!" Kelly said as Adam held the paper up to the camera and

showed his new pay grade.

"Instead of two thousand a month, we now get two thousand five hundred a month."

"Wow! That's a big jump."

"I was thinking that if your car goes out again, instead of taking it to the shop, you could just get another car, a good car you know, a Honda or a Toyota or something."

"Oh I don't know, what about a vacation with my favorite soldier?"

"Yeah? Where to?"

"I don't know. I would let him pick."

"How about Green Bay, Wisconsin? We could watch the Packers play."

"Okay, maybe I'll pick instead," Kelly said with a laugh.

"You mean a beach with clear blue water and drink service to your lounge chair?"

"Something like that," Kelly smiled and watched Adam lean in and kiss the camera, momentarily blacking out the picture.

"Anything for my beautiful girl."

Kelly ate the last bite of her eggs and drank the last sip of her orange juice before leaving money on the table and a generous tip.

After returning to her room and packing up her duffel bag, Kelly checked out of the hotel and paid the sizeable bill. While it was a necessary expense and she felt she needed the additional amenities, she hated spending the money.

With her rental car packed up, she thought she would inquire if she could stay in Alma and Grant's bonus room above the detached garage, a small space where she and Adam lived for a week after they married. If anything, she thought Alma would make arrangements for her to stay even if Grant put up a fuss. Even if it was only a month, Kelly could use that time to figure out what to do next.

She drove down McTavish Drive and turned onto the familiar Grider Pond Road. She parked her rental car in front of her in-laws' home. The quaint, two-story house was inviting with a solid, concrete porch and two wide windows to the right of the door. With little space between houses on Grider Pond Road, only a small driveway ran beside each home and into the backyard, which was where the White's detached garage was located. Kelly got out of her car and walked up the poured concrete path. Once on the porch, she hesitated a moment and then rang the doorbell. Kelly stood still and listened closely for movements inside. She was rewarded by the sound of the door latch being released. The door opened, and Alma's distressed face appeared.

"Hi," Kelly said. Footsteps could be heard coming up behind Alma. Alma moved out of the way, putting Grant White in full view of Kelly. With an expression like a thunderstorm, his eyes appeared to be a dark, electric gray. In his left hand was a kitchen knife. In the other was a jar of mayonnaise. Grant had been making a sandwich when Alma answered the door. Forgetting what was in his hands, he trudged to the door. Unsure of what was to come, Kelly stood in complete shock as Grant reached out for the door and, without saying a word, shut the solid oak door in Kelly's face. *SLAM!*

Kelly covered her mouth in shock and sobbed as she hurried off the front porch and into her car. Inside, Alma had heard her daughter-in-law crying but did nothing. *Grant is right*, she thought. *Kelly is responsible.*

Chapter 35

Abbey stood up on the school bus and waited for the driver to stop outside the gate.

"Look at that," the bus driver said, "The gate is gone."

Abbey looked up and saw that the pillars and wrought iron gate were gone and left a wide, open area for the school bus to drive through.

"Oh. The owner wanted to ask if you would pick me up and drop me off in front of the inn."

"Well, sure."

Excited to see the exterior of the inn, Lanny turned the wheel and drove down the gravel path and onto the cobblestone driveway. Relieved to see a circular drive, he was glad it would be easy to get in and out of the driveway.

"Is he around?"

"Doubt it," Abbey said. She limped off the bus, thanked Lanny and made her way to the front door. He watched until he realized he wouldn't see Jim and took his bus round the circled driveway.

Abbey walked inside and could hear the faint sound of fast, rhythmic footsteps. Jim was running. She made her way to the back porch without being noticed. She watched Jim as he stared at the old barn in the distance while he made long, reaching strides. Rhythmic and fluid movements combined with firm leg muscles afforded him a seven-minute mile. Jim moved his feet with robotic form, each step causing a *thump, thump, thump, thump.* Abbey stared, wishing she could run like that. Without warning, Jim looked over and saw Abbey.

"Hey!" he said barely out of breath, "How was school?"

"Could've been better," Abbey said, somewhat crestfallen.

"What? Why?" Jim said as he stopped the treadmill. He noticed that Abbey was carrying a piece of paper. Jim grabbed a towel, wiped the sweat from his brow and stepped off the treadmill. "What is it?" Jim asked as Abbey handed him the piece of paper. Jim took it from her hands and read it.

Bear Creek Science Symposium
Student: Abbey Creeson
Teacher: Mrs. Watt
Grade: C-
Comments: Student did not complete own work

"You have to be kidding me."

Ring. Ring.

The phone at the front office of Bear Creek Elementary rang as the secretary was getting ready to leave for the day. Once Jim asked for Mrs. Watt, he was immediately put through to her classroom.

"Hello? This is Mrs. Watt."

"I'm calling about Abbey Creeson's grade for the science symposium."

"Yes, sir? What about it?"

"She completed the assignment and went above and beyond for her report. I want to know why you gave her a C minus."

"It is clear that she didn't put her presentation together herself and didn't learn about the required material. The words used in the presentation were not typical of a fourth grade vocabulary and is not inline with her previous work."

"Did you speak with Abbey?"

"I did not. And who are you may I ask?"

"I'm her foster parent," Jim said without hesitation. He continued his questioning, "You are certain that Abbey didn't learn the required material? You never had a conversation with her about it? You didn't give her a quiz or ask her?" Jim fired off these questions like rounds of ammunition. Taking a moment before she answered, she shot back with curt responses.

"I saw her presentation."

"And that was all *you* needed to arrive at a C minus?"

"Yes."

"Okay. Thanks," Jim said and hung up. Instead of fighting with a caged animal, Jim opted to deal with the person in charge. While he navigated the school's website for the name of the principal, Abbey shouted from the lobby.

"Mallory's here," Abbey had seen the headlights pull up through the window while watching cartoons on TV.

"Can you make sure the door is unlocked?" Jim shouted from the dining hall. Abbey left her prosthetic leg behind and hopped on one leg over to the front door, unlocked it and hopped back to the couch and plopped down on the soft leather cushions.

Jim found the name of Principal Phelps and typed the number into his phone. In the lobby, the front door opened. Instead of Mallory, Kelly Mae White entered.

"Oh. Hello," Abbey said.

"Hi. Is this place open?" Kelly asked. Jim heard the strange voice and looked up from his phone. He stood silent, not moving an inch.

Kelly looked at the little girl on the couch. She was missing her right leg and her prosthetic leg stood upright on the floor next to her.

"No, it's not open," Abbey said.

"Abbey, can you come here please?" a voice said from inside the dining hall. Kelly watched as the little girl put on her prosthetic leg and *step, clonked* toward the dining hall. Muffled voices could be heard behind the door until finally the little girl took two steps out of the dining hall and looked at her.

"He said 'we're closed'." Abbey said and then improvised a friendlier response, "Sorry for the inconvenience."

"Could I speak with the owner?" Kelly asked. She watched as Abbey leaned half of her body into the dining hall and spoke with someone on the other side of the door.

When she re-appeared, she reported, "This inn has been closed for ten years and will be closed for another ten years. Sorry." Kelly didn't want to leave without discussing all the options. The thought of getting back in her car and going to the next town seemed unbearable. Kelly could tell that the person behind the door could hear her.

"I was wondering if there was something I could do. I could clean rooms, sweep, mop or something...I just...I would help out in some way. I just need a room and I'll pay for it. I mean, I'll work for it." Kelly wasn't quite ready to beg for a room, but did speak in a pleading tone. She watched as the little girl poked her head into the dining room. More muffled voices and then Abbey quickly popped back into the lobby. She noticed that the little girl's eyes glanced up and to the right as if trying to remember each word of what she was told.

"If you take highway one-fifteen to..." Abbey recited until she was interrupted.

"Please," Kelly pleaded to the door. "It is getting late, and I don't know where else to go. I saw the sign and pulled in just hoping for someone to be nice to me."

"The sign? What sign?" the voice from behind the door seemed to shout out the questions in a demanding tone.

"Bear Creek Inn? Isn't this Bear Creek Inn?" Kelly asked. The construction company that demolished the front gate had four workers on the project. One of those workers found the wooden sign that welcomed guests to Bear Creek Inn lying on the ground behind a tree. Thinking a storm had misplaced it and not an unsociable astronaut who desired total privacy, the worker had picked it up and leaned it against a tree. When Kelly had left Wilkes-Barre, she wanted an inexpensive room to stay in until she figured out what to do and where to go. When she traveled up Bear Mountain Road looking for a lodge, she saw the sign for the inn and turned onto the gravel path.

When the voice behind the door asked about the sign, she looked down at Abbey, "Is that your dad?" Kelly asked.

"Nope. That's Jim. He looks after me," Abbey explained.
Confused as to who this little girl was and why she only had one leg, her thoughts were interrupted when the voice came back from behind the door.

"Miss? I'm sorry, but I am unable to let out a room. Good luck to you," the voice said.

"Sir, were you by any chance in the military?" Kelly asked in an exasperated tone and almost yelling. Jim was thrown off by her question, but quickly answered.

"No." Jim said.

With a quiver in her voice, Kelly shot back, "Well, my husband was. He was a marine, and he was killed overseas, and his funeral was last week. Then I lost the baby I was carrying, and when I got out of the hospital, my in-laws disowned me," Kelly covered her mouth and began to cry, "They blame me for two deaths in their family. I left Wilkes-Barre, and I've been looking for a place to stay, and I need help. Can you help? I'm not crazy, I promise," Kelly said as she wiped her tears and realized she was begging.

Jim slowly cracked the door to look at Kelly, a thin brunette wearing jeans and an un-tucked white shirt. Her hair was a frilly mess. "I just need someone to be nice to me," she said as she turned around and headed for the door. Abbey looked up at Jim with an expression that implied he should do something. Jim rolled his eyes and exhaled, while slightly shaking his head. He looked through the crack in the door and raised his voice.

"I'll give you a room for tonight and tonight only," Jim said, "Wait in your car for now. Give me fifteen minutes."

Kelly nodded her head and continued to wipe her tears and nose as she put her hand on the door.

"Thank you. Thank you so much," she said as she left the lobby. Jim turned on the lights in the dining hall and turned to Abbey.

"Do you want to help her?" Jim asked. With a sympathetic look, Abbey nodded her head *yes*. "She seems genuine, but you never know," Jim said as looked at the closet in the dining hall, then back at Abbey. "Help me get a room ready."

Jim opened the closet door and removed cleaners in spray bottles and grabbed rags by the handful. Jim went to the front desk in the lobby and grabbed a key with the room number 001. The key unlocked the only handicapped-accessible room available at Bear Creek Inn. While every room was located inside the inn, the handicap room had its own parking spot and ramp that led to a door accessible from the outside. He carried a bucket of cleaners and rags and walked out the back door of the dining hall. After passing a row of windows on the porch, he pulled out the key and unlocked the handicapped room. The first thing Jim did was remove plastic coverings on the dresser, floor, TV, bed, and small desk.

"You take care of the bathroom. Just use spray cleaner on everything and give it a once-over. Just make it decent," Jim explained. Abbey nodded and thought she could easily handle the task. In fifteen minutes, the room was dusted and cleaned with fresh sheets, pillows, and a comforter covering the bed.

Kelly was sitting in her rental car when the front door opened, and the little girl stuck her head out. She waved a "come here gesture" and Kelly got out of her car. When she walked up the stairs to the front porch, she saw the little girl was holding a key.

"The room is around back. The door is cracked so you know which door. Here's the key." Abbey placed the key in Kelly's hand.

"Thank you." said Kelly. Just before Abbey removed her head from the door, she uttered two more words.

"No charge."

When Abbey closed the door, Kelly felt like crying once again. Feeling defeated, lost and useless, she managed to bring her duffle bag into the spacious room at Bear Creek Inn.

Chapter 36

"Hey, Jim," Mallory said as she answered her cell phone.

"I need a little help."

"What is it?"

Jim explained the unfounded grade Abbey received from Mrs. Watt. He had called Mr. Phelps and arranged for a meeting with Abbey, Mrs. Watt, Mr. Phelps, and Mallory.

"At 3 P.M.? You didn't even think to check with me first? What if I had an appointment?"

"Do you?"

"No, but that's not the point."

"You would really be helping me out here."

"I have to drive all the way to Bear Creek and then back to Wilkes-Barre."

"You asked me to do you a favor, I did. Now I need a favor, and you complain?"

"Ugh. Fine. Three o'clock?"

"Yep. In the principal's office. I want you to ask three questions. You have to ask the principal and not that old bag that somehow slipped into the education system. Get a pen and paper."

"Bag?"

"Abbey's teacher. Now write this down."

"Please? A please would be nice," Mallory said as she reached for a pen and an old envelope.

"One. What was Abbey supposed to learn about?" Jim asked and waited a sufficient amount of time for Mallory to write. "Two. If a student learned the required material and beyond, what grade would they get?" Mallory scratched on the paper. Jim continued.

"Three. Please ask Mr. Phelps to ask Abbey about flagellum and what its function is," Jim said. Mallory stopped writing.

"That's it? That's what I'm driving all the way there and back for?"

"I think it will work," Jim said confidently.

"Three questions. I'm driving there for three questions? Couldn't we just do this over the phone?"

"No, you are driving there to correct an injustice forced upon a little girl who is being educated by a bridge troll. Abbey has endured an amputation, non-existent parenting, death and being moved around, and you think this is somehow…" Jim's rant was cut off by a single, loud response.

"OKAY. ALRIGHT!"

"Thank you. You're doing a good thing here," Jim said calmly. Mallory exhaled in exasperation.

"Gosh. I don't even know why I bother arguing with you."

"Me, either."

"What was the third question again?"

The rest of Mallory's day was uneventful until she walked into the principal's office and was directed by the secretary to go into the conference room. When she walked in, Abbey was already seated at the table.

"Hey, Mallory."

"Hey, kiddo. How are you?"

"Good," Abbey replied as Mallory leaned down to give her a quick hug.

"Thank you, Mrs. Cain, for coming," Mr. Phelps said to Mallory as he entered the room with Mrs. Watt behind him.

"No problem," she replied as she took a seat next to Abbey. Mr. Phelps seemed as if he was ready to end the meeting before it began. Mrs. Watt sat across from Abbey with each wiry, gray digit interlocking on the table. Like a snotty, first-class passenger, she looked at Mallory as though she was carrying a ticket to a coach seat.

"Abbey, could you please step outside in the waiting area? We need to speak with Mrs. Cain alone for a moment," Mr. Phelps asked. Without a word, Abbey slipped on her prosthetic leg and *step, clonked* out of the room. As soon as she closed the door, Mr. Phelps started the meeting. "I received a call about refuting Abbey's grade from Mrs. Watt on the report Abbey gave for our science symposium," Mr. Phelps said.

"Yes," Mallory said. She refused to make eye contact with Mrs. Watt and kept her attention on Mr. Phelps.

"I have never changed a grade on my teachers' books. I rely on my educators to grade their students. This is merely a discussion," Mr. Phelps said.

"I can make this meeting go faster if I get answers to three questions," Mallory said as she unfolded the envelope and looked at her chicken scratch on the back, "What was Abbey to learn about?"

Mr. Phelps looked at Mrs. Watt who nodded and answered.

"Abbey was to explain what flagellum is and how a cell uses it," Mrs. Watt answered with a condescending tone. Mallory looked at Mr. Phelps.

"The next one is for you, Mr. Phelps," Mallory said as she looked down at her list. "If a student in your school learned the required material and beyond, what grade would they get?" After Mallory asked the question, Mr. Phelps shifted in his seat.

"Well, if a student learned material required of them and went above and beyond, well, that student would most assuredly get an A," he answered. Mrs. Watt opened her mouth like a dying, baby bird asking for worms and uttered her caveat.

"But if that child didn't do any of the work and the parent or guardians were to do the work for her, that would be reason enough to assign a lower grade." Mallory continued to look at Mr. Phelps and ignored Mrs. Watt.

"Last and final question. Mr. Phelps, will you please ask Abbey about flagellum and what its function is?" Mallory asked. Mr. Phelps shifted his weight to one side as he rubbed his hands together.

"I don't know. I see what you're getting at. I suppose if she demonstrates a real understanding of the material, we would be open to a discussion of changing her grade, but at this point I am content with leaving things as they are."

"I, too, am content with her grade," Mrs. Watt stated.

"I'll ask her the question though. We've come this far. Ask her to come in."

Mallory opened the door and asked Abbey to come back into the room. She took a seat and Mr. Phelps started in.

"Okay Abbey, I'd like for you to tell me what you know about flagellum," Mr. Phelps asked with a pleasing smile.

"Everything?"

"Sure."

"Okay," Abbey said, her eyes darted to the left searching her mind for where to begin, and then came back with: "When we swim in a swimming pool, we use our arms and legs. When a cell swims, it uses its flagellum." Abbey began to recite her report, but was quickly interrupted.

"No. She mustn't recite what she remembered. Having a good memory isn't enough." Mrs. Watt said. Mr. Phelps sensed an uneasiness in his educator, but allowed her to press on. Mallory sat back in her chair and crossed her arms, now fully involved in the fight.

"If she needs to prove what she learned, how do *you* propose she do it?"

"I will ask her a few questions. We'll go from there." Mrs. Watt said. Mallory didn't respond, neither did Mr. Phelps. They both watched as Mrs. Watt looked at Abbey and asked her questions.

"What is flagellum?"

"They are little appendages that help the cell move. They are responsible for helping the cell move."

"Go on."

"Flagella aren't just responsible for locomotion, but they are sensory organelles as well. They can recognize temperatures and chemicals and know when they are in environments that contain moisture."

"I never taught what organelles are, nor did I teach words like locomotion." Mrs. Watt said as if she had just won a trial in a courtroom.

"Where did you learn these words, Abbey?" Mallory asked.

"From Jim and Dr. Woodward."

"Dr. Woodward?" Mallory asked. She had thought she would simply hear Jim's name. Her face looked puzzled as she leaned forward and waited for Abbey's answer.

"Dr. Woodward at MIT. We spoke with him on a video confer-ence."

"Who is Jim?" Mr. Phelps asked both Abbey and Mallory. Before Mallory could answer, Abbey spoke up.

"Jim is an astronaut. Dr. Woodward teaches at MIT and engineers bone and tissue."

"MIT? An astronaut here in Bear Creek? This is ridiculous," Mrs. Watt said as she crossed her arms and looked at Mr. Phelps. He nod-ded, but didn't think it was ridiculous. He had put it together in his head. *Was the man who lived in Bear Creek Inn real? Was he really an as-tronaut?* Mallory was ready to speak up about her brother when Mr. Phelps asked another question.

"Abbey, is that all you know about flagellum?"

"No."

"Please, continue."

"Well, both prokaryotic and eukaryotic flagella have vast differ-ences…" Abbey said as she continued to explain everything she had been taught. The look on Mallory's face turned from dumbfounded to elated, with a hint of a giggle. She knew her brother well enough to recognize that he not only took it upon himself to educate little Abbey, but had taught her with the same level of brilliance she had experienced from him her whole life. Once Abbey explained everything she knew about the subject, Mr. Phelps cleared his throat and glanced at Mrs. Watt.

"I think Mrs. Watt and I will discuss this further. Thank you, Abbey, for your detailed and informative explanation. We will be in touch." Mr. Phelps smiled at both Mallory and Abbey, but appeared to be more embarrassed than pleased with the situation. While Abbey didn't see

it, Mallory witnessed Mrs. Watt's desire and possible attempt to man-
ifest lasers from her eyes as she stared at her student. Mallory played it
up as they left the room in an overacted and obnoxious tone.

"You're so smart, Abbey, you did a great job! Do you wanna go get
ice cream?"

"Yeah! Ice cream!"

Chapter 37

Kelly Mae White had overstayed her welcome, as she hadn't yet left the inn. Hidden away in her room, she played out the scenario from the night before in her head. It was surreal walking into the inn and seeing only a little girl with one leg. Then there was the voice behind the door. *Who was it? Why didn't the man reveal himself?* It was an odd encounter that made her think she could get away with staying one more night. *Would the voice confront me?* Her stomach, still sensitive to even the slightest touch sent whips of pain along her skin. She unzipped her suitcase and found a piece of paper and a pen.

> *I have nowhere to go and I am*
> *still recovering from surgery.*
> *Please allow me to stay one more day.*
> *God bless. Kelly.*

She thought the phrase *God bless* might incite a better response, but it wasn't that she didn't mean it. Unable to find a spare piece of tape, she opened the door to Room 001 and tucked it firmly into the space between the door and the tarnished brass knocker. The paper was flimsy, but it appeared to hold and serve its purpose. She closed the door quietly and locked it before looking through a grocery bag of granola bars and bottles of water. Hunger was masked by pain, and she decided it was time to take another pill. Kelly ate two granola bars, downed a half bottle of water and a pill before she got back in bed and turned out the light.

. . .

Mallory turned onto Bear Mountain Road with Abbey in the front seat. She questioned Abbey about her assignment on flagellum.

"So Jim helped you learn everything about flagellum?"

"Yeah. Jim said it's more like solving a puzzle."

"How's that?"

"Well, we would come across the words *sensory organelle*. We wouldn't know what that was, so we would stop and learn about what an organelle was. When we didn't know what the textbook meant, we'd have to find that missing piece. It was like solving a puzzle."

Ring. Ring. Mallory reached for her cell phone as Abbey continued. "Jim said learning about anything is more like solving a puzzle."

"I suppose he's right," Mallory answered the phone, "Hello?"

On the other end was Miss Philhours. After she dialed the number, Miss Philhours had taken a sip of tea. When Mallory answered, she could hear a strange clinking noise as the cup returned to the saucer.

"Mrs. Cain, this is Miss Philhours. I have a court order in front of me to be signed in the morning."

"I'm sorry? A court order for what?"

"This court order is to transport Abbey Creeson to Arizona on a temporary visit so that she can be introduced to the parents that may wish to adopt her," Miss Philhours explained. Mallory sat silent on the phone, unsure of what to say, until—

"Could I get you to delay the court order for a few days?"

"Oh? A few days?"

"Yes, I need to speak with the foster parents. I think they showed interest in adoption. I wouldn't want a complication."

"Always good news when a child is adopted. I will stave off for a few days."

"Great. I appreciate it."

"May I ask where the child is residing at this time?"

"An inn in Bear Creek."

"She's still at the inn. Okay."

"Thanks so much."

"Of course," Miss Philhours said before she hung up.

It didn't sound right to Mallory. The phone call was cryptic. She sounded too accommodating. Mallory had hoped the woman pushed the file aside and left it alone. The phone call lingered in her thoughts as she approached the entrance to Bear Creek.

"The gate. Where did the gate go?"

"Jim had it torn down, and now the school bus picks me up at the front. I don't have to walk all the way to the road anymore."

"I thought that gate would stay that way forever."

Inside, Jim was carving a slat for the back of the rocking chair. Using pure, brute strength and every muscle in his hands, he carved the slat while the peels of Bubinga fell to the floor. When he heard the front door, he set down his carving tool and walked into the lobby to greet them, still wearing his woodworker's apron.

"So how'd it go?" Jim asked.

"No problem. I think it'll work."

"I had to talk about flagellum again, but this time in front of the principal."

"I am sure you did just fine," Jim said. He looked at Mallory and nodded in the direction of the dining hall. "Hang tight, Abbey, I need to speak to Mallory for a second."

"Okay," Abbey said as she picked up the remote and turned on the TV.

Once in the dining hall, Mallory followed Jim to the back porch door. She watched him with curiosity as he cracked the door and looked out as though he was an assassin spy, searching for his target.

"What's the deal?" Mallory asked.

"I have a guest."

"What? Who?"

"I don't know. Some lady was looking for a place to stay, and because the gate is down she wandered up here." Jim said as he looked toward the front of the inn and spoke softly to himself, "I knew I shouldn't have torn it down."

"Why did you let her stay? I thought you would've sent her a paper airplane and told her to get out," she said as an ornery grin appeared on her face.

"Shut up. She said something about her husband being killed in the military, and she lost her baby. She was crying so I gave her the hand-icapped room. She's supposed be to be gone by now."

"Oh, is she still there?"

"I think so. Would you go check?"

"Yeah okay," Mallory said and walked out onto the back porch. She could see a piece of paper stuck to the door as she walked up to it. Removing the note carefully, she walked back to the dining hall while reading the four lines. When she told Jim what the note said, he exhaled deeply and regretted helping the woman.

"There's another problem," Mallory said as she handed him the handwritten note.

"What now?"

"Do you remember the social worker that wants to take Abbey to Arizona?"

"Yes. What about Arizona?"

"Seems the family out there wants to see her."

"And do you know who they are? You didn't know last time."

"I still don't. Doubt I'm able to find out."

"Tell them no," Jim said. "She's fine where she is."

"You're a funny guy, Jim."

"Why?"

"Tell them no? You act like it's your call. It isn't."

"I don't like it."

"I can't help it."

"What can you do? Can't you just work it out?"

"Work what out?"

"Just tell them she isn't available. Tell them something. Anything. Don't let her be carted off to some unknown family." Jim was getting angry. His voice was becoming louder each time he spoke.

"This is how adoption works."

"Don't you know she's better off here? Just let her stay here!"

"Jim, it isn't that simple."

"Well, I'm asking you to do something. Can you do something? Can you prevent this?"

"Well," Mallory said as she came up with an idea. "I can try to file a form that states due to her medical condition, she needs to stay in

Bear Creek."

"Is that possible?"

"I don't know. Slim chance, and I doubt it will even work. I put the lady in Philly off for a few days, so I have some time."

Jim looked down at the note from Kelly in his hand. "Geez. I shouldn't have let her stay here."

Chapter 38

Abbey and Jim stood in the kitchen and ate from bowls of peeled fruit and drank water from clear glasses.

"I saw a deer outside my bedroom window."

"You did?" Jim asked as he popped a banana slice into his mouth. "During Summer, you can look out any window in this place and see a lot of wildlife."

They talked at length while keeping an eye on the time. When the school bus stopped in front of the inn, the driver waited patiently until Abbey opened the door and stepped off the front porch and onto the bus. After the short drive toward Bear Mountain Road, the driver applied his brakes when he saw the sheriff approach the bus on foot with his hand out, signaling him to stop. The sheriff came up to the bus with a paper in his hand. The bus driver then saw an unmarked car on the side of the road. Nervous, and curious as to what was happening, the bus driver opened the doors as Abbey looked on.

"Yes, Sheriff?"

"Abbey Creeson on board?"

"Yes, sir."

"She is a ward of the state and needs to come with us," the sheriff said. When Abbey stepped off the bus, both the sheriff and Miss Philhours greeted her.

. . .

Just after ten o'clock that morning, Jim was fitting dado and rabbet joints together for the seat and rails on his rocking chair. The phone rang and within three rings, he answered Mallory's call.

"Hey."

"Jim," was all Mallory could say. It sounded like she was running and panicked.

"What? What's wrong?"

"Abbey. They took her to Philadelphia."

"What? What do you mean?"

"The child protective services agent in Philadelphia filed a court order even though she told me she would wait. Abbey didn't even make it to school. They took her off the bus this morning."

"She's on her way to Philadelphia?"

"I just got a call from their office. They have all the proper paperwork because I sent it to them before you decided to look after her."

"Can you get her back? Can you file something or talk to a judge?"

"Probably wouldn't fly. I was already kind of bending the rules by letting her stay at the inn as long as I did. It was supposed to be temporary. Like, a week, max."

Jim took off his woodworker's apron and set it aside.

"Mal, what would I have to do to become a foster parent? What would I have to do to get Abbey back?"

"Classes. Weeks of classes and lots of paperwork, and you have to go through background checks, home visits, it takes months. And even then you would have a slim chance of getting Abbey placed in your home. She could be adopted by then. Apparently this agent is taking her to Arizona to meet with a prospective family this week." Mallory's explanation caused Jim to nearly panic. Then he said to Mallory what she never expected to hear, "What would it take for me to adopt Abbey? What's the process?" The words coming from Jim took a while for Mallory to take in. She started to say something, but she hesitated a moment before she finally responded,

"Jim? You sure about this?"

"Yes. What would it take?"

"Probably about the same time as being a foster parent, if not longer. Some paperwork and approval can take up to six months before placement. It's different with everyone."

"Can you notify the Philadelphia office? Can you put her on hold or something so I can get through the red tape?" Mallory was still stunned. It wasn't a *"what if"* question; he seemed determined.

"I'll see what I can do. I can't believe I'm hearing this."

"There's no one in this world who can take better care of her than I can. She needs me."

Jim hung up the phone and conducted what research he could on his computer. He searched for adoption law, attorneys who specialized in adoption and the process of adoption. The day wore on with endless research until the phone rang. Not his cell phone, but the phone at the front desk. Normally the ringing phone would be ignored, but this time Jim ran to the desk and answered.

"Hello?"

"Jim?" Abbey said. She was crying.

"Abbey? Where are you?"

"In an orphanage in Philadelphia." Her voice was a near whisper.

"Are you okay?"

"No, I don't want to be here. They're taking me to Arizona to meet a family tomorrow," Abbey said as she sobbed into the phone. "They didn't let me take anything with me. They didn't let me go back to the inn and get my things. I didn't get to say 'goodbye' to you."

"Abbey, listen to me. You'll be back here at the inn as soon as possible. You hear me?"

"Yes," she said with a sniffling, congested nose as she still maintained her near whisper.

"I will not let this happen."

After reassuring Abbey and calming her down, he hung up and ran back into the dining hall and called Mallory. Instead of getting her on the phone, he heard noises coming from the front porch. Mallory burst in and ran into the dining hall.

"Jim, I had to tell you in person. I am sorry."

"What? You already told me."

"I found out that Abbey is being transported to Scottsdale, Arizona to meet with a prospective family tomorrow morning."

"I just talked to Abbey. She told me she was going there."

"You did? She called you?"

"I just got off the phone with her. Now, how do I stop this?"

"Stop it? The process is already in motion and I'm sure that paperwork has already been filed if they are transporting her tomorrow."

"You're telling me there is no way?"

"I'm sorry. I don't know what to do. The system is set up so that prospective parents can claim a child, just as you wanted to do," Mallory explained. Jim stared at the floor, his hands on his hips as he thought of a solution. Mallory did her best to console her brother. After a full minute, he looked at her as if he was giving her military orders.

"Keep your cell phone by you at all times. Don't turn the ringer off."

"What do you mean?" Mallory asked.

"Please do as I ask. I need your help. Don't turn the ringer off. Even at night." Jim walked over to the computer, and Mallory watched him as he lingered in thought.

"Please, go home. I'll be in touch."

Chapter 39

When the phone rang at the desk of Dave Thomas, he didn't expect to hear the voice of Jim Mayfield. Thinking it was probably an internal call, he lifted the receiver and answered with a dull tone of voice, "Hello?"

"You still need a spaceflight engineer?"

"Jim?"

"Yep."

"Uh, well, actually we are looking at a narrow list of candidates this week. Why? Are you reconsidering?"

"I am. But I want a different compensation package."

"Oh well, of course. We would certainly negotiate, or at least I think Frank would entertain the idea. We'll have to hurry up though, he's pressing me pretty hard to come up with a selection committee."

"I'm open to discussion."

"What did you have in mind?"

. . .

The following day, Abbey woke up in an unfamiliar room in St. Nicholas Orphanage. Her eyes opened with her head resting on a old, used pillow that had been donated to the orphanage by a nearby hospital. The other three beds in the room were occupied by sleeping girls in pajamas: one older, two younger. During the night, a slight chill had come over Abbey and stayed with her since. Instead of blankets, she had been given a stack of white cotton sheets that weren't thick enough to keep her warm.

The door to the room opened, and Miss Philhours stuck her wrinkled, raisin head inside and looked at Abbey. With a slight whisper she said, "Please get ready, and meet me in the lobby." She reached into the room and set a stack of new clothes and a toiletry bag on a nearby desk and closed the door.

After getting up and moving around dirty shirts, jeans, and stuffed animals belonging to the other girls in the room, she walked out as she grabbed her things off the desk. She stood in a cold and uninviting communal bathroom and hurried into donated jeans and a warm, gray sweatshirt. She opened the assembled toiletry bag and found toothpaste, a toothbrush, and a hairbrush. No meeting in the big industrial kitchen with Jim. No bowl of fruit and conversation that she had become accustomed to. She took the hairbrush out of the bag and began running the prongs through her hair. There was a knock at the bathroom door followed Miss Philhours' head peeking inside. Instead of smiling at Abbey, she glared at her. The same glare that Mrs. Watt's cold, dead, shark eyes possessed.

"Did you brush your teeth yet?" Miss Philhours asked.

"No."

"No, *Ma'am*. I can't abide by rude children. You will address me as Miss Philhours or Ma'am."

"Yes, Ma'am," Abbey said out of fear.

"Have you ever been on an airplane before?"

"No, Ma'am," Abbey replied. Miss Philhours opened the door further and walked inside. She stood as straight as a pole and placed her crusty, old hands in front of her, one hand delicately resting on top of the other in a very proper fashion.

"I will give you a dose of dimenhydrinate. It helps with motion sickness, and it may make you drowsy. We have a long flight ahead of us, so let's get going. Please brush your teeth, and meet me in the lobby in five minutes."

. . .

The phone rang once again at the front desk at Bear Creek Inn. Jim knew it would be Abbey. A mad dash from the dining hall to the lobby ensued.

"Are you okay?" Jim said as soon as he picked up the receiver.

"Yes. This woman is taking me to Arizona now. We're getting on a plane," Abbey said in a near whisper.

Click. The thin, veined finger of Miss Philhours plunged down on the disconnect button and ended the call.

"We are in transition, and no phone calls by the child to be adopted shall be placed. Follow me to the lobby."

Back at Bear Creek Inn, Jim hung up the phone thinking that the disconnection wasn't an accident. She had been whispering as if she wasn't supposed to be on the phone. Either way she wasn't in a good place. Jim looked at his watch. He had forty minutes until his conference call with Frank Navasky and Dave Thomas.

Unable to concentrate or bear the pain of waiting forty minutes, Jim jumped on the treadmill. His thoughts drifted over Abbey, and he asked himself if he was doing the right thing. *Without a doubt*, he answered in his head. *Without a doubt.* Jim ran for a full thirty-five minutes and jumped off and paced in the dining hall to cool off. When the phone rang, it didn't make it to the full ring.

Jim greeted both Dave and Frank, and then the questions began.

"Are you reconsidering, Jim?" Frank asked as he stared at the speakerphone.

"I am."

"Dave tells me that you want to negotiate your compensation package."

"Correct."

"What part of it exactly?"

"All of it. I only want 2 things."

"Two?"

"Yes. As far as money goes, you can keep the money. Every penny." Frank looked at Dave with a confused look.

"No money?" Frank asked.

"Just two things. First I need assistance with adopting a little girl. She is the one you saw at the meeting."

"Excuse me, Jim. We don't have anything to do with things like that. I'm sorry." Frank glanced over at Dave and looked annoyed.

"Nope. You don't," Jim quickly confirmed. "But you do know Senator Keeler of Pennsylvania. He can help. He's a big proponent of funding NASA, and we can consider him a friend. Speak with him and see what he can do," Jim explained. Frank sat back in his chair and stared at the ceiling. His eyes darted towards the mute button, "Hang on, Jim," he said before he pushed the button. His eyes were now on Dave. "You know Keeler. You think he would do something like this? What can a senator even do with adoption?"

"I don't know. It's a little far-fetched, but he does do favors for people. He reminds me of The Godfather. He'll do you a favor, but he might call upon us at some point. Worth a phone call, I guess," Dave said. "How bad do you want Mayfield on this?"

"I would sleep better at night knowing Jim is on this. We all would. Any other candidate would be a coin flip. Jim's our guy."

"Good point." Dave said. Frank nodded in acknowledgement as he pushed the mute button.

"Okay, Jim, we do this for you, and you will do what in return?"

"Everything. Training, sims, pre-mission planning, retro fitting the coupling, perform the EVA repair and assist afterward post-mission. Everything." Jim explained. "But, if it doesn't happen with this little girl, I'm out."

"Jim, we don't know if Keeler will do anything. Let us call him, feel him out, and we'll get back to you," Dave said.

"Jim, what's the second thing?" Frank asked hoping it wasn't something else out of reach.

"I want to borrow your jet. From Bear Creek to Scottsdale, Arizona."

"I understand you are giving up your initial compensation package, Jim, but this is still a tall order. To be matter of fact, it would be preferable to just give you your salary."

"While I admit I could do without the jet, I would consider an extended contract as an as-needed consultant from here on out," Jim said. Dave and Frank exchanged looks.

"We will see what we can do," Dave finally answered.

"Call him now. Right now," Jim demanded. Dave shrugged his shoulders at Frank. "I want this sewed up by tonight, tomorrow morning at the latest," Jim added.

Dave spoke up, "I'll call you back."

Chapter 40

"Jim Mayfield the astronaut?" Senator Keeler asked. He strolled around his study on his cell phone while drinking from a water bottle. "I don't know anything about adoption, but a district judge would be able to help in this situation," Senator Keeler explained. He took a swig from his water bottle while he listened to Frank Navasky. To Keeler, sitting at a dinner table and bragging to others about his assistance with a NASA matter intrigued him. More than a casual story to tell on the golf course, it could add it to his list of accomplishments. Perhaps it would become a story to tell at a campaign fundraiser that would talk up his support of NASA and reinforce his commitment to scientific research. Once the phone call ended with Frank, a call was placed to Chief Judge Harkin.

. . .

Abbey looked out the window as the plane flew above the clouds. While the flight itself was pleasant, sitting next to Miss Philhours was not. An odor crept around Abbey that radiated from her captor's decaying body. A scent reminiscent of sulfur and burning hair greeted Abbey's nose and she discretely covered her nostrils with her index finger. *Clink. Clank. Clink. Clank.* Repeated, high-pitched sounds emanated from Miss Philhours' teacup as she stirred a single serving of creamer into her hot tea. Abbey turned her head away from the window and looked at the cup and saucer.

"The airplane has teacups?" Abbey asked as she looked at Miss Philhours. She waited for a response to her question and when it was apparent she was being ignored, she turned her head back toward the window. Abbey's first flight wasn't as fun as it could have been due to her frail kidnapper and the fact that she had no interest in meeting with prospective parents. She didn't want to be adopted. She wanted to stay at the inn with Jim. She looked at a break in the clouds and could see a river cutting through the land before another cloud covered up her view. Keeping her index finger in front of her nose, she kept her face out of view of Miss Philhours and continued to stare out the window.

. . .

Chief Judge Harkin sent two clerks spinning into the abyss of adoption law after his phone call with Senator Keeler. Documents were downloaded, scanned, emailed, and reviewed. A copy of Abbey's birth certificate was placed in a manila folder along with thick packets of stapled documents. In a separate folder, data was collected on James W. Mayfield that displayed his educational background, former drivers' licenses and driving records, with background checks, bank statements and credit reports. The director of St. Nicholas Orphanage was contacted, interviewed, and questioned.

At six o'clock in the evening, a PDF file was emailed to Frank Navasky. Upon opening it and attempting to read the legal jargon, Frank could see that Senator Keeler had delivered.

At 7 P.M., Tom and Jerry had gotten a call from Dave Thomas who explained the situation and discussed a pre-approved flight plan. An hour later they were taking off for Bear Creek.

. . .

Jim Mayfield looked at the PDF file emailed to him from Navasky. He read it line by line, taking in the legalese with a smile. After five minutes of reading the document, he opened his email and read it again.

From: 'fnavasky'
Sent: Friday, 5:51 PM
To: 'dthomas'Jim Mayfield[mailto:Jim.Mayfield@canyonmail.net]
Subject: Compensation

_____

Jim,

Senator Keeler came though. Attached to this email you will find a document that gives you full custody of the child. I am told you will be required to sign a truckload of documents before all of this is 100% official. Your local social services office will contact you. Please advise.

Jim received another email and immediately opened it. This one was from Dave Thomas.

From: 'dthomas'
Sent: Tuesday, 1:12 PM
To: 'dthomas'Jim Mayfield[mailto:Jim.Mayfield@canyonmail.net]
Subject: RE: Proposal

_____

Jim,

Congratulations. Your ride is in the sky on its way to you. See you soon.

-Dave

The phone rang and Jim immediately answered it.

"What is going on?" Mallory asked.

"What do you mean?"

"My boss just called me and said that someone just adopted Abbey Creeson and that someone is MY BROTHER!"

"I just got the papers emailed to me."

"How in the world did you get around all the red tape that everyone else has to go through? Somehow I knew it. I just knew it."

"I'm flying to Arizona tonight."

"Apparently there are adoption papers already at the office. Wait… you're leaving the inn?" Mallory asked.

"Mal, can you do me a big favor? Can you get those papers and fly with me to Arizona?"

"Tonight?"

"I'll explain everything. I'd like to get all the paperwork out of the way as well."

"You're flying out of Philly?"

"Nope. NASA's jet out of Pocono Municipal. You'll be back by to-morrow morning."

"Wow. A NASA jet? Well I would need to make a few quick arrangements with Barry."

"Thank you. Seriously, I need your help with this."

"Uh…tell me one thing though, and be honest. Did you leave the inn to get Abbey new glasses?"

Silence. Jim tapped the table in an anxious rhythm before he answered.

"Yes."

Mallory smiled and exhaled while shaking her head.

"I knew it."

Chapter 41

Kelly Mae White heard rustling outside and a car door opening and closing, and what sounded like someone in a hurry. She confirmed it when she took a few steps out of her room and looked around the porch. She watched a truck speed off before retreating into her room. She turned off the TV and listened for sounds of movement. Silence. Kelly developed a plan in her head that she would go to the lobby in hopes of explaining to someone that she would be leaving tomorrow with many apologies. She had hoped that the voice behind the door had just left, and she could talk with the little girl. She seemed nice, and maybe she would divulge more information that could lead to a longer stay. She walked around the porch and toward the front door.

Ready to say her line, she tried to open the door only to discover it was locked. She peered inside and could see a small lamp sitting on the end of the check-in desk. It was the only light source. The rest of the lobby was dark. She stood silently and pressed her ear to the window and listened for signs of life. Kelly bit the fingernail on her index finger, a nervous tick that surfaced at the thought that she might be able to stay another night. After a full minute of silence, she decided she was alone. Kelly walked back to her room and closed the door.

. . .

Tom and Jerry glanced at the instrument panel, noting that they would need to ready for approach soon. They discussed their passenger as Tom ate a tuna salad sandwich and Jerry sat in the co-pilot seat looking at his tablet computer in his lap.

"Why, all of a sudden, are we taking him to Arizona?" Jerry asked.

"No clue. Why don't you ask him when he boards?"

"You ask him," Jerry suggested.

"What'll you give me?" Tom asked before he took a monumental, and possibly, record-breaking bite of his tuna salad.

"What do you want?" Jerry asked. Tom responded with a mouthful. Jerry could see the gross, half-chewed sandwich as Tom answered.

"Ten dollars."

"Just for asking a question?"

"Then you ask him. I'll give you five," Tom said, still chewing.

"Five? You wanted ten."

"Yeah, it's a five-dollar question." Tom said.

"If it's no big deal, then why don't you ask him?"

"I'll tell you what. Whoever asks him first pays the other ten dollars," Tom said with a smirk.

"So, we're back to ten dollars?"

"Yep. Ten bananas."

"So this is a ten dollar bet?"

"Yeah, a bet."

"Okay, fine. Ten dollars."

"Fine," Tom confirmed as he shoved the rest of the sandwich into his mouth. He washed down the sandwich with a swig of water and spoke into his headset mic and readied for approach.

In the quaint terminal at Pocono Mountains Municipal Airport,

Jim was seated facing the automatic doors that lead to the runway. He felt at ease since there wasn't anyone around except for a twenty-something kid that sat behind the desk. The young attendant spent nearly every workday looking at his smartphone and even though having someone in the terminal was an oddity, he kept to himself hoping he wouldn't have to answer any questions. A light came from behind Jim and he could see his shadow for a brief moment. He looked over his shoulder out the window toward the parking lot and saw headlights as a car parked next to Jim's truck. Mallory got out of her vehicle, walked through the automatic sliding doors, saw Jim, and stopped. She stared at him with a smile as he stood up.

"First of all, you're out of the inn. This is incredible."

"Calm down," Jim said with a slight smile. The attendant at the desk looked up briefly before looking back down at his phone.

"And second, you're a father. I feel like I'm going to the hospital after your baby has arrived. This is a big moment for me."

"There you go, making this all about you again," Jim said. Mallory ignored her brother's sarcasm and wrapped her arms around his neck. "I'm finally an aunt." When she pulled back, tears were present in her eyes.

"Why are you crying?"

"I don't know. I guess I'm just overwhelmed," Mallory said as she wiped her tears away and chuckled. "I have so many questions. Like, how in the world did you adopt a child in a flash?" Mallory asked. Before Jim could answer, he noticed from the window that their plane was taxiing.

"I'll tell you on the plane."

When the plane came to a full stop, the door opened, and the stairs lowered. Jerry looked out from the open door and could see a man and a woman walking toward the jet. Jerry turned his head toward the cockpit: "There's two."

"What?" Tom asked as he slightly raised his voice.

"There's two. Jim and a woman," Jerry said in a quieter voice as he turned around.

"Who is it?" Tom asked as he tried his best to get a look out the front window of the jet.

"I don't know. We're only supposed to pick up Jim." Thinking that they could board at any second, they lowered their voices to a whisper.

"You gonna ask him?" Tom asked.

"Yeah, sure, for ten dollars I'll ask," Jerry thought about the question, "Wait. What am I asking him?"

"Why he's…" Tom started to say when Jim boarded and looked into the cockpit. His full, unkempt beard and flannel shirt shocked them into silence.

"Fellas," Jim said as he nodded. Tom and Jerry could only nod back. Mallory smiled at both of them as she passed by. They returned the smile until she headed toward her seat. Tom slapped Jerry on the shoulder and spoke through his teeth.

"Nice job, Charlie Chaplin," Tom whispered.

. . .

When Abbey arrived at Phoenix Sky Harbor Airport, she and Miss Philhours retrieved their luggage and found their ride waiting for them, a fifteen-passenger van with the words *Kingman Home for Children* scrolled across the side. Miss Philhours rode up front with an obese woman who drove the van while Abbey found a place in the back seat and fell asleep. The ride to Kingman was three hours on a desert highway. Unbeknownst to Abbey, there was a jet flying at thirty thousand feet and headed in her direction with a flight time of four hours and thirty minutes. Jim was on his way.

Chapter 42

The Kingman Home for Children looked more like a retirement home than an orphanage. The van pulled up in front of the sprawling, ranch-style structure and parked underneath a canopy. Abbey had been awake for twenty minutes as the last leg of the trip was bumpy and had jolted her awake. Miss Philhours spoke with the obese driver of the van while unloading luggage. Abbey made her way toward the double doors of the van and opened them to exit, seemingly invisible to both the plus-sized driver and Miss Philhours. Abbey limped over to them with her pink backpack.

"I will arrive no later than 9 A.M., and we will meet with the prospective adoptive parents at noon."

"Oh, good," Miss Philhours replied.

Abbey listened to them speak until she saw something from the corner of her eye. A black woman wearing a white polo shirt, khakis, and a lanyard with a nametag walked through the front door and toward Miss Philhours. The white polo shirt and khakis seemed to be more of a uniform than a fashion choice since both the driver and the black woman matched perfectly.

"Hello, you must be Miss Philhours."

"I am."

"My name is Ginny Reece. I am the assistant director."

"Oh, yes, Ginny."

"I wonder if we might have a word in private," Ginny said, to the surprise of Miss Philhours.

Minutes later, Abbey was seated next to a secretary's desk. She looked over the telephone, a jar of pens, and a lamp. Next to the lamp was a bottle of pills with the words *Caffeine Alertness Aid.* She looked up from the desk and could see Miss Philhours through the window as she spoke with Ginny. Unaware of what was going on, she watched Miss Philhours' mannerisms.

"I am afraid I have some bad news. Maybe not, depending on how you look at it."

"Oh?"

"The good news is that Abbey Creeson has been adopted, and the bad news is that you had to make a trip out here for nothing."

"I'm sorry. That can't be right."

"I received a call from the district court of Pennsylvania."

"When?"

"Earlier today."

"I don't see how this is possible," Miss Philhours reached for her large purse on the ground next to her chair. She pulled out a file and held it as she spoke. "I have all the proper documentation right here. Prospective parents have been notified."

"I called off the meeting. I wanted them to know immediately."

"You did what?" Miss Philhours nearly shouted. Abbey watched from the secretary's desk and could see that she was clearly upset. Abbey continued to watch and couldn't help but crack a smile when Miss Philhours stood up and walked out of the office steaming mad.

. . .

Once Mallory got over the fact that she was flying in a private jet and was sitting in a plush, white leather swivel seat, she focused on Jim and the mountain of paperwork before her. She asked many questions which Jim answered, telling her the whole story, including the deal with NASA. Mallory spent much of her time filtering through forms she had brought with her and having Jim sign many documents. After about twenty minutes of Mallory highlighting spaces for Jim's signature and handing the pages over to him, they both got into a rhythm.

"In a million years, I never thought I would be doing this for you."

"What? Filling out adoption papers?"

"Yep. This is crazy."

"There's no one that can take better care of her than me," Jim said. Mallory stopped and looked at her brother, frozen by his sincerity and matter-of-fact tone. "What?" Jim asked. Mallory thought it through: Jim looking after Abbey, protecting her, teaching her, and guiding her. Who better than her brother? He had practically raised her since they were kids back in Bear Creek.

"I believe you. I do. I believe you, Jim."

. . .

Instead of heading off to the hotel, Miss Philhours decided to wait and meet the agent that was taking her case away from her. She sat in the lobby and read an old newspaper from four days ago.

Abbey had been escorted to a playroom with colorful carpet, an array of beanbag chairs, and long tables filled with rows of computers. While the other children slept at the other end of the orphanage,

Abbey turned on a computer and navigated to a math game where she solved problems to help a monkey reach bananas in a tree.

Knock, knock.

Abbey turned around and saw Ginny standing in the doorway.

"Hello, Abbey," she said with a pleasing, soft voice. Ginny approached Abbey and asked her about the game she was playing. When the small talk was over, Ginny explained that she would no longer be meeting her prospective parents. Instead, she was going back to Pennsylvania. Abbey had a question:

"Is it Jim? Is Jim coming to get me?"

"I'm sorry. I don't know. This is all the information I have, but you should know soon enough. Okay?"

"Probably not," Abbey said.

"What?"

"Well, Jim doesn't leave the inn. He doesn't like to go out," Abbey explained. Unaware of who Jim was or what Abbey was talking about, Ginny simply nodded her head and smiled.

"We should know something soon. Okay?" she said as she put her hand on Abbey's shoulder.

"Okay," Abbey said. Ginny left, and Abbey went back to her game.

As Abbey solved a multiplication problem, Jim and Mallory stepped off the jet at Kingman Municipal Airport. They walked a short distance to a black Lincoln Town Car, arranged by Jim through a pre-paid website. He chewed on his fingernails as the car made its way through traffic and finally to the Kingman Home for Children. The car pulled up under the canopy and came to a stop just before Jim exited with Mallory behind him. Ginny saw the man walking through the front door and briefly wondered if he was kin to Paul Bunyan.

"Hello. I am the assistant director, Ginny Reese," she said to Jim, but it was Mallory who took over.

"Hi. I'm Mallory Cain, social services agent, and we are here to pick up Abbey Creeson," she said while gesturing to the mountain of paperwork under her arm.

"Nice to meet you. Can we step into my office? If you have all the documents, this won't take long."

"Sure," Mallory said with a smile. She turned and looked at Jim. "Wait here," she added while patting him on the shoulder. Jim nodded and strolled over to the lobby. On the other side of the room was Miss Philhours. She looked up from the newspaper to see a tall, thin man with a beard. She sized him up quickly: working class, low household income, gruff, and possibly cruel to animals.

"Are you here to pick up Abbey Creeson?" she asked. Jim nodded his head. Unsure of who the woman was, he quickly ascertained that she was not friendly. Miss Philhours folded the newspaper with her wrinkled hands and set it aside. She looked him over once again. "I'll have you know that I have a family lined up for Abbey. He is a physician, and his wife is the CEO of her own company. They can afford to look after a handicapped girl. They have not just a house, but a large estate. This is a perfect match."

"Okay," Jim said. He turned around hoping she was finished.

"She needs to meet with these people. She doesn't need to be taken back to Pennsylvania. This little girl needs to be adopted," Miss Philhours explained.

"Abbey is adopted."

"Oh, I don't see how. An adoption takes time."

"She's taken care of. Thanks," Jim said as he turned his back, a vain attempt to try and end the conversation.

"And whom, may I ask, adopted her?" Miss Philhours asked.

"That would be me," Jim answered. Although he couldn't see Miss Philhours, he could tell that she was in a state of disapproval.

"I'm not sure who you think you are…" Miss Philhours started to say until Jim walked toward the administrative offices. Up until that point in her life, Miss Philhours had never been ignored like that. Blatant, sociopathic, level-99, major-league ignoring. Jim didn't hurry. He simply took several steps, opened the door and walked inside the administrative offices. She stood in shock and anger. Her mouth was slightly open, taken aback in mid-sentence.

Upon finding Mallory, he looked at Ginny. "Could I see Abbey, please?"

"Of course. We will all go back together. First, there is a social services worker that wants to speak with Mallory here."

"Is that the lady in the lobby?"

"Yes. She's quite insistent on seeing the documents that prove the adoption's validity. She believes it's impossible. Just let me make a quick copy."

After sitting in the lobby for some time, Miss Philhours was relieved to see the lumberjack, Ginny, and Mallory, who seemed to be the social worker in charge, walking toward her. She stared Mallory down.

"I'm Miss Philhours, and I require a signed document issued by a judge to release this child you have so callously removed from my care."

"I'm Mallory Cain. You spoke with me on the phone."

"Yes, I remember," she replied curtly as she was handed the judge's order.

"She has what she needs?" Jim asked Mallory. Mallory looked at

Miss Philhours who was reading the papers.

"She does."

Jim looked at Ginny who immediately turned around and led the way down the hall. Miss Philhours combed through the papers from Judge Harkin's office. While she couldn't believe it, she finally admitted defeat when she saw the signatures and the official stamp by the judge's name. "How can this be?"

Abbey had grown tired of computer games and resorted to looking around the room for a place to lie down. Perhaps if she moved two beanbag chairs side-by-side, she could rest. She limped over to a cluster of red beanbags and pushed them together. When the door opened, Abbey looked up and saw Jim. He wasn't timid about walking through the door. He came toward Abbey with long, rapid strides as if the room were on fire and he were rescuing her. Before she knew it, before she could even come close to the realization that it wasn't a dream, Jim had crossed the room and knelt down. He quickly wrapped his arms around her.

Letting go of stress, she sobbed into his shoulder while he held her tightly and gently whispered, "I'll never let you go, Abbey. I'll never let you go again." Mallory had stopped at the door and looked at her brother as he embraced Abbey. Mallory's hand was clapped over her mouth as tears swelled up in her eyes and streamed down her face.

Abbey's voice was muffled as she spoke with her face pressed against the fabric of Jim's T-shirt.

"I missed you, Jim. I missed you so much."

"I missed you too, Abbey. You have no idea."

Chapter 43

The flight back to Bear Creek was quiet and dark. Jim had turned the cabin lights off and reclined his seat back after Abbey had fallen asleep. She had curled up in the seat across from him after he covered her up with a plush cotton blanket and checked to make sure her seatbelt was fastened. Mallory had followed suit and had gotten comfortable in her cushy, white leather chair.

Up front in the cockpit, Tom and Jerry couldn't help themselves.

"Okay, so who's the girl?" Jerry asked.

"Which one?" Tom replied.

"Which one? There's only one."

"No, there are two."

"You mean the woman?" Jerry asked.

"Well, okay, you mean the little girl."

"Of course. Why would I call a woman a girl?"

This conversation continued for another ten minutes before it changed to what fast-food chain had the best French fries. Jim, Mallory, and Abbey awoke when the cabin shook briefly as the wheels met the asphalt at Pocono Mountains Municipal Airport.

Upon their return to Bear Creek Inn, Mallory and Abbey slept in the same room as before. Jim adjourned to his room and did the same for a couple hours.

Even though school was in session, Jim thought it best to keep

Abbey out until the following week to give her time to rest after her long ordeal. Jim sat at his desk and read an email from Dave Thomas to many people at NASA.

From: 'dthomas'
Sent: Monday, 7:13 AM
To: 'ISS Team 7', 'GCrew 7', 'MTeam 7'
Subject: Team Announcement

We have received confirmation that Mission Specialist and Flight Engineer Jim Mayfield will be joining us for the repair of the Zarya module and implementation of a new coupling ring. He will be meeting with everyone next week and will be officially working as Mission Specialist beginning May 31st.

Jim had been completely focused on Abbey until he read the email from Dave. It didn't seem real until then. He would be training for months at Johnson Space Center before the mission. His thoughts were interrupted when he heard someone enter the dining hall. He turned around to see Mallory walking toward him.

"Hey. She's still asleep," Mallory said.

"I bet. I would be too."

"I'm headed off to her school to take care of her enrollment."

"She has to be enrolled again?"

"All the paper work that the Philhours woman did removed her from Bear Creek Elementary. It's a headache, but it's expected. Don't worry. I'll take care of it. I've done it before," Mallory said as she bent down and kissed Jim on his forehead.

"Thanks."

"You know, I don't think you've really thought about it, but Abbey Creeson is now Abbey Mayfield," Mallory said.

"Really? That's pretty cool."

"I'm taking the paperwork with me, but I will give you a large folder with copies and her original birth certificate. I also have some of her medical records," Mallory said as she started to walk out of the dining hall.

"Hey," Jim said. Mallory turned around.

"When is school out for Abbey?"

"End of May. Why?"

"I have to go to Houston for the summer. Just wondering how I'm going to work it out with Abbey," Jim said as he stared off into the distance.

"Are you wanting to take her with you?"

"Of course, but we'd have to move down there. When does school start?"

"September."

"Can I enroll her in a school there and then transfer her up here in December?"

"Well, there's Christmas Break. You would just enroll her before she starts back in January, but what about the school play?"

Knock. Knock.

The knocking came not from the front door, but the back door in the dining hall. Jim looked at Mallory.

"Can you answer that?"

Mallory crossed the room and opened the door to Kelly Mae White.

Chapter 44

Kelly Mae White stood on the back porch in a white top, jeans and white Keds tennis shoes.

"Hello. I'm sorry. I heard talking, and I thought I would see if I could speak to the owner," Kelly said as she fidgeted with a charm on her silver necklace. The way Kelly spoke and her delicate tone made her immediately likeable.

"My brother owns this place. I'll get him for you. Just a sec."

"Thank you," Kelly said as Mallory closed the door to a thin crack.

"No. Come on," Jim yelled in a whisper.

"What? She wants to speak with you," Mallory whisper yelled back.

"I don't want to see anyone. I have rules here," Jim said a little louder. "What do you want me to do?"

"Take care of it," Jim said flinging his arms.

"Fine. Hang on," Mallory said as she walked out onto the back porch and closed the door behind her. Jim listened to the muffled voices coming from the porch. After a few minutes, Mallory came back.

"She's gonna stay for a few weeks."

"Weeks? She was supposed to be gone several days ago."

"She has no nowhere to go."

"I know. I heard her story, but she can't stay. I don't want her here at all."

"You wanted me to handle it. That's how I handled it. She needs help and seems sweet. If you want her gone, go tell her yourself. You know you're gonna have to start talking with people when you go back to work."

"Yeah, yeah, but not here. This is my home."

. . .

Knock. Knock.

This time the knocking came at Kelly Mae White's door. She stood up and walked to the door and opened it to Jim Mayfield.

"Hi," Jim said. He seemed in a rush to leave. His hands were in his pockets the whole time and he couldn't stand still.

"Hello."

"Look, my sister said a couple of weeks, but the best I can do is one."

"Oh, okay. I'm sorry I overstayed my welcome. You were so nice. I can pay you if you like?"

"No, no. Just one week. No more. I'm sorry."

"Okay. No problem. One week, I promise," Kelly said. She closed the door when he left, sat down on the edge of the bed and reached for the remote. She muted the TV and considered where she should go next. What city? What state? She briefly considered somewhere tropical, but then thought about seeing all the happy tourists and how unhappy that would make her—families walking along the beach while she worked a menial job at a beachside bar.

Unsure of what to do, Kelly decided to make a run to the store for groceries. Then it hit her. The rental car. Today was the last day she had the car. Making out a plan to turn the car in and get groceries, she picked up her phone and began searching for a nearby cab company.

Inside Bear Creek Inn, Abbey woke up to familiar surroundings. She moved to the edge of the bed, attached her prosthetic leg and stood up. After fifteen minutes of getting ready, she slowly walked out into the lobby. *Step, clonk, step, clonk.* The sound of her walking wasn't the only repetitive sound. She could hear a methodical thumping. *Thump. Thump. Thump. Thump.* Abbey walked into the dining hall and found Jim running on the treadmill next to his desk. He was facing a half assembled rocking chair and didn't see Abbey until she walked to the side of the treadmill.

"Hey!" Jim said as he pressed the stop button.

"Why are you running in here?"

"Well, you know that woman that we helped out?" Jim said as he stepped off and grabbed a towel.

"Yeah."

"Well, as it turns out, she is staying for another week." Jim wiped the thick beads of sweat from his forehead.

"She is?"

"I'd rather not run on the porch while she is staying so close by, so I brought the treadmill in here."

"Oh," Abbey said. "Can I ask you a question?" Abbey asked.

"Shoot."

"Why do you not like other people?"

"Oh. Well, it's not that. I do like people," Jim said as he walked over to his desk and pulled up a chair. He sat down as he continued to wipe the sweat off his head. "I like people, but what I like even more is privacy. In fact, I love it."

"So should I…" Abbey said and then paused before continuing, "…

leave you alone?" Jim smiled and dropped the towel to his side.

"Abbey, I didn't want you here at all at first. I really didn't. But, as I got to know you, I came to like you. A lot, actually," Jim said as he looked her in the eye. Abbey acknowledged him by nodding her head. Jim continued. "I like privacy, but lately I've come to like having you around."

"You do?"

"I do. When you were taken away from me…" Jim started to say, his head tilted toward the floor and he collected himself before he continued. "I felt…alone." Jim looked up at Abbey. He placed his elbows on his knees and leaned slightly forward. "I haven't felt alone in over ten years. I missed you, and I didn't want you to go. So, no, you shouldn't leave. You should never leave. And don't ever think that I don't want you around, because I do. I mean that," Jim said as he reached out and placed his hand on her shoulder.

Abbey smiled and nodded her head as she spoke.

"Okay."

Across town, Charlie Park, 61, of Bear Creek had sold his grocery store and was ready for retirement. Selling the store was a relief and having the money and freedom to live out his dream of fishing in Florida was coming true. The hardest part about leaving would be telling Jim. He wouldn't necessarily call Jim a friend even though he seemed like it in the emails they exchanged back and forth. When he drove up the cobblestone driveway, he got nervous, even though he could never have known Jim was looking at him from the lobby window.

"What is Charlie doing here? I didn't send him a list yet," Jim said to himself.

In over a decade, Charlie had only seen Jim once. He walked up carrying a box full of groceries and saw him cutting firewood, but by the time he got close to the inn, Jim was gone. After he set the groceries on the porch, he walked back toward the gate. Just before the trees and shrubs cut off his view, he saw Jim as he walked back to the stump and bent over, collecting split logs in his arms.

Charlie had hoped to meet Jim but considered it a slim possibility. If the knock on the door didn't pan out, Charlie thought he would just send him an email.

Knock. Knock. Knock.

Jim had watched as Charlie made his way to the front porch and knocked. He bit his fingernails and thought a moment before he approached the door.

To Charlie's amazement, a man in a flannel shirt and a full beard opened the door.

"Charlie, come in," Jim said. He wasn't overly friendly, nor was he rude.

"Jim?" Even though Charlie had looked him up online and had seen photos of him, he still wanted to make sure.

"Yeah, Charlie, it's me," Jim said with a grin.

"Just making sure. I wanted to come by and tell you in person, but I wasn't sure if I would be able to."

"Well, you're catching me on a good day, I suppose."

"Good. I am sorry about coming up here unannounced, but I wanted to tell you face to face that I just sold the store to a foods company in Wilkes-Barre. I'm moving to Florida."

"That's gonna be a long drive for you to bring me my groceries."

"No problem. I'll just up my price," Charlie said with a smile. Jim grinned and nodded. "I figured it would be better than telling you in an email."

Jim stuck out his hand. Charlie did the same and they shook.

"You really helped me out, and I'm grateful."

"No problem. It was my pleasure. Maybe you can find someone to bring you your groceries. I'd make some suggestions, but I know how particular you are."

"Don't worry about it. I'll find someone. You live it up in Florida. Catch some fish."

"Will do. It was nice meeting you. Finally."

"You too, Charlie."

Jim watched as Charlie walked down the steps of the front porch and considered his new predicament. Food.

Chapter 45

Knock. Knock.

Kelly Mae White awoke from a nap to someone at her door. A bit dazed, she walked to the door and opened it. Abbey stood before her holding a piece of paper.

"Hello, again," Kelly said.

"Hello. Jim wanted me to ask if you would do us a favor."

"Oh. Of course."

"Could you get these things on this list at the grocery store?" Abbey said as she held up the list. Kelly took it from her hands.

"Sure. I was just there. No problem going back. Gives me something to do."

"Thank you," Abbey said as she handed Kelly a fifty-dollar bill.

"Oh wait! My car. It was a rental. I took a cab back here."

"Um...okay, hang on," Abbey said and went back inside.

Kelly put the grocery list in her pocket and thought about having to buy another car. She would have to. She had some money, most of it came from the military's casualty benefit. Interrupting her in midthought, she saw Abbey limp out of the back door with keys in her hand and another fifty-dollar bill.

"These go to the red truck over there. He asked if you could fill it up too," Abbey said as she handed her the keys and the additional money.

"Sure, no problem," Kelly answered with a smile.

Ring. Ring.

Jim's cell phone lit up on the desk next to him as Abbey came back inside.

"Was she nice about it?"

"Yeah, she was nice. She will fill it up, too."

Ring. Ring.

Jim didn't recognize the phone number but answered anyway.

"Hello?"

"Hello, Mr. Mayfield? This is Tilda Harris, Abbey's guidance counselor."

"Oh, hi," Jim said.

"I don't think I've ever had the pleasure of speaking with an astronaut before." Tilda seemed polite on the phone, but Jim abhorred conversations about his profession. A flight engineer could only answer "What's it like floating in space?" and, "How do astronauts go to the bathroom?" so many times. The incessant questions became a constant that Jim would rather have done without. Tilda's comment brought back memories of conversations he wanted to avoid.

"Well, this is my first time speaking with a guidance counselor in over 35 years," Jim said. Tilda laughed, but quickly got to the point.

"Well, I am calling for two reasons. I wanted to inform you that Abbey has been selected to portray Peter Pan in our school play."

"Mallory had explained to me that you were trying to get her the role. I'm sure she'll do just fine."

"I know she will do great. When she returns to school, she will be given a packet that includes costume information and the script with her lines highlighted. There are a lot, so make sure she is prepared.

"Sure, I can do that."

"Also, with the school year coming to a close, we have Career Day coming up on the second to last day, and I would like to invite you to speak. It's in the auditorium, and you would only have to talk for five or possibly ten minutes.

"Oh. I see."

"We have bankers and accountants and butchers and bakers, but it would be something if you could visit us and tell us about being an astronaut," Tilda explained. Jim didn't even have to think about it. Snotty-nosed kids, a spotlight on him, while talking about going to the bathroom in space.

"No, thanks."

"Oh. We understand. It's just that the past two years I've seen Abbey disappointed when the kids ask if someone is going to show up for her on Career Day."

"For her?"

"The people that attend are the parents of the kids. The parent on stage usually points out their child, and he or she stands up when their name is called, and for an astronaut, the star of Career Day, I assure you, to call out Abbey's name would make a big impact on her."

"Oh. Well, I don't know. I'll email you if I can make it."

"Please do."

. . .

At the grocery store, Kelly Mae White looked at the list of items. Some items on the list were familiar; some were not.

Navel oranges

Red Delicious apples

Unsalted cashews

Kale

Romaine lettuce

Broccoli

Wakame seaweed

Penne Pasta

Extra Virgin Olive Oil

Kids Toothpaste

Bar of Dark Chocolate

"Seaweed?" Kelly said out loud, although no one was paying attention. She looked around the store as she pushed her cart through the aisles. Pulling out her phone, she typed the words *Wakame Seaweed* into a search engine.

Back at the inn, Jim was sitting with Abbey in the dining hall. He explained his arrangement with NASA and how he managed to get her back so quickly. Details were not spared. He remembered what it was like to be nine and felt Abbey was entitled to know everything.

"So, we will be moving to Texas until the end of the summer?"

"Well, I'll have to stay in Texas, and you'll have to come back for school."

"When do you come back?"

"Before Thanksgiving."

"So from the beginning of school to Thanksgiving, I won't see you?"

"Well, we can video conference, and you can come down for fall break. It won't be that long."

"Can't I go to school in Texas?"

"You can. That's an option, but there is something else. Something that may change your mind, I think."

"What is it?"

"Well, I got a call from your guidance counselor."

The front door opened, and the rustling of bags could be heard. Jim got up and walked over to the doors that led to the lobby. Looking through the crack, he saw Kelly struggling with groceries. Jim turned and looked at Abbey.

"Can you thank her for going out for us?" Jim whispered. Abbey did as asked and walked out into the lobby while Jim watched through the crack in the door.

"Thank you for going to the grocery."

"You're both welcome," Kelly said as she set the bags down. "Do you need help getting these to the kitchen?" Kelly added. From behind the door Jim watched Abbey turn down the assistance.

"No, thanks. We got it from here."

"I'm sorry. I don't know your name."

"I'm Abbey, and Jim is the one who owns this place."

"Well, it is some place," Kelly said as she looked around the lobby.

Jim continued to watch through the crack in the door as she took out two fifty-dollar bills out of her pocket. "Here, give this to Jim. Tell him I paid for the groceries, and I filled up the tank. I'm thankful for him letting me stay here."

"Oh. Okay. I will," Abbey said, taking the money. Jim watched Kelly leave before going into the lobby to collect the bags.

After putting the groceries away and making dinner, Jim and Abbey sat on the couch and finished their conversation.

"Your guidance counselor was telling me about the school play."

"The big one?"

"I guess. It's in November."

"Yeah, that's it."

"Do you know what the play is?"

"Uh huh. Peter Pan."

"So when you were talking about going to school in Texas, I think you might change your mind when I tell you that you'll be in the school play."

"Really?" Abbey said as her eyes lit up.

"If you want to. It's your choice."

"Of course I want to. It's a big deal."

"Your guidance counselor told me the part she wants you to play. Do you want to know what it is?"

"Uh huh."

"She wants you to play Peter Pan."

"Really?" Abbey shouted as she stood up. Her eyes and mouth opened wide in excitement.

"That's what Mrs. Harris said."

"He's the main character. He's the name of the book."

"I didn't know you would be this excited about it."

Abbey limped around and talked as her hands made animated gestures.

"It's the biggest show in the whole school. Everyone goes, and the auditorium is packed." Abbey stopped and then shouted with excitement. "Do you think they're gonna let me fly? They have a thing where they hook you up to it, and it can make you fly around the stage."

"Sounds exciting."

"I bet I will get to fly in front of the whole school!"

"Apparently you're going to get a packet of info when you go back to school next week. Maybe you'll find out then."

"This is amazing."

"Mrs. Harris also told me about Career Day. What is that about?"

Abbey sat back down and picked at her food. "We have Field Day and Career Day at school. Career Day is the second to last day of school, and Field Day is the last day. Career Day is boring, but Field Day is awesome."

"What do you do on Career Day?"

"We sit in the auditorium and listen to parents talk about their jobs."

"Mrs. Harris said you seemed disappointed last year."

"I did? I don't remember."

"Your aunt and uncle never came by?"

"No. It wasn't a big deal, but one kid on my bus teased me about not having real parents last time we had Career Day."

"Well, let's just focus on Peter Pan. Do you know the story?

"Of course."

"Does it bother you to play the role of a boy?"

"No way! It's Peter Pan. I just hope they let me fly."

The following days were filled with Abbey sleeping in and taking naps on the leather couch with rays of sunshine from the skylight that kept her warm. While Jim worked inside, her evenings turned into exploration adventures outside as she found scurrying chipmunks and squirrels, and became more familiar with the grounds around the inn.

When Monday morning came, Abbey got ready for school and walked through the lobby and then the dining hall. Jim was nowhere to be seen. Abbey headed toward the kitchen in hopes of finding him there. Upon opening the stainless steel swinging door, she saw him standing over two bowls of oatmeal and sliced fruit on a cutting board.

"Breakfast?" Jim asked when he looked up and saw Abbey. She suddenly felt comfortable and at ease. It was the kind of familiarity someone developed when they felt safe and secure in their own home. Eating breakfast with Jim had unknowingly become a routine, and it was a routine she missed when she was away. It was comforting to see him in the kitchen waiting for her. While it wasn't something Abbey realized fully, eating breakfast with Jim in the kitchen would stay with her the rest of her life.

When the bus pulled up to the front of the inn, Jim walked Abbey to the door and bent down and hugged her. He watched out the window as she held tightly onto the railing and stepped down each stair carefully. After Abbey boarded the bus, Jim watched as it drove away. He worked most of the morning on the rocking chair until his phone rang.

Chapter 46

"So, the girl was a foster child?" Dr. Stanton asked.

"Hey, Stanton. Yeah, long story."

"I think I got the gist of it from Dave. You, by far have the weirdest compensation package of any astronaut."

Jim laughed while he examined the headrest of the rocking chair and looked intently at the joints.

"Guess I'll be seeing you soon," Jim said.

"Yeah, I got the email. Bring a few of those beers for me, will ya?"

"I'll see what I can do."

"You know the whole facility is buzzing about you coming back."

"Is that a good thing or a bad thing?"

"I don't know. I'll be honest, a lot of people think you're crazy. They have a name for you."

"I can only imagine."

"Wanna hear it?"

"I suppose."

"Crazyfield."

"Nice."

"Could be worse."

"Yeah, I don't really care. I just want to do what I agreed to and move on."

"I thought it was clever."

"I figured."

"Not everyone thinks you're off your rocker though. Get it? It's a rocking chair reference."

"Yeah, good one. Any tips from a shrink on how a crazy recluse should enter society again?"

"I don't know. I'm sure you will figure it out. You aren't that bad off."

"Oh I don't know. I shiver at the thought of being around people."

"Start small, I guess. Try going out to eat or something."

"I don't think that's my thing. Maybe I'll just drive around."

"I once had a patient who was terrified of public places. I told him to go to small restaurants and gradually work up to a food court at a shopping mall."

"Did it work?"

"Nope. He got real fat though." Jim's laughter echoed throughout the dining hall. When they hung up, Jim went back to work. He had taken a scrap piece of Bubinga wood leftover from carving the headrest of the rocking chair and had sanded it to a smooth surface. He uncapped a jar of boiled linseed oil and applied it to the surface of the wood with a cloth. Once a matte and dull scrap piece of wood, the oil brought out the vibrant and detailed surface. Each grain line weaving and flowing down the length of the Bubinga wood could be seen in rich detail. He held the wood under a lamp and closely examined the deep red color—when the phone rang. He answered his cell phone hoping it would be short.

"Hi, Mr. Mayfield. Did Abbey inform you that she is to be picked up at school today at four?"

"She didn't."

"With everything going on, she might not have remembered. We meet today with the students and faculty until four o'clock. We'll go over the play and the roles, and then speaking lines will be distributed."

When the conversation ended, Jim thanked Mrs. Harris. He walked over to the open jar of boiled linseed oil and picked up the cap. He screwed the cap on the jar as he exhaled and considered one of his few options.

At Bear Creek Elementary, packets were distributed to the cast members with instructions not to open them until they were at home with their parents. The students were led to the front of the school where their parents were waiting for them, and Abbey was unsure of who would be picking her up. She glanced around and saw Mrs. Harris talking with Kelly Mae White as she stood next to Jim's truck. Confused, Abbey step clonked toward them. Kelly was holding her cell phone and talking with her hands as she spoke with Mrs. Harris who turned and looked at Abbey.

"Hey, Abbey. Do you know Kelly?"

"She's staying at the inn," Abbey answered. Mrs. Harris continued, "Jim called me and explained he couldn't pick you up so he made arrangements with Mrs. White."

Kelly looked at Abbey with a friendly smile. "I have to text him as soon as you get in the car and then when we are on Bear Mountain Road," Kelly said as she gestured with her cell phone. "He told me to make sure you were buckled in. Twice."

"You have your packet, Abbey?" Mrs. Harris asked.

"I got it," she responded as she reached around with her left arm and tapped her nylon, pink backpack. They said their goodbyes, and when Abbey was buckled in, Kelly texted Jim as instructed. She received a text back immediately.

Please drive carefully

Kelly looked both ways before pulling onto the main road.

"Jim spoke to you?"

"He did."

"He doesn't like being out. He likes the inn," Abbey said. Kelly had questions about Jim and why he acted the way he did, but she didn't want to seem like she was prying.

"You like school?" Kelly asked, trying to appear casual.

"Yeah, I am going to be in the school play."

Their conversation dwelled on the play and how excited Abbey was to be the lead character. Turning onto Bear Mountain Road, Kelly handed her phone to Abbey and asked her to text Jim. Abbey navigated the phone and sent the text.

We are on Bear Mountain Road.

When they arrived, Abbey and Kelly parted ways on the front porch. Kelly went to her room and Abbey walked in the front door. After walking into the dining hall, she could see Jim talking to people on the computer screen.

Abbey left to watch cartoons in the lobby and returned to the dining hall once she heard Jim stop talking. She walked over to him and sat in the chair by his side.

"How was the ride home?" Jim asked.

"Fine."

"Did she drive carefully?"

"Yes."

"Was she nice?"

"Yes."

"Good."

"She let me text you when we were on Bear Mountain Road."

"Well that's good. I don't want her texting and driving with you in the truck. I was thinking about that after she left. Did you get your packet?"

"Uh huh!"

"Do you want to look through it?"

"Uh huh," Abbey said as she stood up with a smile.

The thick packet was opened, and the contents spilled onto the coffee table in the lobby. Abbey reached out and picked up the script and flipped through the pages, seeing her lines highlighted.

"You have a lot of lines," Jim said, before picking up two papers stapled together with the title: *costumes*. Jim read the first line.

Parents are responsible for their child's costumes. If you have difficulty providing a costume for your child, please contact the director.

I know nothing about costumes, thought Jim. He put the papers aside and looked at the script with Abbey. She flipped through the pages, using her finger to follow along with paragraphs that gave stage direction. Her movements seemed frantic, prompting a question from Jim.

"What are you looking for?"

Abbey kept looking and finally found it. She gasped and threw her fists in the air.

"Fly! I get to fly! It says right there," Abbey said as she read the sentence again with her finger underlining the words. This time, Jim read with her. "Support cables lift the harness and float Peter Pan from stage left to stage right. I get to fly! They're going to let me fly!"

Chapter 47

Knock. Knock.

Abbey needed another ride from school back to the inn, and once again, Jim had to use his last resort. Kelly Mae White answered the door to Jim who was wearing a blue flannel shirt and jeans with bare feet. His jeans were covered in fine-grain sawdust, as were his hair and beard.

"Hi," Kelly said.

"Could you help us out again?"

. . .

When Abbey left play practice, she stood outside with the other kids until she saw Jim's old, red truck pull up with Kelly behind the wheel.

Once Abbey was seated and buckled, Kelly texted Jim before pulling out onto the road.

"How was your day?"

Abbey talked with Kelly all the way back to the inn and even lingered on the front porch as they continued their conversation. When Abbey eventually went inside and spoke to Jim, she asked him a question that would push Jim to his limit.

"Can Kelly eat with us tonight?"

"I'd rather not."

"She's really nice."

"I know, but I don't think I can handle it. I've already extended her stay way beyond what I first agreed to."

"Could I bring her something to eat?"

"I don't know."

"Please?"

"Why do you want to?"

"She is really nice, and she told me a joke."

"Why did she tell you a joke?"

"We were talking about the woodpecker that pecks on the trees outside. She said she can hear it in her room."

"What was the joke?"

"What's the best way to carve wood?"

"I don't know."

"Whittle by whittle."

"It's not that funny," Jim said as he cracked a smile.

"You're smiling though," Abbey said as she pointed at him. "I also have to be picked up at school next week after play practice. She said she would."

"She's leaving tomorrow."

"I know. She said she would still help out if she found a place in town," Abbey explained. Jim exhaled a deep breath, running his hand through his thick hair. *I do need someone to pick up Abbey,* he thought. He considered allowing Kelly to stay in exchange for helping out, but quickly decided against it.

"Mallory will pick you up. I'll have to beg her, but she'll do it."

"Could we have Kelly for dinner as a way of thanking her?"

"We did thank her. We let her stay here," Jim explained. Abbey hung her head in defeat.

"Oooookay."

"Sorry, I'm just not fond of having other people around right now."

"What about when we go to Texas?"

"That's different. That's a necessity."

"Well, could I bring her dinner at least?"

"I suppose…" Jim was interrupted by a knock on the front door. Abbey leaned over as far as she could without falling over to see out the window.

"It's her," Abbey said as she limped toward the door.

"Abbey, wait. See what she wants, but please don't let her in," Jim said as he watched Abbey open the door and step out onto the porch. Their conversation was lengthy enough for Jim to be curious as to what they were talking about. Since he had already become acquainted with Kelly, even on a limited basis, Jim walked over to the door and took a deep breath before he opened it.

"Hello," Kelly said.

"Hi," Jim returned.

"I was just telling Abbey here that I would like to bring you something from the diner. I thought I could bring you take-out for being so nice to me. I could just take a cab or if you are willing to let me use the truck again…"

Abbey looked up at Jim, stood on tip-toe and waved for him to bend down. She cupped her hand around her mouth and whispered in his ear.

"Can I go out to eat with her?" Abbey asked. Jim stood up straight. *Start small. Try going out to eat,* he thought, hearing Stanton's voice in his head. Instead of pondering on the idea, he jumped at the thought as if ripping off a Band-Aid.

"Why don't we all go?" Jim said to the amazement of Abbey.

"You, too? You would come to the diner?"

"Sure. I need to get out a little before we move to Houston," Jim explained. Abbey was still in shock. Her mouth was wide open. "Go get your green, zippered case though. I'd rather we not leave without it."

Once they were all seated and buckled, Jim started out on Bear Mountain Road. Abbey sat between Kelly and Jim with her prosthetic leg on the floorboard. Abbey held onto the green, zippered case that contained her ipecac syringes.

"Is it still weird?" Abbey asked.

"A little."

"Has it been a long time since you left?" Kelly asked.

"Well, I left briefly to take her to the optometrist, but other than that, I haven't left in ten years."

"Haven't you gotten sick?" Kelly asked.

"Of course."

"Didn't you go to the doctor?" Abbey asked.

"I had a nurse practitioner visit me. I paid her to come to the inn, go get my prescription and bring it to me."

Kelly looked at Abbey's green case. She nodded toward it as she asked Abbey a question.

"What's in the case?"

"It's vomit syrup. I can't eat fake sugar."

"Fake sugar?"

"Artificial sweeteners can damage her kidneys," Jim interjected as he steered the truck. "I don't quite understand it, but if she accidentally drinks or eats it, she's supposed to ingest the contents of a syringe. It makes her regurgitate the contents of her stomach."

"You mean like a syringe with a needle?"

"Yeah, but these don't have a needle. You just squirt it in her mouth."

"I usually just stay away from sugar anyway," Abbey said.

When they arrived at the diner, Jim parked the truck in front of Murray's and looked through the big, plate-glass window. He was relieved to see that only one table was occupied. Three men who appeared to be auto mechanics ate while talking and laughing. The rest of the diner was empty.

Darla Pettigrew had just turned on the coffee-maker, brewing a fresh batch for her three customers. While it was nice to have customers, Darla wished they would leave. Steven Burns and Burt Poole sat across from their friend, Bull, who had a buffet of food in front of him.

Reuben with fries

Cheeseburger with fries

Hot Dog with potato salad

Grilled Cheese

Country Fried Steak with Green Beans and mashed potatoes

Although Murray's Diner didn't have an eating challenge gimmick, Steven Burns started one by offering to pay for Bull's food if he could finish everything from the left side of the menu. Half-way through the hot dog and potato salad, Jim's old, red truck parked in front of the diner. Kelly exited the passenger side.

"Hey, there. She ain't bad lookin'," Steven said as he pointed out the window at Kelly. Burt and Bull looked outside. They watched as Paul Bunyan exited the driver's side and helped a little girl out of the truck.

Steven watched as the girl came into view stepping up onto the sidewalk with a hand from the bearded man.

"A cripple, a lumberjack, and a soccer mom walk into a diner," Steven said as if he was telling the beginning of a joke. Burt and Bull both laughed.

Ding. Ding.

The bell sounded as they entered.

The three underachievers at table eleven watched as the lumberjack with his wife and handicapped kid sat at the counter. Ignoring them and going back to their plates, Steven slapped the hand of Burt Poole.

"Oww! What was that for?" Burt said just after he had stolen a French fry off one of Bull's plates.

"He has to finish all that. I don't need you helping him. I have to pay for all this if he finishes."

"It's just one fry. No big deal."

"If it ain't a big deal, then you pay."

"No way! I didn't start this bet."

"Then keep your hands off his fries."

The outburst garnered a look from Abbey as she sat on a barstool. When Darla came out from the kitchen, she saw three new customers at the counter and whipped out her pen and pad.

"Evening. What can I get you to drink?" Darla asked and wrote down their beverage order. As she disappeared into the kitchen, she thought something was strange about the lumberjack. Without being able to place him, she ignored it and went about filling their order.

Steven Burns and Burt Poole watched Bull finish off the last of the potato salad. As he chewed an enormous mouthful, Steven reminded the challenger of his remaining hurdles,

"Just a grilled cheese and country fried steak to go."

"Green beans too," Burt said as he moved a side order in front of Bull.

"No problem. Be ready to pay up," Bull uttered with a mouthful and a smile.

Darla came out from the kitchen and set the drinks in front of Kelly, Abbey, and Jim before returning back to the kitchen.

Once the atmosphere sunk in and Kelly felt comfortable, she asked Jim a question while snapping a white sugar packet.

"Do you own the inn?"

"I do," Jim replied as he slid the plastic sugar packet container across the counter. He eyed the yellow and pink packets of artificial sweeteners and noted the proximity to Abbey.

"For how long?" she asked as she poured the sugar from the packet and stirred her tea.

"Well, my parents owned it, and my sister and I grew up there."

"She's the one who talked with me before?"

"Yeah, that's her," Jim answered. Abbey's thoughts stopped when Jim said "my parents".

"Jim?" He looked down at her sitting on the red bar stool, swiveling slightly. "Are your parents my grandparents?" Abbey asked. Jim thought about it, another part of a quick adoption that wasn't realized until much later.

"Yes. They are," Jim said with a smile.

"Where are they?"

"Well, they passed, many years ago," Jim said with a subtle grimace.

"Oh," Abbey said, not remembering her conversation about his parents during her first encounter with Jim.

"I thought she was your daughter."

"She is, but only as of a few days ago. I adopted her."

"Oh. Wow. I didn't know that."

"It's a long story," Abbey said.

"I see."

The conversation halted when Darla returned to take their orders. "Okay, what can I get you guys?"

"Cheeseburger and fries," Kelly said.

"Fruit and yogurt," Abbey ordered.

"Same," Jim replied. Kelly remembered the grocery list of healthy items and looked at her iced tea. Both Abbey and Jim were drinking water. Their orders compared to her unhealthy choices made her feel somewhat out of place. Trying to move on, Kelly asked another question.

"You have any big plans for the summer?" Kelly asked Abbey.

"Uh huh! We are going to Johnson Space Center in Texas. Jim is going back to space."

Abbey's response travelled from the counter and floated toward Steven Burns who caught the words in his ear and sparked the one percent of his brain that only fired on one cylinder.

"Hold the phone. Uh oh," Steven said as he leaned over his table to get a good look at the lumberjack. "Burt, Bull, we're sitting amongst a celebrity here."

Jim could see the look in Steven's eyes. Like a visitor at a zoo, Steven stared at him as though he was looking at a captured animal behind glass. "We've heard about you. We've heard about you for a long time."

"Thanks," was all Jim could say. Steven and Burt laughed at Jim's response.

"Thanks?" Steven said under his breath as he laughed. "Hey! You ever see anything weird or strange up there?" Steven asked, showing off for his friends. Jim ignored his question and considered leaving. Kelly looked disturbed, as did Abbey. Steven, Burt, and Bull talked and laughed over their plates of food, glancing periodically at Jim. When Darla brought out a pitcher of iced tea and refilled Kelly's glass, she could tell her counter customers appeared a little disconcerted. Her eyes turned toward the peanut gallery as they looked Jim's way and laughed and spoke softly.

"Oh great," Darla said. Steven had resorted to whispering to his cohorts while looking in Jim's direction.

"Steven, I think it's time you leave."

"Bull still has half a grilled cheese and a whole 'nother plate to go. Plus we asked for coffee and still haven't got it yet."

"Excuse me, could we get this to go?" Jim asked Darla.

Darla nodded and disappeared behind the silver-swinging door.

"To go?" Steven said overhearing Jim talk. "You just got here." Steven said amidst laughter from his friends. Jim just stared straight ahead, wishing he hadn't left the inn. "Let me ask you somthin'," Steven started in. "You see anything up there that made you lock yourself up for ten years? Somethin' that scared you?"

"Like what?" Jim asked.

"I don't know, aliens or somethin'?" Steven said causing Bull to nearly choke with laughter as he ate the last of his grilled cheese. Burt just smiled and looked on, waiting for a response. "What'd you see up there?" Steven asked. Jim ignored him and didn't even look in his direction. "You gonna answer me or what?" Jim continued staring straight ahead until he reached for his ice water. As he took a drink through the straw, he looked at Steven full in the face, never saying a word. Steven utilized one of the few expletives in his vocabulary, which caused Jim to glare in his direction.

"Hey!" Jim raised his voice. "I've got a little girl here, watch your language."

Darla emerged from the kitchen with a tray of coffee for her unsavory customers. Three steaming cups. She set it on the counter near Kelly and Abbey with the intention of walking around and taking the tray from the other side. She stood by the tray and pointed at the three clowns: "Coffee and you're all out. Bull, hurry up."

"Don't forget the cream, Darla."

"I'll get your cream. Calm down."

Darla then turned and spoke in a melodious tone to Jim. "I have your orders to go. Just let me put them in a bag for you." She once again disappeared into the kitchen.

"I expect an answer, Spaceman. You've already got a reputation around here for being crazy. Don't be jackhole, too" Steven said.

Bull looked over at the lunch counter and saw Abbey peeking around Kelly and looking towards their table.

"What happened to your leg?" Bull asked as if he was holding back from laughing. Jim looked at Abbey and shook his head *no*. Steven saw the exchange.

"Why won't you let her talk? All he asked was a question. You and your family should be more sociable."

Jim looked at Abbey and spoke just above a whisper, "Tell them." Abbey stared at him. "Go ahead," he added.

Abbey looked back at their table and began to explain. While she spoke, Jim reached for her green ipecac case, removed three syringes and simultaneously plunged a syringe into each cup of coffee.

"Shhhh," Jim whispered quietly to Kelly who was conveniently blocking the coffee cups from view. With one fast motion, he shoved the empty syringes into the green case and stood up. He grabbed the tray just as Abbey finished explaining.

"Guys, allow me to serve you and apologize. I'm just not a sociable person," Jim said as he set the cups of coffee down in front of them. "Also, allow me to pay your tab," Jim said as he took out a hundred dollar bill and a fifty-dollar bill. He slapped them on the counter near the register. Jim looked at Kelly and Abbey as if they had just robbed the place and needed to escape.

"Okay. That's more like it," Steven said.

Darla came out from the kitchen and handed Kelly a plastic bag with Styrofoam to-go boxes inside. Jim leaned over the guys' table and talked to them as if he was sharing a secret.

"And by the way, just between us, I did see something up there," Jim whispered as he looked out the window and up at the sky. "It was green. It was big, and it I can still hear it scream in my head—scared me to death," he whispered as Abbey and Kelly walked out the door. Jim followed behind them as he turned and looked at Darla, pointing to the two bills on the counter. "Keep the change."

Ding. Ding. The bell sounded as they left.

Chapter 48

With school coming to a close in a week, Abbey had more play practices which required more rides from school to the inn. With very little twisting of her arm, Kelly agreed to stay at the inn until school was out, with the caveat that she pick up Abbey and make runs to the grocery. Jim was looking over a PDF of a mission plan Dave Thomas emailed him earlier in the day when the phone rang.

"Hello?" Jim answered.

"Hi, Mr. Mayfield, it's Mrs. Harris."

"Oh, hello…what's wrong?"

"Oh. Nothing is wrong. I just wanted to ask you if you would be able to attend Career Day," she asked. Jim exhaled in frustration, reliving his last outing of ridicule and torture.

"I'd rather not. I don't know what I would say."

"Well, we would prompt you with questions, and I'm sure the other kids would have a question or two."

"I'm sorry. I have to turn you down."

"Well, I don't know if it helps, but we only have four other parents coming, and two of them are computer programmers."

"Yeah, that does sound like fun."

"The others are a pharmacist and an accountant. You would certainly be the star of the show."

"And that's exactly the kind of thing I try to avoid."

"Well, if you are the star, Abbey would be, too. I know it would make her very happy to see you there."

"I will consider it. But I won't promise anything."

Jim didn't give Career Day much thought until Abbey brought it up at dinner.

"Did you know that Career Day is coming up?"

"I have heard that, yes." Jim said without trying to sound as if he had been hounded about it.

"Do you think you could come and talk to us about being an astronaut?"

"I've thought about it, and I would rather not if it's okay."

"Uggghhhh!!!!" Abbey said as she leaned back, her eyes looked up at the ceiling in desperation.

"What?" Jim said.

"It's so frustrating."

"What is?"

"It's like having a really cool car, but you can't be picked up in it at school."

"Is that why you want me to come? To show me off?"

"Yeah, kind of."

"I don't think that's a good reason."

"Well, what if you could video conference? They could set it up and show you on screen in the auditorium."

"Hmmm… I guess I would do that."

"Really? You'd do that?"

"Yeah. I'll do it."

"This is great. It'll be awesome. Will you say my name? Everyone knows by now my last name changed to Mayfield," Abbey explained with pure excitement.

Talk of Career Day dominated the rest of their conversation. After eating dinner, Abbey got out a piece of ruled notepaper and a pencil. They stayed up late into the night and laughed while they wrote down a long list of questions the school could ask Jim.

The next morning at breakfast, Abbey was a little sluggish as she walked into the kitchen.

"I shouldn't have let you stay up so late," Jim said.

"It's okay. It was worth it. It was fun."

"It was. What was your favorite, silly question to ask?"

"Are there alligators in space?" Abbey recited as Jim laughed.

"Are you really going to ask that?"

"No, but I can get Gillian or Hannah to ask it."

"You think the other kids would laugh?"

"I know they would."

When Jim saw Abbey off to school, he went back to the dining room and made a phone call.

"Dr. Stanton," Stanton answered.

"I went out to eat," Jim started in.

"Hey, Jim."

"It sucked."

"You went out to eat? Where?"

"Murray's Diner. I was pounced on by an ignorant local."

"What happened?"

"Eh, he was asking me something about an alien in space, goading me into answering."

"I bet I know who you're talking about. So what did you say?"

"Nothing really, he got a little belligerent. Not the kind of first interaction I had hoped for when slipping back into public."

"I bet. What did you do when he became belligerent?"

"I put ipecac in his coffee."

"What? Where did you get ipecac?"

"Long story. I need a favor from you."

"Wait. What happened?"

"To the guy? I don't know, he was sitting with two other guys, and I put it in all their coffees. I left before it got messy," Jim said as he heard a faint wheezing and a deep, hard chuckle coming from Stanton. After twenty seconds, Stanton composed himself and asked another question. "You don't know what happened?" Stanton asked. Jim replied: "No," offering little satisfaction. "Well, hang on, I'll call them. Stay on the line and you can listen in. I have to hear this."

Across town at Murray's diner, the phone rang and a burly old man wearing a white apron set his spatula down near the steaming hot griddle and answered the phone.

"Murray's"

"Hello, I'm calling about some fellas that may or may not have gotten sick at your diner there," Dr. Stanton asked. Jim could hear every word.

"Yeah, you from the health department?"

"No, just a curious citizen."

"Well, from what I heard three guys came in, and before they left they threw up all over the place. One guy had eaten quite a bit, too. I was told it looked like someone sprayed their table with a food hose," the burly man said. Stanton tried to contain his laughter as the man continued: "Lady that works here took her week vacation then and there. Took her apron off and left. Took the cleanup crew a full hour."

"Are the guys okay?"

"Yeah, I suppose. Just sick is all. We don't even know what happened."

"Well, thanks for the info."

"Yuh huh."

Click.

Stanton hung up and only Jim remained on the line. As they both imagined Steven and his friends spraying food all over each other, they laughed until they were out of breath.

"Great story. Never heard anything like it," Stanton said.

Once the laughter subsided, Jim finally got to the point.

"Do you think there would be a way for me to borrow a promo spacesuit?"

"Why?"

"Abbey has Career Day at school, and we're going to video conference so I can do a question-and-answer session. I thought it would be nice if I could do it in something else than a plain, old shirt."

"Well, I don't know but I will ask. You mind if I give out your email address or phone number to the marketing department?"

"No. No problem."

Later that day, just before Abbey got back home, Jim got a phone call.

"Mr. Mayfield?" a voice asked.

"Yes."

"My name is Clay Perkinson and I'm a marketing assistant for NASA."

"Hello."

"I was told you wanted a suit?"

"Yes. For a school career day."

"I have a few suits here in storage. The best promo suit we have is available, and I could sign it out for you and send it your way."

"That would be great."

"Okay. I will send you an email and when the boxes arrive, use the four-digit code in the email to open them. There's a keypad on the side. When you are done, just do your best to re-pack it and use the shipping label provided inside."

"Great. No problem."

When he hung up, Jim heard Abbey come in through the front door.

"Guess what?" Jim said as he walked out into the lobby.

"What?" Abbey asked as she set down her backpack.

"NASA is sending me a space suit to wear on the conference call."

"Oh! wow! That'll be great."

Jim had imagined the delivery would arrive in a suitcase-sized box, and he would simply unfold the suit, attach the helmet and be done. Much to his surprise, a few days later, Jim opened the door to two silver, metal boxes on wheels. One with the word *Washer* and the other with the word *Dryer* stenciled in black. Jim wasn't sure who would believe that a washer and dryer came in metal boxes locked with coded keypads on them, but it was understandably better than stamping "NASA" on the sides.

He quickly discovered the boxes weren't as heavy as they looked as he rolled them into the dining hall. Once the codes were entered into the keypad, the boxes were opened, displaying more black foam than space suit. Jim first grabbed a set of papers which read: *NASA Promotional Space Suit with Voice Box.*

Voice box?

He read through the instructions and proceeded to remove the upper torso followed by the arms. The nylon material looked brand new and even had a fresh nylon smell, a material not found in a suit crafted for the vacuum of space. Then Jim spotted the top of the helmet among the formed, black packing foam. He reached in, took a hold of the helmet and lifted it out of the box. It looked real, but a lighter version, as this one only weighed ten pounds. While a genuine space suit weighed 280 pounds, this one was a considerably lighter version made to appear authentic.

Impressed with the suit, Jim spent the next hour getting into it, putting on each piece with great difficulty. Struggling and fighting to get into the suit, Jim finally managed every piece except the helmet and gloves. He reached down and took the heavy helmet in his hands. Before putting it over his head, Jim noticed a label inside the helmet that read *Voice Box audio switch*. Remembering he read a section in the manual about a voice box, Jim looked at the helmet and realized that the integrated lights on the helmet had been taken out and replaced with speakers. Jim flipped the switch to the *on* position, hearing a slight hissing noise. He put the helmet over his head and turned it to lock it in place.

"Hello?" Jim said. His voice was broadcast through the speakers and throughout the dining hall in a boisterous, deep voice. "Oh, this is cool," he said as he stood in the middle of the large, empty dining hall. "I sound like Darth Vader."

Jim reached up and felt the tab of the sun visor on his helmet and pulled the sun shield over the clear bubble, giving him complete anonymity. Suddenly, Jim had an idea.

Chapter 49

On the second to last day of school, Abbey awoke early and ate breakfast with Jim. The excitement of Career Day was upon her, and she was eager to see Jim on the big screen in the auditorium. While Jim had led her to believe that he was going to be attending Career Day via a videoconference, Jim had made other plans.

Once Abbey had left, Jim enlisted Kelly as his assistant to help him get dressed in the suit before taking him over to Bear Creek Elementary. Forced to leave a few sections of his suit off for the ride to school, Jim held his helmet, sleeves, and gloves while Kelly drove.

Abbey had just finished lunch and was heading to the auditorium with her class. Her classmates bustled and scurried to their favorite seats once let loose among the empty chairs in the auditorium. Within minutes of being seated, Mrs. Harris took the stage.

"Good afternoon, students. Settle down, and please be very quiet."

Out in the parking lot, Jim and Kelly exited the truck.

"Here. Can you help me put these on?" Jim asked. Kelly assisted Jim by attaching the gloves and arm pieces of the suit over his flannel shirt. Once he had squeezed into the rest of the suit, he reached into the passenger seat of his truck and grabbed his helmet. "I'm not going to be able to see very well once I put the visor down, so you're going to have to guide me."

Inside the auditorium, a parent had just tried to present their unfortunate career choice as a computer programmer as enlightening and enjoyable as possible.

The front doors of Bear Creek Elementary were opened and in walked a man from outer space. Kelly guided Jim through the doors and to the window of the front office. Once the secretary saw the astronaut through the window, she picked up her walkie-talkie and spoke into it, never taking her eyes off of him.

"He's here."

While Jim waited in the entrance hall of the school, Mrs. Harris made her way from the auditorium, to where Jim was standing near the front office. A short, flimsy gentleman with a wispy mustache walked by her side.

"Wow. Look at this," Mrs. Harris said with a long, drawn out, excited voice. "Hello, Mr. Mayfield, can you hear me in there?" she asked.

"Hi, Mrs. Harris," Jim said with his booming voice coming from the speakers.

"Oh, goodness," Mrs. Harris said with laughter, placing her flattened palm on her chest. "This is great. I never expected it to be so impressive," she added. Unable to see Jim through the copper colored tint of his sun visor, she stared at her own reflection as she introduced the flimsy gentleman, "This is Mr. Wallace. He is our audio-visual tech, and he has a great way for you to enter the auditorium."

"Okay," Jim's voice said through the speakers. Mr. Wallace's wispy mustache wiggled with every word he spoke.

"I'm going to play the theme from *2001: A Space Odyssey* and have a spotlight on you as you enter. It'll be great," Wallace said with excited eyes as he enthusiastically nodded his head.

"Sounds good!" Jim said as he gave him a thumbs up.

Abbey sat through the first four parents impatiently, waiting for Jim to appear on screen. She imagined the moment when Jim would call out her name, and she could wave to him through the camera. Finally it seemed the fourth parent, a pharmacist, was wrapping up and Abbey began to get excited. The lights dimmed down, but the screen was not lowered. Mrs. Harris took the stage as the parent walked off to a sparse smattering of applause.

"Students, I am pleased to announce a special guest, and I ask that you remain in your seats. Do not leave your seats."

"Leave our seats?" Abbey said out loud to her friends.

Suddenly, the backdoors opened and the music began. Children near the door shouted and screamed as a man in a space suit walked in. Abbey's attention was directed toward the back and saw a man in a space suit walking down the aisle with a spotlight on him. The music became very loud, and the ruckus from the kids was slightly unsettling. *Is it really him? Is that Jim?* Abbey thought, in disbelief, as she watched the spaceman walk up on stage. The music continued to roar. The kids watched the space man raise his hands at the music's climax, as if he was celebrating a victory. The entire auditorium cheered and screamed with excitement.

Once the music faded out, Mrs. Harris calmed the children down with moderate success while Jim walked up to the microphone. The entire auditorium could hear a pin drop. *Is that really Jim?* Abbey thought once more, unsure. Finally the astronaut spoke.

"Hello," the deep, unrecognizable voice blasted out from the integrated speakers, sending the kids into another excited frenzy. The teachers shushed the kids, trying to contain their shouts and screams. "I am an astronaut from outer space," Jim said, playing up his role. "I have been in outer space three times and have lived aboard the International Space Station." Knowing it sounded weird to say out loud, still unfamiliar, he said the words, *my daughter.* "I am here looking for my daughter. Where is Abbey Mayfield? Stand up, Abbey," Jim's thunderous voice said.

The spotlight plowed through the rows of kids and stopped on Abbey. Instead of standing up and cheerfully waving to Jim, she stood up with her hand over her mouth as tears streamed down her face. Through the sun visor, Jim could see the spotlight on Abbey and that she was crying. Unsure if she was upset, but wanting to see her, he called for her.

"Abbey, please come up here to the stage," Jim said. Her classmates watched as she stepped out into the aisle and limped to the stage, hand still pressed firmly against her mouth, tears flowing down her cheeks. After struggling with the stairs, she made it to the stage. Jim bent down on one knee and lifted the sun shield. Abbey hugged Jim, and he returned the embrace by squeezing ever so gently.

"I am so glad you came," Abbey said through her tears.

"Me too, Abbey," Jim responded softly through his speakers.

When Abbey collected herself, Jim stood up and took questions from the auditorium while Abbey stood off to the side of the stage with Kelly. Once he completed his Career Day appearance, he walked backstage to take off the suit. With Abbey and Kelly's help, they took very little time getting out to the truck and on their way home.

The events that transpired had been burned in Abbey's memory forever, but it was one single look from Jim that stood out. As Jim was removing the suit backstage and he took off his helmet and gloves, he had casually looked at her and simply asked, "How was that?" with a smile that made her smile back—a moment that meant the most from a man she could unequivocally call her father.

Chapter 50

Once Abbey was out of school, it proved to be more stressful on Jim than he thought. Packing up and getting ready to move to Houston with the added fun of having to integrate back into society and the workplace were intimidating. In preparation for the trip, he was forced to renew his driver's license, which included another driving test that took up an entire afternoon. Turnabouts and parallel parking, followed by a quick photo shoot, and he was back on the road.

Once Jim received the training schedule for the mission, he reviewed it in its entirety. Some days on the schedule looked like they would last twelve hours or more, with time spent in the training pool, mission briefings, and classrooms. Jim thought of what he would do with Abbey while he was working. After briefly considering begging his sister to take Abbey for the summer, he quickly disregarded the idea. He wanted Abbey with him, especially since Mallory could barely boil water, and Abbey would be exposed to the world of fast food on a regular basis.

A thought came to mind that wasn't ideal, but it did make sense.

Knock. Knock.

When Kelly opened the door to her room, Jim could see her suitcase on the bed. It was wide open and stacks of clothes were ready to be packed away.

"You getting ready to leave?"

"Yep. Heading out tomorrow morning. Promise," Kelly said with a smile that was both charming and thankful.

"Where are you going?"

"Well, I don't know. I was thinking Charleston."

"South Carolina?"

"Yeah. I went there once. It was nice."

"What are you going to do?"

"I don't know for sure but to start out I thought I might wait tables or something," Kelly said. Jim nodded and paused before going into the reason for his visit. At first, Kelly thought he had come over to make sure she was leaving, until…

"Can I talk to you a minute?" Jim asked.

"Sure. Do you want to come in?" Kelly asked. Jim took a half-step before stopping. Staying on the porch seemed more comfortable. Kelly opened the door to let Jim through, but he had decided to stand awkwardly on the porch, leaving both of them uncomfortable.

"No, no. Thanks though. This won't take long," Jim said, stepping back.

"Okay." Kelly thought he was about to tell her to leave immediately. Something came up, and he wanted her out. Unsure of his intentions, or what he was about to say made her feel uneasy. Jim leaned his body against the doorframe and crossed his arms while his brow furrowed in thought. Now, awkwardness established, he appeared to be asking her to prom.

"We are leaving for Houston in two days, and Abbey will be there for the whole summer. Then she needs to come back here for school."

"Okay."

"I need someone to be with Abbey while I am working which could be twelve-hour days. So, I would like to hire you to watch her. Just for the summer, and then when you return you will have a free place to stay while she goes to school. At least until I get back."

"Yes," Kelly said immediately.

"Yes? No need to think about it?"

"Yes. I'll do it."

"You'll travel with us to Houston, stay with us the whole summer, and then bring Abbey back here and watch her until November?"

"Yes."

"Don't you want to know what I will pay?"

"I don't care. I'll do it. I didn't know what I was going to do. I like this option better. Better than Charleston," Kelly said. Jim couldn't help but grin and nod.

"Okay. We'll work out the details later. I'm glad you said yes."

Once Jim left, Kelly closed the door and spun around. She leaned her back against the door and breathed a sigh of relief. The feeling of carrying a weight made of lead seemed to have been lifted. Kelly continued to pack her suitcase, although for a completely different reason. When Jim went back inside, he went over the conversation in his head. She was sweet. Charming even. While walking toward Abbey's room, he questioned his decision, but his reservations disappeared when he found Abbey and explained the arrangement.

"Really? She's coming with us?"

"Yep. Are you okay with that?"

"Of course! I think she's really nice."

"Good. If you didn't approve, I don't know what I would do. She's kind of our last resort."

Kelly attended dinner with Abbey and Jim on Abbey's request. Jim felt that if she were to be with them for the rest of the year, eating with her would help determine if he really had made the right decision. If there was the slightest bit of crazy in Kelly, he would send her off without hesitation.

Dinner was grilled chicken, asparagus, and baked tomato wedges drizzled with olive oil, sprinkled with Parmesan cheese and black pepper. Setting their plates on the coffee table, Abbey took a couple pillows off the couch and sat on the floor. Jim opted to sit on the couch and lean over his plate. Kelly decided to follow Abbey's seating arrangement. While it wasn't unusual for Kelly to eat at a coffee table, it was unusual to eat with the TV off. She listened to Jim and Abbey's conversation, grateful for being included and even more grateful for the opportunity to be with them the rest of the year. Kelly compared it to being a dog in a shelter and being rescued by a nice family.

"Are there spaceships there?" Abbey asked.

"At the Space Center?" Jim replied, to which Abbey nodded. "Yes. They're decommissioned though. Some of them are outside, at least the big ones are. Inside, there are space shuttles you can go through."

"We can see them? The rockets and shuttles?"

"Of course. We'll have all summer to look around."

Both Jim and Kelly could see the pure elation on Abbey's face at getting to do something new and exciting. Throughout dinner, Jim watched Kelly, trying to find a flaw or an imperfection that would end their arrangement. Jim found nothing. Kelly was polite and charming as usual.

Later that night after she had gone to bed, Abbey had difficulty falling asleep. She had spent many sleepless nights over the years tossing and turning, as she was constantly worried about something. For the first time in her life, Abbey had difficulty sleeping because of her excitement for the months to come.

Chapter 51

Jim, Kelly, and Abbey boarded a direct flight to Houston from Philadelphia International Airport. Severely missing the private jet experience after long lines and being manhandled by a TSA agent, Jim slid into his uncomfortable seat between Abbey and Kelly. Midway through the flight, Jim got up and entered the tight quarters of the restroom. Once he locked the door, the light came on just as he saw himself in the mirror. His beard was out of control and he winced at the sight of his matted, messy hair. A barber was in his near future.

After the five-hour flight, Stanton stood near the baggage carousel and held a sign that read *Crazyfield*. Not sure how Jim would take it, he considered abandoning his joke a few times. When he finally saw Jim walking toward him with a carry-on bag over his shoulder, he could see that Jim was smiling at him.

"Very funny," said Jim.

"Yeah, I thought you would like that."

Introductions were made all around starting with Abbey followed by Kelly. Stanton poked fun at Jim's woodsmen appearance, making both Abbey and Kelly laugh at Jim's expense.

Stanton had borrowed a company van from the fleet to pick them up and take them to Lighthouse Drive, a street near NASA's campus. As he navigated the van through traffic, Abbey and Kelly talked in the back while Stanton gave Jim the details.

"We've got you in a nice duplex. It's two stories and overlooks the lake, and before I forget," Stanton said as he leaned to one side and fished out car keys from his pocket, "there are two company cars in the garage," he said as he handed the keys to Jim.

"That's great," Jim responded.

"The entire block was bought up by NASA. All your neighbors are your co-workers. None of these homes have pools, but there is one you can walk to," Stanton said as he pointed his thumb behind him at Abbey and Kelly.

"You hear that Abbey? There's a pool you can walk to," Jim said.

"Really? I love to swim."

Stanton pulled the van up in front of 2899 Lighthouse Drive. Within a minute, Stanton had unlocked the front door and let them in.

"Wow," Abbey said as soon as she hobbled in. Her eyes fixed on the big window in the eat-in kitchen. The lake view was stunning and caught everyone's eye as they walked in. Stanton turned to Jim and smiled.

"I got a little welcome home present for you."

Jim followed Stanton to the stainless steel refrigerator and watched as he opened the door. A full case of Black Bear Alaskan Ale sat on the bottom shelf.

"Hey. That's great."

"Figured you'd appreciate it. Bought a couple cases a few days ago."

The rest of the day, Jim, Abbey, and Kelly moved their luggage and belongings into the house and ordered take out from a sandwich shop. After dinner, they helped Abbey memorize her lines for the play.

"I'll be Captain Hook, and you play the part of Wendy," Jim said to

Kelly who was pleased to be included. Jim read his lines.

"When you see Peter Pan, you prepare to catch him. I want him alive," Jim said. While Jim could design space-qualified mechanical components with electrical and thermal design specifications, he couldn't perform a theatrical role. His acting ability inspired rotten tomatoes and collective boos. Abbey didn't pay much attention, but Kelly noticed, thinking it sweet that he was enthusiastic about helping Abbey, despite his lack of thespian skill.

"Let 'em go, Hook!" Abbey read.

"Why don't you come down here and face me? Cut out the flying around," Jim read and continued with his line. Abbey was focused on her lines and read them without faltering. Kelly watched Jim and Abbey read until it was her turn.

"Watch out, Peter! It's a trap!" Kelly read aloud.

"A trap?" Abbey followed by reading her line before Jim continued.

"Ha ha. I've captured Peter Pan," Jim said as he attempted to conjure up enthusiasm.

The next day, Jim awoke at dawn and slipped out for a run up and down Lighthouse Drive. After thirty minutes of running, he went back inside to find Abbey sitting on a barstool at the kitchen counter. Her back was to him, and she turned her head.

"Hey," she said casually as she looked at a magazine.

"What are you doing up?"

"I set my alarm."

"Why?" Jim asked. Abbey leaned to one side revealing two bowls of cereal.

"Breakfast," Abbey said simply while shrugging her shoulders. He had made breakfast for her before school, now it seemed she was returning the favor.

Jim smiled, "Where'd you get the milk?"

"I didn't. It's dry cereal. Is that okay?" Abbey asked. Jim nodded and walked toward his room.

"Of course it is. Let me jump in and out of the shower. Be right back."

Jim hurried in and out of the shower, quickly returning to the kitchen in a T-shirt and khaki pants. He used a small towel, to dry off his hair and beard.

"What are you going to do today?" Abbey asked.

"I don't know. Get caught up on everything, I guess. Training starts tomorrow so I have to be prepared, and I don't even know when I'll be home. Could be late."

"That's okay. I'm sure we can find something to do."

"This weekend, I will take you on a tour of the facility."

"Can I get in a spaceship?"

"We'll see. Last time I was here a little kid was in a spaceship, and it accidentally took off."

"Nu uh," Abbey said as she smiled and shook her head. Jim smiled back as he popped a grain of cereal in his mouth. "I would have heard about that on the news," Abbey added.

Jim walked into the garage and found two Honda Accords. They looked to be a couple years old, one painted red and the other silver. Jim took the red one and drove a short distance to Building Nine on NASA's campus. Upon entering, he was stopped by a security guard who was certain that Jim was a lost, homeless man.

"Sir, I am sorry, but this is not a building open to the public. Guided tours are handled at the visitors center."

"I'm supposed to be here for a meeting at nine."

"You are? Who are you meeting?"

"David Thomas."

"The mission director?" The security guard's eyebrows lowered and his mouth flinched crooked.

"Yeah. Could you tell him Jim is here?"

"What's your last name?"

"Mayfield."

"Jim Mayfield. You're Jim Mayfield?" The security guard now looked at him as if he might be a threat. "Sir, can I see some ID?"

Jim removed his wallet and pulled out his driver's license. The guard looked it over – a brand new driver's license. Red flag. The photo was the same tattered lumberjack standing in front of him and then he examined the name, James W. Mayfield. It looked to be correct. After making two phone calls, Dave finally came out to the lobby.

"Hey, Jim," Dave said as he walked over. The security guard looked on as they both shook hands.

"This gentleman didn't believe I'm me."

"I don't doubt it," Dave said as he slapped Jim on the shoulder. The security guard handed Jim his license, now looking at Jim as more of a celebrity than an impostor. "Come on. We'll get you a badge later. It's good to have you back," Dave said. Jim followed Dave through the maze of hallways. "How long has it been since you've been here?"

"Over ten years," Jim answered.

"Well, be forewarned that some of these people have known about you coming back for some time. They're all expecting to see you today, so get used to the weird looks."

"Stanton greeted me with a sign at the airport that read *Crazyfield*."

"I know, he told me. He was relieved you took it so well."

"I'm still not sure what I did to deserve that title."

"Well, there isn't an official ranking, but you were the hotshot in the corps. The number one guy. Then you lock yourself away for a decade. Everyone thinks it's crazy to get to the top and walk away."

"They think I went crazy?"

"Who knows? Who cares? If it's any consolation, the crew we're working with look up to you. That's all that matters."

Dave opened a door and walked into a massive warehouse with high ceilings and a full 1:1 replica of the International Space Station.

"We've made quite a few changes since you were last here. We'll do a quick walk around before our conference call with Hatherton."

After looking over various components and reading countless sections of manuals and workbooks, Jim and Dave adjourned to the conference room for a meeting with department heads of the Hatherton Corporation. Once the meeting ended, Jim opted for a quick break. While walking around the facility looking for bottled water, Jim spotted Stanton talking with a man in a flight suit and walked toward him. Once their conversation was finished, Stanton turned to Jim with great interest.

"Do you have a few minutes? You've got to meet someone over at the robotics lab," Stanton said, hoping Jim would say Yes.

Thinking he was about to be showcased to some visitors, Jim followed with little enthusiasm to a nearby building on NASA's campus. Inside, Jim looked at his watch, hoping to make this quick. Stanton hurriedly made his way down a long hallway and turned into a room labeled *Dexterous Robotics R1 R2*. The room smelled like a bag of heavily circulated coins and was lit with harsh, fluorescent lighting. The room was filled with workbenches and desks on which sat robotic armatures under construction with wires that protruded out of open joints. Jim noticed there were only a few people in the room as he walked behind Stanton, and most never even looked up from their workbench. When Stanton saw a thin black man working on a large, robotic rover, he made a beeline toward him, encouraging Jim to pick up the pace.

"Greg," Stanton said, as Jim tried to keep up.

"Hey Dr. Stanton," Greg said. Wearing a grey T-shirt with the word *Army* lettered in black, Greg shook Jim's hand when they were introduced. Greg's bicep was large and protruded from underneath the sleeve of his shirt.

"Greg Thompson."

"Jim Mayfield."

"I know," Greg said just as Stanton jumped in.

"Now, don't show him yet," Stanton said to Greg. "Tell Jim what you do."

"I'm a robotics engineer and member of the corps working on the new model for exterior ISS maneuvers. Specifically on the robonaut three project."

"I see," Jim said, familiar with the project.

"It's an honor to meet you, sir," Greg said with a look full of respect.

"You, too," Jim said with a smile, ready to head back to Building Nine.

"Okay, now show him," Stanton said. Unsure as to what was about to happen, Jim watched as Greg bent down and grabbed a zipper at his ankle. He pulled the zipper up to his knee, uncovering a black carbon-fiber prosthetic leg.

"See that? Just like Abbey," Stanton said.

"How did you lose it?" Jim asked, now completely interested in Greg.

"Never fully developed when I was a kid," Greg said as he looked down at his leg.

It wasn't like Abbey's clunky prosthetic. It was a shiny, black and grey, spiral structure that resembled intertwining strands of DNA flowing down into a tennis shoe. The calf was hollow, with the thick tornado of carbon fiber twisting and narrowing into the form of an ankle before ending at a metallic joint.

"Now tell him where this came from," Stanton said as he led him along.

"I designed it and built it. This is the prototype. Functioning, of course."

Jim looked at the prosthetic leg like a child in awe of his favorite athlete. He looked up at Greg who watched Jim react with great interest.

"May I?" Jim asked Greg as he gestured at his prosthetic.

"Sure," Greg answered. Before Jim could kneel, to get a better look at the prosthetic, Greg reached down and unlocked the leg with a sound like a firearm being separated for cleaning. He set it on the table in front of Jim. "It locks into a base, which is firmly attached to my thigh, see? My leg sits comfortably inside," Greg said as he lifted up his pant leg, revealing the same carbon fiber at the end of his thigh. A white cushion could be seen at the top of the thigh socket where his leg was seated. At the other end was a mechanical locking system that allowed Greg to easily attach and remove the prosthetic. Jim studied it as if he was inspecting a jewel.

"You have an interest in prosthetics?" Greg asked.

"I do now," Jim said.

Chapter 52

Kelly's room was bare, nothing on the walls and no television. Just a bed, closet, and a small bathroom she shared with Abbey. It had been only three days since they arrived and already they had found a routine. Abbey would wake up to an alarm and take a quick shower before heading down to the kitchen for breakfast with Jim. Once Abbey was downstairs, Kelly would shower, get ready and go downstairs when she heard Jim was getting ready to leave. It had become obvious to Kelly early on that she shouldn't interrupt their breakfast. Jim still seemed uncomfortable around her, which robbed Abbey of Jim's full attention.

She stood in front of the mirror naked after her shower and ran her hand along her scar thinking of what could have been. Adam's death continued to sting. Feeling like a part of her had died, the life inside her that was taken amplified her husband's death by a thousand. Holding back tears, she fought against the onset of depression as she got dressed. She walked halfway down the stairs listening for Abbey and Jim. They were talking, but in an unhurried and casual manner. Walking down the last few steps, she turned the corner and was greeted by both Abbey and Jim who turned their heads over their shoulders to greet her.

"Hey Kelly," Jim said.

"Morning," Kelly answered back.

"You ready to go?" Abbey asked.

"Where?" Kelly asked.

"We're going over for a tour," Jim said.

"To the Space Center?" Kelly replied. She had remembered they discussed touring the facility, but thought she would remain behind, thinking the tour was only for Abbey. To her surprise, Jim spoke up.

"I found a barber shop close by."

"Jim's gonna get cleaned up," Abbey said with a smile. Jim continued,

"I thought I'd get a hair cut and a shave, and then we'd take a tour at the Space Center. We can grab lunch and come back here before I go back to work," Jim explained. Kelly smiled as she had wanted to be included, but would never have asked.

"Sounds good," Kelly said with a nod, and squealed in her head.

Within an hour, Jim walked into the barbershop he had found on his phone. Bud's Barber Shop was located at a strip mall which allowed Kelly and Abbey to peruse the shops while they waited on Jim. When he entered, he found himself standing in a small waiting room with wood paneling and a coffee table covered in dated magazines. An elderly man named Bud peeked around the corner from a sitting position while holding a newspaper. Wearing a white coat that complemented his bushy, white mustache, he peered over his reading glasses. When Bud gazed up at the lumberjack, he saw trouble.

"Either you're here for an overhaul, or you're looking for your ox," Bud said, still peeking around the corner.

"Overhaul," Jim answered.

"Okey dokey," Bud replied. He took his time getting up as he tossed his newspaper aside. The shop was empty except for Bud, although two other barber's chairs sat in darkness. Elated that the shop wasn't full of people, Jim tried to relax. Bud made it easier on him as he was polite and full of vinegar.

"What are we doing here?" Bud asked. Jim stood in front of the barber's chair as he answered.

"A close shave. Tight and blocked haircut, active duty hair length."

"Lumberjack special. Got it. Now for the shave, I'm gonna give you a first-class shave, you know what that is?"

"I don't."

"Hot towel, ice cold water, hot shaving foam, and a straight edge razor."

"Sounds good."

"Strap in," Bud said as he slapped the barber's chair.

The room was lit entirely by fluorescent lights and the sharp smell of rubbing alcohol wisped by Jim's nose as he reclined back in the chair. After twenty-five minutes of a straight razor, electric clippers and scissors, Bud spun his customer around so Jim could see himself in the mirror. Jim stared at his haircut and missing beard long enough to worry Bud.

"That okay?" he asked, unable to tell if Jim liked it. Jim didn't answer right away, still touching his face.

"Yeah, it's fine. I just haven't seen myself in a while. Not like this."

"Good to hear. Twenty-two is the damage."

Jim paid and thanked Bud, who then grabbed his newspaper and sunk into the barber's chair, his usual position, without missing a beat. Just as Jim exited, Kelly and Abbey had just walked up. Their eyes fell on Jim at first not realizing it was him.

"Oh my God," Kelly said with a smile. Abbey covered her mouth.

"You look so different," Abbey said.

Jim's jaw line was sharp and defined. Instead of lumberjack Jim Mayfield, Kelly thought he looked more like a version of Clark Kent, minus the glasses.

"Do I look okay?" Jim asked as he touched his face once more. "Feels weird."

"You look great," Abbey said. Kelly noticed his haircut was similar to Adam's. She held back additional comments and just nodded her head.

"Good," Jim answered.

After a quick drive to the Space Center, Jim struggled with the thought of being around tourists, but he wanted Abbey to get the full experience. In his mind, he had planned out the day omitting the tram tour and decided instead on entering through the visitor's complex and letting Abbey see some of the exhibits.

As they entered the visitor center, Abbey wished she could walk faster. Her prosthetic leg prevented her from rushing into the Plaza like the other kids around her.

"Wow. This place is huge," Abbey said as she limped inside and gazed at a replica lunar module hanging from the ceiling.

"Is that real?" Abbey asked.

"No, but it looks to be about the same size."

The focal point of the massive room was a large banner of the moon spanning an entire football field. Surrounded by hallways and possibilities, Abbey looked around not knowing where to go. The sounds of other kids and parents echoed throughout the massive building. Feeling uneasy, Jim decided to take the lead in an effort to escape the crowd.

"Let's go look at the shuttle and the astronaut exhibits. I can answer pretty much any question you might have."

Jim and Kelly watched as Abbey hobbled from one exhibit to another while they followed her. Kelly looked on in fascination and took it all in and watched how Jim interacted with Abbey. At one point, Abbey tripped. Kelly watched Jim spring to her aid, much like what she imagined a secret service agent might do protecting the child of the President. Throughout the tour of the Space Center, Jim kept looking at his watch. Kelly had noticed him keeping time, but didn't question him. Once Abbey saw a shuttle simulator, she hopped inside. Kelly watched as Jim poked his head in and looked at the displays.

"Could I learn to fly the shuttle by doing this over and over?" Abbey asked as she looked at three computer screens showing the curvature of the earth. Jim looked at the displays.

"Nah. There aren't any gauges, and the display is wrong. This is just for fun. See if you can land it though."

Abbey maneuvered the controls for a while before relinquishing them to another kid waiting to climb inside. Once Abbey exhausted all of the exhibits in the plaza, they walked through the hallways and looked at moon rocks and decommissioned space suits, including one that looked similar to the suit that Jim had worn at Career Day.

"Is that the same one?" Abbey asked.

"It's the same model, yes."

The tour concluded outside with the Saturn V rocket. Kelly and Abbey marveled at its massive size. Jim looked at his watch and thought it was time to get Abbey over to her appointment, one that Jim had scheduled and refrained from speaking about.

"It makes all the other rockets look tiny!" Abbey exclaimed. Jim looked at his watch once more.

"Okay. We need to head to the parking lot. I have something to show you."

"What is it?" Abbey asked.

"You'll see. It's kind of a surprise."

Once inside Building Nine, he acquired two visitor passes and led Kelly and Abbey to a massive room with scale replicas of the modules on the International Space Station. The sound of cooling fans on computers and other machinery emitted a droning sound that filled the room. A few people walked around in blue flight suits with serious expressions on their faces. Focused and determined to complete their task, they moved about while paying little attention to Jim and his guests.

"Wow. What are these?" Abbey asked.

"These are replicas of the modules on the space station. I'll be spending a lot of time here for training." Jim pointed to the American module, a gray cylinder with stairs that led to the interior of the capsule. "This is the American section of the space station called Node One," Jim explained before he pointed to an outer door. "That is the airlock we use for spacewalks. Now what makes living in space a reality is the Russian Service Module," Jim said as he pointed it out.

Kelly spoke up and asked a question, "Do the U.S. and Russia work together on this project or independently?"

"Well, there are many countries involved with the ISS. Russia, Europe, Japan, the U.S. and Canada are the main ones, but there are many other countries that participate."

"China?" Abbey asked.

"Not China. They're trying to launch their own space station."

"Oh," Abbey said.

"Let's go inside the Russian Service Module, and I will show you a few things."

Jim guided Abbey and Kelly inside the narrow hallways of the module and showed them a wall with three laptops that were strapped down.

"We are in the aft end of the space station. These laptops are the commanding control computers for the entire space station. See how they are strapped down?" Jim asked. He looked at both Abbey and Kelly when he spoke.

"Yeah," Abbey answered.

"That's not because we're afraid of anyone taking them. Everything you see in here is exactly like the space station in orbit. If the computers weren't strapped down, they would just float in microgravity."

"Are these the exact same laptops?"

"They are. In fact, we don't have a central computer or server. The entire space station is run with laptops."

"Really?" Kelly asked.

"Yep. Amazing isn't it?" Jim said as he looked at his watch.

Throughout the tour, Kelly noticed Jim was in his element and seemed to be more talkative and had no problem interacting with her. The tour continued as they left Building 9 and walked to a nearby building that housed the Dexterous Robotics Laboratory, which was a long walk for Abbey. Bending down as he reached his arms behind him, Abbey hopped on Jim's back for a piggyback ride. Jim's solid frame carried her with no slack in his step. Once they were close, Jim set Abbey down, and they walked into the robotics lab.

"Follow me."

Jim saw his intended target, and Kelly and Abbey followed his eyes to a black man in a flight suit. Now old friends, Jim responded to Greg with a smile and a handshake.

"Wow. You sure clean up good. I didn't recognize you at first," Greg said. Jim felt where his beard used to be as he answered.

"Yeah, I'm still getting used to it."

"This must be Abbey," Greg said as he looked at her. Surprised to hear her name, she looked at Greg and noticed he was dressed in a flight suit with patches on his left arm.

"How do you know my name?" Abbey asked. Greg brought out a small stool on wheels and sat down. He looked at Abbey on her level.

"Jim and I have been talking about you lately."

"You have?"

"Yep. Abbey, I notice you have an artificial leg there," Greg said as he pointed, "How long have you had it?"

"I've had it for a few years," she responded. Jim leaned on a table nearby and watched them interact with each other.

"I was born with a weak leg. My muscles were underdeveloped and the bone structure was too weak from the knee down. So when I was very young, it was amputated."

"Really?"

"Yep," Greg said as he unzipped his right pant leg and rolled up the cuff in order to reveal his glorious prosthetic.

"Wow. That's amazing! Is that your prosthetic leg?" Abbey asked with eyes as big as quarters.

"You like it?" Greg asked.

"How does it work? Why is it spiraled?"

"Well, when I was your age I had a prosthetic just like yours."

"You did?" Abbey replied as she looked down at her own.

"Yep. And it was uncomfortable, and it didn't function very well."

"Mine is pretty uncomfortable."

"I bet. Well, now you can have one just like this."

"I can?" Abbey asked with a voice of pure excitement.

"But you have to work for it," Greg said, adding the caveat.

"What do I have to do?" Abbey asked, ready for anything.

Jim bent down on one knee and looked at Abbey.

"Greg here is gracious enough to teach you about his design and how he made it. Then, he will help you build yours."

"You mean I get to make my own?"

"Yep. Jim and I have worked it all out," Greg said.

"For one hour a day, you can come here, and Greg will guide you through what's necessary to make yours."

"I can't wait," Abbey said.

"Now it will take some time, several weeks or so. Are you up for it?" Greg asked.

"Yes!" Abbey said—with a smile.

Chapter 53

For almost a week, Kelly had been dropping off Abbey at the Dexterous Robotics Laboratory every day. The first two days, she stuck around while Greg and Abbey worked on a computer. After the third day, she left the campus and drove to the grocery store to stock up before she returned to get Abbey. Upon returning, she walked into the building and was greeted by Jim. Normally, Kelly had waited in the lobby for Abbey to walk out, but this time Jim was waiting for her dressed in a flight suit.

"Hey. I'm on a quick break. Abbey wants to show us something, so I thought I would come up and get you."

"Oh, okay." Kelly said. On the way back to the lab, to her surprise, he initiated a conversation.

"I haven't seen much of you or Abbey the past few days. I've been so busy and working late."

"I know. She falls asleep around ten."

"At least I get to see her in the mornings," Jim replied.

"Do you have any nights off? I could arrange for something we could all do."

"Yeah, I don't know. The schedule is pretty hectic. We are starting training in the pool soon. I should have you both come and watch."

"The pool?"

"Yep. Have you heard of the the Neutral Buoyancy Laboratory?"

"I think I've heard of that before."

"It's the largest indoor pool in the world. I'm sure you've seen pictures."

"Is that where astronauts train with full space suits underwater?"

"That's it. I'll see about getting you both inside. Shouldn't be a problem."

"Sounds like fun," Kelly said with a smile. She looked at Jim who was smiling back. It was a small conversation for Kelly, but a milestone in socializing with Jim. They walked into the lab and found Abbey and Greg as they looked at a computer screen.

"Hey, guys," Greg said standing up. "Glad you could make it," he continued. On the computer screen in front of Abbey was a wire frame design of the double-coil prosthetic. "Now, Abbey wants to show you what it looks like fully rendered," Greg said as he pointed to the mouse. Abbey maneuvered the mouse and clicked on a tab labeled *Render*. A loading bar appeared on the screen for a brief moment before showing a carbon fiber version complete with lighting and shading, making it look realistic.

"Wow. Abbey that is great," Kelly said.

"That's yours?" Jim asked.

"We designed it in the computer first," Abbey said.

"The software we are using is pretty complicated, takes years to even get the hang of it, so we have been working together, taking measurements of her leg and getting it right. Abbey has a few of the commands down already," Greg said. He nodded at Abbey as he spoke, "Tell them what comes next."

"We send the plans for the armature to a company with a C and C machine." Abbey said.

"Okay," Jim acknowledged. Abbey continued,

"Then we coat the armature in carbon fiber resin."

"What type of resin?" Greg prompts.

"There are two types that are used. Polyester and Epoxy. We will use epoxy," Abbey said, reciting what she had learned.

"And why is that?" Greg asked, as if giving a quiz.

"Epoxy is very flexible."

"And where would you be most likely to find this type of carbon fiber in use?"

"Formula one racing."

"Wow," Jim said, pleased that she had learned a lot.

"That's great, Abbey," Kelly added.

Jim asked Abbey many questions, most of which she could answer. Feeling intelligent and important, she enjoyed the attention and talked about the prosthetic as they walked out of the Dexterous Robotics Laboratory.

"Greg said in a couple weeks I will be able to try it on."

"Will you retire your old prosthetic? Never look back?"

"Yes. I can't wait," Abbey said as she tapped on the now substandard prosthetic.

After dinner that night, Kelly sat with Abbey and went over her lines for the school play while Jim worked on campus.

"Wendy, you can't leave. You should stay forever," Abbey read from the page while putting inflection in her voice.

"But Peter, we were going to leave in the morning," Kelly read the lines of Wendy in a monotone voice, making Abbey's acting better by comparison.

"Fine. You can all leave, but you should know that if you do, you can never return. When you leave Neverland, you grow up. I will never leave for good. I don't ever want to grow up."

Close to midnight when Jim got home, he found Kelly asleep on the couch. On the floor next to the couch was the script for Peter Pan. Being careful not to wake her up, he picked up the script that was wrinkled from being folded and held so much. Some of Peter Pan's lines were marked with an X. Some weren't. Jim looked over the script and then heard Kelly's voice.

"What time is it?" Kelly asked as she woke up.

"Almost midnight."

"I guess I fell asleep."

"Why do some of these lines have an X by them?"

"Those are the ones that she has memorized."

"Oh," Jim said, holding up the stapled script, "All these?" he said pointing.

"Yeah, she's doing really well."

"Well, thanks to you. I wish I could be here to help," Jim said as he laid the script back on the couch. He walked into the kitchen and took a bottle of water out of the fridge. Kelly got up and stretched.

"You doing okay with Abbey?" Jim asked.

"Yeah, she's doing great. She won't stop talking about her prosthetic leg. She's excited about the school play, and keeps asking to go swimming."

"She sounds busier than I am," Jim said after he took a swig of his water. Kelly walked over toward Jim and crossed her arms as she looked at the floor.

"You know, she talks about you," Kelly said as if she was revealing a secret.

"She does?"

"She asked me about your birthday. So we looked up your bio on NASA's website, but it didn't list when you were born. So then she asked if we could call Mallory."

"Mallory?"

"Yeah, we called the office where she works, and Abbey talked to her for ten minutes or so."

"What'd they talk about?"

"When your birthday is and how old you are and what kind of things you like."

"What? Why?"

"We started talking about birthdays at the grocery store when we saw a woman carrying a huge birthday cake. She wanted to know when your birthday was. She mentioned something about buying you a gift."

"A gift? What is it?" Jim asked. Kelly laughed quietly and smiled.

"Well, I am not going to tell you."

"Did you talk to Mallory, too?"

"No, just Abbey, but she did take a few notes," Kelly said as she reached over and placed her finger on a piece of paper Abbey accidentally left behind. She slid the paper across the counter and showed Jim. He picked it up and read Abbey's handwriting.

Jim's Birthday is September 3rd

He is 48 years old

Jim loved baseball as a kid

Always talked about test pilots and rockets

Jim looked over the notes that had been scribbled down and set them back on the counter where Kelly had found it.

"I just thought I would tell you. Something that I thought you would want to know," Kelly said as she strolled over to the stairs. "Goodnight."

"Kelly?" Jim said. It was the first time he had used her name. She stopped and turned around. "Thanks," he said. "Thanks for telling me." Jim nodded. Kelly gave him a slight smile.

"You're welcome."

Chapter 54

Jim sat in a room that resembled a smaller version of a college lecture hall with stadium seating. Dave Thomas stood next to a projection of a cross-section of the ISS. He highlighted certain modules with a laser pointer. He casually looked over at Jim who was in the middle of eleven people scattered around him.

"Commander Anatoly Grechko and Science Officer Benjamin Akers will operate the birthing mechanism which is the latch point shown here on the Zarya module. Once in position, Mission Specialist Jim Mayfield will remove the damaged coupling and replace it by retrofitting the new coupling. This could take many hours to complete."

Those in the stadium seats asked questions about the new coupling and the retrofitting process for which Dave turned to Jim for answers. While his explanations tended to be long, Jim gave thorough and detailed responses. If there were any doubts about Jim's understanding of the mission, all concerns were quickly erased.

Dave Thomas turned the meeting over to the EVA task group leader who oversaw the training at the Neutral Buoyancy Laboratory. Beez Steinway, 45, wearing a blue button-up shirt and a tie, walked up to the front of the room. Speaking with a German accent, he led the meeting beginning with Jim Mayfield.

"I congratulate Mr. Thomas for securing one of the most qualified men for this mission," he stated in a display of regard for Jim. "I am looking forward to working with you, Jim. It is an honor."

"Thank you," Jim replied.

"I will work you like a dog. By the time you make it to the ISS you will be able to repair the coupling in your sleep," Beez stated. Laughter briefly filled the room and then it was down to business. The meeting lasted over an hour and a half, ending with the training schedule for the Neutral Buoyancy Laboratory that would start the following week.

On his way back to Building 9, Jim thought about Abbey and how he would like for her to come see him work underwater. He checked his watch. Abbey was nearby with Greg. With enough time before he had to return, he decided to pay them a visit. He walked to the Dexterous Robotics Laboratory and made his way to where Greg worked.

Taking quiet steps, Jim walked through the room past workbenches and other busy people with headphones stuck in their ears. At the back of the room, he could hear Abbey's voice. A few more steps and he could see her facing a computer screen. Greg was holding up a spiral armature. Next to him was a cardboard box with a mailing label and packing materials that protruded from inside. Abbey watched as Greg held it up next to the computer screen.

"This is one of my favorite parts. We created this in here," Greg explained as he pointed to the screen, "and it became a reality here." He held up the metal armature, "Here, take these," Greg said as he handed her an electronic blade micrometer. "Now measure the thickness of the armature at the top like I showed you," Greg asked. Jim decided he didn't want to interrupt and slipped away quietly.

Over the next few days when he would come home at night, he sometimes found Kelly on the couch and sometimes she would be asleep upstairs. Jim would find the script for the school play and look at the lines marked with an X to see how Abbey was doing. He flipped through the pages and saw that she had only about six lines left to memorize. He nodded in approval and set the script down and headed toward his room.

The next day, Jim woke up, ran three miles and took a shower before Abbey got up. When she finally came downstairs, Jim was waiting with a bowl of grapes, sliced kiwi, and oatmeal.

"You're looking sluggish this morning. No shower?" Jim asked.

"We were up late playing card games."

"What were you playing?"

"Hand and Foot."

"What's that?"

"A card game that Kelly taught me. It's fun."

"Well, maybe you can teach me sometime."

"When are you going to be here next?"

"I don't know. I thought you guys could come see me today. I'm headed for the pool."

"Swimming?" Abbey said in excitement, the first lively expression since she woke up.

"Not exactly," Jim said with a smile.

After lunch Kelly drove into the parking lot of the Sonny Carter Training Facility and was greeted by Dr. Stanton.

"Hey guys, remember me?" Stanton said with a smile. "Jim asked me to be your tour guide today."

Once they signed in and visitor badges were distributed, Stanton made small talk while he walked them through the doors to the pool deck.

"Abbey, what do you call Jim? Just Jim or do you call him something else?"

"Just Jim," Abbey said with a smile.

"I couldn't believe it when I saw him. He cleans up nice."

"I didn't recognize him at first," Abbey said.

"Me either. He looks a lot younger."

Kelly and Abbey followed Stanton as they walked away from the front entrance and through two separate doors before smelling the faint aroma of chlorine. They followed him up a large ramp and finally entered the pool deck, overlooking a clear body of blue water in the shape of a rectangle. Looking down into the water, it appeared that giant, robotic insects were lurking at the bottom. Stanton noticed Abbey as she looked intently toward the bottom and anticipated her question.

"He's down there now. Hard to tell from up here though."

"How will we see him?" Abbey asked.

"From up there." Stanton pointed to what appeared to be a press box at a baseball stadium. The long, white structure nearly spanned the length of the pool, but instead of overlooking a baseball diamond, the large windows looked down over the pool.

"There are cameras in the water so they can see what's going on, so we will be able to watch what Jim is doing on the displays up in the box," Stanton explained as they headed toward another door and into a stairwell.

Beez sat at the controls and looked up at a wall of large monitors as he watched Jim drill into a coupling ring. Jim had told the guys in the control room that his daughter would be coming by and to help her with any questions.

"Hey, Abbey," Beez said from his seat at the main console.

"Hello, Abbey," a woman said as she turned away from a large monitor while wearing headphones. Several other people in the room welcomed her while she smiled from ear to ear and tried to keep up with all their greetings.

"Hello," Abbey said, still taken aback.

In his thick German accent, Beez stood up and approached Abbey as he spoke with a smile.

"Abbey, my name is Beez, and I am the EVA task group leader."

"Nice to meet you," Abbey said. Beez leaned over and pulled up a chair next to his. The rest of the room acknowledged Kelly who stood nearby and watched Abbey interact with Beez.

"Now, I want you both to look up at the main monitor there," Beez said as he pointed to a large display. One of the many cameras in the pool showed Jim in a full space suit working on the exterior of the international space station. "That is Jim right there," Beez explained. "Take a seat in my chair," he said as he patted the seat of his captain's chair. As Abbey sat in front of the controls, Beez took his headset off and placed it on Abbey's head and adjusted the microphone in front of her mouth.

"Here. See this button?"

"Yeah," Abbey said.

"Press it and you can talk to Jim," Beez explained. Abbey pressed the button.

"Hey Jim," Abbey said. With all the attention on her, she didn't know what else to say.

"Hey, Abbey, glad you could make it." His voice could be heard throughout the entire control room and inside each headset. "Beez, are we at a place we can break for a bit, and I can show Abbey a few things?" Jim asked. Beez leaned over to another control panel, and pushed a button for the microphone,

"Sure thing, Jim."

"Alright. Abbey, you see the divers swimming all around me here?" Following Jim's lead, Beez used the controls in front of him to zoom out from Jim's position. Suddenly, Abbey could see three divers hovering near Jim.

"Yeah."

"These are the safety divers. They assist us with many aspects of our task. Today they are watching over me while I train for a spacewalk that requires me to repair a module on the space station," Jim explained. "Beez, can you bring up the camera for Abbey that shows the coupling ring?"

Beez made a quick adjustment that showed a different camera angle.

"Okay Abbey, the reason I am even going up to the ISS is to repair this metal ring here. This is a mock-up, but the one in space was damaged by orbital debris," Jim explained.

"Okay," Abbey said.

"Right now, the module is shut off from the rest of the space station. They can't use it until it's repaired."

"Can it be repaired from the inside?" Abbey asked.

"Sometimes, but this module has severe damage and requires a full replacement which is why I'm in here. We train for all spacewalks in this pool which gives us a general idea of what we are facing in terms of difficulty."

"Okay," Abbey responded.

"We're going to resume the procedure, so why don't you and Kelly stick around and watch."

"Okay," Abbey said with excitement. Sitting over to the side, Beez handled the controls and watched Jim for nearly an hour as he removed the coupling ring. Beez and Jim communicated back and forth through each step with many people sitting in the control room advising both of them.

Before Jim was taken out of the water, he and Abbey spoke.

"Do you remember the suit I showed up in at your school?"

"Uh huh," Abbey responded.

"Well, that one wasn't real. I couldn't use it in space. The one I am wearing now, I could wear it in space. It's just like the one I will be using in November."

"I like it."

"While it protects me, the downside is that on Earth, it is very heavy. It weighs almost three hundred pounds."

"Wow," Abbey exclaimed.

"They have to use a crane to get me out and even then it takes a while. If you all want to watch, Stanton will take you by the pool, and you guys can hang out and I'll see you when I finally get out of the suit. Okay?"

"Okay," Abbey said.

Sitting on a small section of bleachers near the pool, Kelly and Abbey talked about watching Jim on the monitors in the control room while Stanton looked at his cell phone. After about twenty minutes, the massive yellow arm located on the side of the pool began to move.

Abbey and Kelly watched as the bright yellow crane positioned its arm over the water with a mechanical hum and whirring noise as it lowered the cable. Once the safety divers attached the hook to the platform, the whine of the motor now sounded strained as the cable pulled

Jim to the surface. At first they could see the top of his helmet crest the water. Slowly, Jim rose up as the water fell off his suit, seemingly in slow motion. He appeared to Abbey and Kelly as both heroic and valiant. Once the crane had brought him out of the water and over to the side of the pool, a small team of people gathered to help Jim out of the suit. The upper portion of the suit was locked onto a metal bar while shiny metal latches were unlocked and released by the small team in the same fashion a NASCAR pit crew serviced a stock car. Eventually, Jim wriggled out of the spacesuit and once he was free of the torso, he sat down on a white mat where two staff members removed his EMU pants.

Once Jim was freed, he sat in a chair while a physician looked Jim over. Without saying a word, the doctor removed a penlight from inside his coat pocket and clicked it, before he shone the light in Jim's eyes. Next he listened to his heart with a stethoscope. When he was finally cleared, he stood up and walked over to see Abbey.

"That was awesome."

"I thought you would like that," Jim said.

"How long were you under water?" Kelly asked. Jim looked at the clock on the wall.

"Well, I went under before nine this morning, and it's twelve-fifteen, so a little over three hours. We worked on the robotic arm at first and then moved over to the panel repair."

"Where do you go now?"

"Briefing room. We'll be there until one thirty or so and then it's back to Building 9 for an intervehicular training class. We break for dinner and are back at it by six."

"Wow. That's got to be strenuous," Kelly said.

"We joke that we have to be in shape for training and not the actual missions."

"Do you have to go now?" Abbey asked.

"Well, I thought we would jump over to see Greg. I want to see what you've been up to."

"We'll have to go to the engineering building."

"What? Why?" Jim asked.

"We've been applying the carbon fiber. It's in a room with a vent."

Once Jim changed clothes, they all walked over to the Engineering and Technology building. Inside, Abbey led the way to a room labeled, *Application Workroom*. She turned the doorknob only to find it was locked. Standing on her tiptoe, she looked inside and saw her prosthetic standing up with the aid of a clamp.

"Doors locked, but you can see it there. In the corner," Abbey said. Both Jim and Kelly looked inside.

"Is it finished?" Jim asked.

"No. We still have many more coatings to go. Greg ordered the shoe insert and he still has to take a cast of my leg," Abbey explained. Jim could see that the amount of work involved in this had taken Greg a long time. Knowing what Greg's schedule was like, his respect for him grew even more.

After returning to the Sonny Carter Training Facility, they parted ways after Abbey hugged Jim goodbye, a gesture that caught Jim off guard. She initiated it without a second thought. Her arms wrapped around his neck and squeezed tightly.

While on his way to the briefing room, Jim walked a little faster, hands in his pockets, and felt better than he had in years.

Chapter 55

When the day finally came for Abbey to try on her new prosthetic leg, Jim had made adjustments in his schedule to take part in the trial fitting. After breakfast, Jim, Abbey, and Kelly were ready to head over to the Gilruth Center. Before they left the house, Jim had grabbed a suspicious box off the counter. Abbey didn't ask about it until they were on the road.

"What's in the box?" Abbey asked.

"I can't tell you."

"Why?"

"It's a surprise. You're not supposed to see it until later."

The Gilruth Center is a full-service activities center at NASA that includes weight rooms, baseball fields, running tracks, and gymnasiums. One of the gyms with a full-size basketball court was very familiar to Greg as he spent many of his off-nights there playing pick-up games. Knowing that the court would be clear, Greg asked for Abbey to meet him there for the trial fitting.

Once inside, they walked over to a row of metal bleachers and sat down. Jim set the box beside him.

"Are you getting excited?" Jim asked.

"Yep. I can't wait to take this off for good."

"What did you learn when making the prosthetic?" Kelly asked. Abbey talked about the carbon fiber and the process of applying each coat and almost finished her explanation when Greg walked in carrying a metal briefcase and a small backpack.

"Hey, Greg!" Abbey shouted across the basketball court. Greg shouted back.

"You ready for the big day?" he asked as he walked over to the bleachers. "Here, open this up," Greg said as he set the metal briefcase on the bleacher seat with a *clunk*. Abbey, unlatched the metal hinges and opened the top, exposing the prosthetic leg inside. The interior was mostly black foam except for the portion cut out so that the prosthetic fit firmly and securely inside. Seeing the prosthetic with the hinge at the top and the bottom made it look real and completed, ready to wear.

"Wow. It looks so good," Abbey said. Her eyes glanced over the inside of the case where there was a section cut out. In place of the foam was a black, plastic shaped foot. "Is this the foot?"

"Sure is. Take it out and get a good look at it," Greg said. Abbey took it in her hands and felt the weight of it.

"Wow! It's so light!" Abbey said.

"Yeah. That part I didn't design. That came from a company in California that makes spring assisted prosthetic feet. Push where the toes are," Greg instructed. Instead of individual toes, a black bar at the end of the foot acted like one single toe. When Abbey pushed on it, the bar flexed. Greg looked at Jim.

"Did you bring them?"

"Yep, should I give them to her now?"

"Sure."

Kelly watched as Jim brought out the box and handed it to Abbey. Excited to know what was inside, she quickly opened the top flap and exposed a brand new pair of running shoes, sky blue and gray in color.

"Wow. I get to wear these?"

"Those look great," Greg said.

"Kelly picked them out," Jim said.

"I love them," Abbey said as she took them out of the box.

"Well, let's get the shoes on you, and put your new prosthetic on," Greg said ready to start the show. While Abbey laced up her shoes, Greg set up a video camera.

"You recording this?" Jim asked.

"Yep. This design is going to the University of Washington prosthetics and orthotics department. They want video of this fitting."

"Did you sell your design?" Jim asked.

"I didn't. I gave it to them. After clinic they are going to use this design in a government prosthetic program for veterans."

"You're just giving it away?" Kelly asked while Abbey put her leg in the comfortable thigh socket.

"Yeah, the university will patent it and everything, so no one else can make any money off of it," Greg said as he put the camera on the tripod. "But they will improve upon this design someday, and I will get the benefit of that. So will any other person with this type of prosthetic. Plus, they are going to call it the GT Helix. GT for Greg Thompson," he said with a prideful smile.

Once the camera was set up and Abbey had put on her shoe, Greg locked in the prosthetic to her thigh, sounding like a gun chambering a bullet. Fitted and laced up, it was finally time for her to take her first step.

"Abbey," Greg said before she stood up. She looked at Greg and hung on every word. "It might take a little time to get used to this. Don't get discouraged and if you feel like you need to go back to your old prosthetic for a while, that's fine. I had to use my old one for a while before I got used to this one. Okay?"

"Okay."

Greg motioned for Abbey to stand. With a hint of hesitation, Abbey made the move to stand up. Looking down, her right leg looked like a futuristic marvel. Putting her hands out to the side for balance, she took a step. Before, Abbey had to seemingly drag her prosthetic behind her. This one sprung back into form, ready for the next step. One step, two steps, and finally three. The sound of each step was much different. In fact, there was hardly any sound at all. The *step-clonk* was gone.

Abbey was still and had stopped moving. She turned and looked at Greg.

"You have the whole gym to walk around. See if you get a feel for it. Take your time," Greg said. Abbey took several more steps, trying to be careful and not fall. With the determination of making it to the other side of the court, she headed in that direction only stopping once to gain her balance. Jim watched as she turned around and started to head back. Even though she was still getting the hang of it, she already looked better. Her stride looked more natural than before. It seemed that with practice, she could someday walk with the same stability as Greg.

With a look of focus and concentration, Abbey walked around the gym while Greg hollered out cues from time to time.

"Take a longer stride. See how that feels," and, "Don't pick up the leg with your thigh. Try to let it return back to you."

After ten minutes, Jim stood up and walked over to Abbey.

"What's wrong?" Abbey asked.

"Nothing," Jim smiled. "I just want to walk with you. You're doing good."

"It feels much different than I thought it would. But I like it."

"You are moving along just fine. No doubt you'll get the hang of it."

While Jim and Abbey walked and talked, Greg continued recording with the camera.

"How long have you known Jim?" Greg asked.

"About a month," Kelly responded. Greg looked at Kelly, confused. "I was staying at his inn and it turned into me watching Abbey while he is training for the mission."

"I see," Greg answered. "Dr. Stanton told me that he just adopted Abbey. Is that right?"

"Yeah, not too long ago, she was living with two alcoholics and barely eating. Wasn't a good situation."

"Looks like she's doing good now," Greg said with a smile as he nodded in her direction. When Abbey returned from walking all the way around with Jim, Greg looked at her prosthetic.

"Now, look at the hinge at the top and the one at the bottom. They both have a spring return, as does the toe bar. Remember the toes that flex? The toe bar?" Greg asked. Abbey nodded her head. "That toe bar is a key element to help you run. Now, if you feel up to it, try to jog. Not a full-out run, but an easy jog. If you're not comfortable, you can try later."

"Run? I can run?"

"Of course," Greg said. "I play basketball here on this very court. I run up and down with no problem."

Abbey looked down at her leg as she turned toward the open floor of the gym. With plenty of room, she decided she would try. Taking normal steps at first, she built up to long strides. Abbey's weight was forward enough that when she tried to stop, she fell onto the floor with a *thunk*. Jim got up and before he could start toward her, he felt Greg's hand grabbing his arm.

"Hang on," Greg whispered. Jim watched as Abbey collected herself and stood up. Jim sat back down and watched. "Try again Abbey. You're doing good," Greg said.

Once again, Abbey set out by taking regular steps, followed by long strides. With ten long strides behind her, she was in a full out jogging motion. Just as she began to get the slightest bit of confidence, she started to cry while she was jogging. Audible sounds of sobbing and quick draws of breath accompanied each stride, while tears streamed down her cheeks. When she stopped and fell to the floor, Jim leapt up and ran to her side. Abbey was kneeling on the floor as she cupped her face in her hands.

"Abbey? What's wrong?" Jim asked. She sat upright, and Jim placed his hand on her shoulders. With a soft tone of voice, "What's the matter?" he asked again. With tears filling her eyes, she uncovered her face.

"I never thought I would be able to run again," Abbey said. She leaned into his shoulder and cried. Jim could feel her tears through his shirt. He reached his hands around Abbey and held onto her as she sobbed. Jim looked over at Greg who had heard Abbey's statement— Greg nodded and hung his head.

Chapter 56

Jim had spent weeks in class and in training, both in Building 9 and in the pool. The time was fast approaching when he would wake up and Abbey would no longer be waiting for him at breakfast. School in Bear Creek was starting in a few days.

Both Kelly and Abbey had begun packing on Thursday after Jim left for work. Having arranged to be home for dinner, Jim was greeted at the front door by luggage next to the staircase. Looking up toward the kitchen, he saw bags from a local restaurant still packed with food. The voices of Kelly and Abbey come from upstairs followed by giggles and sporadic laughter.

"Hello?" Jim said, hollering up the stairs.

"Don't look in the refrigerator," Abbey hollered back. Confused, he responded, "Okay," and walked into his room.

Abbey and Kelly came downstairs just as Jim emerged from his room after changing clothes. The looks on their faces were suspicious.

"What are you two up to?" Jim asked.

"We'll show you after dinner," Abbey said while maintaining her suspicious look. At the counter, they all grabbed a barstool and took the plastic containers out of the bags. Inside were mandarin oranges and almond salads drizzled with balsamic vinegar. Instead of talking about the inevitable departure, they focused on the school play. While Jim and Kelly read from the script, Abbey said her lines from memory.

"These are the Lost Boys. They hunt, swim and eat all day." Abbey recited the lines nearly word for word. Jim read the part of John Darling, while Kelly read the part of Wendy.

"Hunt? What do they hunt, Peter?" Kelly read aloud.

"Why they hunt bears and sometimes tigers."

"There aren't any bears or tigers around here, are there?" Jim recited. Abbey was silent for a moment as she thought of her next line.

"Oh no, if there were, Tinkerbell would tell us," Abbey said.

After dinner, they set the scripts down and the suspicious expressions appeared once again. He watched with curiosity as Kelly and Abbey stood around the refrigerator and both reached inside. After a few minutes, they removed a birthday cake with candles and carefully walked it over to the counter. After Kelly and Abbey sang "Happy Birthday," Jim blew out the candles while Abbey distributed party hats.

"I haven't had a birthday party in over ten years."

"We know it isn't quite your birthday, but we wanted to celebrate it since we wouldn't be here," Kelly said.

"Better early than never," Abbey added. "We've got presents, too."

"You do?" Jim asked. Abbey walked over to the laundry room and removed two presents wrapped in colorful paper. She handed them to Jim with a smile.

"Open the small one first," Abbey said. Jim set the larger present aside and began picking at the wrapping of a small box. The box was cubed and felt solid, but very light for its size.

"This was Kelly's idea, but we both made it."

"You made it?" Once the wrapping started to come off, he could tell that the box was black with a removable top. Jim opened the box and inside looked to be a bracelet.

A bracelet? I've never worn a bracelet. Ever. Jim thought.

He took it out of the box. A half circle of metal with leather straps completed the other half. The metal was scratched and old, looking more like a bracket to a mechanical device than a bracelet. While inspecting it closely, he noticed an engraving.

"What's this?" Jim said as he looked at a heart and triangle design. *Is this a scientology symbol? Why would I wear this?*

"That piece of metal came from my old prosthetic leg. Kelly and I removed it, took it to the mall and had that design engraved into it."

"What does it mean? A heart and a triangle?" Jim asked.

"It's the symbol for adoption," answered Kelly.

"We hope you don't think it's weird," Abbey said. Jim was still looking it over and appeared stunned.

"Do you like it?" Kelly asked. Jim looked up after he closely inspected the bracelet.

"I didn't know what to think at first. It kind of hit me all of a sudden. The more I think about it, the more I like it. Thank you." Jim exhaled a deep breath. "It's very thoughtful."

Abbey reached for the bigger box and set it in front of Jim as he put the bracelet on his left hand. Just now coming to the realization that all attention was on him, he hurried to open the next present.

Within seconds the box was unwrapped, revealing a model airplane. For nearly a full minute, he was twelve again. The airplane was a Bell X-1 model. The same model Captain Chuck Yeager broke the sound barrier with. The X-1 was a rocket plane and was also the seed that was planted in Jim's mind—the idea of becoming an aeronautical engineer or an astronaut. His parents had heard enough of Chuck Yeager by the time Jim was thirteen. He had read all the books and watched every TV interview. Jim was hooked on jet airplanes and astronauts.

"Do you like it?" Abbey asked. Jim snapped back from being a kid to holding the box of a model X-1 hobby kit.

"I do. I love it. You have no idea," he said as he looked at the model airplane and the bracelet. "I never expected this. I don't know what to say. Thank you both. Really, I can't thank you enough." Jim set the model airplane on the counter and leaned toward Abbey and gave her a hug, squeezing her tightly.

"I called Mallory," Abbey said.

"You did?"

"Yep. I asked her what you liked. She told me that when you were a kid, you liked test pilots and airplanes."

"Why did you pick this model?" Jim asked as he pointed at the box.

"Mallory said you wouldn't shut up about the X-1 when you were a kid. She also said she knows more about it than she wants to," Abbey replied. Jim laughed.

"She's probably right. Do you know anything about this airplane?" Jim asked as he pointed to the bright orange airplane on the box.

"No."

"This airplane is really a rocket. It was piloted by a man named Chuck Yeager and one of the many interesting facts about this great man and his historic flight was that two days before he flew this plane, he broke his ribs just before breaking the sound barrier."

"He did? How?"

"He fell off a horse."

"Really?"

"Yep. He didn't tell anyone except for a friend and his wife. If he had let on to the Air Force that he was injured, they might have replaced him."

"And he still did it?"

"He did."

"Wow," Abbey said.

"I've never heard that story," said Kelly.

"We'll have to look it up," Abbey said as she looked at the box again, now thinking differently of the plane.

Kelly stood up like she had somewhere to go.

"I have a gift for you as well," she said to Jim.

"You do?" Jim asked.

"Well, sort of. Abbey and I have to go upstairs for a moment. We'll be right back." While Kelly and Abbey went upstairs, Jim looked at his bracelet.

It wasn't feminine, but it wasn't masculine either. It didn't matter, he thought. It was true what he said, the more he thought about it, the more he liked it. While he appreciated the gifts bestowed upon him, he smiled at the thought of Abbey making the effort to learn more about him though Mallory. He could feel that Abbey genuinely cared for him through her efforts. In mid-thought, Kelly shouted down the hallway.

"Okay. Close your eyes and face the back porch."

Jim spun around on his barstool and closed his eyes.

"Okay, they're closed," he shouted. He could hear the rustling and whispering as they came downstairs but didn't know what they were doing.

"Okay, turn around and open your eyes," Kelly said.

When Jim turned around, he saw Abbey wearing green tights, a green shirt cinched at the waist with a thin belt that held a small, plastic dagger. On her feet were brown pointed ankle boots. On her head was a green woodsmen's cap that featured a long red feather. Abbey stood smiling in front of Jim.

"Look at that. It's Peter Pan," Jim said as he stood up and admired the costume. The detail on the costume looked to be well thought-out and appeared authentic, as if Abbey was somehow wearing the original outfit worn by Peter Pan himself.

"This is incredible. Where'd you get it?" Jim asked. Kelly spoke up.

"I knew she needed a costume, and I didn't want you to have to worry about buying one or renting one so I made this."

"You made this?" Jim asked.

"I did. Mostly at night. Well, except for the peasant shoes, we found those shopping while you were at the barber shop."

"Wow," Jim said.

"My mother taught me to sew."

"Well you did a great job. It's amazing. It's looks so real."

Jim looked down at Abbey's legs covered in green tights and took notice that it was difficult to tell she even wore a prosthetic. Genuinely pleased with the way she looked, Jim jumped at Kelly's question.

"How about a dress rehearsal?" Kelly asked.

After Jim moved a few pieces of furniture, Abbey took to the makeshift stage. Kelly began the play with Wendy Darling's line.

"Who's there? Is someone by the window?" Kelly said. Abbey delivered her lines on cue, nearly word for word. They laughed as they pretended to fly around the room during the scenes in which Abbey would be attached to the harness. They pretended to fight with swords and used a flashlight to depict Tinkerbell in the scenes that Abbey spoke to her. While Jim recited the lines from the page, he couldn't help but feel a bit of the coming sadness brought on by Abbey's impending departure.

Chapter 57

Returning to school at Bear Creek Elementary was hard at first, but the lingering "cool factor" of living with an astronaut made for an easier return. Also contributing to the ease of her first day of school was the carbon fiber, prosthetic leg with the futuristic helix design. Classmates touched and stared at her appendage, spouting off words like "Bionic" and "Super strength".

While Abbey was adjusting smoothly, Jim was in Houston fifteen feet below water in a space suit retrofitting the new coupling ring on the module for the tenth time. When he got home late at night, he missed looking over at the couch, thumbing through the script to see how far Abbey had gotten in memorizing her lines. Video conferencing with Abbey helped alleviate missing her, but he still felt alone when he came back to an empty house. On the mornings when Jim ran, he would take his time getting in and out of the shower since breakfast was only for one. After spending over ten years by himself at the inn, he thought it wouldn't be a problem being alone once again. Instead he felt an emptiness he hadn't felt in a long time.

Spending twelve hours a day in training didn't leave much time for anything else. Eventually the days flew by, and before Jim realized it, the first week of October was approaching. The launch date was only a few weeks away. After they had made plans for Kelly and Abbey to fly to Houston for fall break, Jim had to call with bad news.

"Hey. I didn't think I would hear from you until later tonight," Abbey said as she sat in front of the computer.

"I have something to tell you. Actually, can you get Kelly in there with you?"

"Sure, hang on," Abbey said as she walked out of view from the camera. Momentarily, she came back with Kelly at her side. As they both sat down, Jim began.

"So, they have moved our flight to Russia up an entire week. We were given an additional training schedule to complete over there. I'm sorry, but I have to leave the states just as your fall break begins," Jim explained.

"So we're not going to Houston?" Abbey said in a disappointed tone.

"No. I'm sorry."

"So if we're on our own, we just need to find something fun to do," Kelly said, trying to save Abbey's fall break.

"Right," Jim said. "I want you two to find somewhere to go or something to do, and then we'll talk about it," Jim said. Abbey looked at the camera and nodded her head.

"Okay," Abbey said before pausing. "I choose Russia," she added with dead-set eyes. Kelly smiled.

"That would be great, but you don't even have a passport yet, and flying to Russia is a little expensive."

"I thought I was gonna get to see you."

"Well, just think, in six weeks you won't be able to get rid of me until you go to college." Abbey and Kelly laughed. Ideas were thrown around as to what Abbey could do for fall break. Toward the end of the conversation, Jim surprised Kelly when he asked Abbey a simple question.

"Abbey? Would you mind going out in the lobby, so I can speak with Kelly for a moment?"

"Okay."

Jim watched as Abbey turned around and walked smoothly without the *step, clonk* and closed the door behind her. Never knowing what to expect, Kelly readied herself like an employee meeting with the CEO.

"Hey."

"Hello," Kelly responded.

"I wanted to ask you about your plans for when I return. Do you know what you're going to do?"

"I don't. So far I haven't been very good at making any plans."

"Well, something I didn't think about when I asked you to watch over Abbey is that she would become so attached to you. I suppose I just thought that you would just leave, and we'd never hear from you again," Jim explained. Kelly nodded and took in a deep breath. Jim continued, "Now, I suppose that you've become somewhat attached to Abbey, as well, and you would rather not leave her behind. Am I right?"

Kelly started to tear up, but held back and focused on her answer.

"I have. I thought that maybe we could keep in touch or email or something."

"Do you think you could find a job in Bear Creek? Or even in Wilkes-Barre? You could try looking around Wilkes-Barre," Jim suggested.

"I could do that."

"And then you would have a place to stay, as well."

"So, instead of leaving Bear Creek, I could stay…" Kelly cleared her throat before she finished her sentence, "…at the inn?"

"Look, I know you've been through a lot, but I don't want you just running off to nowhere. You need to figure out what you want to do, and I don't want you being rushed into anything," Jim explained. The tears she tried to hold back could no longer be contained. Wiping away the streams, she continued to listen to Jim. "For now, I want you to look for employment, so see what you can find, and count on a place to stay at the inn. And go ahead and move into the room next to Abbey. No need to remain in the handicapped room. Okay?"

Later that night while lying in bed, she replayed the conversation in her mind. It felt to Kelly as if the hand of an older brother rested on her shoulder. As if someone was watching out for her wellbeing, a feeling she hadn't felt since Adam. It wasn't stress keeping her awake, instead it was the feeling of belonging somewhere and the anticipation of a clear path to a new life.

Chapter 58

"I had three things that were on my list," Jerry said while sitting in the cockpit of a Gulfstream G550.

"Just three?" Tom asked.

"Well, three things that were immediate disqualifiers."

"So if a girl had one of these three things, you were out."

"Right."

"What were they?"

"The first one was, if she loved horses."

"What? Horses? What do you mean?"

"Well if a girl I was dating loved horses enough to have figurines in her room, she was gone."

"Wait. Just horse figurines?"

"Well, if she liked to ride horses or owned a horse, it was a deal breaker."

"Okay, weird. What else?"

"If she drove a sports car that was a deal breaker."

"Why?"

"Well, if she wanted a sports car, she would cost too much in the long run. Tastes are too expensive. No, thanks."

"That makes more sense than the horse thing."

"My third was if she ever read a book, and then wanted to tell me about it, that would end the relationship right there."

"That is weirdly specific."

"It's my list."

"I always hated it when a girl would have a dream at night and then want to tell you about it."

"Oh, I know. Who cares right? It doesn't mean anything. It's a stupid dream. Keep it to yourself."

"I used to have a reoccurring dream about Abraham Lincoln."

"Really? What was that about?"

"I don't know, but every time I went to start my car, it wouldn't start."

"How does that have anything to do with Lincoln?"

"He was sabotaging my car. Something about him getting under my car and causing problems."

"See, that's weird. No way he could fit under your car."

The clanging of men's dress shoes smacked the metal steps of the ladder going up into the jet. Dave Thomas entered the cabin followed by Frank Navasky and then Mike McCara. Outside the plane, rugged men with thick biceps loaded the underbelly of the plane with large suitcases.

Tom and Jerry watched as several other officials from NASA board the plane, but no sign of Jim Mayfield. Tom listened to Dave and Frank talking about the press conference and the mission.

"Is this thing a big deal? They're talking about a press conference," Tom said.

"I don't know. When is going into space not a big deal?" Jerry responded.

"Seems like people don't care anymore."

Two large gentlemen that spoke to each other in Russian boarded the plane wearing jeans and button-up dress shirts. They walked to the rear of the plane and took their seats.

Chapter 58

Chapter 58

"Now who are they?" Jerry asked.

"Russians."

"Well, I know they're Russian. Look at the passenger list," Jerry demanded. Tom grabbed a clipboard and looked at two names on the list of Russian decent.

"Looks like Yuri something and Oleg, I think. I can't read these names. Am I saying it right? Oh leg?" Tom asked.

"Who knows? Sounds all the same to me. Oh, here comes Jim. Look at him. All cleaned up."

"You gonna say something to him?" Tom asked.

Jim walked up the steps and into the cabin.

"Hey, Jim," Jerry said.

"Fellas," Jim nodded as he walked back to his seat. Jerry slapped Tom on the shoulder.

"You owe me ten bucks," Jerry said.

"What do you mean?"

"We made a ten dollar bet. I win."

"No way. That was a few months ago."

The flight included a long dragged-out meeting led by Dave Thomas as they went over the plans and diagrams on synced tablet computers. The fourteen-hour flight ended at 1:00 P.M. and landed in Star City in Oblast, Russia.

. . .

Walking down the hallway of Bear Creek Elementary after school, Abbey found her way to the auditorium with Kelly in tow. She held Abbey's costume and was careful not to damage her sewing accomplishment. Many of Abbey's classmates and their parents crowded around the bottom of the stage and looked at each other's costumes for the first time. Since no one was fully dressed, all the characters from Peter Pan were deflated and lifeless, a tragic scene that Kelly considered funny, but she kept her morbid humor to herself. Abbey could see a Smee costume and a crocodile costume. When she and Kelly walked up to the group, they saw that Kelly was carrying the costume for Peter Pan with a red feather protruding from the ensemble.

"Wow, Abbey. Looks like you're all set," Mrs. Harris said looking at her costume.

"I can't wait to put it on and see everyone else's."

"Do you know your lines?" Mrs. Harris asked.

"Every one of them," Abbey replied proudly.

"Well since this is only dress rehearsal, it's okay if you need any help," Mrs. Harris said with a smile. She then walked up on stage and raised her voice to teacher level, speaking above the crowd of kids. "Okay, students, I know you are all ready to begin your fall break, but we need to get through this dress rehearsal and once we do, we can all go home."

The total running time of the play was thirty minutes, however the dress rehearsal took about two hours. Kelly sat patiently in her seat and watched the play she had been rehearsing all summer.

. . .

On the other side of the world, Jim was sitting in a briefing room listening to the mission plan being discussed in both English and Russian. Dr. Elena Rhyzkov, the mission director and Dave Thomas' Russian counterpart, stood at the front of the room and discussed the rocket launch and procedures for bad weather. She wore a gray skirt, red high heels and a white blouse with the top button undone. Her hair was swept up with bobby pins and several strands dangled over her glasses. Anytime she spoke English, her accent sounded like a large truck going over a series of speed bumps at high speed. Jim couldn't help but notice that Dave looked at her the way a child might covet a shiny new bicycle. Combining the fourteen-hour plane ride with the hour-long meeting, the visiting crew from the U.S. was officially exhausted. Upon being shown to his room in a cosmonaut dormitory, Jim took a quick shower before lying down on the bed.

Ding.

His email notification on his phone alerted him of a new message in his inbox. Reaching for the phone, he silenced all notifications and checked his email. Among six emails was one from Kelly Mae White. He opened it and read a single sentence.

Thought you would want to see this, Kelly wrote. Jim saw an attachment and clicked on it. A video loaded and Jim could see that Kelly was sitting among rows of empty theater seats with her camera phone pointed at the stage. While it was difficult to see the kids in costumes from so far away, Jim could make out Abbey as Peter Pan. He smiled as he watched the other students say their lines and Abbey respond with hers. The video ended. Jim set his phone aside. On his left arm was the bracelet given to him for his birthday. He grabbed the metal bracket on his wrist and slid it down from his forearm as he thought of Abbey and how fun it would be to see her on the night of her performance. Tired from the long flight and mission briefings, he got ready to turn in for the night. Before he did, he watched the video of Abbey one more time.

Chapter 59

Fall break for Abbey consisted of driving ten minutes to the Poconos and zip lining with Kelly at a nearby woodland attraction. With her new prosthetic leg, Abbey was able to go hiking for the first time in her life. Chipmunks, squirrels, and other critters darted off the path as she and Kelly made their way up the trail.

Meanwhile in Star City, Russia, Jim was deep underwater in the Cosmonaut Training Pool wearing a cumbersome spacesuit with two safety divers on each side. Jim was removing the coupling ring under the watchful eye of the Russian Space Agency. Instead of a baseball press box overlooking the pool, Star City has its control room on the side of the tank. Thick pane windows looking into the pool along with video cameras covering every angle gave the training director a spectacular view.

Dave Thomas watched closely as Jim detached the old coupling ring for what seemed like the hundredth time. Just as he was admiring Jim's skill and control, Vitali Popov entered the control room. Vitali was thin, yet bulky with muscles and veins popping out of every square inch of his arms. Sporting a five o'clock shadow and a razor sharp jaw line, he personified the stereotypical cosmonaut. His accomplishments, jagged good looks and perfect physique made him the ideal spokesman for the Russian space program and he had been seen in countless television interviews and appearances. In his thick Russian accent, Vitali asked the training director a question as he looked through the window at an astronaut suited up and floating in the water.

"Is that Jim Mayfield?"

"It is."

Dave watched as Vitali smiled and bent down while pushing a button on the control panel. As he spoke into a microphone, his thick Russian accent poured into the mic.

"You're doing it all wrong, Jim. You should let a real man do that. Perhaps a good-looking Russian with a grip like iron." Vitali let off the mic and waited for a response with a grin. Jim knew who it was immediately. Over a decade ago he had spent several months on board the ISS with Vitali. Without missing a beat, Jim answered,

"Whoever this is, you're probably right. I know someone who has a grip like iron but he looks like an ugly bulldog, so don't ask Vitali Popov." Vitali breaks out in laughter from deep in his stomach, as did the rest of the control room. Jim continued, "Vitali, when did you get in? I'm surprised I hadn't seen you yet."

"I've been at the Cosmodrome trapped in briefing rooms. I heard you were taking a ride up so I thought I would go with you, keep you safe," Vitali said with a big open smile.

· · ·

Fall break went by quickly, and before she knew it, Abbey was back in school. Speaking with Jim on the computer became more and more sparse as the weeks wore on and the launch date grew closer and closer. Halloween came and went, and the launch date was only a week away. Abbey began initiating calls to Jim to no avail.

"He's just really busy. He'll call soon," Kelly would say. Abbey would continually check NASA's website for updates and was surprised to see a photo of Jim sitting at a table with a cosmonaut. The caption read: *Jim Mayfield and Vitali Popov answer questions from the International Press.* She looked at Jim's face compared to the cosmonaut. Vitali was smiling, Jim was not.

The next day after school, Abbey sent Jim an email that gave him an update on the school play and then a plea for him to call soon. Within ten minutes of her sending the email, the computer began to sound an alert. Abbey ran to the desk in the dining hall and clicked on the screen.

"Hey, Abbey, sorry I haven't been able to talk lately." Jim looked tired with dark circles under his eyes and scruff on his face.

"It's okay. I know you're busy."

"Where's Kelly?"

"In the kitchen fixing dinner. I helped her shuck the corn."

"You did? What is she making?"

"Sante Fe salad and some kind of soup."

"Sounds good. So in your email you said you did a read through?"

"We did. I got all my lines right."

Jim could tell that Abbey was excited to talk to him. While it made him smile, at the same time he worried about letting her down. He hadn't called as he had been too caught up in training for the mission. When the conversation fell into a lull, Jim changed the subject with the intention of rectifying his error.

"I have to get on a plane to Baikonur, Kazakhstan tomorrow."

"Kah-zeck-stahn?"

"It's the launch facility, and we lift off from there. We'll be pretty busy up until we leave, but I promise you this. Before we launch, I will call you."

"You will?"

"Of course. I meant to a few times before, but every time I thought about calling, it was in the middle of the night over there. But there is no way I am leaving without talking to you, okay?" Jim said playfully pointing at the camera, causing Abbey to smile.

"Okay."

. . .

BAIKONUR COSMODROME, KAZAKHSTAN

Jim stepped off the plane with Vitali while a team of escorts wearing flight suits guided them into a building. They walked through a maze of hallways and ended in what looked like a dormitory. Each room was wallpapered, carpeted and featured a comfortable bed. Once the escorts took Jim and Vitali to their rooms, Jim stretched out on the soft bed, almost succumbing to exhaustion. Dave and Frank had already left for the States, and Jim felt as if the end were near. No more training, no more briefings, and the thought of his own bed at the inn seemed closer. In mid-thought, Jim was interrupted by Dr. Elena Rhyzkov knocking at the door. Without waiting for Jim to answer, she walked in and spoke in her sultry, heavily-accented English.

"Your room should be satisfactory. It is designed to make cosmonauts more comfortable."

"It's great. Thanks."

"We will have a pre-launch briefing in the conference room."

"Of course, I'll be there."

"Ten minutes," she added before leaving.

The night before the launch, Abbey was sitting on one of the lobby couches doing her homework when a call came through the computer in the dining hall.

"Hey, I just got home," Abbey said.

"I figured I was calling right on time."

"Are you going to be in space tomorrow?"

"Yep. I will be there for five days, then I will be back in Russia for another two, then Houston for two more days, and then home."

"Nine more days."

"Yep. Not too long now."

"How long does it take to get there?"

"Well, it used to take nearly a full day from launch to embarking on the ISS, but we're taking a Fast Track flight."

"You fly faster than normal?"

"No, not faster. The method was developed by the Soviet Space Program, and it involves timing and task compression. I should have gone over some of this before I left. I'm sorry I didn't think of it."

"That's okay," Abbey said. Then she thought of a question she had been meaning to ask Jim. "What are we doing for Thanksgiving?"

"I haven't thought that far ahead. What do you want to do?"

"I don't know. Eat turkey I guess," Abbey answered. Jim laughed. "A friend of mine in school said she and her family play games all day and all night. Can we do that?"

"Board games?" Jim asked.

"Board games, card games, charades, stuff like that."

"Yes. We will play all kinds of games if that's what you want. Just know that if Mallory plays with us, we have to destroy her. She is a little too competitive, and she'll rub it in your face if she wins." Abbey giggled as she fidgeted in her chair.

"Are you going to be able to call me tomorrow?" she asked.

"Well, once I get up there, we have to go over the mission plan. I suppose I'll call you whenever I get a free moment."

"I can't wait to see you floating in space," Abbey said. Jim replied by recounting his experiences in space and being weightless. Then he asked about Kelly,

"Have you and Kelly been having a good time?"

"Yeah, we've been doing a lot together."

"Did she tell you she was going to stick around?"

"Yeah, I've been helping her look for a job."

"Any luck?"

"I think so. I'm just really glad she's staying here. I didn't want her to leave."

"I know."

"We went to the cemetery today."

"Why?"

"She went to see Adam," Abbey said.

It was raining when they drove up to the gates, but by the time Kelly was ready to get out of the car, the rain had stopped.

"Would you mind waiting here?" Kelly asked.

"Sure," Abbey replied. She watched as Kelly got out of the car and searched through the rows of military tombstones with a dry towel tucked underneath her arm. After a few minutes of searching, she finally found where Adam was buried. Kelly knelt down on the dry towel and folded her hands in her lap.

"I'm sorry I haven't been here sooner," Kelly said. "I'm still having a hard time. Mostly at night, 'cause we keep so busy during the day," Kelly said.

From inside the car, Abbey could see that Kelly was talking out loud.

"I wanted to tell you about what I've been doing," Kelly said in a somber tone. "I have been watching over this little girl. Her name is Abbey. You would like her because she's very strong and has a great attitude about everything. Just like you did," Kelly said as she wiped away a single tear. "I have been living with her and this man named Jim. He's nice to me, and he is Abbey's adoptive father. He's especially nice to her. Sometimes I watch him with her and think that is how you would've been with our daughter. We had a baby girl, did I ever tell you that?" Kelly said as tears streamed down her cheeks.

Abbey could see that Kelly was crying. She wanted to get out and go over to her, but she decided it would be best to give Kelly some space. After all, she asked Abbey to wait.

"When she got back in the car, she didn't say much."

"I'm sure she's still having a hard time. The thing to do when someone is depressed or grieving, or having a hard time is to ask how they're doing. Not often, but every once in a while."

"Okay. I will. I just hate it that she is sad."

"I do, too."

Jim and Abbey spoke for another fifteen minutes before they hung up. Jim spent the rest of the day in briefing rooms before being subjected to a press conference with questions delivered in Russian. Sporadic flashbulbs ignited, temporarily burning spots into his vision. The translator took up most of the time, relaying Russian to English.

When it was time for Jim to retire to his room, he was provided a single blue pill as a sleep aid. While it was only 7:00 P.M., Jim was to go to sleep as soon as possible before the big day.

Chapter 60

Knock. Knock.

Jim woke up to a man opening his door and walking in his room.

The sleep aid produced a hazy outline of a man who was holding the crook of a clothes hanger with one finger. On the hanger was a blue flight suit that was encased in an opaque, vinyl garment bag. The man was a thin, bald fellow wearing a white jumpsuit and standing at the foot of his bed.

"It is time to get ready. We will be outside," the man said softly as he placed the hanger on a hook next to the bathroom and left promptly. After taking a shower and getting ready, Jim put on the blue flight suit with an American flag patch on the right sleeve, a welcomed sight in the midst of all the Russian flags surrounding Star City and the Cosmodrome.

Once outside his room, photographers, dignitaries, and families of the cosmonauts greeted Jim Mayfield and Vitali Popov. Still standing outside their rooms, they were each handed a black Sharpie marker and were asked to sign the wooden door to their rooms, just as all previous astronauts and cosmonauts had done. It was a tradition that had become somewhat ceremonious and was considered good luck. Everywhere Jim and Vitali walked, eyes locked onto them as if they were celebrities.

After a quick pre-flight briefing in the conference room, Jim and

Vitali's escort led them down a long hallway toward the front of the cosmonaut dormitory. Once outside, they walked onto an empty charter bus for a quick ride to the integration and suit-up facility at Building 254.

. . .

Back in Bear Creek, Abbey was getting ready for bed while Jim was once again putting on a space suit, moments away from being propelled into space. Before she went to sleep, she checked NASA's website and found a photo on the home page. It showed a rocket sitting on the launch pad at the Cosmodrome and a caption that read:

> *A Soyuz rocket is erected into position at the Baikonur Cosmodrome's Pad 1/5 (Gagarin's Start). The rocket will launch the newest expedition's team for crew transfer, supply delivery, and a major repair on the ISS.*

Abbey looked for more information, but found nothing else. She turned off the computer and walked to her room.

For nearly a full hour, men wearing surgical masks assisted Jim and Vitali with each piece of their Soquel launch entry suit. After pressure checks and oxygen fittings, Jim and Vitali walked like children in their father's clothes as they took awkward steps while carrying their oxygen supply in a metal box.

Outside Building 254, Vitali's family, the media and colleagues looked on and cheered as the two men walked out of the building, and headed toward the charter bus. Everyone shouted out their well wishes while Jim and Vitali nodded, waved and made the graceless walk to the bus.

The ride to the launch pad was escorted by six police cars for the twenty-five minute drive while Jim thought back to when he left Earth in a shuttle at Cape Canaveral. While the Russian procedure for launch was similar to NASA's, it still felt rigid and cold. The second Jim stepped off the bus, more flashes from cameras ignited while escorts walked alongside Jim as he made his way toward a row of politicians and department heads of the Russian Space Agency. Photo ops commenced as Jim and Vitali were acknowledged and well received before climbing the ladder to the elevator. Camera crews shot video of them rising to the top of the rocket until they could no longer be seen.

While Abbey was sound asleep in her bed, Jim was laying down in the capsule with his back to the earth and his head facing the sky. The thrust of the rockets propelled Jim over seventeen thousand miles per hour through Earth's atmosphere.

. . .

While some days at school were fun for Abbey, this wasn't one of those days. English wasn't her favorite subject. Learning about antonyms, homonyms and idioms was not her idea of a good time. When school was finally over, Abbey walked outside to find Kelly waiting in Jim's red truck.

Once inside the cab, Kelly used her thumb to point over her shoulder.

"Look in the back. It's mulch," Kelly said.

"What's it for?"

"The flower beds around the front porch. I've already planted quite a few flowers, too."

"Can I help?"

"Of course," Kelly replied.

Within the hour, Kelly and Abbey were unloading mulch with a shovel. Kelly had been quieter since she had visited Adam's grave.

Remembering what Jim had told her, Abbey spoke up.

"Is everything alright?" Abbey asked.

"Yeah, I suppose," Kelly responded. Not knowing what else to say, the conversation ended somewhat abruptly. After a few moments, Abbey spoke up again.

"Do you miss Adam? I mean, more than normal?"

"I do. But I don't know what normal is. I don't think I've felt normal since he died."

"I was only asking because you seem different since coming back from the cemetery."

"I know. I still don't know how to feel. It's strange saying that, but I can't let go. I feel bad, because I haven't thought that much about him in the last month or so. I am just having a hard time."

"I'm sorry you feel that way. I am sorry that happened to you," Abbey said. It was the first time anyone had really spoken to Kelly about Adam's death. If anyone spoke to her at the funeral, she didn't remember. The haze and numbness that had set in created a filter that blocked out everything around her. All she remembered was what the Whites did to her and the sound the door made when it slammed in her face.

"Thank you, Abbey," Kelly said, setting down the shovel. "You want to continue this tomorrow? I don't really feel like doing this right now."

"I'm sorry. I shouldn't have brought it up," Abbey said.

"No, it isn't you. Really, I've been doing this for most of the day, and I just keep thinking about him, and I don't know. I'd like to do something else. Take my mind off of whatever it is that I am feeling."

"What do you want to do?"

"I think maybe I'd like to order a pizza and watch a movie."

. . .

At Papa John's, the busy store bustled with workers pounding out fresh dough and distributing fresh ingredients before sliding the pizzas into the oven.

"Okay, your order with coupon is $14.77. We'll have it out to you in about forty-five minutes," Melissa said and thanked Kelly before hanging up. Melissa printed the ticket, peeled off a piece of clear tape and stuck the ticket to the wall before she walked away. Her co-workers watched her as she did this, thinking that she had lost her mind. They were surprised when she simply stood out of the way and said, "Bear Creek Inn."

Two delivery drivers scrambled toward the ticket on the wall. They grabbed and held each other back. Gil Bernstein fended off his opponent and reached out, ripping the ticket off the wall.

"It's mine! It's mine!" he yelled out. When he drove up to the inn and walked up to the front porch, it was a woman, a little older than him, who paid in cash and closed the door.

"Come on!" Gil said out loud to himself. "Where's the astronaut guy?"

While watching a movie and eating pizza, Abbey thought she could hear something.

"What is that? Do you hear that?" Abbey asked Kelly.

"What?" She responded before muting the TV. The sound was faint, yet familiar. A strange ringing sound.

"Oh. That's Jim!"

Once they were connected, the first image Abbey saw was Jim opening a small pouch.

"Hey, Jim!" Abbey said.

"Hey there, I'm trying to get this open so I can show you something," Jim said, struggling with the small pouch.

"Did you make it up there okay?" Kelly asked.

"Yep. No problem. We're on schedule," Jim said as he finally got the pouch open. "There we go. You wanted to see what it was like when I float in space, well I am doing it now. See?" Jim said as he backed away from the camera and moved about in mid-air.

"That's amazing," Abbey said.

"Now, I wanted to show you the best part about living in microgravity," Jim said before squeezing the small pouch and letting several drops of orange liquid float freely in perfect spheres.

"Wow. Cool," Abbey said.

"This is a sports drink. And usually we just drink through a straw. I'm sure you've seen something like this on TV or in a video online, but I thought I would show you anyway," Jim explained before he chomped the beads of free-floating liquid spheres in the air. He squeezed even more of the drink out and chomped the beads like Pac-Man.

"That's great," Kelly said, smiling.

"I love it," Abbey remarked. Jim proceeded to show Abbey and Kelly other cool tricks he had learned before nearing the end of their conversation.

"I can't be taking up all the bandwidth so I need to be going soon, but we still have a few minutes."

"I got a new assignment in school."

"What is it?"

"We are making bridges from wood, and we have to build a bridge that can hold five pounds."

"Wow. That sounds like fun. When is it due?"

"The final day before Christmas. We have a demonstration in the gym. It's kind of a competition. The teacher said that if the bridge we build supports the five pound weight, we automatically get an A plus."

"Okay, we'll have to find a structural engineer, and we'll ask them some questions."

"Like we did with Dr. Woodward?"

"Exactly."

"I can't wait."

Kelly had a question, but was afraid to speak up. When there was a slight lull, she decided to jump at the opportunity.

"How do you get back home?"

"Well, decades ago the Soviets designed a capsule for reentry. It's called the Soyuz and it's a very small capsule that can easily transport us back to Earth. I'll try to show you the capsule before I have to get inside. Sometimes we detach our camera and take people around the ISS on a tour."

Jim looked at the clock on the laptop and decided he had surpassed his allotted time. He ended their call after they said their goodbyes. He smiled to himself recalling Abbey's excitement about the bridge project as he floated through the space station. He gripped handlebars that were placed along the walls of the ISS and pulled himself along with little effort, gliding to the U.S. Lab.

Tapping randomly on a keyboard, he woke up a sleeping laptop and launched the main command software for the ISS. Jim wanted to keep the mission on schedule. The sooner his mission was complete, the sooner he would be home.

Chapter 61

Dr. Elena Rhyzkov sat in front of a camera in Russia while Dave Thomas stood in front of his camera in Mission Control in Houston. Waiting to be connected to the ISS via videoconference, engineers and specialists meandered behind Dave as he stood close to the camera and looked at Elena on the screen.

"Your hair is down," Dave said.

"It is. Thanks for noticing," Elena answered in her thick accent.

"Looks good," Dave said as he nodded.

"I'm married, Mr. Thomas."

"I didn't mean, I mean, I didn't…"

"…But not happily," she said with a wink. Dave looked behind him at the staff of mission control. They tried to hide their smiles, but their efforts were in vain. Suddenly the ISS came on the screen. Taking the opportunity to move on, Dave smiled and spoke loudly.

"Hey! How's everyone doing today?"

The crew smiled back at Dave's enthusiasm and the briefing began. Vitali and Jim floated to the right of the screen with Benjamin Akers and Susan Basset. In the middle of them all was Anatoly Grechko. Anatoly had been on the ISS for six months and was scheduled to leave with Jim in the Soyez capsule. He was the tallest and thinnest of the group and was the commander of the ISS.

"We're doing great," Anatoly said through his accent.

"How you doing Jim?" Dave asked.

"It's like old times up here. We all work hard, and Vitali sleeps all day."

Once the laughter subsided, Dave and Dr. Rhyzkov led the meeting by going over the mission plan and the EVA. The crewmembers hovered, bounced, and reached out to hang onto handlebars as they floated about during the briefing. When the call ended, Jim began saying goodbye to the crew, as he was scheduled to sleep in a separate module. Performing an EVA required the astronaut performing the spacewalk to sleep in the Quest module, which had a separate atmosphere and helped prevent decompression sickness. After his goodbyes to his crewmates, he floated through the station and glided into the Quest module. Once inside, he locked the doors and opened a laptop, starting the pressurization process.

Four hours before the mission was to commence, Jim awoke to a piercing alarm. Red flashing lights and the sound of yelling coming from his crewmates gave Jim an instant dreadful feeling. Keeping calm, though unsure of what was happening, he grabbed a nearby laptop and looked at the ISS software for the quickest answer.

Chapter 62

3:21 A.M.

Ring. Ring. Ring. Ring. Ring. Ring. Ring. Ring. Ring. Ring. Ring. Ring. Ring. Ring. Ring. Ring.

The phone on the front check-in desk at Bear Creek Inn finally woke Kelly up from a deep sleep. It was an unfamiliar ring to her. She got up out of bed and walked out of Room 102 toward the lobby. The phone continued to ring as she walked barefoot across the hardwood floor. The moon above the inn cast rays of light through the skylight, illuminating the long rectangular desk.

"Hello?" Kelly answered.

"Is this Ms. White?"

"It is."

Abbey was asleep in her bed. Kelly walked in and turned on the lamp on the nightstand and gently woke her

"Abbey. Abbey, I need you to wake up."

After she was awake enough to attach her prosthetic leg, Kelly guided Abbey out into the lobby.

"What's the matter?" Abbey asked. Kelly sat her down on the couch and held the remote in her hand. The lobby was still dark, with the only light in the room coming from the moon via skylight and the banker's lamp on the check-in desk. While she looked into her eyes, Kelly spoke softly,

"Right now, Jim and the crew on the space station are okay, but there was a problem. Something went wrong. I received a phone call from Dr. Stanton."

"He called here?"

"I don't know anything other than that, but he said to turn on the TV for more information," Kelly explained before pressing the power button. The TV screen illuminated the lobby with a soft glow. Kelly changed the channel to a popular news network where a fuzzy photo was being broadcast from outside the space station. Both Abbey and Kelly look closely at the screen that displayed the white structure of the ISS with a portion blackened and shredded. A man reporting on the incident delivered the story.

"Moments ago, there was an explosion aboard the International Space Station. We are unsure as to what caused the incident but it is believed that there are no casualties from the blast. What you are seeing is live video from the exterior camera aboard the space station."

"Jim's okay?" Abbey asked, looking for reassurance.

"Yes. No one on board was injured," Kelly answered as she put her hand on Abbey's back.

The reporter on TV continued to speak over the live shot of the international space station.

"If you are just joining us, at approximately 2:45 A.M. Eastern time there was an explosion aboard the International Space Station." The reporter continued to repeat the limited details for nearly an hour. Several different camera angles of the exterior of the space station were shown. At 4:00 A.M. more information was reported.

"We have a confirmed report of..."

Abbey and Kelly sat on the edge of their seats until the video cut to an animated graphic of the space station with a photo of a NASA spokesperson named Alan Nagel. A bearded man wearing a polo shirt represented the voice that sounded like he was speaking from a cell phone. The reporter introduced him.

"With us now is Alan Nagel, a spokesperson for NASA. Alan, can you tell us more about the incident?"

"I can. Early this morning the structure received a shower of space debris, which came into contact with the ISS at a high velocity. The debris punctured the Research Module, destroying an oxygen tank, which caused an explosion. Now, the tanks were designed so that if they were compromised, the explosion is minimal—a lesson learned from Apollo 13. Right now the Research Module is depressurized and closed off from the rest of the station. Orbital debris is by far the biggest danger to the ISS, and today the full effects of that danger was felt by the crew on board."

"Alan, are the astronauts lives in danger?"

"At this point, everything is okay, but if action isn't taken immediately, this incident could result in major issues."

"Thank you, Alan, for that report. From the Space Station only moments ago, is specialist Benjamin Akers. Here is what he had to say in a recorded message."

Benjamin Akers, a man with a thick build and sporting a flat-top haircut read from a note pad while floating about.

"The crew members of the ISS are uninjured and are managing the situation. We are assessing the damage cause by the debris and will be up and running again in due time. We believe we are not clear of danger yet but are working diligently to rectify the situation."

. . .

On board the ISS, Jim put on his spacesuit and transitioned through the airlock, talking to Houston the entire way.

"Houston, I am opening the outer door."

"Copy that, Jim."

After a series of latching on and off safety points on the ISS and floating over to the Research Module, Jim surveyed the damage.

"Significant damage to the coolant hose and the hull around the hose access point, but looks to be something we can manage. Hull integrity seems to be intact at the moment. Looks like someone threw a handful of rocks at the side of the module. I only see one side that appears to be compromised."

"Copy that," Dave said. Inside the Research Module, Anatoly looked around and surveyed the damage and spoke in his native language.

"Interior of the Research Module is sound; however, the coolant hose on the inside is separated from the exterior. There is a definite leak."

"Copy, Anatoly," Dr. Rhyzkov acknowledged in Russian.

After taking in all the data, Dr. Rhyzkov and her staff developed a plan of action and relayed their suggestions to NASA.

. . .

For the better part of the morning, Abbey and Kelly slept off and on while waiting for more news reports to come in. The volume was turned down enough to allow them to rest, yet loud enough to hear key words such as "astronaut" and "NASA". Abbey had stayed home from school as she couldn't attend with the possibility that something could happen to Jim. Kelly had woken up before 9:00 A.M. and saw a live shot of the space station with a man in a space suit outside the ISS. The reporter spoke over the video.

"We are being told that this is astronaut Jim Mayfield…"

"Abbey. Wake up, wake up. Look," Kelly said, pointing to the TV. The reporter continued.

"…an American who is an engineer performing an emergency spacewalk. Ironically, Jim was assigned to the ISS for a repair of the Zarya module and is now performing a similar repair. We are told that the ISS is in good hands as Mayfield has repeatedly trained for months for this type of refurbishment at Johnson Space Center."

"That's Jim? That's him right there?" Abbey asked. Before Kelly could comment, the reporter on TV confirmed it by repeating Jim's full name.

For five hours, Jim remained outside the Research Module. With his gloved hand, he reached into the white, rectangular tool bag and brought out a small socket wrench in the shape of a silver gun. Jim heard Dave in his helmet as he worked.

"Jim, once you have this panel bolted, we advise you to return inside before tackling the Zarya panel."

"Copy that, Houston. I have six more bolts to go. Anatoly? How are you doing inside?"

With the power shut off inside the Research Module for safety, Anatoly worked in the dark with light coming from a flashlight strapped to his head. As he spoke out loud to communicate with Jim, his thick Russian accent was difficult to decipher.

"We should see the pressure increase once you finish with the bolts on the plate. The hoses should hold. There is no sign of a leak inside at the moment."

"Anatoly, where are you on the repair?" Elena asked.

"I am wrapping up. Less than a minute," he responded.

The repairs to the Research Module took over six hours total to complete. Once they were given the go-ahead, Houston cleared Science Officer Susan Basset to initiate a pressure check for the entire ISS.

"Go for pressurization," Dave said over the radio.

"Copy. Testing pressurization," Susan replied. Using the software on a laptop, Susan initiated the sequence.

While the repair of the space station was underway, Abbey and Kelly stayed glued to the TV in the lobby.

"Why do they keep showing the same thing over and over?" Abbey asked.

"I don't know. They do this all the time when there's a big incident. We just have to wait until they get more information, I guess," Kelly explained. The sound of a car approaching the inn could be heard followed by a car door slamming shut. Before Kelly could get up and look, Mallory burst through the front door.

"Is Jim okay? I didn't even hear anything until an hour ago," she said as she slammed the door behind her and whipped around the back of the leather couch. She stopped and stared at the TV. Abbey went through a play by play of what had occurred while Mallory soaked it all in.

For the entire day, all of Bear Creek had their TVs on watching the updates on the space station. So far, the town of Bear Creek had been mentioned twice when talking about Jim. The patrons in Murray's Diner ate their food in slow motion with their eyes glued to the screen above the lunch counter, when the latest update came through.

"It seems that the Research Module has been repaired. The ISS has been pressurized and returned to full function once again. Astronauts are taking a break and resting before focusing on less threatening damage."

By 9:00 P.M., the stress and nerves caught up with Abbey and Kelly. Mallory looked at their tired and exhausted faces, deciding that they should go to bed.

"Looks like everything is okay up there. It seems to be anyway."

"You think so?" Abbey asked.

"I don't think they would be resting if they were in immediate danger. Plus, they said that the damaged module is functioning again."

"I wish I could talk to him," Abbey said.

"Well, I need to get back to Barry and the kids. I will keep watching the news. If you do hear from him, call me."

Mallory hugged both Kelly and Abbey before leaving. Still watching the TV, Abbey decided she wasn't leaving the couch.

"Why don't you go to bed? I'll sleep out here," Abbey said. "I'll yell for you if something comes on," she added.

"Well, I was thinking that I could sleep out here and come and get you if there were any updates. You need to get some sleep," Kelly suggested.

"I don't think I can just go to bed," Abbey said.

"Me neither. I'm staying out here."

"Me, too."

While they made their beds of quilts and pillows for the night, Jim was already asleep trying to get some rest before the next spacewalk.

Back on Earth, teams of engineers discussed the damage of the space station via videoconference.

"We have elevated levels of O_2, and we are running a risk of over pressurization."

Another alarm went off. The jumbo screen in mission control showed data from the ISS. Dave stared at the screen and looked for a cause for the alarm.

Dr. Rhyzkov heard the same alarm and looked at her systems analyst.

Simultaneously both Dave and Dr. Rhyzkov were informed of the danger.

Ammonia.

Dave looked up at the large screen.

"Where is that coming from?" Dave asked. "Ammonia? That's the Research Module, isn't it?"

When the Research Module was struck by orbital debris, the strength of the hull was strong enough to take the hit, except where the coolant hose ran outside. Orbital debris the size of kernels of corn damaged the coolant hose, cooling pump, and heat pipe. While the tank didn't blow right away, it was only a matter of time.

Anatoly floated through the station and into the RM. There he could smell the ammonia instantly, as if he hit a wall.

"Houston, there is a significant…"

BOOM! The tanks exploded.

Cabin depressurization…Fire…Screaming.

Chapter 63

Jim depressurized the Quest module and opened the door to the ISS. Since depressurization should be done over a period of hours and not minutes, the biggest side-effect set in quickly—his head felt tight and ached and throbbed. Dizzy and briefly disoriented, he glided through the tunnels of the space station. On his way, he saw Susan Basset and Vitali Popov carrying an unconscious Anatoly who was bleeding from the head, out of the Research Module, .

"What happened?" Jim yelled above the alarm.

"We don't know. He was inside. There's a fire," Vitali said as they moved Anatoly toward the first aid panel in the Unity module. Jim grabbed an extinguisher and glided into the Research Module and sprayed the base of the flames. Instead of bright orange and yellow flames, the flames were green and blue, and seemed resistant to the fire extinguisher. Benjamin Akers came to Jim's aid with another fire extinguisher. The flames spread over a counter and began to melt a plastic incubator.

"I'm out," Jim said as his extinguisher emptied. He exited the module and yelled over the alarm. "Let's just close the hatches. The hull has been breached," Jim said. Benjamin nodded and floated out of the RM..

"Houston, we are going to close the hatch to the research module. Can you confirm that the oxygen is shut off inside the RM?" Jim yelled out. Dave responds,

"Station, this is Houston. We have cut oxygen to the RM yet we are seeing elevated readings of O_2 inside the research module,"

Ben looked inside the RM. Between the smoke and fire, he could see what looked like air jetting out of a tank.

"Houston, I can see air escaping out of one of the tanks. O_2 seems to be flowing freely into the RM." Ben yelled out.

Jim put his hand on the lever of the RM hatch and pulled it closed. He tried to lock the hatch, but the lever wouldn't move.

"Dang it. Ben, help me out here. The hatch is stuck," said Jim. Ben floated up next to him and helped attempt to force the lever.

"It's not moving," Ben said shaking his head.

"Hang on," Jim said as he opened the hatch to the RM. He pulled himself inside among the smoke and fire.

"What are you doing?" Ben asked. Jim didn't answer. He watched as he reached for the lever to the RM and shut it. From the inside, the lever worked. The hatch was sealed. Jim opened it up again and floated out of the RM as he addressed mission control.

"Houston, the hatch to the RM will only seal shut from the inside. There is an issue with the outside lever." Jim glided into the Quest module and grabbed a spacesuit, hugging it as he floated back to the RM.

"Station, we are getting high readings of heat, rapid depressurization in the Research module," said Elena, "An explosion appears imminent. Get the door shut and move to the far end of the station. Please advise,"

Houston's control room was buzzing with alarms. Interior cameras around the space station showed very little, and exterior cameras showed nothing but calm and silent space.

"Kill the alarm, will ya. I'm sure they hear it," Dave Thomas said among a room full of mission control staff. With a controlled voice, Dave spoke to the ISS.

"Station this is Houston. Explosion imminent. Please advise." Dave's voice carried through the ISS on a multitude of speakers. Jim grabbed a laptop and glided past Ben and into the Research Module.

"What are you doing?" Ben asked.

"Seal the door now. I will get this from the inside," Jim said, closing the hatch to the RM. Dave's voice came back on the loudspeakers.

"Station, explosion is imminent. Please advise."

Susan Basset arrived just as Ben closed the hatch. She looked at Ben who had an expression of a lost child in a department store.

"Is the fire out?" she asked.

Inside the RM, Jim opened up the laptop, the fire raging behind him. After a few clicks, the coupling ring around the module released. Jim put the laptop to the side and reached up around the hatch. He gripped a silver bar at the top, and yanked it out. Jim repeated this with the bar at the bottom. The module was now free from the ISS. The lights flickered and then powered down. The glow of the widespread fire was the only light source.

"Houston, Research Module is separated," Jim said as he started to put on his spacesuit.

"No!" Benjamin yelled out, "Houston, Mayfield is inside the RM. He is inside the module."

"Jim, can you confirm your location."

"Houston," Jim said. "I am inside RM. It was the only way to close the hatch. I have my suit with me, and I am putting it on. I will extinguish the fire by opening the hatch and closing it…" *Static.* Jim's voice could barely be heard.

"Jim?" Dave said.

Static.

"Jim, do you copy?"

Static.

"Communication is severed, sir," A staff member said in Mission Control. "We lost him, but he is able to receive the Wi-Fi signal from the ISS."

Jim turned on the exterior lights on his helmet and looked at the LED display on his wrist for radio signal strength. Still trying to communicate with mission control, he spoke in a calm tone, "Houston, do you copy?"

Frank Navasky had been called down to mission control. He rushed into the room and stood at Dave's side. Dave started with a quick recap,

"There was a fire in the RM, and they couldn't extinguish it. The hatch wouldn't close from the outside, so Jim grabbed a suit, went inside the RM and released it from the station.

"He's untethered?"

"At the moment, yes." Dave said as he pushed a button on the console in front of him, and spoke loudly.

"Station, do we have a visual on the RM?"

"Houston, I am on my way to the robotic arm," Benjamin said as he gripped the handlebars on the ceilings and walls of the ISS and propelled himself through the station at an unsafe speed.

Inside the RM, the lock on Jim's helmet slid shut. He opened the hatch to empty, black space. The fire subsided immediately, and Jim closed the hatch, and breathed shallow breaths. After finding a crescent wrench in a cabinet, Jim removed the bolts and hoses from the ammonia tanks and once again opened the hatch and then threw the tanks outside. After closing the hatch, Jim activated the only full oxygen tank and waited for the O₂ to reach 14 PSIA. While he waited, he noticed something on the wall. Something was wrong. The air coming from the oxygen tank streamed across the RM and out a hole that led to the vacuum of space.

"Houston, do you copy?" Jim asked.

Static.

"Houston, there's a leak in the RM. Cabin is still depressurized. The escaping O2 could be acting as a propellant. I'm going to try to repair it," Jim said in case they could hear him.

With thick-gloved fingers, Jim rummaged through a toolbox looking for something to repair the small hole with. While continuing to breath shallow, he found nothing of use in the toolbox but saw a white case strapped to a workbench. Inside the case was a supply of liquid adhesives. One of them was a two-part industrial mechanical resin adhesive.

When the news reported that an alarm had sounded on the ISS, Abbey and Kelly waited with their eyes glued to the TV.

"We are just learning of yet another incident developing aboard the International Space Station. A fire broke out in the Research Module, an addition to the space station put in place by the Russian Space Agency just a few years ago. After attempts to put the fire out, the module was released with an astronaut inside. At this time, we are unaware if the detached module was an accident or if it was planned. Again, a module was released and is now free-floating away from the space station, and there *is* an astronaut inside."

Both Kelly and Abbey watch the screen intently, not saying a word.

Jim held a metal plate against the wall of the RM that covered the hole. Between the plate and the hole was a resin adhesive he mixed together and applied to the interior wall. Unable to leave the plate and reach out to grab the laptop to communicate with Houston, he applied pressure and waited for the resin to set.

Dave stood in front of his control panel with Frank Navasky looking over his shoulder. Dave clicked on video cameras set up around the ISS while looking for the RM module from different angles, but was unable to locate it. "Station this is Houston. Do you have a visual on the RM?" Dave said as he nervously stroked his tie and waited for an answer. Benjamin Akers looked through the windows in the cupola and saw the Research Module float off the back of the space station, seemingly in slow motion. Benjamin confirmed the visual.

"Houston, we have a visual on the RM, what looks to be about fifty yards off the back end of the station with an estimated speed of a few centimeters a second. The robotic arm is not an option at this point. Over."

"Copy that, Station," Dave acknowledged.

The staff of mission control turned their heads and focused on Dave. "Let's keep trying to reach Mayfield via the laptop. I need all cameras on the station to be pointed off the back of the ISS. All eyes on Jim. Let's get him back."

All of mission control scattered like cockroaches the second Dave set the course of action. A trajectory of five centimeters per second was calculated and loaded into a simulator while another engineer figured out propulsion speed and directional control of the ISS.

In Bear Creek, Abbey and Kelly sat side by side on the leather sofa, eyes on the TV.

"We have learned that the hatch to the module malfunctioned, so to prevent a fatal explosion, an astronaut who's name is being withheld at this time, climbed into the module while it was on fire and closed the hatch. The astronaut then released the module from the space station to protect the crew in the event of an explosion. We now have a live feed of that module as seen here."

Gasping and covering their mouths, Kelly and Abbey stared at the TV thinking that it could be Jim, although no one mentioned his name.

In the Research Module, Jim looked at his watch and back at the metal plate he had glued to the wall. He eased up on the pressure ever so slightly, and the plate seemed to stay in place. He kicked off the wall, and glided to the floating laptop and quickly returned to the metal plate. He continued to apply pressure while attempting to connect to the space station and Houston.

Dave Thomas was hovering over the shoulder of an engineer looking at a computer screen when the video feed of Jim popped up on the jumbo display in the control room. He was still wearing his suit although he had taken off his helmet.

"Dave, Mayfield is on screen."

"Houston, this is Mayfield. Do you copy?" Jim said. Several members of Mission Control applauded and cheered, but Dave was all business.

"Jim, we are looking at your trajectory and configuring a rescue. Is the fire out?"

"The fire has subsided. I opened the hatch and closed it again which put it out. I discovered a leak on the wall and I used a resin adhesive and a metal plate to temporarily seal the hole. I am breathing on a single back-up tank as the other one is depleted, and I have the back-up power running on the RM. The laptop battery is running low, and I am looking for a power source."

"Copy that, Jim. Give me a PSIA update."

"I'm at about 10 to 12PSIA currently, hoping to get to 14 soon. When I heard the alarm, I left the Quest module without depressurization so I can't tell if my dizziness and headache is from that or from the low PSIA, or both."

"Copy that Jim. Hopefully we will have you back on the ISS in no time. We'll have medical review your situation. Good job on the seal."

"Jim?" Benjamin said, "there should be a power adapter for the laptop strapped to a compartment near the shelves. Do you see the shelves?"

"Copy that, Ben. Checking for the adapter," Jim said as he floated up to the shelving in the RM, looking for a black adapter and cable. Seeing the adapter, he quickly grabbed it and plugged it into a utility outlet port. "Got it. Power is good for now."

"How much power does the RM have currently?" Dave asked an engineer sitting at a systems station.

After looking at his monitor he replied, "We've got at least eighteen hours worth of power. If he conserves, it could go a little over twenty-four," the engineer explained.

"Jim? Go ahead and turn off all the lights in the RM. Just use the light from the laptop for now. We don't know how long you will be in there, but we are working quickly."

"Copy. Lights out.

Aboard the ISS, Susan Basset tended to Anatoly as he began to wake up. She removed the oxygen mask and reported to Houston, giving them an update before she returned to his side.

"Anatoly, take it easy," Susan said.

"Bullet."

"Bullet? Anatoly, are you saying, bullet?" Susan asked as she held up a pouch of water with a clamped straw in front of his mouth. She let him take a few sips before he tried to speak again. The gauze wrapped around his head and hands had already been changed once since the blood seeped through and soaked the first bandage. Before Anatoly spoke, he put his hand to his head in pain and signaled to Susan to turn off the lights.

"Gun fire. Is that what happened?" he asked, still disoriented.

"We don't know what happened."

"Was there a fire?" he asked in Russian. Susan answered him in Russian as she held his hand.

"Yes, the fire is out."

Chapter 64

"Jim, we are having some difficulty," Dave said.

"What is my velocity?" Jim asked as he took the cap off of a permanent marker. Dave relayed how fast the RM was moving and explained that it had increased in speed. Then came the propulsion measurements and requirements needed for the ISS to exceed Jim's speed and catch up to him. Jim wrote in permanent marker on the wall of the RM.

"We use seven thousand kilograms of propellant for altitude maintenance and control, and have a total of eight thousand one hundred and twenty kilograms on board."

"Copy, Houston," Jim responded. While he wrote out a formula on the wall of the RM, Dave hung his head knowing that Jim was calculating the outcome and would come to the same conclusion. Taking into consideration the velocity versus the burn rate, the end result didn't look good. Jim completed his permanent marker calculation and stopped. The possibility of the ISS coming to get him wasn't viable, not even close. Jim would not be returning back to the space station.

In mission control, silence had fallen on the sea of engineers and specialists. Dave looked at the screen as Jim came back in front of the camera.

"Houston, what is my trajectory?" Jim asked. No one moved. They all knew the answer. Jim knew the answer. Was he in complete shock? Denial? Maybe Jim just wanted to hear it said out loud.

"Your trajectory, Jim, is the atmosphere," Dave said taking his eyes off the floor and looking at the screen. Jim's eyes were glazed. He stared off into the distance for some time before he eventually spoke.

"Copy, Houston."

. . .

Hearing the news about an astronaut floating away from the space station, Mallory hurried back to the inn. She had once again parked herself in front of the TV with Abbey and Mallory. The news reports kept reporting more details, but no mention of any crew member.

Ring. Ring.

The phone on the check-in desk rang until Mallory answered. Both Abbey and Kelly followed behind.

"Hello?"

Standing in a room adjacent from mission control in Houston was Dr. Stanton.

"This is Dr. Stanton with NASA. Who am I speaking with?"

"Mallory Cain, Jim's sister."

"Do you currently have the television on?"

"Yes."

"Is Abbey with you?"

"Yes."

"Mallory, I am to ask you per a request from Jim to turn off the TV."

"Turn it off?"

"Jim asked for it to be turned off," Stanton repeated.

Mallory held back tears as she heard the significance in Dr. Stanton's voice. With Abbey looking on, Mallory quickly collected herself and spoke with a casual tone, "Will do. Thank you for calling."

. . .

Dave looked out over the engineers and specialists in Mission Control. Dave nodded at a staff member in front of him who opened his mic to the ISS, RM, Russia's control room, and other space agencies.

"Listen up. Jim is heading for our atmosphere, and should we not intervene, he will not survive. We know the ISS can't catch up to him. We know he can't return to station on his own. So, what else? What else can we come up with? If there is a way to rescue him, we need to find it."

Dave's voice was strong, and adamant. Jim felt as if there was hope. After about twenty minutes, Jim appeared on the large screen in Mission Control.

"Houston, is there a possibility of releasing the Soyuz Capsule with a redirected trajectory? What if we redirect it past the RM?" Jim asked.

"Jim, we are already figuring that one out. It's a long shot but possible. We also have Russia working for viable solutions, as well. We're going to upload a couple of sims to your laptop shortly."

"Copy that, Houston."

. . .

Mallory turned the TV off and sat down with Abbey and Kelly sitting next to her. Seconds after she turned it off, Jim's photo was broadcasted with his full name. The words at the bottom of the screen read: *Lost in Space*.

"Abbey, Jim asked for us to not watch the TV right now."

"Why?"

"I don't know, but it's probably because they are reporting things that are inflated or sensationalized."

"What does that mean?"

"It means that they make a bigger deal out of this than it is. Jim asked for us to turn it off, and I am sure he has a good reason."

"Okay," Abbey said as she stood up. After locking in her prosthetic leg, she started for the dining hall.

"Where are you going?" Mallory asked. Abbey turned around and spoke over her shoulder.

"If Jim calls, he'll call on video conference."

The couches that once resided in the lobby were quickly moved to the dining hall. Kelly sat on one end of the couch with Abbey on the other, covered up with the same long blanket while Mallory lay on the other sofa under an afghan. Everyone was asleep.

At three in the morning, the call came through. Abbey was the first to wake. She sprung up off the couch waking Kelly, and hopped over to the computer.

"Jim?" Abbey said. She saw nothing but a dark room and Jim staring at the camera. He had been wiping away tears of frustration before he showed his face. His eyes were red and bloodshot, but it was difficult to see in the video.

"Hey there," Jim said with an improvised smile. Kelly stood up, took a few quick steps and sat next to Abbey. Mallory was still zonked out on the sofa.

. . .

In Houston, Dave picked up the white binder that outlined the entire mission and threw it at the wall. The rest of the staff members hung their head while Dave spouted off curse words, letting the situation get the best of him. Frank Navasky chewed on his fingernails while he stared at the ground.

. . .

"Are you okay?" Abbey asked.

"I'm fine. You guys watching TV?"

"No. We were told not to."

"Is that Mallory behind you?" Jim asked as he saw her asleep in the background. "Shove her real hard. She won't wake up otherwise."

. . .

In Houston, both Tom and Jerry received late night phone calls, rousing them from bed. Unbeknownst to them, an emergency flight plan had been filed with the tower. They were scheduled to fly to Bear Creek in thirty minutes.

. . .

After rousing Mallory up off the couch and once she was fully awake, Jim spoke briefly with Abbey and Kelly before asking to speak to Mallory in private.

"It'll be brief. I promise," Jim said.

Kelly and Abbey left the dining hall and closed the door behind them. Before Jim could even say anything, Mallory spoke up.

"I already know," Mallory said as her eyes started to glisten with tears.

"I thought you said you turned off the TV."

"We did. I can tell. I can see it in your eyes," she said as tears started to fall.

"I am inside the Research Module, and I am separated from the station."

"You're just floating away?"

"Yes."

"Why?"

"There was a fire, and someone had to put it out."

"You can't make it back to the space station?"

"No. All possible options have been considered. At this point any rescue attempt would result in more danger."

"It had to be you? Why are you the one in the module?"

"I didn't think about it really. It just happened. It was either me or all of us," Jim explained as Mallory wiped her tears away. Jim continued, "I wanted to tell you first because I need you to get over this. You and I had many years together, and we were fortunate to have spent that time with each other. I didn't get the time I thought I would with Abbey."

"I'll take her. You know I will."

"No. I have plans for Abbey," Jim said without hesitation. Mallory froze. The thought had already crossed her mind. She would adopt her. *Where else would Abbey go,* she thought.

"Plans?" Mallory repeated as she continued to cry.

"She'll be fine, but I need your help. She needs your help to get through this."

"What do you want me to do?"

. . .

Hannah Parsons, a thin woman with red hair boarded the flight to Bear Creek at 3:30 AM with two attorneys in tow. Hannah, 38, wore a skirt and blouse with her hair wrapped into a tight knot held together by twelve bobby pins. Both Tom and Jerry stared at her as she walked toward her seat, one hip at a time.

"I've always liked redheads," Jerry said.

"Yeah. Me, too."

The attorneys on the plane both worked for NASA and had been ordered to go to Bear Creek to assist with a few legal issues. Dressed in blue jeans and T-shirts, they slouched in their chairs as if they were used to the private jet scene. Hannah, however, was already dressed up and wished she had thought about being more comfortable. While the sharks slept, Hannah tried her best to relax.

. . .

The doors to the dining hall opened, and Abbey looked toward Mallory, wondering what was going on. Mallory looked at Abbey, trying not to cry.

"You can talk to Jim now."

Once in front of the monitor, Abbey looked at Jim who was doing his best to smile. As soon as Mallory closed the door to the dining hall, a sickening feeling came over Abbey, and she didn't understand why.

"How are you?" Jim began.

"Fine. Nervous since you told us to turn off the TV."

"Abbey, I have something to tell you, and it's going to hurt. I would rather not…" Jim started to say. He cleared his throat and took a deep breath while Abbey came to her own realization that he was trying not to cry. "Abbey, I am inside a small module that is detached from the space station, and…" Once again, Jim nearly broke down but then swallowed, cleared his throat and refused to give up. "I'm not coming home."

"You're not coming home?" Abbey repeated.

"I am floating away from the space station, and I will not be able to return," he explained, omitting the part about him burning up in the atmosphere. Seeing Abbey's tears stream down her face caused him to look away from the screen. She did nothing to wipe them away. She just stared at the screen in shock. "I am so sorry," he said as he looked back directly into the camera.

After Mallory had broken the news to Kelly and answered her questions, they sat in silence. The sound of the TV would have been better than hearing the echoing sobs, cries, and pleas from Abbey in the dining hall. After twenty minutes, the door to the dining hall swung open and hit the wall. Abbey stood in the doorway with tears flowing freely down her red, puffy cheeks. Mallory and Kelly rushed to her side and embraced her.

At 7:30 A.M., Tom and Jerry landed the jet at Pocono Mountains Municipal Airport. A black Lincoln Town Car waited for the two NASA attorneys and Hannah Parsons. After utilizing the lavatory to change clothes, both attorneys stepped off the plane dressed in suits. Hannah didn't get much sleep on the flight due to her uncomfortable attire but considered the lesson learned. Once seated in the car, they sped off to Bear Creek Inn.

Chapter 65

At 7:45 A.M. the phone rang on the desk of Mrs. Harris at Bear Creek Elementary.

"Hello?" she answered.

"Mrs. Harris, this is Frank Navasky, and I am the administrator of NASA. I was wondering if I could speak with you for a moment."

"I'm sorry. Who?"

. . .

Standing on the front porch of Bear Creek Inn, Hannah opened the door to the lobby while the two attorneys followed closely behind. With no one in sight, Hannah walked over to the desk and rung the bell. Mallory opened the door from inside the dining hall.

"Are you all from NASA?" Mallory asked.

"We are," Hannah answered.

"Please, come in," Mallory invited as she walked back into the dining hall. Hannah and the attorneys walked through the French doors and immediately gazed at the couches surrounding the desktop computer. Jim looked back at them from the screen. They looked at Abbey who was red-cheeked with bloodshot eyes from crying. Hannah started the conversation.

"Hello, I'm Hannah Parsons, and I'm the director of public relations at NASA. These gentlemen are Daniel Stovall and Callan Yeoman," Hannah said as she looked at Kelly, Abbey, and Mallory. They nodded their heads at Hannah as Jim spoke up.

"Hannah, could you please excuse us for a moment. I know you just got here, but please allow Mallory and Abbey to show you to the lobby. I need to speak with Kelly White for a moment."

"Yes, sir," Hannah said without missing a beat. "I have to get over to Bear Creek Elementary anyway."

Without warning, Kelly had been singled out. She could feel warmth in her chest as if she just ate a hot pepper. Jim nodded and thanked Hannah, while Abbey and Mallory left the room with the attorneys, closing the door behind them. Once they were in the lobby, awkwardness fell upon the attorneys as they watched a little girl with a prosthetic leg sob into Mallory's shoulder.

In the dining hall, Jim collected his thoughts and looked at the camera.

"I wanted to talk to you in private, Kelly."

"Okay."

"I suppose Mallory told you that I am not coming home."

"Jim, I am so sorry. I don't know what to say."

"I know. At this point, neither do I, but I have something I want to talk to you about."

"Okay."

"I want to say, first of all, that you have done a great job with Abbey. She has a good time with you, and she listens to you, and you have been a big help."

"I appreciate you saying that," Kelly said.

"Now, what I really want to talk to you about is this," Jim said, trying to find the words. "You lost your husband and child so close together and you have said that you feel lost. You used that word before, lost. Remember?"

"Yes."

"As of right now, I can relate to becoming a parent and having it taken away from you, but it seems that you have an opportunity in front of you," Jim said, taking a break and collecting his thoughts before continuing. When he looked back at the camera, his eyes were piercing and glazed over. His lip quivered slightly as he said, "I would like you to adopt Abbey." Kelly's hand began to shake and moved slowly toward her mouth as she began to cry. Jim continued, "I need you to promise me something. Right here, right now. I want you to promise me that you will love Abbey, not just as a person," he said as he pressed forward trying not to break down, his voice cracking and shaking. "but as your daughter. She deserves that, and I think you have it in you to love her," Jim explained. Kelly nodded her head before she spoke.

"I do. I do love her."

"I want you to promise me you will love her and protect her and help her become the person that I know she can be. Promise me."

"I promise. I promise you, Jim."

"The two men that are in the lobby," Jim said as he pointed toward the door behind her, "are here to help with my estate. I am giving you and Abbey my estate, which includes the inn. I recommend that you renovate it and open it up. It will provide a good and steady income for both of you. If for some reason you decide it isn't for you, shut it down and figure something else out. I know you will do what is right."

"I will do everything I can, Jim. I will not let you or Abbey down," Kelly said as emotion overcame her speech. While it couldn't compare to having a child, she felt a sense of motherhood she had felt only once before.

"I don't hug people, well maybe Abbey and Mallory, but if I was there, I would hug you now. I would if I was there," Jim said.

"I would hug you too," she said with a slight smile, still tears in her eyes.

. . .

Mrs. Harris was sitting at her desk waiting for the arrival of Hannah Parsons when the secretary at the front desk beeped in on her intercom.

"Mrs. Harris?"

"Yes?"

"I think your people are here."

"My people? I am waiting for Mrs. Parsons."

"You should come see this."

Mrs. Harris walked out of her office and toward the front of the school. As she approached the front doors, she could see three white semi-trucks parked in front of the school. Beside them were two satellite trucks. The NASA logo was splashed all over the vehicles with Hannah Parsons walking in black high-heels between the trucks toward the front doors. Mrs. Harris took a few steps outside and walked toward Hannah who had extended her hand for a handshake long before she was close enough to Mrs. Harris.

"Hi. Hannah Parsons."

"I'm Mrs. Harris. Mr. Navasky told me you were coming," she said as she looked past Hannah at the array of massive vehicles parked in the parking lot.

"Of course. Do you have somewhere we could talk?" Hannah asked.

"Certainly."

When the parents of the cast members of Peter Pan began getting phone calls, the word around town started to spread. While the play wasn't scheduled for another week, there would be an emergency performance. The word "emergency" rightfully confused and mystified the parents of the performers.

Chapter 66

The large semi and satellite trucks parked in the back of Bear Creek Elementary. Cables ran out the back of the trucks like anacondas snaking around a parked school bus, up a ramp, and into the back of the school. Cameras were being set up inside the auditorium while a crew that resembled a biker gang began taping down video and audio cables. Hannah Parsons walked around the stage and looked over everything before walking out the large bay door at the back of the stage and into the parking lot. The four-inch heels on Hannah's shoes *click-clacked* on the asphalt before reaching the aluminum staircase to one of the trailers attached to a semi.

Inside, technicians plugged in and tested equipment while a director and producer went over the script for the play. Hannah was making sure that everything was on track and would be ready for the performance.

Inside the auditorium, parents escorted their children down the aisles as they held their costumes high in the air to keep them from touching the ground. Mrs. Harris stood on the stage and yelled out over the technicians running cable and setting up cameras.

"All actors and actresses up on the stage without their costumes. Let's hurry and run through the play. Peter Pan is not here at the moment so I will be filling in and reading Abbey's lines until she gets here."

. . .

Jim looked at the screen of his laptop at a document sent by the two attorneys. While he reviewed the legalese, he heard a familiar voice coming through the speakers.

"If teleportation were real, I'd send you an Alaskan Ale."

Jim used the touchpad on the computer to maximize a window to the video feed of NASA. Standing in front of the camera was Dr. Stanton.

"Hey, Stanton. You know, if teleportation were real I could get out of this mess."

"That's true. How you doing?"

"Not good. I'm reviewing documents and taking care of my estate. You want in?"

"Just leave me your stockpile of beer."

"Already did," Jim said with a grin.

"Jim, I am sorry about this. I can't help feeling like part of this was my fault."

"Nah, if it wasn't you, it would have been someone else. Plus, I did this. I did this for Abbey."

"I know you did. Dave told me to tell you that he wanted to speak with you in a few minutes. I told him I wouldn't take too long. I just wanted to say hello."

"I'm glad you did. I really am," Jim said. He noticed Stanton's background didn't look like mission control. "Hey, where are you right now?"

"In Mission Control, but I am in the booth."

"Do you know how to record my feed?"

"Your feed is being recorded non-stop."

"Oh. Well, I need a favor from you if you're up for it. A big favor."

"Name it."

"I'm going to talk into the camera and I want you to deliver the video to Abbey in person. Will you do that?"

"Of course. It would be an honor," Stanton said. "Whatever you want."

"Okay, hang on," Jim said as he grabbed a note pad and flipped a few pages. He read a few lines to himself and then looked into the camera. "Okay," Jim said and then began.

. . .

Kelly, Mallory, and Abbey arrived at Bear Creek Elementary with the Peter Pan costume in the back of Mallory's car. Once they entered the school, a man wearing black pants and a black shirt greeted them. Holding a walkie-talkie down by his side he asked, "Is this Abbey Mayfield?"

"Yes, sir," Mallory said.

The man held up the walkie-talkie and spoke, "Hannah Parsons, come in." When she responded, he continued. "Abbey Mayfield is in the lobby."

"I'll be right there."

In less than two minutes, Hannah's *click-clack* steps could be heard coming down the hallway. When she was visible, she looked tired, but determined.

"Hello again. I am to take all of you out back to our communications truck. If you would, please follow me."

Moving at a speedy pace, they followed Hannah through the school and into the auditorium. As they all walked toward the stage, Abbey's classmates and their parents looked at her with expressions of concern and sorrow. In too much of a hurry to notice, they followed Hannah up the steps. The stage was decorated like the inside of Michael's, John's and Wendy's bedroom with a bay window that overlooked a night sky painted on a large piece of cardboard.

Once they were backstage, Hannah took them out the back door and into the parking lot. She guided them to the white communications trailer. Hannah took a few steps up the aluminum stairs and poked her head inside. She looked at the director and nodded. The director yelled out to his crew.

"Okay, everyone out. Everyone out for fifteen minutes." Suddenly, a team of people walked out of the trailer.

"Mrs. Cain, you're first. You may sit in the director's chair," Hannah said as she held the door for her. Mallory walked inside and made her way to a console of monitors. She walked up to the director's chair and came into view of Jim on a monitor. Mallory started crying.

"What's the deal? I haven't even said anything yet," Jim said with a slight smile.

"Is this the last time we are going to talk?"

"It is." Jim's expression became solemn and his smile subsided.

"That's why I am crying."

"I understand. I want you to look after Kelly and Abbey. I know you already know this, but I have to say it."

"I promise you I will," Mallory said. "I just hate this for you, I just hate it."

"Me, too," Jim said. Silence fell between them. Mallory composed herself just before Jim spoke up, "Do you remember when we were kids, and we would put on plays for Mom and Dad?"

"Yes," Mallory said with a smile.

"We'd use the bed sheets for capes, and we would be super heroes, and we would re-enact scenes from movies and TV shows."

"I remember it like it was yesterday," Mallory said.

"We did a lot together. We had a good childhood."

"We did," Mallory said.

"You were a good sister to me. I guess that's what I wanted to say. I've always thought that," Jim said, unable to look directly at the camera. Mallory nodded her head.

"And you were a good brother. You looked out for me. You always looked out for me."

Mallory and Jim talked for a few more minutes while Kelly and Abbey waited outside. Their heads turned when the door to the trailer opened. Mallory was in tears.

"Mrs. White, you may go inside now," Hannah said in a soft, calm voice.

Kelly got up and walked up the steps and went inside. Mallory bent down to Abbey and embraced her niece and sobbed into her shoulder.

"How are you doing?" Kelly asked.

"I could be better. Could be worse too."

"I didn't know if I would get an opportunity to talk to you again, and I thought if I did that I would want to say something. Is that okay?"

"Of course."

Kelly nodded and fished a folded piece of ruled notebook paper from her back pocket before clearing her throat. She read the lines she wrote down, looking up at the camera every so often.

"For the past six months, I have been a witness to how a man can love a little girl as if she were his own child. At one point in my life, I thought I was going to be a mother, but that was taken from me. After watching you with Abbey, it is now my goal to not be just a mother figure to Abbey, but a real mom to her. I wanted to let you know that you have inspired me and have given me hope to be a mother again. And concerning our arrangement we made in the dining hall, I will keep that promise I made to you."

Jim was quiet as he looked off screen. He nodded his head, seemingly to himself, and looked back at the camera.

"You know, Kelly, you had thanked me for helping you by letting you stay at the inn, and you thanked me for taking you to Houston and letting you watch over Abbey, but the truth is, is that you were the one helping me. If it wasn't for you, I wouldn't be so calm and composed right now. It makes this easier on me, so thank you. I have no doubt in my mind that you will be a great mother to Abbey," Jim said. Kelly nodded her head as she wiped the tears from her eyes.

"I know. I will be a good mother to her. I won't let you down."

"Whenever you hug her, please hug her again for me."

"I will."

"As much as a girl likes pink princess stuff and playing dress-up, know that there is so much more to her than that."

"I know."

"Help her learn and grow. I know you will, I just have to say it."

"I know. I will. I promise. I promise."

Inside the auditorium, the seats were filling up quickly with anxious parents. They looked around the room at the six camera operators while the students of Bear Creek scrambled and dashed around back-stage. Make-up was applied hastily while children squeezed into costumes and recited their lines. Mrs. Harris ran about asking questions and relaying information on her walkie-talkie. She peeked through the curtains from backstage, and saw that nearly every seat was filled.

Ring. Ring.

Hannah answered her cell phone while standing next to Mallory and Abbey.

"Hello?"

"Hannah, this is Dave Thomas. Where are we?"

"We are set to start, right on time."

The door to the trailer opened and Kelly exited. She held the door open for Abbey who maneuvered up the stairs and hurried inside. Kelly closed the door and stepped down the metal steps and embraced Mallory.

Inside, Jim smiled at Abbey as she came into view.

"Hey, kiddo."

"Hi, Jim."

"Are you ready for tonight's play?"

"Yes. My costume is inside."

"I'm pretty excited about seeing the play. You worked so hard on it, and I think you will do very well."

"I hope so," Abbey said. Jim cleared his throat and started to say what he had been thinking about since he had learned of his fate. He looked at the camera as if he was looking at Abbey's eyes.

"Abbey, I have lived more than 40 years. I have made many decisions in my life. Some were bad decisions, but mostly good. Out of everything I have ever done in my entire life, the best thing I ever did was adopt you. From now on, I want you to remember that for the rest of your life. No matter what you hear about me, no matter my accomplishments, *you* were the best thing in my entire life. You hear me? You understand that?"

"Yes."

"I don't ever want you to forget that. Ever."

"Okay. I won't."

"One last thing, I want you to know…" Jim stopped. He hadn't said these words since he was a child. It was foreign to him, but he wanted to say it. He wanted her to hear him say it, "I want you to know that I love you. I love you as if you are my own child."

"I love you, too, Jim. I love you so much," Abbey said with complete sincerity as she began to cry without reaching up to wipe away her tears. When Jim had come to terms about the end of his life, he had told Dave Thomas that he wanted a few things to occur before his death. A list was prepared, but one item Jim kept to himself. Jim had wanted to hear Abbey say the words she had just said to him. It was those simple words that made him instantly at peace with his situation. Tears fell down his cheeks as he smiled.

"It's going to be so difficult to say goodbye, Abbey. I almost wish I hadn't requested to see the play. I almost would rather just sit here with you until I can no longer see you."

"I would do that," Abbey said finally wiping away her tears.

"I know you would. I know you would."

Chapter 67

The crowd in the auditorium quieted down when the lights dimmed. Hannah Parsons took the stage and stood in front of a microphone.

"Good evening. My name is Hannah Parsons, and I am the director of public relations at NASA. Thank you for being here under these circumstances. Tonight you are helping fulfill the final request of NASA astronaut Jim Mayfield. Tonight, his daughter, Abbey Mayfield, is playing the lead role, and we are broadcasting this performance to space so he can see it, hence all the cameras around you," Hannah said as she pointed around the room.

While she continued her speech, Mrs. Harris was standing outside, waiting to approach Mallory, Kelly and Abbey. At that moment, Abbey had left the trailer and was crying loudly into the shoulders of Mallory and Kelly. Not wanting to interrupt their moment of grief, Mrs. Harris remained at the stage door and waited until she could no longer do so. The play was about to begin.

. . .

Jim had found three pouches of water in a cabinet and already drank two by the time Dave appeared on his laptop.

"Jim? Before we move you over to the school play, I wanted to share a few things with you first."

"Okay."

"We had a team of engineers work with the crew aboard the ISS to determine the malfunction and the RM module fire. We have determined that if you had not gotten the door shut, there could have been a fatal explosion that would have ended the lives of everyone on board," Dave said just as someone off screen handed him a single sheet of paper. Dave read from the paper, "The report we are filing reads: the actions taken by Flight Engineer Jim Mayfield led to the prevention of a fatal explosion. He sacrificed his life in order to do so. By removing the RM module and extinguishing the fire, Jim Mayfield may very well have saved the lives of the crew members on board. His actions have also extended our scientific endeavors for future space exploration," Dave dropped his arm to his side, paper still in his hand.

"Well, I'm glad to know that it wasn't for nothing."

"I'm sure we aren't telling you anything you don't know. We just didn't want you thinking that we weren't sure of your actions."

"I understand," Jim said as he hung his head and stared at the keyboard.

"Jim, all of us here honor you and your courageous and selfless act. You will be remembered as a friend, colleague and hero to all of NASA." Dave looked up at the big screen as Jim replied.

"Thank you," Jim said just before Dave gave the go-ahead to switch him over to the school play that was just beginning.

Chapter 68

"Who's there? Is there someone at the window?" Wendy asked. A little eight-year-old girl spoke the first line of the play. Jim watched on his laptop and waited impatiently for Abbey to appear. He listened to the story, as did Mission Control, in Houston.

The play could be seen on the largest monitor in Mission Control with the sound of the performance booming over the loudspeakers. Staff members in the room were quiet and paid close attention while looking off to the right side of the monitor where they could see Jim's face as he watched the play unfold.

The audience in the auditorium listened to the lines spoken by the other children, but it seemed everyone was waiting for Peter Pan to appear. Before the play began, the parents in the audience talked about what they had heard and what they had seen on TV.

"He's going to burn up in space?"

"Can't they do anything?"

All of the conversations and rumors led up to the single moment when Peter Pan appeared on stage. Everyone in the theater and at Mission Control knew that Abbey was playing Peter Pan and that she was coming up next. It was the collective silence in the room that made her lines come through clearer than the other performers. Jim had waited long enough. It was time. Wendy flicked on the light switch, turning on all the lights on the stage, revealing Peter Pan.

"It's you. It's really you. You're Peter Pan."

"Of course, I'm Peter Pan. Who'd you expect?" Abbey said.

"Are you here looking for your shadow? I knew it was yours when I saw it." Wendy responded. Jim watched Abbey move around without having to *step-clonk* everywhere. She had gotten pretty good at walking around on her new prosthesis.

In the white trailer behind the auditorium, the director sat with the script in front of him. All of Abbey's lines were highlighted. He directed the cameras and punched the keys that gave Jim a different camera angle. Hannah Parsons stood behind the director and watched the show unfold. Her job in Bear Creek was finished. She listened to the skilled director as he spoke to his camera operators though his headset.

"Zoom in with a half-shot. Focus. Camera three, take three."

Jim watched the play as if it were a TV show. The audio came in clear and crisp, and the camera angles changed frequently.

On stage, Abbey was flying with the aid of a harness and a strong P.E. teacher pulling one rope while another teacher tugged on another. They set her down on a makeshift rock while the Lost Boys gathered around her.

"We have to save Wendy, John, and Michael, and I have a plan to get them back," Abbey said.

After a quick set change, a massive pirate ship took up the entire stage. Abbey flew all over the ship, delivering her lines while battling Captain Hook. Jim watched and listened to one of the lines he had said over and over for Abbey while practicing with her.

"You fly all around yet, you won't face me. Face me like a man, Peter Pan!" The sound effects of clinging metal *ping* and *clang* as they brawled dagger against sword played over the loudspeakers while they fought. The music swelled as Captain Hook was finally defeated and fell into the arms of a crocodile waiting at the side of the pirate ship.

"Hooray! Hooray for Peter Pan!" the Lost Boys said. The cast members cheered and carried on.

"Where are we sailing, Captain Pan?" Wendy asked.

"We sail to London!"

The lights dimmed and the set was quickly changed to Wendy's home in London. Peter Pan brought the Lost Boys to Wendy's home and convinced her mother to adopt them. Wendy looked out her bedroom window as Peter Pan began to fly away in the last scene.

"You won't forget to come for me, Peter? Please, please don't forget," Wendy said as Peter Pan flew toward the other side of the stage.

In Mission Control, Dave was alerted to the fact that Jim was about to enter Earth's atmosphere. With a whisper, the flight technician asked Dave a question.

"Do you want me to display the time to re-entry on his screen?" he asked. Dave simply shook his head no. They had timed the end of the play to coincide with the re-entry. The play was planned out using all available time. In fact, a small portion of the script was removed in order to make the time frame work. Dave looked at the screen where Jim was watching the play. They could see the look in his eyes of pure pride in Abbey's performance, especially as she said her last line. Jim reached for his left wrist, felt the bracelet given to him by Abbey and held on to it with a tight grip.

"I'll return for you, Wendy. I promise." Abbey flew off the stage behind a curtain. Jim watched as the spotlight faded.

The lights faded down, and the cast gathered at the front of the stage. Abbey wriggled through the cast of characters to the head of the stage and was crying uncontrollably. She bowed while the audience cheered and applauded.

Everyone in Mission Control wiped their eyes as they looked to the left. Jim's eyes were filled to the brim with tears. The microgravity caused his tears to fill his eyes like the glassy surface of a swimming pool, never falling on his cheeks. The staff of Mission Control could hear Jim's last words as he said,

"She did so well." The monitor began to crackle, and the video feed was disconnected as the RM entered Earth's atmosphere, burning up and dismantling over the Pacific Ocean.

Just before the cast broke apart on stage, some of her classmates walked over to her in their costumes and embraced Abbey as she cupped her face with her hands and cried uncontrollably.

Chapter 69

The idea of having a funeral service for Jim was considered but ultimately decided against, since NASA had decided to honor Jim with the placement of a statue in front of the visitor's center in Houston. The ceremony for the unveiling would be mostly in honor of his heroic efforts, but would also serve as a memorial service.

Mallory drove her mini-van up Bear Mountain Road while talking to her husband. Barry's clothes fit snug on his ample body. He stroked his graying facial hair as he asked a question from the passenger seat.

"When is the ceremony?"

"Memorial Day weekend. I am not sure of the date and time yet."

"How's Abbey doing?"

"I don't know. I spoke with her yesterday. She said she was doing okay, but Kelly told me otherwise."

"Like what?"

"Crying in her room. Not eating a whole lot."

The mini-van pulled into the driveway of Bear Creek Inn. Mallory steered the vehicle onto the cobblestone and pulled off to the side, passing where Jim's red truck would normally be parked. Navigating carefully, she approached the back of the inn and drove up to the old utility barn and backed up to the doors.

"What are we doing here again?" her husband asked as she put the van in park.

"A favor for Jim."

Barry used much of his strength to move the barn door, sliding it to the left. Mallory walked in and found the barn in order. Her eyes scanned over landscaping supplies, bolts of carpet, two old lawn mowers, and two wheelbarrows. Looking for something in particular, she walked over to a door with cans of wood stain stacked up outside a small room. Opening the door, she found what she was looking for.

"What is it?" Barry asked.

In the middle of the small room, Jim had been using linseed oil on the rocking chair he had made for a client in North Carolina. Cans of woods stain and oil lay empty along the wall with a respirator mask next to the chair. With a polite and apologetic email from space, Jim had explained to his North Carolina client that it was no longer a possibility to deliver the requested furniture due to a death in the family.

"Help me load it. We need to hurry before Kelly and Abbey get back."

With great care, they removed it from the small room and loaded it into the back of the van.

"Why are we taking this?"

"It's for Abbey. We have to keep it for a while."

"For how long?"

"A long time from now. Until she has a family."

Barry closed the back hatch.

Mallory had received an email from Jim while he had been floating away in the Research Module, in fact he had sent out several emails.

From: Jim Mayfield [Jim.Mayfield@canyonmail.net]
Sent: Wednesday, 6:12 PM
To: 'mcain'
Subject: Favor

———————————

Mallory, I need you to pick up the last rocking chair I made and keep it. At some point down the road, should Abbey ever have a child, I want you to make sure she receives it at her baby shower. Please put a tag on it that reads: To Abbey From Jim. I love you.

Mallory had envisioned Abbey twenty-years down the road and attending her baby shower. Jim, always thinking ahead, had already gotten her a present. More than a present. A family heirloom. Mallory decided to keep it hidden away in the back of her walk-in closet after her husband covered it in furniture wrap and foam to ensure it would look brand new whenever Abbey unwrapped it.

Jim sent out three more emails. All pertained to Abbey. The second one went out to Dr. Woodward. After seeing the tragic news on TV the night before, he was surprised to see an email from his fallen colleague the next morning.

From: Jim Mayfield [Jim.Mayfield@canyonmail.net]
Sent: Friday, 6:12 PM
To: 'Woodward.A'
Subject: Favor

_____

Woody,
I need to ask a favor of you. Will you please call Abbey every September and let her know that you can help her should she need any help with anything during the school year? I already know your answer. No way would you let your old roommate down.
Your friend, Jim.

A simple request that would indeed be fulfilled. Dr. Woodward smiled before he took off his glasses and set them on his desk. He read the email one more time and nodded his head in agreement.

Greg was next. His was the longest email of the four Jim sent before his death. In it, he asked Greg to check up on Abbey and assist her with her prosthetic leg. After Greg read the email, he got an idea that would ensure Jim's request. Greg had donated his design to the University of Washington Prosthetics and Orthotics Department. In his agreement, he would receive access to the latest and newest advancements in prosthetic technology. After a phone call to the division head, Abbey's name was added to the short list.

The final email Jim sent out was to Dr. Stanton. After a brief explanation, Stanton printed out Jim's email and handed it to Dave Thomas. Jim's request involved obtaining a small clip from the RM video.

Chapter 70

FOUR YEARS LATER

Kelly Mae White sat in her office behind the front desk of the inn. She typed numbers into a column of a spreadsheet. Bookkeeping wasn't one of her strong suits, but she was managing. On her cork bulletin board was a post-it-note with the telephone number of the local accountant who assisted her with her many questions. While she figured the expenses of remodeling and renovation of the inn, she looked at the clock in the lower right corner of her screen. It was almost time. She typed in a few more columns of numbers and saved the spreadsheet before walking out into the lobby.

The floors had been sanded and finished, the fireplace cleaned, and the old TV was replaced with a flat screen mounted on the wall. The biggest expense wasn't the remodeling of the rooms, nor was it the purchase of the many tables and chairs for the dining hall. It was the payroll. With the staff that she hired for the kitchen and housekeeping, she needed to generate a significant profit.

Kelly used to not sleep well at night with the thought of running the inn into the ground until the reservations started coming in. In the third year of operation, Bear Creek Inn was fully booked for an entire summer, just as it had been when Jim and Mallory were kids. That was the summer that Kelly knew everything would be okay.

She walked out of the lobby onto the front porch and sat down. She looked at her watch and waited for the school bus to drop off Abbey from her last day of middle school. With Abbey's ability to walk and run normally, she requested to be placed on a regular school bus. Kelly watched as it pulled up the cobblestone driveway and opened its doors. Kelly got up and walked toward Abbey with a smile.

"How was your last day of eighth grade?"

"Good. We did a spelling bee with prizes," Abbey said as the bus pulled away.

"Did you win anything?"

"They gave away coupons for free chicken sandwiches. I won two. We both get free chicken because I spelled *Revision* and *Gleaming* correctly," Abbey said. Kelly laughed and walked by her side as they headed toward the front porch. Behind them, they could hear the crunching of pebbles underneath the tires of a car. Abbey turned around and saw that it was Mallory's Honda Odyssey.

"What's Mallory doing here?" Abbey asked. Mallory parked her van and stepped out. "Hey, Mallory."

"Hey, Fabby Abbey!"

Abbey was graduating the eighth grade and a party had been put together to celebrate with a few of her friends. The next few hours were spent hanging streamers and getting food ready for the guests. Needing a shower, Abbey decided to get in a quick run on the treadmill first. Outfitted with track pants, an old T-shirt, and a headband, Abbey ran rhythmically on the electric belt. As she made strides toward her three-mile goal, she stared out over the backside of Bear Creek Inn.

When Abbey reached her distance, she jumped off the treadmill and went to her room to shower. Mallory and Kelly were talking in the kitchen while they assembled a large fruit and vegetable tray.

"Is he coming tonight?" Mallory asked in a low voice in case Abbey was nearby.

"Yep. His plane lands in about an hour, and he'll drive up."

"Does Abbey still not know he's coming?"

"Nope. She has no clue."

"Do you know why he's coming? Did he say? I mean, other than the celebration."

"He said it was part of his promise to Jim."

"I see."

Mallory was familiar with the promises made to Jim. It wasn't just her that he had given specific instructions to.

Of the several people who were fulfilling promises to Jim, no one delivered more than Kelly. The last four years, Kelly had proven her worth by undertaking the task of bringing the inn to life and creating an income for both her and Abbey. Kelly had also proven her worth as an adoptive parent as she slowly and cautiously became a mother to Abbey. It was obvious to Mallory that her sweet and kind nature was what made their relationship strong. She was patient with Abbey and understanding in a way that enabled Abbey to lean on Kelly while grieving over the loss of Jim—being no stranger to loss herself.

When Dr. Stanton arrived, it was near the end of the party, and several of the guests had already departed. To his surprise, he was welcomed with hugs from both Abbey and Kelly. It wasn't until he was the last guest remaining that he spoke about the real reason for his visit.

"The last time I spoke with Jim, he asked me for a favor. He asked me to deliver this to you," Stanton said as he held up an envelope.

"He did? What is it?"

"Well, it's not this specifically. There is a piece of paper inside this envelope. Inside is the username and password to a website, and on the site is a video."

"It's a video?" Abbey asked.

"Yes," Stanton said as he handed her the envelope. "That's it."

"Can I look at it now?" Abbey asked.

"That part is up to you."

The conversation drifted to Abbey's school, to how many people were staying at the inn among other things. When Stanton departed, he received two more hugs from both girls.

Abbey couldn't wait to see what Jim had left behind and adjourned to her room once the party was officially over.

Upon opening the envelope, she navigated to the URL printed on the paper and typed in the username and password.

Welcome, Abbey.

The website had her name at the top and then an icon for files. She clicked on the icon. One single file. A video. The video opened, and Abbey pressed play. On screen, was Jim.

"Hey Abbey. It is the night of your play, and I asked Dr. Stanton to deliver this to you before your freshman year of high school. I hope this message finds you well," Jim said. Abbey took a deep breath and focused on every word. "I'm not sure what to say. This is a last-minute idea that I asked Dr. Stanton to help me with. I asked that this video be delivered to you at this point in your life because you are about to begin a new chapter, and I thought that I could offer you a little advice." A slight grin came across his face as he looked to the side while he collected his thoughts. He looked back at the camera and began again. "When I was your age, my father told me that in four years I would be in college and that, as a freshman in high school, I needed to start thinking about what I wanted to do with my life. He made it very clear to me that I could do or be anything I wanted. Anything. I remember jokingly saying to my dad, "Could I be an astronaut?" Instead of smiling or laughing, he looked at me very seriously and simply said, "Yes." I believe that to be the best piece of advice I have ever gotten in my life, and it is what I think of when I think about my father." Jim briefly paused before beginning again. His face appeared serious, focused on his words. "I now pass this advice on to you. So, be thinking about what you want to do. Be thinking about what interests you and what you love and don't ever let anyone tell you that you can't do something. You are a very bright and intelligent girl, and I know you will be just fine. I just wanted you to know that without a doubt, you have no limits."

Abbey pressed pause on the video. She wiped her tears and used her shirt to clean her glasses. As she looked down, she remembered the day he left the inn to help her get new ones and a new set of tears formed. She remembered feeling safe. Secure. She felt comforted just knowing he was around. She thought the feeling of loss had left her over four years time, but she felt it once again. After she composed herself, she looked at the screen and pressed play. Jim continued.

"The last thing I wanted to tell you is…" Jim stopped and thought about what he was going to say. He looked off camera and finally back at the lens, "…is that I do not in any way regret the circumstances that I am in, if I hadn't come to get you in Arizona, who knows where you would be. I don't ever want you to think that this was your fault because it's not. If this is what it takes to give you the life you deserve, I would do it all over again. Kelly is good for you. She cares for you, and I have no doubts that you are just as good for her. I keep thinking about how you both came to the inn and how both of you needed help. So, I feel that if this is what it took to bring you both together, then I served a greater purpose."

Jim looked away from the camera and took a moment. Abbey watched while wiping the tears away between her cheek and glasses.

"Abbey, I am so sorry this happened. I can't stand leaving you. But I want you to know that I made sure that you are surrounded by people who love and care about you. Maybe someday you can eat breakfast in the kitchen and talk with your children like we used to. And if you do, think of me. Abbey Mayfield, I love you."

See page 405 for a note from the author

What readers have said about Nick Allen Brown's first novel

Field of Dead Horses

A MUST READ! I am an avid book reader. I read at least 1-2 books per week and I must say this book had me from the beginning. The author weaves a tale of suspense, murder, love, redemption and revenge that at the last page, I was sad that my journey was over. Oftentimes, an author wastes words and rambles. This story set in Kentucky in the early 1930s was well written, grabs you from the first page and doesn't let go until "The End." I can't wait for the next book from Nick Allen Brown. I will be the first in line.

—*C. McCoy, U.S.A.*

The quiet strength and decency of Elliott Chapel, the irrepressible humor and wisdom of Booley, the brutal threat of Sheriff Crease, and the vulnerability of all that the Chapels hold dear against the backdrop of life on a small farm and the excitement of Thoroughbred Racing provide a truly exciting and charming read that will remind some readers of "Bridges of Madison County" and "Seabiscuit"...

—*Caroline McCarthy, London, England*

I loved this book! I didn't know what to expect from the title and found that I absolutely loved it. The characters were all wonderful! The main character, Elliott, had a tenderness that kept me engaged and reading on into the night. The book is full of surprises! Just wait until the end!! Sometimes I will re-read a book—I am certain that I will re-read this one...!!! I look forward to the next Nick Allen Brown book. Maybe even a movie??? ...

—*S. Stark, U.S.A.*

NOTE FROM THE AUTHOR — TO YOU.

What can I do for you?

Do you need signed copies of my books? Do you need me to speak to a book club or a classroom via Skype? Do you need me to visit your school, organization or event? What can I do for you? I will help you in any way I can. I need help with reviews on websites like Amazon.com, Goodreads.com, iTunes and I need people to write blogs about this book and post on social media. Even a nice, simple review of my book on your Facebook news feed helps.

You may contact me directly at *nickallenbrown@gmail.com*

I am a new author and I need your help to continue writing novels, but I am willing to work for your help. Thank you.

Theresa Cotter

Christ Is Coming

◆ ◆ ◆

CELEBRATING ADVENT, CHRISTMAS & EPIPHANY

ST. ANTHONY MESSENGER PRESS

CINCINNATI, OHIO

Rev. Edward J. Gratsch

Imprimi Potest: Rev. John Bok, O.F.M.
Provincial

Imprimatur: +James H. Garland, V.G.
Archdiocese of Cincinnati
June 30, 1992

The *nihil obstat* and *imprimatur* are a declaration that a book is considered to be free from doctrinal or moral error. It is not implied that those who have granted the *nihil obstat* and *imprimatur* agree with the contents, opinions or statements expressed.

Scripture citations taken from *The New American Bible With Revised New Testament*, copyright ©1986 by the Confraternity of Christian Doctrine, Washington, D.C., are used by permission. All rights reserved.

Scripture citations taken from *The New Revised Standard Version of the Bible*, copyright ©1989 by the Division of Christian Education of the National Council of the Churches of Christ in the USA, are used by permission.

The English translation of the "O" Antiphons from *The Liturgy of the Hours*, copyright ©1974, International Committee on English in the Liturgy, Inc. (ICEL); the English translation of *Angelus* from *A Book of Prayer*, copyright ©1982, ICEL, are used with permission. All rights reserved.

The quotation from *The Divine Milieu*, by Pierre Teilhard de Chardin, copyright ©1957 by Editions du Seuil, Paris. English translation copyright ©1960 by William Collins Sons & Co. Ltd., London, and Harper & Row, Publishers, Inc., is used with permission.

Design and illustrations by Julie Lonneman

ISBN 0-86716-157-4

©1992, Theresa Cotter
All rights reserved.

Published by St. Anthony Messenger Press
Printed in the U.S.A.